WINDCHILL SUMMER

NORRIS CHURCH MAILER

Windchill Summer

A Novel

BALLANTINE BOOKS · NEW YORK

A Ballantine Book
Published by The Ballantine Publishing Group

Copyright © 2000 by Norris Church Mailer

Title page and chapter opening illustrations copyright © 2000 by Regina Scudellari

www.ballantinebooks.com

Library of Congress Cataloging-in-Publication Data: 2001116903

ISBN 0-34543533-8

This edition published by arrangement with Random House, Inc.

Manufactured in the United States of America

First Ballantine Books Edition: July 2001

10 9 8 7 6 5 4 3 2 1

FOR NORMAN

AND

MATTHEW AND JOHN BUFFALO

WINDCHILL SUMMER

1. Cherry

In July, even in the dead middle of the night, you can't breathe the air in the Atlas pickle plant. You have to suck it. The smell is sharp and thick and sets the hairs in your nose on end and makes you feel like your lungs are getting as slicked over as your white Keds tennies, their laces green and pungent from dragging through puddles of pickle juice.

It was three in the morning, and it had been a bad night for Baby and me. Alfred Lynn Tucker—a tub of lard with bright red hair, glasses, and big, dirty-looking teeth, who was, unfortunately, our boss—had been on our case the whole night long. Not that he wasn't on our case most every other night. Just tonight was worse than usual.

When we came on shift at eleven, he started us off squirting brine into glass jars full of cucumbers that rolled past us on a conveyer belt. The brine came out of an old black rubber hose contraption connected to a wooden vat, and had a nozzle kind of like a garden hose. I bet we weren't on that job even fifteen minutes when he pulled us off, because we didn't let go of the trigger on the hose between squirts and a lot of brine somehow got wasted on the floor. It was an old rusty squeezer that a big man would have had trouble pumping, much less a girl, and it was just impossible to keep letting up on it. Our hands would have fallen off. You'd think Alfred Lynn personally paid for the brine out of his own pocket.

Then he put us to setting empty jars on the automatic packer belt where they passed under a chute that poured the cucumbers into them, but the stupid belt went so fast that we had to practically throw them on, and a few got broken. Not that many—they only had to stop and clean it out twice. Which might have been all right, but on top of that, the speed of the jars passing by right under my nose made me sick, and I threw up on the belt. Ever since I was a little girl, I have had a problem with motion sickness, so it wasn't that big of a deal. Most of it went on the floor. Baby went and got me a Coke and I felt better, but Alfred Lynn had no pity whatsoever. He yelled at me, like I could have helped it or something, and then he moved us to the machine that cut pickles up into the little crinkled disks they use to put on hamburgers.

By that time, Baby and I were getting a case of the simples—which is not unusual for us at four in the morning—and we started giggling and throwing pickle slices at each other. I admit this time we were in the wrong. It's just hard to take a job seriously that you know you'll be leaving when September rolls around. I didn't want to think about all the regular hands that have to work here the whole year, summer and winter, day in and day out, all their lives. I mean, not that there's anything wrong with it, but can you just see Baby and me in forty-five years at the pickle plant Christmas party they hold in Sweet Valley's concrete-block community room, stepping proudly up to the podium and accepting our Timex retirement watches? On our tombstones, it would say SHE WAS A GOOD PICKLE PACKER. A whole lifetime spent putting pickles into jars. Not these girls, thank you muchly. It was bad enough working here in the summers to make enough money for a few school clothes.

———

Alfred Lynn passed by and, as luck would have it, got hit on the back of the neck with a piece of pickle. It stuck there like a round green wart. He had a really loud voice.

"All right, y'all two nitwits! You think this is fun and games? I'm going to show you fun and games. Y'all can just peel onions the rest of the night."

"Oh please, Alfred Lynn. Don't send us to the onion room," Baby pleaded. "We'll try real hard. We promise not to get in any more trouble. Please, please, please!"

I hated to see Baby grovel, but it was better than going to the onion room. Baby kneeled down on the floor and put her hands together like she was praying. I tried as hard as I could not to laugh.

Alfred Lynn's face swelled up and turned blue-purple with rage, he wanted to hit Baby so bad. He would probably have done her some real damage if he had—Baby is only four-foot-ten and weighs eighty-six pounds with all her clothes on. She is Filipino, but you couldn't tell if you only heard her talk. Her daddy was with the American army during the war, and somehow they ended up here in Arkansas when she was five. When she first got here, she couldn't speak a word of English, and of course she learned from all the little redneck kids she played with—mostly me—so she sounds just like everybody else. She kids around about it—calls herself a Filbilly. Get it? A Filipino hillbilly? Well, I think it is funny. Whatever she is, she is the most beautiful girl I have ever seen in my life—cute little pug nose, creamy tan skin, and big chocolate eyes; long straight shiny black hair that hangs down to her waist. And she might be little, but as the guys say, she is stacked. She wears tight white short-shorts to work, and makes grown men nervous. Including Alfred Lynn, as much as he would hate to admit it. So, since he couldn't hit her, he just sucked in his breath, clenched his fists, and gave us one more chance.

"All right. You get one more chance. I'm putting you out on the relish belt, and if you two don't have sense enough to pick out the trash from the cukes and throw it in a barrel, then you will be peeling onions. And I don't mean maybe."

We followed Alfred Lynn out to the dock. He moved pretty fast for somebody that would've dressed out at three hundred pounds at the slaughterhouse. We tried not to follow too close. You could always smell Alfred Lynn fifty feet before he got to you. Him and his old daddy, Walter Tucker, lived together out in the bottoms by the Arkansas River in a tar-paper shack. It didn't have running water or an indoor toilet, so I guess maybe it wasn't all his fault that he didn't wash more often. Or it could have been that his sweat had permanently turned into pickle brine from him being the night foreman at Atlas for ten years. Whatever it was, he sure did stink.

—

It was, at least, less like a furnace out on the dock. A conveyer belt ran the length of the concrete porch, under a roof, with the sides open to the warm night air. The smell was a lot better out here, too, even though we faced the back lot, with its giant wooden vats of pickles soaking in brine. Some of them had been out there for years, but supposedly they were still edible. At least they still sold them, and I'm sure they didn't want to take the chance of poisoning somebody and getting sued.

Further on out, you could see the glow from the streetlights of Sweet Valley and catch the headlights of the occasional truck on Route 66.

———

We pulled up stools and joined the row of women who were halfheartedly picking out rotten cucumbers and pieces of trash and throwing them into barrels while the good-but-not-perfect cukes rolled on down the belt to be ground up in the chopper at the end and mixed with onions, peppers, and spices to make hot dog relish. Hunching over the belt made your back hurt, but it was the best job we'd had all night.

Linda Sue Miller sat across from me. She was our same age, twenty-one, but had gotten married in the eleventh grade and already had three kids. She had short, curly blond hair with dark roots and still carried around the extra fifteen pounds from her last baby. She was one of the year-round hands. Not much of an advertisement for young love.

"Hey, Cherry. Hey, Baby. Y'all have been on a go-around tonight, I hear." She slapped at a mosquito. "These mosquitoes are eating me alive. They might just as well put regular lightbulbs out here—these old yellow bug lights don't do a lick of good, and they make it hard to see what you're throwing out. I sure as heck wouldn't eat the relish that comes out of this place."

"Oh, it's not bad," Mary Jo Bledsoe said, scratching her nose with the back of her wrist. "That brine purifies it. My kids eat it."

"Your kids would eat a scalded dog, Mary Jo. They can't come in my door without they eat everything that's not nailed down. I never saw such a bunch for stuffing themselves. You'd think they never had a meal at home."

Mary Jo's four kids were famous for dropping in at the neighbors' houses right at mealtime.

"Anytime my kids bother you, Linda Sue, you can just send them home. Although if you do, you might have to hire a baby-sitter or spend time with your three squalling brats yourself."

"Would y'all please not fight? It's bad enough out here without having to listen to y'all two ragging on each other." I said it as nicely as I could. Apparently, the night had gotten to me more than I thought. My nerves were starting to get a little frayed. I changed the subject. "What do you hear from Robert, Linda?"

Linda's husband was in Vietnam, like a lot of other boys we knew. He could probably have gotten out of it, because of the kids and all, but he felt like if he invested two years, he could make some good money and get benefits and education that he wouldn't be able to get as a high school dropout. In a way he was right, because their last baby—which got started on one of his leaves—only cost them something like two dollars with the army paying for it. I wouldn't have done it, though. Too big a gamble. Guys were dropping over there right and left. It was really depressing to watch Walter Cronkite every night on TV and stare at all the pictures to see if you recognized somebody you went to school with. Two boys from our class had already been killed, Jerry Golden and Bobby Richmond. Seven of our classmates—we only had fifty-four in our class—had been drafted or had volunteered to go over there in the three years since we graduated, but Bobby was the first to be killed. He hadn't been over there even a week and was in Saigon at the dentist's office fixing to get his checkup when a kid on a bicycle rode by and threw a satchel bomb into the waiting room. Ten guys were killed, plus the dentist and the girl who cleaned teeth. A little kid did it. Is that crazy or what?

Then Jerry Golden got killed by a booby trap somewhere, I think in Quang something, or someplace that sounds like that. I don't really know a whole lot of details about it, but it was doubly horrible because he was the president of our class and a really great guy, and even though we liked Bobby a lot, Jerry was one of our gang. We had a big memorial service at the high school for him, and practically the whole town turned out. All of us kids took it hard, not to mention his parents, as you would expect.

That whole war is insane. I know there are a lot of people who are for it because of the fear of Communism spreading and all, but I mean, really, what does it matter if Vietnam is Communist or not? Cuba, which is a heck of a lot closer, is Communist and it hasn't harelipped any Americans yet. And what about China? I didn't notice us invading China when it went Communist. We didn't study Vietnam at all in geography class. So now our guys have to go and die for a country they can't even find on the map?

When they held that big peace march on the Pentagon year before last, in '67, we had our own protest rally at the university. A lot of kids turned out in spite of the fact that it rained and there were rumors that the FBI had spies taking names and photographs with little hidden spy cameras. Most of the kids who came to the rally were art majors, like Baby and me, and English majors, but you saw science majors and even a few guys who were in ROTC. It was getting to where more and more kids were against the war, and Baby and I were two of them. I mean, who would be the next to go? The war hung over all our heads like the shadow of a hawk on the chicken yard.

—

Linda tried to act like she wasn't worried, but she wasn't too good at it.

"He was all right two weeks ago. At least that's when the last letter I got was dated. He said he was going to send me a set of dishes and a Japanese movie camera. They can get that stuff real cheap from over there. He already sent me a cocktail ring and a Vietnamese housecoat, and little ones for the babies. It's real pretty—red, with one of those stand-up collars. Lot of embroidery making out dragons and things on the back. I think it's silk, or at least a real high-quality polyester."

"Do you think he could get me a set of dishes?" Mary Jo wanted to know. "Can you pick out the pattern, or does he just have to take what he gets?"

"I don't think so, Mary Jo. It's just for the families." Linda yawned and threw out her gazillionth rotten pickle of the night.

Baby yawned and so did I. So did Mary Jo and everybody else on down the line. A big drop of sweat ran down my neck, and I wiped it off with my shirt collar. Only two more hours until quitting time. A breeze came up. We all turned our faces for a breath of moving air.

"Oooh, feel it. Here comes the windchill." Baby sighed.

Mary Jo snorted. "What are you talking about, Baby? It's hot summertime. There ain't no chill in that breeze. You won't hear the weatherman talking windchill until way up in the winter."

"I don't see why they don't," Baby said. "It's the same thing. All it means is that the weather is fooling you."

"Fooling you?"

"Yeah. See, Mary Jo, like, there you sit, here in this pickle-plant shed, sweaty and hot as all get-out, when the old wind whips up, blows on you, and makes you think it's got cooler. Of course that's great, but then just as soon as you're nice and comfortable, the wind dies down and the heat slaps you in the face again, and that makes it worse than ever."

"So it feels good while it lasts but it was a lie all the time, right?" It made sense to me.

"Oh, I get it," Linda said. "That's cute. Well, I don't care. I never minded a little lie if it felt good. Especially from a guy. Guys have been lying to me ever since I can remember."

"Don't feel like the Lone Ranger—you and all the rest of us," Mary Jo put in. "Every man I know is a born liar. Not a one of them will ever be honest with a woman. You just gotta figure they're all the time blowing hotter or colder than they say they are. And it's durned hard to know which it is."

We all agreed.

"In fact, I think most men would *rather* lie, even if the truth would serve them better," Linda added.

"Amen." We all nodded. Wisely. Like we had a lot of experience. I nodded too, even though I probably had the least experience of us all. I didn't have a boyfriend at the moment, and it was sort of embarrassing.

More cucumbers rolled down the line.

"Looky here, Cherry. There's an old rotten potato. I swear, I think Alfred Lynn throws junk in these cucumbers just as a test to see if we're asleep or not." Baby reached out to take the potato, then pulled her hand back.

"Baby, why didn't you get that old thing?" Now I'd have to get it when it came by me. "You are just worthless as a trash picker. I'm going to tell Alfred Lynn on you."

I reached out, but Baby put her hand on my arm to stop me.

"I don't know what it is, Cherry, but it's not a potato. What are those little things sticking up out of the sides? They look kind of like . . ."

"Legs! Baby, it's a rat!" I have to admit that I screamed my head off. I never was too crazy about mice, much less rats.

When I started screaming, so did everybody else. Stools went flying, and Baby jumped up on top of me and knocked me over. We both landed on the grimy concrete as the rat drifted by above our heads on the conveyer belt. It was lying on his back, legs stuck straight out of its bloated belly like black twigs. Its mouth was open and a blue, swollen tongue was wedged between its sharp little teeth.

All of us huddled together and watched in silence as it slipped off the end of the belt into the grinder. There was a sick, soft pop. Foul-smelling pink spew sprayed up. With a gritty screech as the steel blades bit into its bones, the machine stopped. For a minute more we stared, our mouths open, not moving a muscle. Then, like a group of dimwits, we all turned, as one, to see Alfred Lynn thundering down on us like the wrath of God.

2. *Cherry*

 The sun had just begun to pink up the sky when the whistle blew for the shift change two hours later. It was already ninety degrees outside, and in spite of the fans blowing fresh air into the onion room, you could barely breathe. My tear glands had long ago drained dry, swelled shut, and quit working, and I guess that was for the best.

We had gone through two or three of the big piles of onions that were mounded up around the room, and bushel baskets full of them, peeled clean and white, waited on flats for the guys to pick up on their forklifts and carry to the different parts of the plant.

That's what I really wanted to do—drive a forklift. Those lucky guys got to whiz in and out of the warehouse on their cute little go-carts that had hard-rubber wheels and two steel forks sticking out in the front like the arms of the Sphinx. They pulled a lever and slipped the forks under wooden flats of pickles or onions, screeched around corners, and scared all the old ladies out of their hair nets with their hotdogging. But girls didn't get to drive forklifts. Girls—especially summer-hand college girls—peeled onions.

—

Baby stood up and stretched. I reached out and picked off an onion skin that was stuck to the back of her leg. Even standing knee-deep in onion peelings, she was cute. I knew I shouldn't, but I envied her. I am five-foot-eleven-and-a-half—well, all right, five-foot-twelve—and feel most of the time like Big Ethel, the giraffe down at the Little Rock zoo. I stretched, too, and uncurled my fingers from my paring knife. They practically creaked with pain.

"You look like a big ol' lazy cat, Cherry, with that wild white hair and those yellow-green eyes of yours. You got eyes just like a lion."

"Oh, get out of here, Baby."

But I smiled. That's one of the reasons I love Baby. She thinks I am as beautiful as she is. To her, my size-36-inseam skinny legs are gorgeous, even though I think they look like white ropes with knots for knees. The boys in the fifth grade used to call me Chicken Legs, and Baby, little thing that she was, would put her hands on her hips, get right up in their faces, and say, "She does not have chicken legs! They're like a deer's. She has Bambi legs." Baby has always thought she was my protector.

We do look kind of strange together. Every once in a while, we'll be walking down the street and pass a mirror or a store window, and it comes over me how bizarre we must look to people who haven't watched us grow up together. We get a lot of Mutt-and-Jeff jokes, which we don't think are the least bit funny.

——

"Durn that Alfred Lynn. This smell will never come off my hands. I'll have to sleep with them under my pillow." Baby pulled off her hair net and shook out her hair. It fell down like a black satin curtain. I took off my own net, undid the knot I had tied my hair into, and got a strong whiff of onion.

"Even my hair smells," I said. "I hope that onion juice didn't bleach it out any worse than it already is."

As if that was possible. I was very nearly an albino when I was little. The only thing that saved me were my eyes, yellow-green instead of pink, but my hair was stone white, and I never had any eyelashes or eyebrows that you could see. My mother started dyeing them when I was six, before I started to school. She didn't want the kids to make fun of me any more than they had to.

Mama and I would get it done at Dottie's Kwik Kurl, in what used to be the old bank, on the other side of the railroad tracks. It was a little weird that the bank was now a beauty shop, but it was kind of elegant, with the marble floors and wooden counters and all. The shampoo bowls were in the front, where the bank customers used to stand in line. There, Miss Dottie would lay you back and scrub your head, digging in with her pointy red fingernails until your scalp tingled and nearly bled, and then she'd towel you off and take you around behind the teller cages, which still had bars on them, where she rolled you up and put you under one of the hair dryers. They looked like silver Martians' moon helmets and blew out scalding-hot air that burned your ears to nubs and made you deaf from the noise. You had to sit there, no matter how much pain you were in, until the bell went off and Miss Dottie took you out.

Off in the corner, she had one of those old-fashioned permanent-wave machines—the kind where the hair is rolled onto wires that cook the curl into it. Since they'd invented cold waves, though, hardly anybody wanted the electric kind anymore, so it just sat there like some Dr. Frankenstein contraption. I guess it was expensive and Miss Dottie hated to haul it off to the junkyard.

Not that I needed a permanent wave. Besides being white, my hair was curly to the point of kinkiness. Miss Dottie used to roll it on the biggest brush rollers she had, to try to tame it down, but it was hopeless. It would be almost smooth for about a minute, then gradually I'd feel it start to draw up and spring back into its old shape.

Every week Mama went and got a shampoo and set, and every other week I would go with her for my eyelash dye job. While Mama was under the dryer, Miss Dottie would set me on a stack of towels, pump me up high with the foot pedal and, with the tiniest brush they made, she'd paint Dark Eyes dye on my lashes and brows. Sable brown. When she first started doing it, I was scared it would get in my eyes and make me go blind, but it didn't, and after a few years I learned to do it myself. Not many people know I don't really have sable-brown lashes and brows. My hair is still Pillsbury white, but I call it platinum blond. Unfortunately, people who haven't known me all my life think it's bleached, on account of the dark brows. You never can win.

———

We waded through the squishy old onion rinds, out into the sweet-smelling morning, and gulped in that clean air like we had just been pulled from the river. Lord, there's nothing like watching the sun come up over the mountains. At first, the sky is all kind of dark hazy blue and cool. Then a blush of pink starts to warm it up—like the tail end of Picasso's blue period, when he finally began to get out of his depression and paint clowns and things in pink instead of those scrawny blue beggar people. I like Picasso a lot. At least his earlier stuff—before he started making women look like monsters with their mouths open, screaming, and sharp, spiked tongues. Even if he offered, I wouldn't let him paint my portrait for love nor money, but he's eighty-eight years old now and still going strong, so that says a lot for him. Actually, there's quite a few painters who have lived to be really old, if you think about it. Not the worst reason to go into it.

Baby and I are going to be taking our third year of oil painting at DuVall University in the fall. She likes Van Gogh the most. Maybe I do too. I can't decide. Picasso has more styles to choose from. But Van Gogh's color is wilder, and I love the way he made all those thick swirls of paint. You can tell from the way he piled on the paint that he was crazy—even then, paint couldn't have been cheap. The fact that he lopped off his own ear is also a clue. I bet the girl he sent it to was never quite the same after she opened up that little package! Kind of sweet, though, that he loved her so much. I never met a boy who would lop off his ear for me.

But then, to complicate the issue of who I like best, there is Gauguin! And Rousseau. And Peter Max. Actually, I like them all. I haven't really found my own style yet, but then it took Picasso a while before he found his.

Painting makes you look at things differently. You start thinking of everything in terms of paint colors—the cerulean blue of the sky, the sap green of the trees. The Payne's gray of the rat.

———

"Do you think Alfred Lynn actually threw out that relish?" I asked Baby as I dug around in my purse for the car keys.

"I doubt it. He probably trucked it out one door and in the other. You can bet I'm eating my hot dogs with just mustard for a few years. Let's go and get us some breakfast. Smelling onions always makes me hungry."

3. *Cherry*

We pulled up to the Deep South in my Volkswagen. It was a great car—still painted its original green, and it had a radio that worked and a heater that blew full blast all the time, summer and winter, although in an Arkansas summer the car's heater felt cool compared to the air outside. Baby had one just like it—same color, same year: '56. What is really freaky is that we got them on the same day, and neither of us knew the other one had it until we talked on the phone that night. I almost think sometimes that we were twins in a previous life, if you believe in that stuff, and I kind of do. We were always together in one car or the other, and nobody could tell them apart unless they looked close and saw that the dents were in different places. My daddy bought mine for a hundred dollars three years ago, so I could drive back and forth to college. I wanted to live on campus, but we only lived ten miles away, and we couldn't afford it anyhow. One reason he got the Volkswagen was that it was the cheapest on gas. I could go a whole week on a dollar's worth.

At least Daddy gave in about me being an art major. At first he carried on about how I would never be able to support myself by painting and what I really should do was to become a pharmacist. There was always money in sick people. Mama agreed, but she thought maybe I should be a nurse—they stand more of a chance of marrying a rich doctor, being around them all the time. I told her in no uncertain terms that I didn't plan on having to marry some man, especially a doctor, to make me a living. I figured I'd be able to do that myself. Plus, the very thought of a hospital or medicine makes me gag.

We fought back and forth, but they finally knuckled under on the condition that I get an art-teaching degree so I would have a steady paycheck. People raised during the Depression are just obsessed with steady paychecks. Daddy wasn't even forty-five yet, and talked all the time about saving for retirement.

Baby's parents didn't care what she did. They are great people, but I'm not real sure they even know what an art major is. They've tried hard to stay Filipino and not mix too much in modern America. Baby's father runs a fish-and-bait store out by the lake, and her mother—Baby calls them Tatang and Manang—was all the time drying fish up on the roof or cooking fish-head stew and rice. She's a good cook, and eating over there is interesting, but you don't want to inquire too closely what's on your plate. She makes dishes like barbecued chicken intestines—I kid you not. Once I grabbed a handful of what I thought were nuts and they turned out to be some kind of foul-tasting dried octopus testicles or something. Frankly, if she didn't look exactly like her parents, I would think Baby was adopted.

—

Nestled among all the big trailer trucks in the parking lot of the Deep South was a deputy sheriff's car. What bad luck. It had to be Ricky Don Sweet. I sure didn't feel like making light conversation with Ricky Don, looking the way I did and smelling to high heaven of onions. He was enough of a pain without me giving him more ammunition to rag on me with.

Me and Ricky Don have a history. Besides our going to school together since the first grade, he was my first real boyfriend, in the tenth. He was a big football player—got to be captain our senior year—and had a reputation for meanness on the field. If you ever played against him, you knew that he'd pull your leg hair or twist your arm in a pileup. He was the only one I knew that really wanted to go to Vietnam. "I'm gonna show those gooks what a real American is," he'd say. "I'm gonna go over there and kick some butt."

Whether he kicked any butt, I couldn't say. He didn't talk about it much after he came back, at least not to me, but I think he was an adjutant in a two-star general's office and, as far as I know, never saw any combat. The only scar he had was from football. He got the top of his nose scraped off at the beginning of the football season his junior year, and the scab kept getting knocked off during every game or practice. It was bloody for a whole solid year. Now he had a scar, but it made him look kind of sexy. Dangerous. Like a cougar, with his sandy hair and pale gray eyes. He scared me a little bit then—if I'm honest, he still does—and when he asked me to go steady at Christmas our sophomore year, I took his ring, even though it was the last thing I wanted to do. The fact is, I sneaked around and dated other boys, and on at least three occasions that

I knew of, he found out and beat the guy up. That cut down on my social life considerably. Every time he'd beat one up, he'd turn up at my house sorry and crying and begging me not to leave him, claiming that he'd kill himself if I did. It was pitiful. There's nothing worse than a big, scary football player crying around over a girl, especially if it's yourself.

Usually, I promised that if he would shut up I wouldn't leave him, but after a while it got to be kind of a drag. Finally, when he had done it for the second time in a month, I said to go ahead, that I didn't care if he killed himself. And I didn't.

He slammed out the door and got into his old beat-up truck. He was going to drive off the bluff and end it all in a tangled heap of steel on Nehi Mountain. How like him to pick a method of suicide that left a big mess for somebody else to clean up.

After he left, I sat quietly thinking about what I'd say to his folks at the funeral. I would have to convince them it wasn't my fault, which might not be easy. They would be mad at me for not trying to stop him, I was pretty sure.

I had just about decided to call somebody and tell them when he knocked on the door and said he couldn't get the truck started. He wanted me to come out and give him a push. Can you beat that? I was quite a bit put out, to say the least, that not only was I the cause of him killing himself, but I had to help him get his old truck started so he could go and do the job.

Needless to say, since he was sitting here this minute in the Deep South, he hadn't done it. I would have probably thought more of him if he had, and he knew it.

———

Baby and I went on in and sat down in the back booth. The Deep South was a truck stop open twenty-four hours a day, and it was the gathering place at one hour or the other for just about everybody. At night, after out-of-town ball games, the buses used to stop off there on their way back to the school, and everyone—football players, cheerleaders, band, and spectators—would take over the whole place. We'd invariably order a Deep South salad and lemon icebox pie. The salad was ordinary iceberg lettuce with tomato, ham, and cheese cut up in it, but the dressing was spectacular—creamy garlic so strong it made your nose run. The bus windows would fog over with the smell of our breath when we got back on.

The early mornings belonged to the truck drivers, and now, they packed the place. It was pretty rowdy at six o'clock, with all those truckers getting tanked up on coffee for their runs to Tulsa or New Mexico, carrying loads of frozen chickens, TV dinners from the Swanson plant, or crates of Atlas pickles, whose trucks were painted with their red logo of a muscle-bound Atlas holding a giant pickle on his shoulders. Along with the locals, there were a lot of out-of-state guys, on their way through to California or points north. They all gave us the once-over. Some, the twice-over. Ricky Don was at the counter telling jokes in that big loud donkey voice of his. He was swiping at his greasy eggs with a biscuit when he spotted us.

"'Scuse me, boys. I got to pay my respects to some ladies here." He popped the biscuit into his mouth, chewing as he got up, and carried his coffee cup with him.

He swaggered over to our table with that walk they teach them at sheriff school, hitching up his big brass belt buckle. In the three years since we'd graduated, his tight athlete's body had gone just the tiniest bit to fat. I could see him at our ten-year reunion with a real gut. He still slicked his hair back with Wildroot Creme Oil, even though most of the guys at college were letting theirs grow long and natural. He sure would never be mistaken for a hippie. The shiny name tag on his shirt said SWEET. Sweet Valley was named after one of his great-great-great-grandpas or something, and there were a zillion Sweets living around the county, but in relation to Ricky Don, the name always struck my funny bone.

"What're you laughing at, Highpockets?" He started calling me that when I was twelve, and still did.

"I'm just happy, Ricky Don. Peeling onions all night long always makes me laugh."

"I'm glad to see you're just as nutty as you ever were. Mind if I sit down?"

I scooted over, and Ricky Don settled his six-foot-two self into more than his share of the red Naugahyde booth.

"Y'all do smell. Phew! I'll try to hold my nose long enough to finish this coffee. Although after what all else I been smelling tonight, onions smell pretty good."

"What's that, your left armpit?" Baby never could resist.

"No, Miss Wiseass. A body."

"A body? Whose body? What body?" we said together.

"You remember Carlene Moore?"

"Yeah—sure."

Of course we remembered Carlene. She was in our class but dropped out in the eleventh grade because she got pregnant by Jerry Golden, the one who was killed in Nam. It was a big scandal at the time.

"It wasn't her, was it?" Baby looked scared.

I guess I did too. "Ricky Don, don't tell me that."

"Yep. It sure was. We found her floating in the lake this morning about four o'clock. Ol' John Aldridge and some boys were running trotlines and she was snagged on one of the hooks. She hadn't been in the water for more than a few hours, they think. But even so, I can tell you it was not a pretty sight. We had to take the boys and go get Doc McGuire out of bed to treat them for shock over it."

I looked over at Baby, who had all of a sudden gotten quiet. She looked a little pale. "Baby? Are you all right?" I said.

She took a deep breath, like she couldn't get enough air into her lungs. "I'm okay. What happened to her? Who did it?"

"Y'all don't want to know what happened. And if we knew who did it, we'd have him thrown under the jail already. But I will tell you this: She died hard. Horrible as they were, they don't think she died from her wounds. They think she might have been alive when they throwed her in. She drowned."

Ricky Don paused for effect. He got what he wanted. We sat there with our teeth in our mouths, too stunned to say a word. He looked at one of us, and then the other. He smiled, satisfied with himself, and got up, flipping a dime onto the table.

"Coffee's on me. I'll see y'all. Be careful now."

He went on out, and the waitress came over to take our order, but it seemed like neither one of us was too hungry. We had known Carlene since we were six.

———

She was one of those carrottop flaming redheads with a jillion freckles. As if that wasn't bad enough, she came to school one day in the third grade with her hair dyed coal black. It made her skin look kind of pale green. The kids started calling her Spook. She acted like she didn't care, and even seemed proud when she said her mother did it so they would look alike. Her mother's hair was black. I don't know if it was dyed or not. Nobody ever saw her but rarely. Frannie Moore was a little odd, bordering on card-carrying crazy. She wore filmy nylon dresses, even in the wintertime—black, with red and yellow flowers. I don't know where she bought them, but she must have had a bunch, because that's all I ever saw her wear. She used to cut her old ones down for Carlene, but she wasn't much of a seamstress, because some of them came down to Carlene's ankles. I can still see her skinny little white feet in scuffed patent leather shoes sticking out from under the hems. Kind of strange-looking on a third-grader, to say the least.

Carlene couldn't run very fast or skip rope or hang from the tommy-walkers in those long dresses. She always had bruises or cuts on her, too, so I guess she was pretty accident-prone, and must have tripped a lot. She mostly stood off to the side at recess, chewing on her fingernails. When we tried to play with her, she just shook her head and kept gnawing. Coming to school, she sat alone on the backseat of the bus, and she ate her lunch out of a brown paper sack, by herself. Maybe she was ashamed of what she brought—usually a cold, greasy biscuit left over from break-fast; once in a while, a pack of Twinkies.

I remember one time we had to do a book report and Carlene brought in a picture book that belonged to her daddy. The teacher paddled her and locked the book in her drawer, so we never did exactly know what was in it, but the boys said there were pictures of naked women.

After the black started to grow out, she really did look funny, with red-and-black-striped hair, until one day she came to school with it cropped almost in a burr, and it was totally red again. I guess the kids kind of made fun of her, although I didn't. I knew what it was like; I'd had all I needed of them laughing at me and my long skinny legs and frizzy white hair.

But Carlene was pretty tough about the teasing; she ignored it and acted like it didn't much bother her. Finally, the novelty wore off and gradually we stopped thinking of her as weird. Still, she was quiet and hardly ever spoke up in class unless the teacher asked her a direct question, even though she usually knew the answer. I don't know who she ran around with, but I don't think she had many friends. She lived out by the lake in a trailer, and her mother worked. Her daddy ran off and left her and her mother when she was thirteen or fourteen. She didn't say much about it, but that was the rumor. He wasn't much account, anyhow, from what they said.

Once she got to be a teenager, though, she started using makeup to cover the freckles and was really not that bad-looking, given the fact that she was a little too fond of blue eye shadow. Then, to our surprise, in the ninth grade, she went out for the girl's basketball team and made the squad. She was good at it—a real hustler. The coach loved her, and Carlene made all-district her sophomore year. The coach tried like crazy to get me to join the team, too, for the obvious reason that I was the tallest girl at school. I finally agreed to try it, but after running two miles—and lagging two whole laps behind everyone else—then running up and down the bleachers until I nearly blacked out, I realized I wasn't cut out to be a basketball player and quit. I was never too sure which goal I was supposed to be shooting at, either, and I felt stupid and ugly in the shorts. But I remember Carlene ran those miles like a sturdy little horse and didn't seem to be overly out of breath, in spite of the fact that she smoked. She was really kind of a jock, I guess. At least she liked to act like she was—independent and tough.

So all in all, it was a surprise when she started going out with Jerry Golden, who, as I said, was president of the class, an honor student, quarterback of the football team, and a really great guy: tall, dark, and the proverbial handsome. His dad was the pastor of the Church of Christ, and he was one of the leaders of our in-crowd, so to speak, although I hate that term. I mean—don't get me wrong—we were happy for Carlene, but they seemed like an unlikely match. All of a sudden, here was a girl we had never thought much about before and she had landed the prize catch of the class. Even if he was going out with her for the obvious reason, we had to give her a second look.

While she never got to be a close friend of Baby's or mine, after Jerry hooked up with her, he brought her to a lot of our parties. I remember talking to her at one, and she told me she was a big admirer of Shirley MacLaine—probably because they had the same color hair. In fact Carlene did look a little bit like her—and she said that she wanted to go to Hollywood and be a movie star. Of course I didn't laugh at her right to her face, but I remember thinking it was a pretty far-fetched dream. I mean, she was cute, but sort of—oh, I don't know—hard somehow, or something, bless her heart. On the other hand, maybe hard is good in Hollywood.

The movie-star ambition was short-lived, because they weren't together more than a year when her luck ran out and she got pregnant. This is where it gets pretty bad, because Jerry, who made straight A's and talked about being a lawyer, denied that it was his. I mean, you can't really be sure with anybody, but Carlene told us it was Jerry's, and she was so crazy about him that it couldn't have been anybody else's. We never heard of her going out with anybody else. They were stuck all day like glue, sitting together in assembly, taking all the same classes, eating lunch side by side. He drove out to the lake every morning to pick her up for school. They used to talk to each other nose to nose, like they were about to kiss at any minute. It made you feel uncomfortable, like maybe you should look away. I wondered if they were ever concerned that their breath wasn't fresh.

After he denied it, as much as we liked him and wanted to believe him, it was hard to see her at school, getting bigger every day, crying as she walked down the hall, and him just ignoring her. She wore a long brown coat, even though it was nearly May, thinking that it hid her belly or something. Jerry tried to act normal, joking around with all of us and try-ing to pretend nothing was wrong, but it got to be pretty tense.

Then the principal called her into the office and "suggested" that she drop out. I guess he figured she was a bad influence on the rest of us, like we were all going to run right out and get pregnant ourselves because we could see how great it was for her. She did drop out, even though there was only a month left of school. Instead of Jerry finishing high school and going on to the university like he planned, he left right after our junior year, bummed around over the summer, and joined the army. Even though he tested really high and could have probably gotten OCS and gone in as a second lieu-tenant, he didn't. He just went into the infantry, like anybody who'd been drafted. That was a sure bet he'd be headed for Vietnam, but he didn't seem to care. It just about undid his parents, plus being the biggest and last mis-take he would make. After Carlene had the baby—a boy, I think—she didn't come back for senior year, and I kind of lost track of her.

—

I couldn't get over it. The baby was an orphan. He must be nearly four now—not a baby, but a big kid. Amazing. I couldn't imagine having a four-year-old. I still felt like a kid myself, most of the time. I wondered where the boy was and who was taking care of him. Probably Carlene's mother, if she could do that and still work. I wondered if Jerry's mother and daddy would acknowledge now that the baby was his. I hoped so. They'd lost Jerry, but at least she had his son. Assuming it was his son. That was something. In that way, it was good they'd had the baby—a little piece of both of them was still alive. On the other hand, if Carlene hadn't gotten pregnant, Jerry wouldn't have joined the army and gone to Vietnam, and she probably wouldn't have gotten into whatever it was she got into. Both of them dead because of one little moment in time, one wrong choice. That is so scary. Even one sentence can sometimes change a whole life. Gives you something else to worry about, and right then I was starting to worry plenty.

———

"The third one of us," Baby said. "The third one of our class to die. First Bobby, then Jerry, and now Carlene."

It was bad enough to have our boys fighting in that insane war clear on the other side of the world, horrible enough that Bobby Kennedy and Martin Luther King had both been murdered in cold blood last year, but now some maniac right here in Sweet Valley, Arkansas, had killed Carlene Moore.

"What do you reckon he did to her, Baby?"

"Ricky Don is right. I don't know, and I don't want to know. Let's just keep our car doors locked when we go home and look in the backseat before we get in. No telling who did it or where he is now."

We got into my car and headed to Baby's house, out by the lake. The sun was up and the hot smell of cut grass from the mowers on the highway blew in through our open windows as we turned down the dirt road that ran along the lake shore. Neither one of us had much to say. I dropped Baby off and headed home. I just wanted to take a hot bath and crawl between a pair of cool sheets to sleep. And try not to dream about Carlene Moore.

4. *Cherry*

 When I got up later in the afternoon, the whole family was at our house clumped around the TV watching the moon landing. I sat down with them, and we all stared at the screen. For what seemed like hours.

It was phenomenal that we were able to go that far and try to actually land, but frankly, there was just nothing to see up there. Even on a color TV, all you could make out were some fuzzy black-and-white pictures of rocks and dirt. Although the earth looked pretty cool from that perspective, you couldn't just keep staring at rocks and dirt forever. They were supposed to get out and walk, but that might not be for ages.

The aunts had brought over stuff for a picnic out in the backyard, and my mother had custard simmering on the stove to make ice cream. I stirred it for a minute, then wandered outside to see what the cousins were up to. They had burned out on the moon landing a while ago.

—

Most of us in my family are big and blond-headed. Daddy—David Marshall—and his brothers, Ray and Jake, are six-five or six-six, and Mama and her sister, Rubynell, are five-ten or more. My mama's name is Ivanell. Now that I have just said their names, it hits me again how awful it must have been for them to grow up with those names. I don't think Grandma even had a sense of humor about it. She just liked how they sounded. It's a good thing they are good-looking women. Can you imagine if they were ugly and had those names? Or, worse, if they had been named some little-girl cutesy names, like Debbie or Tammy? (Cherry, at least, stands for Cheryl Ann, and I never think of it as cutesy.)

Aunt Rubynell and Uncle Jake only had one girl, a year younger than me, named Lucille Desiree, after some book Aunt Rubynell was reading at the time she had her. We are double cousins, obviously, because Aunt Rubynell is Mama's sister, and Uncle Jake is Daddy's brother. They aren't twins or anything; they just happened to marry brothers and have names that rhyme. In fact, it was a double wedding. The only thing they didn't do together was have babies. Mama beat Aunt Rubynell to that. Growing up, Lucille and I were like sisters, but now that I am in college at DuVall, we don't see each other all the time like we used to, although we're still pretty close.

Part of the reason, too, is that Lucille got married and pregnant, not necessarily in that order. Her husband, Jim Floyd Hawkins, worked at Wilmerding's Funeral Parlor, and had ever since he was sixteen. When they were dating, Jim Floyd's job was to stay all night with the bodies—I think there is a rule in this state that you can't leave a corpse unattended or something—and Lucille would keep him company. They spent their evenings making out on the couch in the grieving room. The baby was more than likely conceived right there in front of some dead person. It kind of gives you the creeps. Now he had worked his way up to assistant embalmer and was doing so well that Mr. Wilmerding was going to send him to mortuary school in Dallas in the fall to get his diploma.

After all those years of making out around dead people, Lucille got real comfortable with them, and Mr. Wilmerding gave her a job doing the makeup and hair of the corpses. I can tell you that some of those old ladies would turn over in their graves—if they were in them yet—at the amount of rouge and lipstick she puts on. They look like shriveled-up Las Vegas showgirls. But most of the families don't complain. Either they are too much in shock or they don't want to hurt Lucille's feelings.

The two of them, Lucille and Jim Floyd, live in a trailer out in Aunt Rubynell and Uncle Jake's backyard. Lucille was about to deliver any minute, and had spent most of the day lying around in the shade hollering for Jim Floyd to get her glasses of ice tea. Talk about paying for your sins—Jim Floyd sure was.

———

"Come on out here, Cherry. Pull you up a chair and tell me what Ricky Don said about Carlene. Jim Floyd didn't get to see her when they brought her in."

Lucille had her legs all splayed out, lying back on the webbed-nylon chaise, and didn't even care that anybody who looked could see all the way to China.

I unfolded a blue-and-white lawn chair and joined them in the shade under the pecan trees.

"Ricky Don didn't tell us much of anything, just that it was awful. To tell you the honest truth, Lucille, I didn't ask him any details. I have enough nightmares as it is from the pickle plant."

"Do you think he cut off her tits?"

Lucille herself had just about the biggest boobs I ever saw. They were enormous before, but since she had gained eighty pounds with this baby, they looked like they were going to pull her off the chaise every time she turned over. I didn't want to think about the sweat somebody would work up trying to cut them off.

"I don't know, Lucille. Can't we talk about something else? I bet whoever did it is long gone from here."

"I bet he's not. I bet it's somebody right here in this town. I bet it was a sex maniac. Sex maniacs are often the most common, gentle people you know." Lucille's eyes glowed just thinking about it.

"It could be somebody we went to school with, or even somebody like old Mr. McRae down at the post office," she went on. "On the surface just quietly minding his own business for forty years, but underneath—a raving sex maniac."

I didn't think old Mr. McRae could do much in the sex-maniac department. He worked with Daddy down at the post office, was at least seventy-five years old, and had lost a leg in the First World War. He wore khakis with safety pins pinning his empty pants leg up and hopped back and forth on his one leg from the window to the mail bins. But in a way, Lucille was right. It could be anybody.

———

"Don't y'all want to come in here and see these astronauts? They're getting closer to getting out," Mama yelled at us from the back door.

"No, Mama. Just you watch and tell us when they're about to." I felt a little guilty that I was missing one of the great moments of history, but enough is enough. After *Star Trek* and all the wonderful worlds that Kirk and Spock had conquered, the moon, even though it was real, seemed a little bare and boring.

George Wesley came out carrying the ice cream freezer. G. Dub, as we called him, was my only other cousin. His father was Daddy's brother uncle Ray, but his mother wasn't related to Mama or Aunt Rubynell, even though they all acted like sisters.

G. Dub set the freezer down, poured it full of cracked ice and salt, and started turning the crank.

"Why ain't you over at Wilmerding's, Jim Floyd? I come by early this morning and there was a gang of cars, cops and all, parked outside. What are they doing with her?"

"She's gone. They've done took her to Little Rock, G. Dub." Jim Floyd flicked his cigarette butt. "This thing's too big for these local boys. They've called in the state boys. They wouldn't even let me in to work this morning. Wouldn't let any of us even see her. This thing is big."

"Well, they'll have to bring her back here to bury her. Her folks are all buried up at Shady Vista." Lucille drained the last of her ice tea with a slurp and fished out a piece of ice to chew. "I'll probably have to do her hair. Even if they have her all fixed up, we'll still be able to see if he cut off her tits."

"I wish to goodness we could change the subject." I probably spoke a little louder than I should have. This whole thing was creeping me out.

"All right, all right." G. Dub stopped cranking for a minute. "Let's talk about something else. Here, Cherry, reach over and get that sack of salt and pour some more in this ice."

I got up and gave him the salt bag. G. Dub could see that the conversation was getting to me, and from the way he was turning that crank, it looked like it was getting to him, too. To Lucille and Jim Floyd, dead people are perfectly normal. They don't mean anything by it. It is just their life.

G. Dub and I have always had a cousinly crush on each other, probably more on my side than his. When I was six or seven, I used to think I would marry him when we grew up. But it would be impossible, since it's probably against the law, and our kids would likely be retards. He was two years older than me, and so good-looking that I always caught my breath when I saw him. His mother, Aunt Juanita, is a full-blooded Cherokee from Vian, Oklahoma. Uncle Ray met her on one of his truck runs—he used to drive an eighteen-wheeler for Atlas until they got married and Aunt Juanita made him quit and start farming. She knew the kind of trouble those truckers get into on long runs. She is little and dark, with the whitest teeth you ever saw. Eats hot peppers right out of the jar like they were peanuts, and has a temper to match. There is no question about who wears the pants in that family.

G. Dub got all the good stuff from that mix of genes. He is not as big as Uncle Ray—or even me—but where all the rest of us are blond, he has coal-black straight hair and that dark kind of complexion that tans in two minutes.

Lucille and I used to lie out in the sun trying to get a tan until we were boiled red in our own sweat and had clear blisters all over our bodies. In spite of greasing ourselves up with baby oil and iodine, a mixture *Glamour* magazine guaranteed would give you a golden tan, we peeled off twice every time, and neither one of us ever got darker than unbleached flour. Then this cream stuff called QT came out that was supposed to tan you without the sun, and I was the first one in line to buy some. Ha. I don't want to even describe the awfulness of the week it took to wear off. Let's just say my new nickname was Sunkist for a while.

When we were little, G. Dub was pretty nice to us, given the fact that we were girls. He played games with us, like touch football, baseball, or tag—even though he was good at everything and Lucille and I were too uncoordinated to walk and chew gum at the same time. It wasn't our fault. We just grew too fast for our bodies to keep up, and it seemed like my legs got a head start on the rest of me. I looked down one day when I was about twelve and noticed the longest, skinniest thighs I had ever seen sticking out of my Bermuda shorts. They seemed to have sprung out overnight. And let me tell you that growing pains are not a myth. My knees ached and hurt until Mama got scared and took me to see Doc McGuire. He X-rayed and poked and pinched and couldn't see anything wrong.

Finally, he said, "Ivanell, the girl's body is just growing too fast. You can expect her to be another big-boned Marshall." And I sure was. The rest of my body gradually caught up with my legs, but they are still far and away the longest part of me.

But G. Dub never made fun of me or Lucille, even when she turned thirteen and her flat chest ballooned out to a size D in what seemed like weeks and everyone called her Boober. He told her she looked like Jayne Mansfield. She did, kind of, but I'm not sure he did her any favors by pointing it out to her.

G. Dub thought up great games. Every Saturday, we'd go out to his farm and ride horses bareback with just a rope bridle, playing like we were Sky King and Annie Oakley, galloping over the fields screaming like wild

Indians. One game G. Dub and me played, when Lucille was not around, was hiding up in the top of the barn loft and playing doctor, or whatever else the excuse was to look at and feel of each other. We would practice kissing with our mouths closed tight, and sometimes we would take off our clothes and he would lie on top of me and put his soft little weenie against my leg, where it lay like a fat worm. Neither one of us knew exactly what we were doing, but it's funny—even little kids have instincts. Preservation of the species, I guess. When we were eight and ten, we stopped doing it and neither one of us ever mentioned it again. Come to think of it, I wonder if he and Lucille did the same thing. It would be just like her. She would never tell me the truth, though, so I might as well not ask.

———

As he turned the crank on the ice cream bucket, G. Dub's hair swung back and forth, shiny and black, with every rotation of the handle. His hair was almost to his shoulders. His daddy said he was going to catch him asleep and cut it off one night, but I don't think even Uncle Ray had the nerve to do that. G. Dub worked at Uncle Jake's Esso station and was in pretty good shape from hefting tires all day.

"Jim Floyd, would you mind running in the house and getting me a glass of ice tea? I am just parched, and it would take a derrick to get me up off of this." Lucille already had three empty glasses sitting on the ground beside her.

She reached down, with some difficulty, to get them, but gave up and fell back.

"Here, take in these glasses. You don't have to get a new glass every time."

Jim Floyd slowly gathered up the glasses and ambled on into the house. If you ask me, Lucille is lucky to have bagged him. He is the most easygoing man I know—if you can call a nineteen-year-old a man. Nothing ever gets him too excited, and it seems like he moves in slow motion all the time. They used to call him Lightning on the football team, as a joke, and he never got in the game unless we were six or eight touchdowns ahead. He's not good-looking—he's a shrimp, not more than five-six, and skinny to boot. He has stringy hair-color hair and a long George Armstrong Custer mustache that droops like the rest of him. But he is wild for Lucille. He can't believe his luck at getting that blond mountain of woman to fall in love with him.

A lot of little guys are like that—worker bees buzzing around their queen. They love parading their woman down the street and thinking everyone is admiring them for the sheer guts they have to copulate with all that flesh. I tried not to think about Lucille and Jim Floyd doing it in the funeral parlor. It is just too obscene.

Sex is such a weird business, isn't it? I have to confess right here that I am still—you certainly can't count G. Dub—a virgin. Not that I'm holier than thou or anything. It just hasn't hit me yet. The closest I ever came was with Ricky Don Sweet our senior year of high school. We had broken up two years before, after that night he tried to drive his truck off the bluff, but there was still that little attraction. It's a long story . . . but I might as well tell it now. It will explain a lot about Ricky Don and me.

There has always been a certain kind of guy who really went for me. Not many, because most guys are put off by somebody as big and gawky and strange-looking as I am, but the ones that aren't—they really aren't. Ricky Don was one. Maybe it started when we were kids. Until we were twelve or thirteen, I was bigger than him, and he always had to prove that he was the strongest or fastest or whatever. No matter what game we played, he had to beat me. Even after he caught up and passed me in size, he was like that. I don't know what the big deal was. He never had any trouble beating me at anything, unless it required some brains, like Clue or Monopoly.

When we were seniors, we started dating again—almost by process of elimination, since Sweet Valley is not that big and we had gone through nearly everybody else around. At first it was just friendly—going to the movies, riding around or out to the Freezer Fresh to get a Coke. I never intended to get in the position of having to take that ring again, and we, of course, never mentioned him trying to kill himself. But somehow, maybe because we were older, this time it was different. We started kissing one night when we were parked up on the bluffs of Nehi Mountain, and before I knew it, he had figured out a way to get my bra off without removing my shirt. It involved unhooking the back and pulling it out through my sleeve. Ricky Don always was good with his hands. I think I let him just to see if he could.

Then we started getting in deeper and deeper. It was crazy—like I didn't know my own self. On one hand, I really couldn't stand him, but when we started kissing it didn't seem to matter that he wore hair oil or that he laughed too loud when things weren't that funny. Parked on the bluffs or out at the lake, he would knead my tiny boobs for hours. I couldn't imagine there was enough there to interest him. I was always as flat as a boy. I sure never got anything out of it except sore nipples.

Probably it wasn't enough for him, either, because he started going for more, and we had some real wrestling matches. I'm pretty strong for a girl, and he never once got to third base, though he tried for months.

Then homecoming came. Baby and I were elected senior maids. That's not as unbelievable as it seems, because the maids and queen are picked by the football players. Since the captain was Ricky Don and he was still trying with might and main to get in my pants, I'm sure he scared them all into voting for us—he knew I wouldn't have done it unless Baby got it, too. Of course, Ricky Don was my escort onto the field for the pregame ceremony.

The queen, Cindy Ragsdale—a cute little cheerleader with bouncy boobs and ratted hair that was sprayed into a concrete-solid, perfect flip— wore a long white satin dress and a rhinestone crown. All us maids wore long dresses with blue velvet spaghetti-strap tops and white satin skirts— Sweet Valley is the Blue Tornadoes, and our colors are blue and white. Under the big, full skirts, I had on seven layers of can-can slips that made me feel like a ringing bell as I swayed across the field with my hand in the crook of Ricky Don's arm. The slips were so big and fluffy that I had a hard time squeezing into our car. They filled up the whole backseat.

During the game, we girls sat next to the field up on a float that had taken us weeks to make out of gazillions of squares of blue and white crepe paper, which we stuffed into chicken wire. It spelled out GO, BLUE TORNADOES! and had a blue tornado in the middle with mean eyes and big teeth.

It was early November, but freezing. The longer we sat on that float, the colder it got. In spite of the mouton coats we had all borrowed from former queens and maids, we turned as blue as our dresses. I must say, though, it really made you feel like something to sit up there and have the whole school—the whole town—come up and congratulate you and stare at you like you are royalty or a movie star. It was especially great for Baby and me, since I was always too spastic to be a cheerleader like the really popular girls. Baby didn't even try out for cheerleader. They probably would have elected her, but she said she didn't want to. I think she was just being loyal to me.

Come to think of it, Carlene came up to the float carrying her baby and talked to us that night. We all said what an adorable baby it was and how we all wished we had one. Of course, none of us meant it, but I think it made her feel a little better. Looking back, I can see how miserable she was, in spite of trying hard to be happy and showing off the baby. She stood by the fence for most of the game and watched the cheerleaders, a lot of whom had gotten friendly with her when she was on the basketball team. They all came over and oohed and aahed, but then they went back and did their routines while she stood there hugging the baby. I felt bad for her, but it was too exciting a night to spend much time thinking about Carlene.

We were in heaven. We won the game. Of course we won the game. We always schedule to play our sorriest opponent at homecoming, to make sure we win. But Ricky Don made three touchdowns and was feeling full of himself. I sat in his truck and waited while he showered and cleaned up, and then we went to the gym to the dance.

The homecoming dance theme was the Blue Grotto, and the cheerleaders and pep club had decorated it like an underwater cave, with blue lights, fishnets, and plastic lobsters and crabs. The crepe-paper flowers at all the tables had been sprayed with Tabu, and they smelled so loud you had to strain to get a whiff of the sweat socks. Ricky Don had even washed the Wildroot Creme Oil out of his hair, and it was soft and fell over his eye in a wave, just the way I liked it.

Baby's boyfriend, Bean Boggs, was the leader of the Draggons, the band that played, and he looked really cool up on the stage with his Beatles haircut and leather pants, like Mick Jagger wore, and little round rose-colored sunglasses. The Rolling Stones were their idols, and they sounded almost as good as them on "Satisfaction."

After we all wore ourselves out dancing to the fast songs, they played "Theme from *A Summer Place*," which always turns my knees to jelly. Ricky Don took me into his arms and breathed on my neck. It just about undid me. I begin to think that there might be a sensitive side to Ricky Don, after all. As soon as the crowd started to thin out, we got into the truck and headed for the lake.

—

The moon was full, and the water was still and smooth as satin. Little fish came up to sniff the surface and made bubbles that went out in rings and rippled the moonlight. It was cold, but we had the truck windows fogged up in about five minutes. Ricky Don had decided that tonight was going to be the big night. No more wrestling like fifteen-year-olds. We were going to actually *do it*. After careful consideration and a half hour of hot, sticky kisses, I thought it might not be such a bad idea. I was going to be eighteen in a few months, and in the fall I would be a college girl. In the back of my mind, I was afraid I might go to hell, but it was pretty far back.

Ricky Don managed to maneuver his pants down in spite of the gearshift, and then went digging through my slips. Under the best of circumstances it would have been a nearly impossible job, and these were not exactly the best of circumstances.

He still had the same old truck he had planned on driving off Nehi Mountain—a '53 Plymouth—and one of the springs stuck up through the vinyl seat cover and poked me in my back. Besides being uncomfortable, I was scared it would tear my dress, which poofed out and filled up the truck cab. I had to fight the slips, which kept billowing up in my face. It was hard to focus on romance. But Ricky Don was one determined fellow. He finally found what he was looking for, and I felt something hard punching in the general direction of my you-know-what, but it was missing the mark and hitting the bone. I tried to tell him, but the slips muffled my voice. Or maybe he was just concentrating too hard to hear.

Then all of a sudden, Ricky Don screamed. He jumped off, flung open the truck door, and grabbed his Jockey shorts, holding them in front of himself. I was a little confused, and by the time I got the dress under control and wedged myself out of the truck, he was down by the water on his knees. He was crying and carrying on like he had just had his weenie lopped off or something.

"Ricky Don, what's the matter?"

"It tore. Goddang! I'm going to bleed to death! It might be broke."

It felt like a cold hand went down my neck, and I remembered a book we girls had found buried back in the dusty stacks of the school library. It had a copyright date of 1896 and was so old that all the lettering had faded from the cover. I can't believe anybody knew it was there, or it would have been burned. It was called *Anomalies and Curiosities of Medicine*. It was a disgusting book, with drawings and photographs of freaks—like Siamese twins, three-legged men, and women who had 135-pound ovarian tumors and things, but one of the worst chapters was on wounds of the penis. We giggled at the horrible stories of men breaking their penises or having them bitten off by donkeys, and thought somebody in the 1800s had a fine imagination, but in this split second, standing on the bank of the lake, with Ricky Don on his knees howling in pain, all the case histories in that book came back to me.

I looked down at my white satin dress. It was covered with blood, and I realized that my legs were sticky with it. It seems that Ricky Don had never been circumcised, and whatever of mine he was trying to stick his tallywhacker into was too small and tough, and peeled the foreskin back until it split. He was a mess. And so was I. Why oh why didn't we wait to try this maneuver on a summer night when I was wearing jeans? If I went home in this shape, I would be dead. Mama and Daddy would kill me for sure. I might as well pack my bags and get on the bus.

The only sensible thing to do was throw myself into the lake. I took a running jump and dove in. Fortunately, there were no logs or snakes where I landed. The water was so cold it knocked the breath out of me, and I gasped for air, bobbing up to keep my feet from miring down in the muck, which was a thick slime of dead leaves and fish poop and Lord knows what else. I treaded water for a minute and then took off, trying to swim, but after a few yards the dress and slips were soaked full of water and started to pull me under. I was headed for the bottom when Ricky Don jumped in and hauled me out. He was cussing like I had never heard anybody cuss before, and when we finally lay heaving on the bank, I thought he was going to pass out.

"I think it's time we called it quits, Highpockets," he said when he got his breath back. "I just don't think I'm man enough for you. I'm gonna wind up dead for sure, one way or the other."

All I could do was nod. Suppose he had really bled to death? It would be my fault. What would they put on the death certificate? Murder weapon: a too-tight you-know-what.

"Take me to Baby's house, will you, Ricky Don? I'll spend the night with her, and think up something to tell Mama and Daddy in the morning."

——

Ricky Don stuck by his word and never did ask me out again—big surprise—and as far as I know, nobody found out about what happened. Except Baby and Bean, of course, who was at Baby's house when Ricky

Don dropped me off. Or dumped me out, would be more like it. You don't want to imagine the look on Baby's face when I dragged in through the door, my satin dress soaked with lake water and blood and my hair looking like the business end of a mop. It took Bean and me both to hold her back and keep her from getting in the car and going after Ricky Don. I don't know what she thought she was going to do if she caught him, but if it came right down to it, I would put my money on Baby to win that fight. Or any fight, for that matter.

Finally, after nearly having to sit on her, I got her to settle down so I could get into a hot tub. I told her I was afraid I'd get pneumonia—not much of a stretch—and she made Bean go home, which he didn't much like, so she could fuss over me.

We got up early the next morning and went back out there to look for my earrings, which I had lost. Although they were nowhere to be found, we did run across Ricky Don's bloody shorts. We wrapped them around a big rock and threw them far out into the middle of the lake. Hopefully, they are still on the bottom, unless some fish ate them. Wouldn't it be wild if somebody caught a big catfish, cut it open, and found Ricky Don's Jockey shorts?

When we got back to her house, Baby's mother had somehow cleaned my dress and was pressing it with a warm iron. If you weren't in a bright light, it looked almost as good as new. I don't know how she did it, and she never asked—or even said one word to me about what had happened. But I ate second helpings of her cooking with a big smile after that, no matter what it was.

—

Anyhow, the point to this story is that more than three years later, I am still a virgin. Of course, I've been out with several guys since then, but I never let anybody else get close enough to get maimed. They don't believe me when I tell them it is for their own good, and unhappily, nobody has lasted more than a couple of months. Sometimes, to tell you the truth, I get scared I will wind up an old maid, like Miss Oatsie at our church, who plays the piano for Sunday school and lives by herself with a pack of cats. I would hate that. I don't really like cats.

—

The astronauts finally walked on the moon. It was nearly eleven o'clock at night, and all of us were pretty worn-out. President Nixon called them on the phone, all the way to the moon, and told them how proud he was. I guess it was worth it, all those hours of watching. It was, after all, pretty exciting. I mean, *Star Trek* was great, but this was *real*. Anyhow, it was something to tell my kids one day.

Just as the president said, "The heavens have become part of man's world," Lucille's water broke. Right in the living room, all over Mama's Persian rug. Lucille just stood there and stared at it gushing out, like it was happening to somebody else. Aunt Rubynell ran to get towels, and Jim Floyd danced around, saying, "Honey, what can I do?"

Mama said, "Jim Floyd, what you can do is go get the car and get this girl to the hospital. She's fixing to have the baby right here in this living room."

I had never seen him move so fast. He took off running, and we got Lucille's stuff together.

She seemed real embarrassed. "I'm sorry, y'all. I thought it was all the ice tea I drunk. Aren't you supposed to have pains or something?"

Mama and the aunts laughed. "Don't worry, Lucille," Aunt Juanita said. "You'll have a pain or two. I promise." They seemed to be having a great time.

Jim Floyd was out front honking the horn like a crazy man, and they finally got Lucille out the door. The aunts and Mama went with her, but I had to go to work.

It is so strange to think of Lucille having a baby. She's younger than me—just a kid herself. I probably won't ever even have a boyfriend—at least not as long as I have to peel these stupid onions. Only a little over a month left until school starts, and I can quit this job.

I wondered if the astronauts would be able to sleep up there on the moon. On my way out to the car, I stood in the yard and looked up at it. It looked like the same old moon—silver and cool. But it would never be the same again. There were men up there, walking on its face.

I pulled out of the driveway and headed to the pickle plant, wondering what Baby had done all day. I had tried to call her a time or two during the afternoon, but her mother said she was out, and then when I finally reached her a little while before I left, she didn't really want to talk, which was not like her at all. Baby said that she hadn't watched the moon landing; she just spent the day thinking about Carlene.

That wasn't really weird or anything. G. Dub had said the whole town was in shock over the murder, and I imagined people would be locking their doors tonight—it was the first murder in Sweet Valley in years, or maybe ever. It was just a little surprising that Baby took it so hard. This morning when I dropped her off after we left the Deep South, I watched her through my rearview mirror and she didn't even go into the house, just stood in the road staring like a zombie or something until I got out of sight.

Well, I'd talk to her about it tonight. At a stop sign, I reached over and locked the passenger door. No point in taking the chance of somebody jumping into the car. You never know where the killer might be lurking out in the dark.

5. Baby

 The morning Ricky Don told them about Carlene, Baby stood in front of her house and watched Cherry drive away in the old green VW. Almost in a trance, she stared as the car boiled up dust and got smaller; stood there a long time after it disappeared around a bend, heading toward town. She wanted to go into the house, but it felt like her feet had grown roots that dug in and held her to the dried-out ground. She was so tired she couldn't move. The sun seemed to ooze over her head and run down her arms and legs, burning like honey poured from a melting pot. Gnats whined around her face, drinking from the sweat drops on her upper lip. She was too tired to brush them away.

By an act of will, she managed to go inside, take a shower, and get into bed, but instead of passing into sweet oblivion from fatigue, Baby lay awake. Every time she shut them, her eyelids popped open as if they were attached to springs. Every noise made her jump. It was hard enough to sleep in that house during the night, much less in the daytime.

Baby was the oldest of seven children, and it seemed like all of her life there had always been a baby crying or somebody screaming. She was the only girl for eight years, until, after three younger brothers, her sister Ana Pilar was born. Pilar was fourteen now, and acted much too grown-up for her age. Baby called her the Pill. She was already sneaking out to neck with boys, and more than once Baby had smelled beer and cigarettes on her breath. Manang and Tatang were oblivious, but they were oblivious to most things that went on right under their noses.

The brothers, Rosario Ronaldo—or Rocky, as he was known to his friends—Demetrio—Denny—and Juan Jesus, who liked to be called J.C., were nineteen, seventeen, and sixteen. They were always off in their own world, using the house mainly to change clothes and grab food from time to time.

Denny and J.C. lived and breathed old motorcycles and cars. If they weren't working on them, they were roaring around the mountain roads or racing down by the river in the middle of the night. One boy or the other nearly always had a cast on some body part.

Rocky spent all his time practicing with the Draggons, the band Bean Boggs had started back in high school. Rocky thought Baby's boyfriend was the coolest guy in school, and since he was always hanging around their house, Rocky kept on at him until Bean taught him to play the bass guitar. His one ambition was to join the band, which was just beginning to get a few paying gigs when Bean was drafted in '66 and sent to Tigerland, the make-believe jungle village in Louisiana where they trained the troops who were headed to Vietnam.

While he was gone, Rocky practiced day and night until the whole family thought they would lose their minds, but when Bean got back from the army early in '69, he took Rocky into the Draggons. They had plans to go to Memphis and make a record as soon as they got the money together; they'd try their luck at Sun Records, where Elvis got his start. Or maybe they would head out to L.A., where the Doors had hit it big. They knew they would make it one way or the other. It would just take time and luck.

The last two of Baby's siblings were the little girls Carmia Concepcion and Anselma Asuncion—Connie and Sunnie—still practically babies, only two and three. Baby hoped to God that Manang and Tatang were through. There was something embarrassing about a woman and man in their forties still having children.

But that was just one more thing for Baby to be embarrassed about. It wasn't easy being Oriental in Arkansas. It hadn't been all that many years ago that the whole Japanese-American population was forced into internment camps—one of which was not too far away, down at Jerome in the Arkansas delta—for the duration of World War II, and when Baby's family had first gotten here, most people thought they were Japanese. Now that the Vietnam War was exploding, everyone thought they were Vietnamese. There was no telling these ignorant rednecks anything.

Maybe being Oriental in Arkansas was better than being colored, but there were days when Baby would have traded places with any of the ten or twelve colored kids she went to high school with. At least they were born in America. Their mothers and fathers spoke the language. It was horrible that they suffered discrimination from the white world, but they had their own world they could retreat into. They had their juke joints and barbecue shacks, their blues and jazz, their own churches, and their gospel music. Their culture was uniquely American, patched together from the days of slavery to a Jim Crow society that begrudged them a seat on the bus or even a cool drink of water from a fountain. They had a shared misery and a shared joy that bound them together and made them part of something bigger than they would ever be separately.

Baby had only her family—one small unit—and they were foreign, even to each other. Manang and Tatang tried to maintain their Filipino culture, but it was an ongoing job, what with their kids, who hated that everything was different at their house. Food, for example. None of their friends' homes had the smells that saturated the Moreno home, like minced garlic, stir-fried with vegetables and shrimp or chicken. Manang cooked the parts of animals that most people threw away. Nobody in Arkansas ate like that. Here, everything—vegetables, meat, and fish—was dipped in flour or meal and fried in lard. Baby and her brothers tried to get Manang to fix food like all their friends ate. She didn't understand, but she tried. She bought Spam, but then cut it into cubes and stir-fried it with mung-bean sprouts; made hamburgers with sweet-and-sour sauce and served them on a bed of rice with steamed broccoli. She really didn't get it. No matter how hard they tried, the kids couldn't get away from their roots—or accept them, either.

Before it was moved, there used to be a little movie theater on Main Street in Sweet Valley, called the Roxy. The white people sat downstairs, and the colored people sat in the balcony. The first time Baby went there alone with Rocky—they couldn't have been more than nine and six—the woman at the ticket window didn't know where to put them.

"What are you?" the woman asked her. "You ain't white, but you ain't exactly colored, either."

Rocky didn't like the woman, and was so afraid she wouldn't let them see Hopalong Cassidy that he threw a kicking fit. To shut him up, the woman let them sit down front with the white people, so from then on they were more or less part of the white crowd. But it was humiliating.

"What are you?"

Baby had never figured it out. Arkansas had been her home for practically her whole life. In a lot of ways, she was southern to the core. She spoke the language with a thick Arkansas accent and dressed like any other girl in Sweet Valley—better than most. Everyone liked her a lot. But in her mind she would never really fit in here any more than she would if she were to go back to the Philippines.

—

Baby tossed on the hot sheets. The sun came in through pin-size holes in the green window shade. One shaft hit her right in the eye. Manang was sizzling something in a wok, and Connie and Sunnie chased each other through the house, screaming at the top of their lungs. Cartoons blasted from the old black-and-white TV. Beany and Cecil. "Ship ahoy, Cecil! I see a whale off the starboard deck!"

Baby put the pillow over her head and got a powerful whiff of onions. There was no way to get rid of the stink. Even after a scalding-hot bath and half a bottle of Jergens lotion, her hands smelled of onions. She was sweating. Her sweat smelled like onions. The old electric fan in the corner was doing its best, but it just smeared the hot air around.

As she twisted on the damp sheet, she fought back the image of a bloated body caught on a trotline hook right in the very lake that lay outside her door. What had happened to Carlene? Why would somebody do something like that? This was Sweet Valley, Arkansas—not New York City, or even Little Rock. And why did it have to be Carlene, who never hurt anybody? Baby knew Carlene a lot better than Cherry thought she did. Baby felt guilty about hiding things from Cherry. She loved her more than anyone in the world. She would stick her arm into the fire for Cherry, and they were as close as sisters in a lot of ways, but there was a line between them that Cherry was not even aware of—and if Baby had her way, Cherry would never know what was on the other side. Cherry was so good and honest and trusting that sometimes Baby trembled for her, wanted to protect her. Cherry had been raised in the Pentecostal Ho-

liness Church by strict, loving parents, and in spite of her backseat
wrestling with Ricky Don Sweet in high school, she didn't know a whole
lot about life.

Baby had had to grow up fast. Manang still couldn't speak English with
any degree of competency, so from the time she learned to read and write,
Baby more or less ran the house. She wrote the household checks and
took care of the books for her father, who made a spare living running the
boat dock and fish store, a tidy shack built next to their house on the edge
of the lake. It was attached to a long rickety pier that stretched out over
the green water and had several small rowboats tied to it, waiting to be
rented out for an afternoon's fishing.

In front of the store, under a tin awning that offered shade in the
summer—mostly to old men who liked to sit and swap stories—were a
couple of picnic tables, two benches, and a red soda chest full of Cokes
and Dr Peppers, which the Moreno children were forbidden to touch.
Above the door was a sign that said MORENO'S FRESH FISH AND BAIT in
green letters under a picture of a bottle of Coke and the flowing script
that said: Drink Coca-Cola.

Inside, on the cool concrete floors, an ice-filled case was laden with
fresh catfish, perch, crappie, and bream that a housewife could buy or a
fisherman could take home if he came back empty-handed. Underneath
sat big buckets of bait that smelled dank and earthy. There were shelves
stocked with picnic foods, like potato chips and sandwich makings, and a
case of candy that was also off-limits to the family.

With the vegetable garden and the fish, they got along all right, but all
the kids had to go to work as soon as they were able. Rocky and Denny
didn't go to college. J.C. probably wouldn't, either. Pilar might if she
could get her head on straight. But Baby was different. She was the valedictorian of her high school class, because she had worked harder than
anyone else. And the kids liked her in spite of it. She had perfected an act
of laughing at herself before anyone else had the chance. She told funny
stories about things her parents would do—like the time her mother was
drying fish and a cat snatched one and ran away. Her mother had thrown
a rock at the cat, and not only did she rescue the fish, they had cat stew
for dinner.

The kids all laughed, but not many except Cherry ever came to visit.
Certainly, not to eat. Baby made them believe she didn't care. She almost

made herself believe it. She had gotten a full scholarship to DuVall University, and next year she would graduate. Like Cherry, she wanted to be a painter, but you had to be realistic. She would become a teacher, paint in her spare time. Get the hell out of Dodge, so to speak, and go somewhere else. Anywhere that didn't smell like fish and onions.

———

Baby couldn't take the noise and heat any longer and got up. Ten o'clock. Less than three hours of sleep. Her eyes were swollen. She stood again under a hot shower and let the water burn her face, burn the puffiness away. Toweling herself, she sniffed her water-pruned fingers. Onions.

Tatang had brought in a string of frogs, and Manang was cooking them for noontime dinner. Fried frogs' legs, rice, and egg rolls. The legs jumped around in the hot wok like they were trying to escape and chase down their bodies. Manang clamped the lid down just as a pair made it to the edge, and they fell back into the sizzling oil.

Sunnie and Connie had taken the little feet out of the garbage and were dipping them into Baby's good oil paints, making cadmium-yellow frog footprints on the wallpaper.

"Sunnie! You and Connie get out of those paints! I'm going to skin you and put you in the wok with those frogs! Those paints cost money!"

In answer, Sunnie grabbed a tube of burnt sienna and squeezed the whole thing out onto her legs. She smeared it onto her shorts and her face and her sister Connie, who was trying to grab it away from her.

"Manang! Do something with them!"

Manang looked up with an uninterested glance and kept fighting the frogs' legs. "Clean them, Baby. Dinner soon ready."

One under each arm, Baby carried the howling, thrashing girls into the bathtub and scrubbed them with turpentine, then with soap. It took three or four washes and a lot of wrestling to get most of the paint off. By then, her rage had spent itself.

Now the two of them sat at the table like cherubs, their skin red and rosy—tender, if not nearly burned to the second degree—eating the delicate pieces of fragrant greenish-white meat.

Baby helped Manang with the dishes and, leaving them all glued to the TV watching the astronauts approach the moon, she went for a walk along the edge of the lake.

—

Sweet Valley Lake was man-made, built back in 1950. They dammed up the Arkansas River and diverted the runoff to the low country outside of town. It was stocked with game fish, and Tatang had opened up the boat dock and bait shop the year they moved here. It was funny to see live trees rising out of the water when the lake was first built, but by now the trees had died and all that remained were jagged black stumps. The fishing was good, and so was the boating, if you kept a careful watch. Some of the kids even water-skied, but if you weren't good at stump-jumping, you could split yourself wide open hitting one at thirty miles an hour.

Not to mention the fact that the lake was swarming with water moccasins. Rocky had once told Baby that water moccasins nested in big wads pretzeled around each other out in the lake, and he knew for a fact of one skier who fell and landed right in the middle of a nest. When they pulled him out, the boy had swelled up to three times his normal size and was so full of poison that his body turned green before they could even get him to the funeral home to embalm him.

Baby didn't really believe it—Rocky not being known for his veracity—but even if it was a total lie, the idea of wads of snakes had kept her out of the lake. Like all other snakes, water moccasins always slithered around the edge of Baby's nightmares. She wondered if snakes would bite a dead person.

It was a bright summer day, but the dark water seemed to have a red cast to it, as if Carlene's blood had colored the thousands of acres of water. The sun moved behind a cloud, shadows suddenly got cooler, and the hair on Baby's arms stood up in goose bumps. John Aldridge's trotline was usually strung right out there, not a hundred yards from shore, among the stumps where the biggest catfish liked to hide.

Baby squinted at something out in the water. She thought she could see hair floating out by the trotline. Long, carrot-colored hair. But it was only red nylon cord still attached to the empty Purex bottles that floated the line.

A set of tire tracks led up to the water, apart from the mass of tracks the police and ambulance must have made. Truck tires. Maybe the very tire tracks of the man who had dumped Carlene like the carcass of a wounded deer.

Baby turned and looked all around, deep into the woods. The silence was alive with the ambient noise that squirrels and crickets and birds make when they are undisturbed. Normal sounds. Comforting sounds. As if nothing more sinister than rain had fallen into the lake since its birth.

They say that a murderer always returns to the scene of the crime. But this murderer more than likely ran away, at least to another county, and maybe as far as Oklahoma or Texas or Missouri. Ran far away. Drove all night and drove all morning and is probably still driving. No, he would never come back here. Never again. In fact, Baby told herself, this was the safest place to be.

Baby saw a flat rock at the edge of the water and kneeled to stack two more on top of it. Then she peeled a clump of damp green moss from under a tree and placed it on top of the rocks, like velvet on a small altar. From her middle finger she removed a fragile ring that Carlene had once admired. It was made from a pink seashell and had elaborate carving.

"That ring looks like you dove to the bottom of the sea and broke it off of one of those big old seashells, Baby," Carlene had said. "I can almost hear the ocean waves in it. When I get to California, I'm going to get me one just like it. Maybe wearing a pretty ring would help me stop biting my nails."

Baby was sorry she hadn't given it to her then. But she liked it, too. And how could she know Carlene would be dead so soon? Now the ring lay on the moss.

"Take it, Carlene. I hope you're somewhere that's like a California beach full of pink seashells. I hope you're happier there than you ever were here." She flung the ring, rock, and moss into the water and tried to pray, but her thoughts kept flitting away, like hummingbirds.

She felt sleepy then. The shade was so cool; the moss, so soft. She lay down and slept until the sun went down and the mosquitoes began to bite. Then she went home to eat supper and get ready for work. Somehow she felt at peace. Like maybe Carlene was indeed someplace better.

6. *Cherry*

 "There's going to be a wedding at the church on Saturday. It seems Rayburn Earl Payton told Marcy Oates six years ago that he'd marry her when man walked on the moon."

Baby and I were still in the onion room. After two nights, Alfred Lynn had not relented and moved us, but we didn't care. They were beginning to pack hot peppers, and if anything is worse than peeling onions, it is packing hot peppers. No matter if you wear two pairs of gloves, your hands still burn like fire. And if you forget and brush your hand over your eye—oh, my Lord, forget it. There is no describing the pain.

Baby threw another onion into the basket. "I don't know why they're bothering. They've been going together for fifteen years. They must have wore it out long before this."

"It's the principle of the thing. He made a promise, and Marcy is holding him to it. There's a pool of guys here at the pickle plant betting that Rayburn Earl will back out, but Marcy's girlfriends have already given her a shower, and they would rip Rayburn Earl's arm off and beat him to death with the bloody stump if they had to take back the mixers and the chip-and-dip sets and stuff they laid out for."

One of the hotdoggers whizzed into the room on his little go-cart with a new flat of onions for us to peel.

"Whooee!" he said. "Y'all ain't never goin' to finish this load if you don't speed it up." He slid the flat off right beside us.

"I'll trade jobs with you, William Lee, if you think you can do any better."

"What? Me do woman's work? Peeling onions is all y'all are good for. Besides something else, that is." He dodged the onion I chucked at him, laughed, threw the buggy into reverse, and zoomed out. Boys can be so ignorant it's not even worth worrying about.

I tossed my pile of onion peels onto the mound on the floor, split one of the new bags open with my paring knife, and filled the pan I held in my lap.

"She probably would like to have a baby. Marcy is already thirty-two, but she might still be able to have one. If they hurry."

"Well, I hope she gets what she wants. Myself, I can't picture marrying that stupid Rayburn Earl, or anybody else right now. Not even Bean." Baby still seemed a little down, but I wasn't worried about her anymore. She said last night that it was just the shock of the news about Carlene that had gotten to her, but she felt better now.

"Me neither," I said, and I meant it. "I want to live a little before I have to settle down with a husband and a squalling baby. Speaking of which, I can't believe I forgot to tell you. Lucille finally had her baby this afternoon."

"Did she? What was it?"

"A girl. Ten pounds and eight ounces. Fattest little thing you ever saw. Her eyes are just slits. She's almost as big as Jim Floyd right now."

"Did Lucille have a hard time?"

"I guess so. She was in labor fourteen hours. You won't believe it, but Mama said that they had just shaved her you-know-what and given her an enema and she was sitting on the porta-potty passing the entire contents of her bowels—which I will try not to think about, given the fact that she had not only eaten two orders of Taco Loco the night before but also three helpings of kraut and weenies—when the whole ladies' auxiliary from our church trooped in to see how she was progressing and to give her moral support."

"I bet that popped their eyes, the old biddies." Baby threw her peelings onto the floor.

"You don't know the half of it. Lucille started cussing at them and throwing toilet paper and everything else she could reach, yelling for them to get out. I bet some of them had never heard of the things she called them."

"That is one thing I just don't understand about the Holiness Church," Baby said. "What's this mania they all seem to have to bust in on people when they're in the hospital? The last thing people need when they're sick is a bunch of do-gooders standing around staring at them and preachers praying over them, making them feel like they've got one foot on the road to glory."

"It gives the preachers something to do when they're not preaching. The Bible says to visit the sick, so it makes the congregation feel like they're racking up gold stars in their heavenly crowns. And let's face it— there's not exactly a whole lot to do around here, so it's entertainment."

"If I ever have to go to the hospital, just make sure none of those Holy Rollers gets near me." Baby was dead serious.

"Well, I beg your pardon. Are you talking about me?" I pretended to be offended. We had gone over this ground before.

"Oh, Cherry, you know you're not a real Holy Roller. You just have to go to church with them because your daddy makes you. You know I'm not talking about you. You better come if I get sick."

"Knock wood."

"Knock wood."

We knocked on the wooden flat.

"What did she name her?"

"Tiffany LaDawn."

"That sounds like something Lucille would pick. It's a pink-sounding name. I can just see all the pink ruffledy outfits she'll make the poor little fat thing wear. Lucille the second."

Lucille had always had rather excessive taste, to say the least. Probably thanks to G. Dub, who once mentioned the resemblance and gave her a swelled head. Jayne Mansfield was Lucille's hero, and she had seen every movie Jayne had ever made four or five times and read everything in *Photoplay* they had ever printed about her and her weight-lifter husband and their gang of kids and her heart-shaped swimming pool. After Jayne unfortunately had her head lopped off a year or two ago when her driver fell asleep and plowed the car under a Mack truck, Lucille went to bed for three days. But the fire in her heart burned on. Pink had been Jayne's favorite color, and the tighter, lower, and pinker the dress, the better Lucille liked it. I knew for a fact that before it was even born, all the outfits she bought for the baby were pink. It was just a miracle that Tiffany LaDawn had not been a boy. He would have had to wear them anyhow. Lucille and Jim Floyd's trailer was all done up in pink, too. It was like walking into a bottle of Pepto-Bismol when you went in over there.

—

"I'm going to get a breath of air. It's nearly time for break anyhow."

I shuffled through the onion peelings to the door that led out to the back lot and breathed in the night air. The moon was still full and lit up the yard. As hard as I looked, I couldn't see any sign of the astronauts.

Off to the left, a night-watcher lamp shone on a railroad siding that ran behind the pickle vats. A bunch of boys were shoveling out a boxcar load of salt into big containers. One of the boys, I didn't recognize. He was blond, with long hair pulled back into a ponytail, and he had on faded-out blue jeans and a white undershirt—the ribbed, sleeveless kind—that showed off his muscles. He was built a little like G. Dub but more slender. Not delicate, though. He was shoveling as fast and hard as the rest of them. He must have felt me looking at him, because he stopped for a minute and looked right at where I was standing. You know that shock of electricity you get when you slide across the car seat and touch the door handle on a cold winter day? I'm not making it up; I felt one when he looked up at me.

The whistle blew for break. Baby put down her knife and got up.

"Come on, Cherry. Let's go down to the break room."

I didn't move.

"Cherry? What are you looking at? Let's go. We only have fifteen minutes."

The boy disappeared into the boxcar, then came back out putting on a blue chambray shirt. He flipped his ponytail out from under the collar and started to button it as he jumped down to the ground.

I followed Baby to the break room, off the main floor. It was painted sea-foam green, lit by fluorescent lights, and had four or five machines full of sandwiches, sweet rolls, candy, Coke, and coffee. The chairs were the tan-metal folding kind, with plastic seats; nearly all of them had cigarette-melt marks and silver tape holding the splits together.

Most of the tables were filled by the year-round workers, who had long ago staked out their territory. Lord help you if you sat in somebody's regular seat. Baby and I got honey buns and Cokes, pulled off our hair nets, and shook out our hair.

Just as we sat down, the blond boy walked in with a couple of salt-encrusted guys I knew. He looked around the room like he was trying to spot somebody. I glanced away before he saw me staring and bit into my honey bun. Baby was saying something, but I'm not sure what it was. She waved her hand in front of my face, like you would to see if somebody was blind.

"Cherry? Yoo-hoo. Anybody home?"

"Huh? What did you say?"

The boy walked over to our table and stood. In his hands were pink coconut Sno-balls.

"Is this seat taken?"

He had blue eyes. No—aquamarine. And ridiculously long eyelashes that looked like he had squeezed them in an eyelash curler. They were a shade darker than his hair. Golden. Honey. Wheat. I would have killed for those eyelashes. I wondered for a minute if my white eyelash roots were showing under the Dark Eyes color job.

"No, not at all. Take a load off." Baby had caught on by now.

He pulled out the chair, turned it around, threw his leg over the back, and sat down. Right across the table from me. I tried to size him up. He was maybe as tall as I am. Maybe not. It didn't really matter.

"Thanks. I'm Tripp Barlow." He put down his Sno-balls and stuck out his hand. We shook it—Baby first, then me. It was hard and gritty from the salt, and warm. I could feel my face flush with hot blood.

Tripp Barlow. That couldn't be his real name.

"I'm Baby Moreno," Baby said after a moment when I didn't say anything. "This is Cherry Marshall. We peel onions."

"Yes, I can tell. I shovel salt." He was serious, but his eyes seemed to be laughing. I couldn't think of a single thing to say. Baby, however, was never at a loss for words.

"Are you new here? I don't think I've ever seen you before."

"Yeah. I just moved here to go to DuVall in the fall. I'll be a senior. Thought I'd get here early and make a little pocket money. I'm from California. San Francisco." His voice was like warm syrup poured over sand. He had an accent that could only be from California. You could hear the surf in it.

"Oh wow! California! That's so great!" Baby's voice squeaked. "We're seniors at DuVall, too. What's your major?"

"Art."

"Oh my gosh. You're kidding. So is ours!" Baby's voice went up two octaves. She was being just a little too effervescent, I thought.

I knew it had to be art. Nobody around here had hair that long unless they were in the art department. In fact, they were still trying to kick kids out of high school if they didn't cut their hair. I got so mad at that. Like, if you don't have short hair you don't deserve an education. Next they could say that if you don't pluck your eyebrows or shave your legs you will be expelled. It's nobody's business but yours how you wear your hair. Tripp's hair was nearly down to his shoulders. I guess they were more ahead of the trends in California than we were in Arkansas. Big surprise.

I could picture him on a surfboard with that hair hanging loose in golden waves. Jesus Christ was the only thing I could compare it to. As soon as the thought entered my mind, I said a little prayer asking Him to forgive me for thinking anybody looked like Him. It's so hard to keep bad thoughts out of your head. The Devil is always putting them in there whether you like it or not. But Tripp did look, at least, like an angel might.

There were so many things I wanted to ask him. Like, for starters, why did he pick little old DuVall University to go to if he was from a great big city like San Francisco? Why didn't he go to Berkeley? That was the hottest school in America to be at right now. But for some reason the words wouldn't come out of my mouth. I just kept staring at those clear aquamarines. Baby was shaking my arm.

"Cherry, the whistle blew. We have to get back to work. Come on!"

I stood up and looked at Tripp with a goofy grin on my face. "See you."

"So it talks. See you later." He laughed and waved and made his way back out to the salt car. Baby and I went back to the onion room.

"You've got it bad, Cherry. I've never seen you like this. Snap out of it!"

"What? He's cute, that's all. I just met him, for Pete's sake!"

"You just remember that ones who look like him are bad news. Don't do it, girl. Run now, while you still can. Save yourself."

Baby can be so melodramatic sometimes. But she was right. I never could fool Baby. I just couldn't admit it out loud yet.

"Oh, the voice of experience. You've been with the same guy for four years, and he's crazy about you. But I hear you. Anyhow, he probably won't even ask me out. I didn't say three words to him. But just in case he does, I promise not to fall for him. Okay? Satisfied?"

"No, I can't believe you. I'm on record: I warned you."

"Great. I wrote it down. You're off the hook in case he breaks my heart."

I moved my chair closer to the door so I could watch the boys shovel salt while I peeled. The rest of the night went really fast.

7. Baby

 Baby was not as charmed by Tripp Barlow as Cherry obviously was, in spite of her having been so friendly to him at the pickle plant. When she thought about it later, she decided that something about him had made her nervous, made her talk too much. Maybe it was because he was so pretty—you couldn't call it handsome. Men that good-looking were usually more in love with themselves than they would ever be with any woman, and it was better not to get started with them in the first place.

Not that handsome men weren't attracted to her. Most men were attracted to Baby, but she wasn't interested in many of them, and she went into senior year of high school with her virginity intact. Then she started going out with Bean Boggs. Bean was small, like she was. He couldn't have been more than five-foot-three. He was nicely built but slight; dark, with deep brown eyes. He acted like he thought Baby's little feet didn't quite touch earth. It seemed that he couldn't believe his good luck that she wanted him—a little guy who the in-crowd didn't even know existed.

That, in fact, may have been a big part of why Baby was attracted to Bean. She and Cherry went to parties and ran with the in-crowd, but Baby never really felt part of it. If Cherry knew how she felt, she would say it was all in Baby's head, but deep down inside, Baby believed the rest of them secretly thought they were better than she was.

She never felt that way with Bean. He was at the bottom of the social totem pole, because he lived on the Ridge—back up on the wild side of the mountain, where the shacks scattered through the woods had outhouses and dilapidated old cars jacked up on concrete blocks in their front yards. The kids who lived up there had rusty elbows and rode the bus to school. They smelled like wood smoke and bacon fat and B.O.

Bean was born and raised up there, but Baby knew he wasn't like the rest of them; he had a gift. He could play any musical instrument he tried—piano, accordion, saxophone, anything. He could hear a song once and play it note for note; he could sing the song with perfect pitch, without even using a pitch pipe. When he played or sang, he wasn't just one of those trashy Boggses from the Ridge. He was magic.

The band director seized him as soon as he hit junior high, put him into a band uniform, and taught him to read music, which was as easy for Bean as football was for the rest of the boys. He played the clarinet, first chair, and could have gotten a music scholarship to DuVall, or anywhere else for that matter, but he didn't care about school. He was going to be a rock star.

He practiced every song the Beatles and the Rolling Stones had ever written, and junior year, he and a couple of the guys in the marching band, John Cool McCool and Clint Murdoch, started a rock band.

It was while they were playing for the first time in public—at the Future Homemakers of America girls-ask-boys dance—that Baby noticed Bean. He was wearing tight leather pants and singing "The House of the Rising Sun." His gravel-and-ice voice went right up her spine. She left the guy she was dancing with, walked up to the stage, and stared at Bean as if she had never seen him before. At the break, he came over and talked to her, and to her own amazement, she told him she thought he was really sexy. She let him take her home, and from that night on, they were a couple.

The band was just beginning to make some money when they all scattered after graduation. Bean was drafted into the army right out of school. When he got back from Vietnam in March of '69, the first thing he tried to do was get the band back together again.

John Cool, big and shaggy, with a full beard and long hair, was happy for a diversion from his job selling used cars at Mountain Motors, but Clint had left for Texas Tech, so Baby's brother Rocky bought a pair of leather pants and yellow aviator glasses and got his heart's desire to play bass. Bean played lead guitar, and growled the vocals in a voice that made the girls scream.

The new band sounded even better than the old one, and before long they landed a regular gig out at Woody's, a roadhouse and liquor store over by the interstate just across the county line. On Fridays after dark, the traffic from the dry town of Sweet Valley to Woody's, in wet Marlon County, was bumper-to-bumper, everyone crossing the line to dance a little and stock up on beer and Boone's Farm for the weekend, hoping they wouldn't pass their preachers or their mothers on the road.

Baby hung out a lot with the band, dancing and having a few beers, but Cherry had never been to Woody's. Ever since Bean had come back and started playing there, it was like Baby had a new part of her life that she couldn't share with Cherry. Cherry was a member of the Holiness Church, which didn't permit dancing, much less at a place where there was also drinking going on. As far as the church was concerned, Woody's was the gateway to hell. One preacher or the other preached about it nearly every week. Members of the Holiness Church would jump off a cliff without a parachute before they would set foot in Woody's. Baby felt the same way about the Holiness Church. It was foreign to her, and she would just as soon keep it that way.

8. Cherry

 Last Sunday night our pastor, Brother Wilkins, announced we would have a revival at church, starting tonight. I hated—well, disliked; *hate* is too strong a word—revivals, because for the entire week I couldn't do anything at night but go to church. It was enough to have to go three times a week.

Daddy was a deacon in the First Apostolic Holiness Church of God, and I think the first thing he and Mama did when I was born was take me straight to service from the hospital. They used to put a quilt down on the floor in between the pews and I'd sleep or nurse during the sermons, my mother delicately covering herself with a lace handkerchief. Getting religion with mother's milk, so to speak.

Being raised Holiness is kind of hard at times. It's a real Don't religion. They don't believe in dancing or drinking or swearing or playing cards or wearing makeup or shorts or even sleeveless dresses, much less swimming suits, to mention a few things. When I was little, Daddy used to make me wear a dress when we went swimming in the creek, but I almost drowned once when it got wrapped around my legs, so Mama put a stop to that. To tell you the truth, Mama wasn't all that keen on the Holiness philosophy. If she had stuck to all the rules like they preached, she wouldn't have been able to use Dark Eyes on me or play cards with the aunts or wear makeup. She, of course, had to leave it off when she went to church, but Daddy didn't seem to care (or maybe he just finally gave up) that when she went anyplace else, she put on the whole nine yards—lipstick, powder, rouge, and Maybelline mascara. That was the best part. The mascara came in a small red plastic box with a tiny drawer that slid out to reveal the weensiest little brush you've ever seen—like a toothbrush, with only one row of tiny bristles—and a brown cake of mascara. Mama would wet the brush with a drop of water and scrub it on the mascara cake, then, with dainty strokes, apply it to her lashes, her little finger bent, her eyebrows stretched upward. In a pinch, she would spit on the brush. It was kind of yucky, but she said your own body fluids are clean to yourself.

I used to love to watch her put it all on when I was little, but I don't wear much makeup myself. False eyelashes sometimes. Eyeliner. Maybe a little pink or coral lipstick once in a while, but if I wear red, I look like a big red mouth wearing a skinny, white girl. Back a couple of years ago everyone was wearing white lipstick, and I tried that, but it was too scary, because it blended right in with my skin and made me look like I didn't have any lips at all.

But makeup looks great on Ivanell. She has real style, the kind you have to be born with. She loves jewelry—big button earrings or gold hoops and bracelets that jangle. She's big into nylon negligees, which she wears around the house with high-heeled marabou slippers. There is no one more glamorous than Mama. She should have been a movie star.

Frankly, if she wasn't crazy for Daddy, I don't think she would be all that much into the church at all. Ivanell loves fun, and the church is against anything that smacks of fun. They don't like it if you go to a ball game or go fishing on Sunday. Most of them think it's even a sin to have a TV.

When TV first got popular, there used to be long debates at church on whether or not it was a sin. They wouldn't admit it out loud, but a lot of the congregation wanted a TV. They were just afraid of it. There were no Scriptures about TV in the Bible to guide them. It was an understood fact, though, that the movies were sin. A lot of movies had drinking and dancing and half-naked women in them. Christians didn't go to movies. I learned that early.

When I was about nine, a girl in our church, Bernadine Taylor, sneaked out to the movies with her friends one night and had the bad luck to come out of the theater just as Brother Wilkins was passing by in his car. He got up in church the next Sunday and preached a whole message about it. He called her by name and made her kneel down at the altar and had the whole church come up to pray with her for forgiveness. She was crying and they all were crying and moaning and talking in tongues and begging for forgiveness for her soul. You would have thought she had been caught naked at the truck stop with a room full of sailors. I think she was thirteen at the time.

I even remember the movie. It was something with Robert Mitchum, who, Brother Wilkins said, was known to drink and maybe even use dope. Not that I particularly liked Robert Mitchum, but I did like Elvis quite a lot, and thought I might get to see one of his movies one day. But not if I would go to hell if I did. It upset me so much that I cried about it after church.

Mama told me to hush crying. She said that God would never send anybody to hell for having a good time, and all of them at church were a bunch of ignorant old fuddy-duddies who wouldn't know a good time if it bit them on the butt. The next night, in spite of Daddy's warnings, she took me to see *Jailhouse Rock*. We bought popcorn and Coke and both fell in love with Elvis.

When the movie was over, we stood in front of the theater for a really long time just hoping Brother Wilkins would drive by. Mama even smoked a cigarette, something she usually never did in public.

"Just let that old S.O.B. try to drag me up to the altar," she said as we looked up and down the street.

He, as luck would have it, didn't drive by that night. But after that we did buy a TV. Daddy rationalized it by saying, "Well, we are doing it in the privacy of our own home. It's not like everyone is watching us."

I'm sure he wouldn't have bought it if Mama hadn't thrown such a fit over the movie thing. I think he did it, in part, so she wouldn't go back to the theater. Or maybe he would have bought one anyhow. She really wanted one. He pretty much did whatever she wanted. She had a hold over him greater even than the Holiness Church.

With the wonder of the TV, it seems like things eased up a little, and by the time I started dating Ricky Don, they didn't say much when I went out to the movies with him. We even went to a dance once in a while. I just didn't make a point of telling Daddy, and he didn't ask: "Ask me no questions, I'll tell you no lies."

And that's more or less the way it has been ever since, about everything. I still go to church Sunday morning, Sunday night, and Wednesday night, and I sing in the choir. But hell has receded a little for me.

The first night of the revival was to be the annual foot washing and Lord's Supper to kick off the week of services. I really dreaded the foot washing. I may have mentioned that my feet are large. I wear size 11, but there is just no place that carries that size, so usually I have to buy a 10, and my feet hurt all the time.

I asked Doc McGuire once if there was an operation to take out some bones in my feet to make them a normal size, and he gave me such a lecture that you would have thought I had asked him to make my boobs bigger. Which, to tell the truth, I would have done if it was possible. But after that tongue-lashing about the feet, I wouldn't dare mention boobs to him. I guess I'll just have to live with big feet and a flat chest. Or find a more sympathetic doctor. I probably couldn't afford it anyhow.

But the foot washing, I could do without.

The way it works is, they line up two benches facing each other on both sides of the church, four benches in all. The men are on one side, the women on the other. We all sit across from each other, and then, taking turns, each woman gets down on her knees and washes the feet of the woman opposite her. I don't mean really scrub them with soap—we just symbolically splash a little water over them and pat them dry with a towel to show humility, like Jesus did at the Last Supper.

I was doubly embarrassed when it came my turn, because Brother Wilkins's wife, Sister Wilkins, plopped herself down right in front of me to be my partner. She was as small as Brother Wilkins was large; skinny, with sharp elbows and a big pink mole on her upper lip that quivered when she talked, bless her heart, so that try as you would, you couldn't take your eyes off it. I suppose the Holiness Church won't let her get it removed. I couldn't imagine kissing her. I was trying to picture Brother and Sister Wilkins kissing when she got down on her knees and I had to put my foot in the basin to get washed. It was so big—my foot, not the basin—that my toes stretched up the side of the bowl. All the water almost sloshed out. I'm sure she picked me because, being the preacher's wife, she wanted to get all the humility she could. More foot for the money, so to speak. She cupped her hands and dipped a handful or two of water over my feet, then dried them with the towel, and I did the same for her poor little skinny size 5's.

Then they passed around the blood and body of Christ—trays of un- leavened bread and tiny glasses of grape juice. We each took a piece of bread and chewed it slowly and reverently, and then a sip of juice from a sip-size glass, putting it back into its stainless-steel holder as the deacons passed by. We couldn't understand how the Catholics could all drink out of the same cup, with the germs and all. And it was rumored that they used real wine. The Holiness Church believes that no one in the Bible ac- tually drank wine and that at the wedding in Cana, Jesus changed the water into grape juice. Nothing will change their minds.

After the bread and grape juice were served and the benches were put back in order, we sang "I'll Fly Away," and Brother Dane Harkness got up to start preaching the revival.

I liked Brother Dane—a lot more than sour old fat Brother Wilkins, with his puckered-up face, chipped front tooth, and unfortunate perspira- tion problem. Too bad Brother Dane was an evangelist and didn't want to take a church full-time as the preacher. I would swap Brother Wilkins for him in a minute.

Brother Dane used to be a hell-raiser in high school. He was in the same class with Mama, and she told me he was the best-looking boy in the class but that it was scary going out with him—which I think she did, al- though she would never admit it to me—because he drank moonshine whiskey and raced his old car around those winding mountain hairpin curves at ninety miles an hour and did every other wild thing he could think of in this little town. Until he found Jesus and reformed and became a preacher, that is.

Nobody ever fell asleep during his sermons. He loved to preach about how bad he was in the old days. It was meant to make us see how horri- ble sin was, but it sounded like he'd had a really great time:

"Brethren, I know sin in an intimate way! The Devil was my closest companion when I was a young and foolish boy. Me and the Devil were just-like-this." (He held up his crossed fingers.) "Inseparable. We drank together in honky-tonks, got into fistfights, played cards, drag-raced, and chased loose women. We got unspeakable diseases together, got shot at, cut with knives, and once the Devil went with me to the hospital at three in the morning to get an ear sewed back on that had got half bit off in a fight." (He stopped and pointed out the scar.)

"There was nothing he wouldn't egg me on to do," he continued. "Nothing. If I hesitated, he dared me. 'Are you yellow?' he'd say. 'Are you chicken?' And I'd say, 'Chicken? I'll show *you* who's chicken!' And then I'd go on and do whatever it was he wanted me to do. Oh, he was a fine companion. So fine that one morning after fighting and drinking moonshine whiskey the whole night long, I woke up in the hog pen with the sun in my eyes and the hogs rooting me around and never knew when or how I got there.

"Brethren, in that hog pen, in that nasty, slimy, stinking muck, I hit bottom. I was as low as any man can go. I was sick at my stomach, covered in my own puke. My head felt like somebody had taken a chopping ax to it, and I could hear my old pal the Devil laughing at me. Brethren— it made me mad.

"If Saint Paul wrestled with an angel, I wrestled with the Devil that morning there in that hog pen. I lit into him like a man possessed—which I was—and he dodged me like one of those greased pigs. The Devil is a dirty fighter, brethren. A tricky fighter. When you fight the Devil, it's Katie, bar the door!

"I called him every name in the book. I ran out of names to call him, and made up a few. I dared him to show his face. Then I would feel him sneak up behind me. I'd wheel around and dive at him, but he wouldn't be there, and I'd just dive into the hogs. The madder I got and the more I rolled and thrashed around with those hogs, the louder he laughed.

"We wrestled until the sun burned down hot at high noon. We wrestled until the sweat ran and the twilight came, and I was wore plumb out. The Devil was still laughing. He was not even winded.

"I gave up then. I gave up and lay right down and waited to die. The Devil had won. The end was coming and I knew I was going to die and get eaten by those hogs. I would become what I deserved to be—hog manure."

Brother Dane was preaching so loud that the windows rattled. He was jumping up on the altar and down off the altar, swinging at an imaginary Devil. His dark hair hung down in his eyes, the color of blue gas flames, and I could see why girls had been scared of him. But he had that congregation in the palm of his hand.

Then he stopped. He stood looking at us without saying a word. There was not one baby crying or one kid squirming. Nobody even breathed. Then he continued on in a quiet, gentle voice:

"But, brethren, something miraculous happened. Just as soon as I stopped fighting, just as soon as I gave up, I heard a still, small voice speak to me. I heard it just as sure as you are sitting there and listening to my voice speak to you here tonight.

"It said that it loved me. It said that it had loved me since long before I was born, and loved me so much that it had died for my sins. It said I didn't have to be in this wretched shape anymore. I didn't have to play the Devil's game and wonder if each day would be my last."

He took out a handkerchief and mopped his forehead.

"All I would have to do is ask Jesus to come into my heart. For that was who was speaking to me, brethren. Jesus. In Luke, Chapter eleven, Verse nine, He said, 'Ask and it shall be given you; seek and ye shall find; knock and it shall be opened unto you.' I asked Him that day to come into my heart. He knocked, and I answered.

"He's knocking at your door, brethren. All you have to do is let Him in. Say, 'Jesus, I have sinned, but I'm tired of sinning. I'm tired of carrying this burden all by myself. I need a little help. I want you to come into my heart, and into my life.' Ask Him now. Invite Him to come in now. And He'll take over from there.

"I asked Him right there in the hog pen. I opened the door. And when Jesus came in, the Devil fled. There's not room in your heart for the both of them, brethren. You don't have to be in a hog pen to accept Jesus. You can do it right here at this altar. It changed my life, and it can change yours. Close your eyes and bow your heads. Come to the altar now. Nobody will be watching you. Come now. Come while we sing."

The choir began singing "Just as I Am," and Brother Dane went up and down the aisles, laying hands on the bowed heads in kind of a blessing. The air was snapping with a crazy energy. I must admit, my own heart was racing. If I hadn't already accepted Jesus as my personal Savior when I was eight years old, I would have gone up and let Brother Dane lay hands on me.

A woman staggered up to the altar and went down on her knees. A skinny boy with big ears followed, and then a man in overalls. Brother Dane knelt down to pray with them, and most of the other women and some of the men in the church came up and joined them, to pray them through.

Then the woman being saved got up and started to shout and jump around, clapping her hands and yelling, "Hallelujah." That led to six or eight others jumping around, too, trying to out-shout each other and speaking in tongues. It sounded like, *"Elisob annodovich, umma umma lo-dano dibbabollo suba,"* and a lot of other sounds that make no sense at all, but it is a special language sent from God. I have never been graced by tongues myself, and have absolutely no idea what they are saying, but there are people who say they know. It's usually something like "God is sending down blessings to you." Never anything too specific, like "You are going to be in a major car wreck on September ninth." That would be really creepy.

Finally, the frenzy died down, and everyone hugged. Brother Dane is a most enthusiastic hugger. He just about cracked one of my ribs. He hugged me for quite a long moment. I could smell his aftershave. Canoe, it was—I can tell them all—and if I didn't know better, I would swear I felt something as he pressed against me. But, no . . . it couldn't be that. There was that old Devil putting evil thoughts in my head again. It must have been his car keys.

He walked back up to the podium, mopping his face with a white handkerchief.

"All minds clear?" Nobody said anything. "Then, Brother David, dismiss us in prayer."

Daddy said a short prayer. He always says the same one if he has to pray out loud—"Heavenly Father, as we come before You today, we thank You, dear Lord, for the many blessings You have bestowed upon us. Guide us and keep us safely as we return to our homes, and forgive us of our many sins. In Jesus' name we pray, amen."

"Amen," everyone said. I bent down to pick my purse up off the floor, and as I straightened up, I looked toward the back of the house. Tripp Barlow was standing beside the back pew. I went stone cold.

He just stood there watching me with this stupid grin on his face. I know I was red. When I get embarrassed, all the blood goes right to my face. It felt like it was on fire. He watched and grinned while I maneuvered through the crowd.

"What are you doing here?" I didn't mean to be rude, but I was.

"I came to service."

"You've been here this whole time? Where were you sitting?"

"In the back, with all the other good sinners. I came in when you were down washing that woman's feet. You didn't see me. That was some show."

He looked at me with that little smile. I was horrified. He must have thought we were all a bunch of crazies.

"You didn't have to come here to make fun of us." I could tell he thought the whole thing was one big joke.

"I'm not making fun of you. I meant it was an interesting experience."

I tried to push past him, but he took me by the arm.

• "Not so fast. It took a lot of doing to track you down. Let's go get a Coke and talk. Then I'll take you home in time to get ready for work. I promise."

I looked over at Mama, who was trying to figure out what was going on. I called out, "We're going to get a Coke. I'll see you at the house."

She nodded. I could see she was curious. So was everyone else. As we made our way out to the parking lot, I could feel all their eyes on us.

———

Tripp's car was a 1957 Chevy painted a rich candy-apple red—the twenty-one-coat kind of custom paint job that looks so deep you could put your arm up to the elbow in it. On the right tail fin was written, in flowing butter-yellow letters, *Ramblin' Rose*. The '57 was one of the most coveted cars on the road. I knew that much from Baby's brothers Denny and J.C.

I got in, shut the door, and sank down into the custom burgundy-velvet seat covers as Tripp revved up the motor and threw it into first. With a loud vrooom, we peeled out of the church parking lot, slinging gravel. My head jerked back, and I grabbed for the door handle. The whole congregation stood together, eyes wide, watching us leave. I promised God that if I lived, I would never get into this car again. Gingerly, I tried to rotate my head. It wasn't too painful, so I probably didn't have whiplash, but I was really P.O.'d.

"You didn't have to burn rubber back there. I think everyone could see what a hot car you have without you showing off for them."

"Sorry. I didn't mean to. I guess it was just all that pent-up emotion from the sermon coming out. Wow! I could get into this church thing. It was weirder than an acid trip!"

"Acid? You've taken acid? Stop right here and let me out of this car." I didn't know who this guy was, but he was scaring me.

"Who, me? Acid? No way! Just read about it."

"You read a lot of good books." I was still a little discombobulated. What was I getting into here?

"Look, let's start all over." Tripp pulled off to the side of the road, killed the motor, and turned to face me. "I'm sorry if I muscled in on something I shouldn't have. I'm new here. I was asking about you, and somebody told me you were at church tonight. I just wanted to see you. I thought I'd surprise you. But if I made you mad or something, I can take you home and that will be the end of it. You never have to see me again."

He had this way of looking up from under his eyelashes with those aquamarines. Like a naughty little boy. For some reason, I wasn't mad anymore. But I pretended.

"Oh, now you're trying to get out of buying me a Coke? I don't think so, buddyruff."

He grinned and started the car, pulling carefully back onto the highway, and I relaxed a little bit.

9. *Cherry*

 The Freezer Fresh was the only place to hang out in Sweet Valley, except for the Deep South on Route 66 and the Town Café on Main Street, where the farmers went to drink coffee early in the morning on their way to buy feed or whatever. But no kids would be caught dead at the Town. It wasn't cool. And everybody, not just kids, went to the Deep South. But the Freezer Fresh was ours.

A couple named Millie and Herman ran it. He was a big fat guy with hairy tattoos of hula girls over both his arms, and Millie was skinny, with a frizzy perm and bad teeth. They were good-natured, though, and they gave huge orders of curlicue french fries for a quarter, and shakes so thick that the straw stood straight up—reason enough to go there.

It was a low white building situated a mile and a half outside of town, in the center of a big parking lot, where everyone congregated, had a Coke and a burger, and then piled into each others' cars to go riding around—the main social activity in Sweet Valley. From there, you'd either go out to the lake (to watch the submarine races, of course) or up on the mountain, to the bluffs under the red airplane-warning lights (to look for UFOs). That's why there were so many young marriages in Sweet Valley—there wasn't much else to do but park.

Four or five kids were lined up at the take-out window waiting for their orders when we pulled up. All eyes took in the car as I waved to them.

The place was packed, and we had a hard time squeezing in. The air was thick with smoke and hormones. "Wooly Bully" was playing on the jukebox, as loud as it could go. That was Ricky Don's favorite song, so I knew he had to be there, as indeed he was, shooting pool with a couple of girls I didn't know, who were wearing hip-huggers and belly-button-baring tops. He gave me and Tripp a long look, then went back to his game.

Baby and Bean were at the corner table. She was sitting in his lap drinking an orange-vanilla milkshake. She waved for us to come over.

"Hey, Cherrykins, I see the salt boy found you. Where y'all been?"

"You know exactly where, Baby. Brother Dane's revival." I couldn't believe it was Baby who'd told Tripp where I was. Actually, yes I could. I would have done it for her.

"You went to church, Barlow?" Bean was surprised. It seemed like he already knew Tripp. He fished out a cigarette and offered one to Tripp, who took it and bent over for the match Bean struck with his fingernail. Then Tripp turned a chair around and slung his leg over it, just like he'd done at the pickle plant. I wondered if he ever sat in a chair the regular way.

"Quite an experience. I can see why people get into the church thing. As the man said, 'Religion is the opiate of the masses.'"

When he took a drag on the cigarette, his eyes squinted up in a way that made him look really sexy. Somehow, I didn't think he would ever be too religious.

Ricky Don kept looking at us with mean little eyes the whole time we sat there. One of the girls in the hip-huggers sat on the edge of the pool table to make a shot and leaned her boobs right under his nose. He didn't even notice. I pretended not to see him.

"Ricky Don's drilling holes in you, Barlow. You're with his girl." Bean was clearly enjoying the idea of the two of them maybe fighting.

"I am not Ricky Don Sweet's girl, Bean, and you know it." I looked pointedly at Tripp. "I'm nobody's girl."

"Let's get out of here and go for a ride." Baby got up and pulled Bean to his feet. We started to follow, and as I passed Ricky Don, he motioned for me to come over.

"Y'all go on out. I'll be right there." I went over to the pool table.

"Who's your new friend, Cheryl Ann? I ain't seen him around here before."

"His name's Tripp Barlow. He's from California. Why are you so curious?"

"He looks like trouble to me. Long-haired hippie. You better watch yourself."

"It seems like you watch me enough for the both of us."

Ricky Don picked up the chalk and squeaked the end of his cue with the blue cube. "I mean it. I don't like that guy. I got a sixth sense about these things. Just watch yourself."

I turned and left without another word. He drove me crazy. He had to butt into everything I did.

We got into Ramblin' Rose, with Baby and Bean in the backseat, and headed up the mountain road.

———

The dashboard lights made Tripp's face glow, and the car radio was blasting "Honky Tonk Women." Another great song. The Stones just can't make a mistake. Tripp took out a pack of cigarettes and offered me one. I shook my head. Now, don't get the wrong idea. Just because I have never drunk or smoked, plus still being a virgin and belonging to the Holiness Church, all that doesn't mean that I am a square or anything. I could do any of it if I wanted to. I just don't want to. Cigarettes and liquor give you really bad breath. But I don't get all weirded out if somebody else smokes or drinks around me—not too much.

The three of them lit up Marlboros, and Tripp reached under the seat and pulled out a can of beer. I have to admit that *did* make me a little nervous.

"I'm not trying to tell you what to do, Tripp, but if you get pulled over with an open can of beer in this county, they don't look too kindly on it. They can arrest you, and us too."

For a minute, he acted like he was going to open it anyhow, but then he put it back under the seat. I let out my breath, which I wasn't even aware I had been holding. It would be just like Ricky Don to follow us.

He would have loved catching us with beer, would probably take us all down to spend the night in jail. I would be dead for sure if that happened. In a dry town like Sweet Valley, even if you are over twenty-one, it's against the law for you to sell or buy liquor, or drink it in public. Certainly not in a moving vehicle.

I looked in the rearview mirror, pretending to fix my hair, but there was nothing behind us except black road and the glow of our taillights.

We wound around the hairpin curves, practically taking some of them on two wheels. I clung to the armrest, gritting my teeth to keep from saying something about his driving. He probably thought I was enough of a baby as it was. But it did seem like he was trying to see just how far he could go.

As we went higher, my ears popped and I swallowed, trying to unpop them. The headlights bounced off the tall, thick trees that had probably been there since the Caddo Indians used this road for a footpath. A possum moseyed out, its eyes wide and glowing green, and just missed becoming roadkill. It was apparent that Ramblin' Rose didn't slow for wildlife.

"Turn here, Tripp." We had come to the turnoff to the airplane lights.

"I know." I guess one of the first things you learn when you move to Sweet Valley is where the best parking places are. I wondered who he had brought up here before.

Like a native, Tripp pulled up and stopped under the red signal lights, high on poles, that warned airplanes of the mountaintop. Baby and Bean were already lying flat out across the backseat, going at it hot and heavy, and didn't know we were in the world. Tripp looked at them for a minute, then opened his door.

"Let's go for a walk."

The moon was beginning to go on the wane, a slightly lopsided ball, but there was still a good amount of light. We made our way over the flat rocks to the edge of the bluff and looked out over the valley. It was like fairyland, all lit up by the streetlamps and the lights from the houses. It seemed unreal that behind each of those little golden glows people were washing their supper dishes and putting the kids to bed, maybe watching *Gunsmoke* or *Perry Mason* before they turned out the lights and went to bed themselves. From up here, the lake was a giant pool of dark liquid silver, attached like a balloon to the shiny ribbon of the Arkansas River.

Seeing Tripp in the moonlight, I imagined that if he stepped off the rock, a pair of white wings would sprout from his shoulder blades and lift him right up to the stars. He had pulled his hair back in a ponytail for church, but now it was loose and wavy. A breeze blew up, and I shivered.

"What's the matter? Cold?"

I tried to laugh, but it never got out of my throat. "It must be the windchill," I said, remembering what Baby had said at the pickle plant. I also remembered what Linda Sue and them had said about guys lying. I didn't know which had made me shiver.

Tripp put his arm around me and rubbed his hand over my bare arm. Hard. The skin warmed up, but I trembled. Not from the cold; from nerves. He turned me to face him and leaned in to kiss me.

It was too soon. I wasn't ready. As his mouth came close to mine, I drew in my breath and turned my head. It was a near miss. The heat almost blistered my lips. It was hotter than any real kiss I had ever had. But then, most guys don't have a clue how to kiss. They either try to swallow your head and gag you with their tongues or they make their mouth into a little round O and plant it on you so it feels like you're taking a swig from a Coke bottle. Then there's the weird ones, like the guy who latched on to my bottom lip like a snapping turtle before I had a chance to pull away. It made a hickey, and I had to wear red lipstick for a week. Needless to say, that first kiss was the last for him.

But Tripp . . . he was at another level. He didn't give up so easy. He looked right into my eyes, put his hands on either side of my head, wound his fingers into my hair, and kissed me for real. It started soft and gentle, gradually gathered heat, and turned my whole body into a limp noodle. My heart and stomach seemed to melt and run right down in a puddle into my you-know-what. My knees started to buckle.

"Let's sit down here for a minute." I managed to get the words out and sit down before I fell. We sat in silence on the edge of the rock, his arm around me, and dangled our legs over the side of the cliff. He kissed me again, and then started to lean me back onto the rocks. If that happened, it would all be over, I knew. What was wrong with me? I didn't even know this guy. I had just been to the revival. Where were my Christian values?

"No. I can't take another one of those." I pushed him back up. "Let's just talk." He leaned back on his elbows, like he had all the time in the world.

"Why did you come hunting for me tonight? I hardly said a thing to you at the plant."

"I think that question just answered itself." He smiled. White teeth in the moonlight. "I liked your looks. I liked your . . . whatever it is that people like about each other. Chemistry, I suppose. I never met anyone like you."

I didn't really know what he meant, but I think it must have been a compliment. He put his hands behind his head and lay back on a patch of grass that grew between the rocks. It smelled like it had been freshly cut. Or maybe it was him that smelled that way—the clean smell that makes you think of Saturday morning and wet wash pinned on the clothesline, blowing dry in the sun. I was tempted to stretch out there right beside him, but something held me back. I didn't need Ricky Don to tell me Tripp was trouble. I knew it. What was worse—a part of me didn't care.

"You really have taken acid, haven't you? Don't lie."

He looked up into the black, bottomless sky full of stars. Considered.

"Yes, I have. A lot of times. Does that bother you?"

"I don't know." We sat without speaking for a minute. "Is that how you got your name?"

He laughed. "My mother was a Tripp. Emily Gibson Tripp. She was a southerner, actually, from Mobile, and you know how southern women like to give their family name to the boys. My whole name is Randall Tripp Barlow. Anything else you'd like to know?"

There was a lot I'd like to know. "What was it like? Taking acid?"

"Hard to describe." He thought about it for a while. "It makes everything more."

I looked at him; waited. He seemed to be having trouble. "More what?"

"I mean . . . okay. Say you're looking at a light. A little green light, like on the radio dial. You drop some acid, and it gets brighter and brighter, until you have never seen such a bright light in your life. You need to get sunglasses to look at it. The very air glows—every molecule vibrates with shimmering green light. The light pulsates and envelops you and becomes the whole world, and you look at it for hours. It is the most incredible, wonderful, fascinating, groovy thing, and you can't take your eyes off of it.

"Or, say your buddy has a big nose. You focus on it, and it gets to be the biggest nose you have ever seen. All you can see is this big nose waving around attached to a tiny face. Sometimes, you can even make somebody's face turn into somebody else's. I remember one time when I was with this guy, we dropped acid, and I stared at his face until it turned into George Washington, and then it slowly changed to Abraham Lincoln, and then I could swear it was John Kennedy, big as life sitting there across the couch from me. It went on all night like that."

"That seems kind of scary."

"It can be. When you feel fear, it is a fear like you have never experienced before."

"Why do you keep doing it if it makes you afraid?"

"It's not that simple. It also makes you believe that you are the most brilliant human being God ever made. You can feel every single nerve in your body. You hear the valves in your heart opening and closing, the blood gushing through your veins. You are exquisitely, painfully aware of yourself and the miracle of life. Even your fear is alive and beautiful. You are a super-human being who can dive into the fear and emerge on the other side. You are the master of the world. There has never been anything like it. It makes you feel a little bit like God."

I said a quick little prayer for God not to take what he was saying too seriously. "How long does it last?"

"It varies. A few hours. Sometimes more. Sometimes less."

"Have you done other drugs?" I couldn't think of the names of any at the moment, but I'm sure he knew all of them. "Have you ever smoked pot?"

"Sure. Haven't you?"

"No."

In spite of being an art major, I never really knew anybody who did drugs. Or if they did, they didn't let me know. Although, of course, I'm sure there were plenty who did. A lot of the kids at school were from out of state. There was even a guy from New Jersey. He probably smoked pot.

"Is that anything like acid?"

Tripp laughed. Not in a mean way, but it made me feel like he thought I was maybe a little ignorant.

"Oh, no. It just makes you feel nice and relaxed. Mellow. No worse than a couple of beers. Would you like to try it? Smoke a joint? There's nobody up here." He started to reach into his pocket.

"No! Are you crazy? You can go to jail for that! You mean you have a joint in your pocket right now?" Oh, Lord. What had I gotten myself mixed up in?

"Okay, okay! I'm not going to light up!" He held his hands up in the air like I had pulled a gun on him. "You really are uptight, aren't you?"

"I'm not uptight. I just can't see spending the rest of my life down at the women's prison at Tucker, that's all. You can do what you want to. Just wait until I'm not around." I couldn't believe he had come to church with a joint in his pocket. Ricky Don and his sixth sense.

"I guess you think we're pretty hickey here in Arkansas," I continued. "I'm sure San Francisco is much hipper, with Haight Ashbury and the flower children and all. Why did you even come here? Why didn't you go to Berkeley?"

"I was at Berkeley, but I got bored spending my best young years in classrooms studying stuff I would never use in my life, like chemistry and philosophy, so I dropped out and spent a couple of years in Nam. For the excitement. To find out what all the noise was about." He smiled a crooked smile to himself.

"Fellow I met in training camp at Fort Benning was from here. He thought this was the most beautiful spot on the planet. Kept talking about Sweet Valley Lake and Nehi Mountain and the red airplane lights and the river, how the people were the nicest in the whole world. He had planned to go to DuVall when he came back home, and eventually to law school at the University of Arkansas.

"When I got back from Nam, I was ready for a change of scenery— someplace smaller, with good air. Sweet Valley sounded like the right place to go. I felt like there was nothing left for me in California. My folks are both dead."

"Oh, I'm sorry."

"Me too." He took a ragged breath. "They were killed in an auto accident while I was in Nam. That's ironic, isn't it? I was the one who was supposed to be in danger. I was the one dodging bullets out in the rice paddies. They were just driving home with a carload of groceries when a cement truck ran a red light and totaled them."

He paused. I didn't know what to say to comfort him, but I felt like I needed to say something to break the silence.

"Don't you have any brothers and sisters?"

"No. I'm a spoiled-rotten only child."

"Me too." I said. He picked up my hand and kissed it. And forgot to let go. There was that electric current again, running from his hand up my arm.

"Anyhow, I felt like there was no home to go back to. So here I am, on the GI Bill, Uncle Sam paying for my education. Couldn't be simpler."

"Who was the boy from here?"

"Jerry Golden."

"Oh my gosh. You must know, then . . ."

"He was in my platoon. I was with him when it happened."

That was a stunner. "You're kidding."

"I wouldn't kid about something like that."

"I'm sorry. I didn't mean to say you were kidding. I just meant that . . . how did it happen? If you don't mind talking about it."

For a minute I thought he wasn't going to say anything; then he started talking.

"We were on patrol in Son My, which was a heavy booby-trap area in Nam. We'd been out in the field for a couple of months with no break, and if you want to know what that's like in the rainy season, just imagine jumping in the river wearing all your clothes and a seventy-pound backpack, then walking twenty miles through mud that sucks at your boots and packs on the bottom so that every step you take is like dragging ten pounds on each foot. Your muscles burn like fire. Each step is torture. Then before you start to get dry, a cloud opens up and dumps a load of water on you and you're soaked again. You go to sleep wet and wake up wet. We'd never take our clothes or shoes off. When we finally did take off our shoes and socks, the skin would come off with them. More GIs were crippled from jungle rot than anything. Sometimes the blood would squish out and leave tracks.

"On this particular day, we had humped more than five klicks through the worst terrain you can imagine—wet and muddy, foliage so thick that visibility was never more than twenty feet. And since it was known to be a bad trap area, you couldn't relax and let down your guard for even a minute.

"Then the guy right in front of me stepped on a mine. I heard the noise, but I couldn't figure out what was going on or why the air all of a sudden had a ruby-red mist hanging in it. But shortly I could see that the guy had gotten his right leg blown off. What was left of it looked like hamburger. He lay there screaming, and a medic ran over and applied a tourniquet as best he could. I was operating the radio and called in for a dust-off, then I yelled for Jerry to come help me pick the guy up and take him to the LZ, which was a klick or so away."

I wasn't sure what a klick or an LZ was, but it didn't matter. I got the gist. Tripp went on, lost in some other place, some other language.

"I heard the Hueys overhead, which is the sweetest song you ever heard in the jungle, but before Jerry made it over to where we were, he hit a trip wire and let off a Bouncing Betty. Those are the worst, because they jump up and detonate right at crotch level. If you make it, you have no legs and no balls. It was lucky Jerry didn't make it. We tried to get him on the slick, but he was already dead."

His voice had gotten thick. I didn't say a word.

He shook his head. Picked up a small rock and threw it out over the trees. It racketed through the leaves of the treetops and hit with a soft thud.

"You have no idea what it's like to be in a place where there's nothing you can trust. Every step you take might set off a trap. The VC have been known to booby-trap lighters they've taken off dead Americans and leave them on bars. They blow off some guy's hand when he's having a drink. Even the kids, the ones who gang around the soldiers looking for a handout—they might be working for the Cong. You know, sometimes the VC actually tape bombs to the kids' bodies, and they blow up right in the middle of a bunch of GIs who are giving them candy bars. The women who wash your clothes in the daytime might take a gun to you at night. Life is cheap in Nam."

He threw a couple more rocks.

"Did you know about . . . Carlene?" I asked.

"One of the things I was going to do was look her up. I can't believe I never got the chance. Unbelievable, isn't it? Jerry talked about her a lot. If it had been me, I'd never have left and joined the army. But he thought he needed to get away and start over."

"Did he say anything about their baby?"

Tripp turned and looked at me.

"Their baby? I don't think he was the father. He said they had never actually gone all the way. That's not something a guy admits to his buddy if it isn't true."

I felt a little guilty. All of us had just assumed it was his and that he was lying. "Look, you didn't know how close they were. They were with each other every single minute—"

"All I know," he interrupted, "is what Jerry told me. But I know he loved her. She wrote to him every day. He told me that he had found out some things and he was going to marry her when he got out, and adopt the baby. After he got out of Nam and they got married, he was going to go to DuVall on the GI Bill. Maybe that's part of the reason I'm going there."

He looked out into the dark, starry sky and was quiet again.

I must say, the story had taken a little of the bloom off the night. But I'm glad he told me. It made me feel more at ease with him. If Tripp was that close friends with Jerry Golden, then he was practically one of us.

I leaned down and kissed him. Just to show him how sorry I was. And to show him that I wasn't a square about the acid and pot. Big mistake. He pulled me down on top of him, and I felt the hardest bulge in his jeans I had ever encountered. I had to do something fast to stop the wild horses that were dragging me away.

I jumped up and ran to a path that angled down the cliff, dusting some gravel off my butt as I went. Miniskirts were not made for sitting on the ground. Or for protecting your virginity.

Down the path, over to the right, was a big boulder we called Sweet Rock, which leaned into and almost touched the cliff. The space between was called Fat Man's Squeeze, for the obvious reason. I ran down to it and called over my shoulder. "I bet you can't get through this!"

He chased me and nearly caught up just before I started through the crack in the rock. But not quite. I slipped through Fat Man's Squeeze and waited on the other side in a little alcove under the bluff.

Standing there, it hit me—I don't know what I could have been thinking. Now we would be totally out of sight in a cozy, dark nook.

Cherry, you idiot, I said to myself. You're asking for trouble. But another part of me knew that already.

The moonlight was pretty bright, but it still was hard to see down under the rocks. Tripp seemed to be having some trouble getting through the crevice.

"I'm going to have to wait a minute before I can make it through!"

Great. It would be just my luck if Tripp broke his pecker in Fat Man's Squeeze. That would make my record perfect. He flicked his Zippo and lit up the rocks, twisted around, and finally made it through.

The lighter flickered on the rock face. He glanced up at it, then stopped and stared. "What is that?"

I turned. In big red letters, it said IDA RED IS DEAD!! The writing shone in the flicker of the flame; shiny, fresh paint.

"Who's Ida Red?" Tripp asked. He touched the paint as if it might come off, wet and red, on his hand. It was dry, but it couldn't have been there long. A feeling of panic washed over me, like some killer had written it. I had to get out of there.

Without a word, I ran back through the Squeeze and up the trail, Tripp right behind me. He didn't have as much trouble getting through it this time. We got to the car just as Bean and Baby were starting to yodel. Tripp yanked the door open and we jumped in. He gunned the motor and backed out, spinning gravel. Baby and Bean were pulling on their clothes, falling onto the floor.

"What's got into y'all? Slow down!" Baby was flung back against the seat.

"Baby, somebody painted something on the rocks down under Fat Man's Squeeze. I don't think it's been there for very long."

Bean pulled on his socks; he looked a little put out. "I wish y'all would give a fellow some warning next time you get scared by a sign somebody painted."

Baby seemed a little on edge, too, although I can't really blame her.

"It was probably just kids messing around. Why would something like that scare you, Cherry? What did it say?"

"It said, 'Ida Red is dead.' It was in bloodred paint. The letters just screamed at us. Who is Ida Red?"

There was a numb little silence. Then Baby said, "I think maybe that was a nickname Carlene had. It seems like she told me that when we worked together out at the restaurant."

10. Ida Red

From the time she was born, Carlene was not a baby you rushed to pick up and cuddle or speak to in baby talk. She would squirm when her mother rocked her; she was prickly and serious, sturdy and pale, with freckles sprinkled on her skin like nutmeg on eggnog. Her hair looked like a lit match out in the wind; her eyes, an odd shade of pea-green-gray. She would look deep inside you with those eyes, stare until you looked away first, feeling somehow nervous and guilty. She herself never appeared to be nervous in any way but one: She bit her fingernails. She slowly and methodically gnawed her nails deep into the quick, chewed them so furiously that they never grew. They remained child-size pink crescents embedded in the fleshy ends of her fingers.

She grew up in a trailer on the other side of the lake from Baby's house. Her father was a strapping, good-looking man named Carl Moore. He worked at the sawmill but never seemed to make enough money to take care of his family. He wasn't stupid, exactly, but he was a good ol' boy who never was too sure of the joke—whether he should laugh, or if they were making fun of him and he should get angry. So he usually got angry, just in case.

Carlene didn't get her red hair from her father. Or her mother. There was a lot of talk, and of course nobody knew for sure, but Alfred Lynn Tucker's daddy, Walter, had bright red hair the exact same color as Carlene's. The same color as Alfred Lynn's. Before Alfred Lynn inherited the job, Walter had been the night foreman at the Atlas pickle plant for twenty years, and Carlene's mother, Frannie Moore, had worked there nights the summer before Carlene was born.

The evidence was not enough to hang anybody. Nobody ever actually saw the two of them doing anything, although he used to tease her and make her laugh a lot. But Walter teased all the women at the plant. Even after he got older and his barrel chest became a potbelly, he had a way about him that the women liked. Maybe it was because he really liked them—all of them. It didn't matter if they were old or young, skinny or fat. Even the women packing pickles who had been married for forty years would squeal when Walter pinched them on their broad rear ends and, with pretended outrage, slap his hand while their cheeks turned red with memories of slipping out behind the vats on long-ago hot summer nights.

No, his working at the pickle plant with her mother was not proof that Walter Tucker was Carlene's father. Sooner or later, everyone in Sweet Valley ended up working there.

But Carl Moore didn't need much to fire his suspicion. Frannie Jones was a fey Welsh beauty from the Ridge, far back in the mountain woods, with wild-blackberry hair and eyes the color of cigarette smoke. Like smoke, she always seemed to be slipping through his fingers. If she said yes to a date, there was no guarantee she would be there when he went to pick her up. Or if they actually made it to the movies, she was likely to go to the concession stand for popcorn and never come back to her seat.

He married her thinking that she would finally be all his and would turn into a normal woman who made the beds and washed the dishes, cooked his dinner and sewed his shirts. She married him because she was seventeen and grown—too old for her widowed mama, with five other kids, to take care of—and she didn't know what else to do with her life. That, and the fact that Carl wanted her more than any other boy ever had. He didn't give up no matter what she did to him. That's hard for a woman to resist.

Frannie couldn't wait to get away from the noise and mess of her family, and she thought marriage would be more freedom, not less; not the unrelenting closeness of a tiny trailer, the sink full of greasy dishwater and the smell of a man's bowels first thing in the morning—a man who was so jealous that he watched her every move. She couldn't even take a bath without him checking on her, or go to see her mother without him being there, too. Sometimes she felt as if she were smothering; then she had to get out of that trailer or go stark raving mad.

Even on nights when they were sitting and quietly listening to music on the radio, sooner or later Carl would turn away to glance out the window or fish in his pocket for a cigarette, and when he turned back to her, she would be gone.

She might have gone to bed without saying a word. Or into the kitchen for a piece of pie. Or she might not be there at all. Then he would search through the trailer, calling her name, and run outdoors to find her swimming naked in the lake. Or standing in the yard staring at the stars. Once, she stripped off her dress and danced with the mailboxes; waving the filmy nylon dress in the air like Isadora Duncan's scarf, she floated up and down the road, moving to some fairy song playing in her head.

"Frannie!" Carl called out. "What's the matter with you? Get ahold of yourself, woman! Get some clothes on and get on in the house!"

"Oh, Carl. You're no fun. Come out with me! Don't be such an old grump-bum!"

"I mean it, Frannie. You're acting crazy. Come on, now. Get in the house."

That time, she gave in and draped her dress over her shoulders, put her hand into his and walked home with him, as if they were lovers out for a stroll. But another time she might run from him and hide in the woods. Then there was nothing for him to do except go back in the trailer, bang his head against the wall, and go to bed. Long after he was asleep, she would creep under the covers, cold and damp, full of the smells of lake and leaves and moss and woods, and curl up as small as she could, against his back.

He would turn and hold her, then, until she fell asleep, and listen all night to the sound of her breathing, afraid that if he went to sleep, she would be gone again.

———

When she was born with a head of bright red hair, it was evident that Carlene Ida Moore didn't look anything like her black-haired daddy. He told the nurses at the hospital that there had been some mistake and accused them of switching the babies. He threw such a cussing fit that they had to call the guard.

After they brought her home, he would sit and stare at her, trying to see something of himself in her, and she would stare right back at him with her old baby eyes.

"What was that story your old grandma Ida Jones used to tell, Frannie, about the elves back in Wales taking somebody's baby and leaving one of their elf babies in its bed? What was it they were called?"

"Changelings, Carl. Why'd you want to know that for?"

"I think they done it to us." He looked at the baby's solemn face. "A changeling," he told her. "That's what you are. An elf changeling."

He used to laugh at Frannie's grandma for believing in the little people, but now it all made sense. The elves had taken his baby from the hospital in the middle of the night and left this red-haired elf-baby in exchange. Because if it wasn't that, his wife was a cheat and this baby belonged to Walter Tucker. If he had ever taken a biology class, he might have known that the gene for red hair is a maverick that can disappear for years and show up a few generations down the line. He or Frannie might have had a red-haired great-great-grandfather or something. But Carl knew nothing about that. He was sure the baby belonged to Walter Tucker, and it ate him up.

"Carl, that's the silliest thing I ever heard. Of course Carlene is your baby. Why would I have anything to do with that old man Walter Tucker? Hold her now while I fix dinner."

"I've never seen hair like this on nobody in my family, Frannie, nor yours."

He leaned down and whispered to the baby, who looked up at him with her big, stormy eyes. "You ain't no part of me, you little red elf changeling, and you didn't have no business being named after me. We should have just called you after your great-grandma, that old Welsh witch Ida Jones. That's what I'm going to call you. From now on, you're not Carlene—you're Ida Red, the changeling."

And he never called her anything else.

11. *Cherry*

 Ten o'clock in the morning. The phone rang. I need eight hours of sleep, can function pretty well on six, but three drags me out of the deepest part of the sleep cycle and I have a hard time coming to, or even figuring out where I am. It rang three more times, and I jumped out of bed and fell flat on the floor. My left leg was asleep from my foot to my hip, like it wasn't even there. I tried to stand up, but it was like my ankle was made out of rubber, and I fell down again.

The phone kept ringing. I crawled across the floor and pulled the hateful thing off the table by the cord.

"Hello!" I said in a mean voice.

Lucille. She was all excited. "They brought her in this morning. Jim Floyd is going to help with the embalming, and I have to go down and do the hair and makeup. I need you to take care of Tiffany LaDawn for me. Mama and the aunts have gone up to Morrilville to that discount furniture store. I know you worked last night, but I wouldn't have called you if it wasn't an emergency."

"Lucille, what are you doing out of the hospital?"

"I'm fine. I got tired of all those bossy old nurses telling me when I could or couldn't see my own baby girl. Besides, they called and told Jim

Floyd that Carlene was coming in today, and I couldn't miss it. Now, can you keep her or not?"

"Are you crazy? She's brand-new! I can't baby-sit her! I don't know a thing about babies. I might break her or something." And I might have added that I really didn't have any desire to learn about those moist little things that cried all the time.

"I thought of that. You can come with me and take care of her at the funeral home. I'll be right there in case anything goes wrong, and I can nurse her. I'll bring her little carry-seat. She can sit in that, and all you'll have to do is watch her. I got Mr. Wilmerding's permission, being that you're family and all. Please? Don't say no."

"Lucille, is there nobody else—"

"Aren't you just a little bit curious about what Carlene looks like?"

"No!"

"You won't have to see her, then. I promise. You can keep Tiffany LaDawn out in the grieving room."

"Well, I . . ."

"Great. You're the best. I knew I could count on you. See you in half an hour."

I hung up and started rubbing my leg. The feeling was coming back, and it felt like somebody was sticking a jillion pins into it.

Why don't I have more backbone? The last thing in the world I wanted to see was the mutilated body of Carlene Moore. Especially after last night. Baby couldn't remember who had given Carlene the nickname Ida Red, but she was pretty sure Carlene had told her about it.

For the two summers before this one, as well as weekends all winter, Baby had waitressed at a place out by the lake called the Water Witch. It was run by a guy named Jackie Lim, and was the only Chinese restaurant in the county. Carlene got a job there after she dropped out and had the baby.

Love of the pickle plant wasn't the reason I didn't try to get a job out there, too. It was because the Water Witch was a private club. That is to say, they had a bar and could serve liquor to you if you were a member. The way to become a member was to buy a membership for five dollars as you came in the door. It was a legal way around the dry-county rule, like the country club was for rich doctors and lawyers, who liked a drink after work or wine with their dinner. Can't you just see me telling Daddy that I was going to work in a place that served liquor? *That* would go over like a pregnant pole-vaulter.

I told Baby she was crazy for quitting that good job and coming to the pickle plant this summer, but she didn't want to go back. She said she'd had it with carrying heavy trays and being on her feet all night, and she wasn't that hot at waitressing anyhow. I probably wouldn't have been, either.

I must say, I was glad Baby was with me to share in the wonders of onion peeling. Next year, knock wood, we would both be teaching in a nice, clean art department somewhere and out of that stink hole forever. We could spend our summers painting. Maybe we would get an apartment together. It seemed like a long way off.

———

The hot water of the shower revived me somewhat. I ran a comb through my wet hair and tied it down with a braided-leather headband wrapped Indian-style around my forehead—there was no time to roll it. It would just have to frizz up. Hopefully, I wouldn't run into Tripp. I threw on a pair of jeans and a T-shirt, stuck my feet into moccasins, and went into the kitchen.

Mama had left a note propped up against the sugar bowl on the table telling me about the trip to the furniture store. None of the aunts ever made a major decision without consulting the other two, and Aunt Juanita needed a new living room suite. At the end of the note was Mama's signature heart with a little arrow stuck through it and a pink lip print where she'd kissed it. She's cute, that Ivanell.

I took down a package of Ding Dongs and poured myself a glass of milk, my usual breakfast. I wouldn't mind gaining a few pounds, if they went to the right places, but nothing I ate seemed to stick. Mama said I'd fill out after I had a baby or two. She did, and she was as skinny as me when she was a kid. I must admit, for thirty-nine, she still looked pretty good.

As I unwrapped the foil off the Ding Dongs, last night came back to me. Nothing made any sense. Who would write something so crazy up there on the mountain, back in that hole? I couldn't let myself even think of the possibility that it might have been the killer doing the writing. Surely the killer had run off to Texas or someplace. And why would he have written it, anyhow? Why would anybody?

I wished Baby could remember who called Carlene Ida Red. It might have been a kind of joke. Maybe it was based on that old country song, "Ida Red, Ida Red, everybody's talking about Ida Red." I used to hear it on the radio when I was a kid and Mama would listen to *The Grand Ole Opry* while she did the ironing. Little Jimmy Dickens or somebody like that sang it. It was corny, but for some reason it stuck in your mind until you went crazy singing it all day long.

I swallowed the last of the Ding Dong and drained the glass. Nearly ten-thirty. If I was going to do this thing, I had better get at it. I mean, it's only a body, right? A piece of clay. It can't get up off the table and grab you, like in the movies. Can it?

12. *Baby and Bean*

Baby didn't go to bed at all the night after they found the writing on the wall. She didn't know how many people knew Ida Red was Carlene's nickname, but that writing must have had something to do with her. It was just too odd a name. Jackie Lim could have known. Maybe Jerry Golden knew and told someone. All night during work, she turned around in her mind every single person who might be capable of killing Carlene and then going up and writing on the rocks in Fat Man's Squeeze. Nobody she thought of made any sense.

She felt guilty, too. After Baby quit the Water Witch, Carlene had tried several times to get together with her, but Baby had always put her off, saying she was too busy, until Carlene quit calling. It wasn't that she didn't like Carlene anymore. She just wanted to get away from everything that had to do with the restaurant. Maybe if she had tried to keep up the friendship, she could have done something to stop whatever it was from happening to Carlene.

By the time she got home from work, she was worn-out with worrying but too keyed up to sleep. She went out on the boat dock and dangled her feet in the water until the sun climbed into the sky and burned the early-morning mist off the lake.

She wondered where Bean and Tripp had gone last night. They had taken her and Cherry home in time to change and get to the pickle plant for work, and then left together. Tripp, apparently, was taking a night off from shoveling salt.

It seemed like they had made friends awfully fast. First, Baby told Bean about meeting Tripp, and the next thing you knew, they were practically bosom buddies. The whole thing was weird. Bean was usually suspicious of new people. Tripp must have been somebody special for him to get so close, so fast.

—

What Baby didn't realize was that fellow dopeheads always managed to find each other. In the Bible Belt South, law-enforcement officers didn't have a sense of humor about drugs. Dopers had to stick together to survive. It was amazing how they could always spot each other. Of course, long hair was a clue. That's why the schools and parents hated it so.

Bean had learned to smoke pot in Vietnam, and he cultivated a patch of it up on the Ridge, deep in the woods behind his house on the far side of Nehi Mountain. It was risky, but there was no road, and nobody much had a reason to go up there. There were still bears and cougars back in those woods, and a few bobcats—not as many as everyone thought, but sometimes when kids were parked on the bluff, they would hear a cougar scream; it sounded exactly like a woman screaming. It would raise the hair on your neck straight up. And Bean mentioned from time to time—not too often, just enough—that he had seen this or that bear out behind his house. So Bean's patch was relatively secure.

He took to marijuana right away when he landed in Nam. Everyone smoked, more or less right out in the open. Technically, of course, you weren't allowed to do it, but most of the time the NCOs and even some of the officers would look the other way. Maybe once in a while they would have a little inspection and look in your trunk and pat you down, but some friendly sergeant would always know in advance when it was, and you could just stash your stash until inspection was over.

And what good stuff it was! You could get the finest in Vietnam: Thai sticks, fat joints the size of your biggest finger for a dollar; party packs of ten rolled joints for five dollars; joints soaked in opium that would lay six guys out for the count, for a dollar apiece. You could even buy whole cartons of what looked like Marlboros, filtered and sealed, except the to-bacco had been taken out and marijuana put in. Bean got to the point that the first thing he did in the morning on his way to breakfast was fire up a J. In the work he did, it helped to be a little stoned. It leveled out his senses.

Bean was a tunnel rat. They zeroed in on him right away when he first got there, since he was one of the smallest men in the platoon. They gave him some tests to see if he was claustrophobic. He wasn't, and passed with flying colors. Then they gave him several tests to see if he had that little bit of craziness you need to spend long hours, without cracking, in tight, dark tunnels full of vicious bugs, snakes, rats, bats, and gooks who are trying to kill you. Out of fifty men, he was one of the five they took.

He was sent to the big army base at Cu Chi, which had been built right on top of a maze of Viet Cong tunnels—a clever subterranean highway, over two hundred miles long, dug by hand from the dry, loamy earth in the 1940s and 1950s, when the Viet Cong were called the Viet Minh and fought against France. The tunnel system was expanded during the American War, as they called it. The tunnels were loaded with booby traps, intended for any GI that tried to find his way through them, and by late 1966, when Bean arrived, they were just beginning to scratch the surface, so to speak, of tunnel warfare.

Bean would have probably volunteered for the Rats anyhow, since he actually liked being underground. Back home, Nehi Mountain was honey-combed with caves that not many people knew about, or at least the extent of them, and Bean had spent his childhood exploring those caves and hiding from his drunk daddy. He practiced walking through the dark passages and rooms, trying not to make a sound, feeling his way with all of his senses, until after a few years he developed something not unlike the radar that bats have. He could judge the height of a ceiling by the change in the air; locate a vent by the smell; tell the depth of a pool by the sound a peb-ble made. He figured if his daddy came looking for him, he would just put out his light and take off.

That bat sense saved his life more than a few times in Nam. He was a legend among the Rats. From the beginning, he always seemed to know which root was actually a trip wire or if Charlie was around the bend hid-ing in a nook, waiting to blast an unsuspecting GI. He got so good that he could hear an eyelid blink in the total darkness of the tunnels.

When Bean first started, he wasn't sure what he would do when it came to killing a man, but after one of his buddies was lowered into a tunnel and had his legs blown off at the groin by a grenade trap, Bean knew he would be able to kill VC.

Even so, the first time was still a shock. Not long after his buddy lost his legs, Bean went down the same tunnel, even more cautious than usual at the memory. Pistol in one hand, flashlight in the other, he inched along. He had practiced searching for traps until his fingers were as sensitive as a blind man's reading Braille, delicately touching the bumps and roots along the tunnel as he looked for a connection, something that didn't feel quite right.

He was concentrating on a patch of earth that seemed too even, when it shifted, almost imperceptibly. Before he had time to react, a trapdoor sprang open not a foot in front of his face and he looked into the startled eyes of a VC. Bean's gun went off, almost by itself. He was nearly blinded by the spray of blood. The VC's body slipped down the hole, and the trapdoor fell back into place with a solid thud, like a Cadillac door makes when it shuts.

Bean hugged the ground, frozen, waiting for others to emerge, but the only sound was the shrill ringing in his ears from the gun blast. An anguished disbelief washed over him at his not sensing it coming, and he vowed to never let that happen again.

—

Even though killing became a more or less regular occurrence and he was no doubt the best in the Rats, it was still a notably ugly business. Right before he went down, even if he had just smoked a joint, he got a rush like a greyhound gets at the first sight of a rabbit. The guys called him Jumping Bean, because he couldn't sit still. His leg would start to jiggle up and down, as if of its own accord. One of the officers would say, "Okay, he's wound up—let him go!" And Bean would enter the tunnel. Only then, when he inhaled the inky, damp air to the bottom of his lungs, would he relax, get deathly still and listen, with all his senses, to what the dark had to tell him.

The longer he worked, the more he respected the Viet Cong's intelligence. That they had fought first the French for twenty years and then the Americans and never given up was impressive. Still, Bean never really thought of them as human. Not like Americans, anyhow. Human beings don't live in burrows like animals or eat rats. Some of the VC spent months underground without once breathing fresh air. If the Cong had souls, he reasoned, they were probably like dog or cat souls—maybe they went someplace after they died, but not to the same place as everyone else.

Even so, he couldn't help but admire them. The tunnel system was ingenious. The top levels of the tunnels were the easiest for the tunnel rats to access. That was where the leaders had their meetings, where the food was cooked, and where the makeshift hospitals were located, lined with recovered silk parachute material to keep out the dirt. There were even underground rooms used as theaters, where girls would sing and dance and perform patriotic plays to entertain the troops, and big rooms with printing presses, where they could produce a newspaper. There were holding pens for water buffalo, and once, to their amazement, the Rats found an American tank. It had been scavenged by the Cong, buried, and used as a command center.

Down deeper were the workshops, where the artisans, working by the light of paraffin lamps or flashlights, repaired weapons and made mines and booby traps, chiefly out of the vast leavings of the American army. Coca-Cola cans and unexploded claymores were favorite materials for mine-making. One good ten-kilo homemade mine could take out an entire platoon. There was a hidden civilization right under the Americans' feet, run to a large extent off the garbage the Americans so casually tossed away. There were always batteries with a lot of juice lying around, and leftover food that was better than the food the VC were able to get in the tunnels, since cooking underground was hard. If the smoke went out one ventilation hole, it was visible; if it was diffused, there were leaks that made the bad air even worse. A major treat for the VC was to be able to cook up in the open, but that got riskier with time, because the Americans learned to spot even a few grains of rice on the ground and know that there was a tunnel nearby.

Only a few tunnel rats ever got good enough to penetrate the second or third level, where the munitions were stored. Bean was one of them. He once broke through a dividing wall into a room over five meters high, full of big mortars. They were disassembled every night and stored underground, then reassembled in the morning, carried through the tunnel piece by piece. It was a lot of work, but this way it was nearly impossible for the Americans to find them.

The gooks never ceased to amaze Bean, and he never took them for granted, like he never took for granted the spiders, snakes, scorpions, and chiggers that infested the tunnels and made life a misery—not to mention the foul air. It stood to reason that the VC had to urinate and defecate in the tunnels, and the body odors, sweat, and gases, plus the low amount of oxygen made the air practically unbreathable at times. Bean would get used to it after twenty or thirty minutes down there, but when he came out and sucked fresh air into his lungs, the shock sometimes made him faint. Still, he got to where he could judge how many people had been there and how long, by the smells alone. It was his world, and he knew it as well as he knew the Ridge, which sometimes seemed like a far-off, fading dream.

—

After he came home from Nam, readjusting was hard. It was impossible to sleep all night and not be on guard, expecting to be awakened by missile fire. For months, he woke up at every noise—deer running through the woods, dogs barking—and reached for his M-16 and his shoes. And all the men and women he had encountered and killed in the closeness of the tunnels paraded through his dreams almost every night, along with the friends he had lost. They haunted him, with their hideous wounds, until he dreaded to go to sleep.

It would have been hard, as well, to break the pot habit. Not that he especially wanted to. Why should he quit? He liked it. It sharpened his senses, improved his music. Smoothed all the hairs in the same direction, so to speak. He had smuggled some fine seeds back in a shaving-soap can and scattered a small patch far back in the woods. Bean's homegrown marijuana was powerful stuff. Everyone said it was the best they ever had. He read an organic-gardening book and kept a compost heap going; made the stingy rock-riddled mountain soil as rich as bottomland. Some of the plants were way higher than his head. He dried them in the old cave, the entrance hidden in a crack in the cliff near his patch, and quietly sold bags of it for ten dollars apiece. Made a nice profit—enough to buy a new guitar, keep his truck running, and have a first-rate stereo system installed.

He could probably have afforded a new truck, but he didn't want to be too much of a show-off and draw a lot of unwanted attention to himself. Which, at times, was almost more than Bean could manage, because he wanted to be famous, like the Stones or the Doors. After coming home from Nam, he wanted it more than ever.

Before he left for Vietnam, Baby had never really seen the wild side of him. She was definitely the beloved, and he was the lover. He tried always to please her, afraid she would get bored and leave him. Now that he was home again, though, the dynamic had shifted. He was centered in a way he never was before, sure of himself. He was crazier than ever about her, it seemed, to the point of obsession, but there were also times now when she had never felt more foreign. He talked about it a lot, comparing her to the Vietnamese women he had seen. It was almost as if he were look- ing at her through somebody else's eyes, as if it were her being Oriental— rather than her being Baby—that turned him on. Bean was like a stranger she had to get to know all over again. She wasn't afraid of him exactly, but if he didn't get his way, he could be cold and cutting. A time or two, he had raised his hand to her. He didn't actually hit her, just gritted his teeth and clenched and unclenched his fist. But it was something he never would have done before.

She blamed it on the pot. There were few waking hours that Bean wasn't high, and he didn't want to smoke alone; he wanted Baby to go with him to the mellow place marijuana took him. The first time she tried it, nothing much happened. It took a few tries until it hit, but it didn't send her to the stratosphere or anything. It just made her horny, hungry, and sleepy. She could polish off a bag of Oreos all by herself when she was high, concentrating for long minutes on the way the black cookie crunched, sticky, between her teeth.

Unfortunately, Bean wasn't much good for the horny part, because when he got stoned, all he wanted to do was talk. And he did. On and on and on. Sometimes about his experiences in Vietnam, which Baby hated, since he usually went into great detail about the vermin and the fetid smells in the tunnels. But mostly he talked about music. Baby knew more about the Doors, the Stones, and Jimi Hendrix than she ever needed to know in her lifetime. After he lectured for a while, Bean would get out the guitar and try to teach her the chords and frets or whatever they were called. He would demonstrate how Clapton did it, how Keith Richards did it. She would stuff another Oreo into her mouth and pretend to lis- ten, nodding and saying, "Uh-huh, uh-huh, uh-huh," as he rattled on for hours. Finally, she would just curl up and go to sleep. He wouldn't even

notice, would just keep talking as though she were still awake and hanging on his every word. She only smoked pot because he insisted. She really
didn't see what all the noise was about.

Of course, she couldn't confide in Cherry about this. It was even hard
to talk to Cherry about sex, since she was still a virgin. There seemed to
be a gulf growing between them, and Baby didn't know how to stop it.
She didn't know what Cherry would think if she found out that Bean had
talked her into smoking pot. Even though she would pretend that it didn't
matter, it would. Things would never be the same between them. Actually, Baby probably wouldn't smoke pot at all if she weren't afraid of making Bean angry. It took so little to set him off these days.

That was why Baby hadn't said anything more last night about the Ida
Red business. She had no idea who might have written that message on
the rocks, but she knew she had already said too much by mentioning the
restaurant. Every time she brought it up, it reminded Bean about Jackie
Lim. Bean hated Jackie worse than poison, because he was convinced that
while he was away in Vietnam, Baby had cheated on him with Jackie.

13. *Baby*

 Bean had been away in the army for nearly a year when Baby
started waitressing at the Water Witch. The summer after graduation, she had worked at the pickle plant with Cherry, but that
was only a three-month job, lasting through the fresh pack season, when
they ran three shifts. But she really needed a job on weekends during the
school year, too, and this was perfect.

The Water Witch restaurant and marina sat on a spit of land that jutted
into Sweet Valley Lake, not too far from Baby's house. Its picture windows
framed the lake in a panorama. Out behind, a deck set with tables under big
green umbrellas faced the view, and a wooden walkway stretched across the
manicured lawn down to the dock. The lake was connected to the Arkansas
River by a deep inlet, and lot of wealthy people from towns up and down
the river kept boats and party barges in the protected marina year round. In
the summer, every night was party night at the Water Witch.

The interior was unlike anything else in Arkansas. Jackie Lim had the bar shipped in from Hong Kong, as well as the rugs and the tables and chairs. They had once been part of a famous old restaurant. The bar was mahogany, hand-carved in an elaborate design of dragons, burnished by countless hands over time so that it had a dark, satin finish. The mirror behind it, heavy beveled glass, rich and old with crackles in the silvered backing, was framed in antique gold Chinese lacquer and reflected liquor bottles on glass shelves, lit by invisible lights that made them glow from inside with amber fire.

Countless coats of glossy, deep persimmon-orange paint made the walls seem liquid, and delicate Chinese art floated on them. It was altogether out of place, as if it had been lifted from the China Sea and set down on Sweet Valley Lake. Baby couldn't believe she would actually get paid to spend her time there.

At first, Jackie was just a guy who was her boss. He was more than ten years older than Baby—thirty-two—smooth, sophisticated, and the first Oriental man she had ever met outside of her family. He wore his hair greased back in an Elvis pompadour with long sideburns, and dressed only in suits, tailored for him in Hong Kong on his trips back home—sharkskin, for the most part, in pearly shades of gray, green, or blue. His shirts had french cuffs and were custom-made of the softest Egyptian cotton, linen, or heavy silk in eggshell colors. He loved jewelry and wore a thick gold ID bracelet with a diamond dotting the *i* in *Jackie* and an enormous diamond pinkie ring. Every day of the year, he put on a different pair of cuff links—solid-gold dice with black enamel dots, owls with emerald eyes, fish with scales made of the tiniest seed pearls. Coral. Jade. Countless other kinds.

He came from a rich family in the export business in Hong Kong, but Jackie was more interested in spending money and partying than in learning the family trade, so in desperation they sent him to America. They checked out schools in different states and finally chose the University of Arkansas in Fayetteville, up in the Ozark Mountains, because they thought it was isolated enough to keep him out of trouble. What they didn't figure was that it was exactly the kind of place that would make Jackie stand out. There was no one at all like him there, and he played the Chinese playboy role to the hilt. He could speak English with very little accent when he wanted, but liked to put on "Chinee-talk" to amuse and throw people off. He would garble a joke, then slap his knee and howl with laughter. Every guy he met was an old "son-a-ma-gun." He had his own apartment off campus and drove a yellow Triumph. There was always a party going on at Jackie's place. Twice, his father had to come over from Hong Kong and convince the school not to throw him out. He dropped broad hints that there would be a Lim Library at the university one day if Jackie was allowed to graduate.

Instead of going back to Hong Kong and the family enterprise when he graduated—magna cum laude in business—he took his graduation gift money and bought a dilapidated restaurant and marina on Sweet Valley Lake, and managed to get a private club license through one of his fraternity brothers, Mark Greer, whose father was a county judge. He found investors, renovated, and advertised, and in nine years had made a nice little fortune. His family was finally proud of him.

The first time he saw Baby was at the roller rink, shortly after the restaurant opened. In Sweet Valley, there wasn't a lot to do for entertainment—one movie house, one bowling alley and the roller rink. Even Jackie would get desperate at times and bowl a few games or take a date out to skate. He got good at it, and liked to show off by skating backward with his arms crossed, while everyone had to leap out of his path or get knocked flying.

On this particular evening, Baby was there with Cherry and several other kids from their seventh-grade class. Except for Cherry, who was already a head taller than everyone else, Baby looked more mature than the others. In fact, she was more than a year older than they were. When she moved to Sweet Valley, Baby was small and didn't speak any English, so the teachers advised her parents to keep her back a year. By seventh grade, she had already blossomed into healthy puberty.

Jackie was startled to see an Oriental girl. He skated over to her and struck up a conversation.

"Hey, beautiful lady," he said in perfect English. "Where did you come from? Would you like to go out to dinner with a poor old Chinese man?" She couldn't believe she heard him right.

"I'm fourteen!"

"Don't fourteen-year-olds eat dinner?" He was trying to be funny, but it scared her.

She looked at him as if he were crazy and skated away. He laughed, like it was a big joke.

Over the years, though, he became a familiar face. Once in a while they would pass each other in their cars and wave, or say hello if they saw each other standing in line at the movies, have a little conversation in the aisle of the grocery store. Not long after she finished her first year at Du-Vall, Jackie ran into her at the gas station and offered her a job. Within two weeks, they were lovers.

Baby wasn't quite sure why she did it. She had never intended to cheat on Bean, who had been gone nearly a year. Maybe it was that she was lonesome and nobody had ever shown her the kind of attention Jackie did—compliments, gifts, dinners out. He said, gazing into her eyes with the most sincere expression, that only she could speak to his soul, because they were two strangers in a strange land.

She liked the way they looked together. So did he. They lay naked on a white bearskin rug in front of a floor-to-ceiling mirror in his house and stared at themselves—two small, creamy, brown muscular bodies with hair the color of coal. They made love and never took their eyes off the mirror, playing for it as if for a camera. It was an incredible turn-on.

The trouble was, unbeknownst to Baby, he used the same line, or a variation of it, on an alarming number of woman, most of the waitresses at the Water Witch included. After she had been with him a few times, Baby came down with a raging case of crabs, and when she told him in a panic, he convinced her she must have gotten it off the toilet seat at the restaurant, from one of the other girls.

It was a holy struggle all summer to get rid of those lice. Just when she thought they were all gone, she would spot some more tiny white eggs and the whole thing would start again.

That's how her friendship with Carlene started. Baby went into the storeroom to get a bottle of soy sauce and found Carlene hiding behind the wine cases, scratching. Carlene's face turned as red as her hair.

"You wouldn't have a few friendly visitors, would you?" Baby asked.

"I wouldn't call them friendly."

"It's all right. I won't tell if you won't." Baby gave herself a healthy scratch.

Carlene raised an eyebrow at Baby. "It seems like more than a few of the girls here have been hit with this problem."

"Really?" Baby was surprised. "Are they that contagious?"

"Well, I guess in theory you could get them from the toilet seat, if that's what you were told, but I would bet that a certain Chinese boss has done more than a little to spread them around. Is that maybe where you got them?"

Baby's face turned red. Suddenly, it hit her how naive she had been. Of course Jackie would have slept with all the waitresses. Why not? And what right did she have to get angry? She had no claim on him. She was supposed to be going steady with Bean, who was off fighting for his country. She felt ashamed, but she couldn't blame Carlene. Maybe Carlene blamed her.

Carlene waited to see what she would say. When their eyes met, Baby knew it would be all right. Carlene wasn't mad at her; she had a half smile on her face, like she had seen it all and nothing could surprise her.

"I guess that white rug must be infested with them, huh?" Baby finally managed to get out.

Carlene laughed. "It must be. Jackie Lim better watch his butt or that mangy old polar bear will bite a piece out of it!"

"I think it already got a piece of his pecker!" They looked at each other and laughed; laughed until they were weak, and clung to each other.

Baby wiped her eyes and sat down on a crate of litchi nuts. "What are we going to do? These little suckers are the very devil to kill. I'm going crazy trying to pick them all off every night."

"Get you some Quell, get in the bathtub, and scrub yourself down. It may take a few tries, but that might get rid of them. If all else fails, shave the whole mess off. I am right past the Quell stage, and I am going to do that, myself, tonight. And I think both of us should stay away from the boss, at least after hours. You can bet he's been out with me his last time."

Carlene lived about a mile from the restaurant in a trailer with her boy, Kevin, and her mother, who took care of the boy at night while Carlene worked. Sometimes, if her old pickup was in the shop, Baby gave her a lift, and after work they would sit outside in front of the trailer and smoke and talk. It was nice to have a friend who knew the score. There was so much she couldn't talk about with Cherry, and Carlene seemed to take to her, trust her. She said she had always thought Baby was one of the nicest girls in their class—not stuck-up, like some of them. For once, Baby felt like the leader in a friendship.

In a strange way, she felt guilty, too. It was almost like cheating on Cherry. But that was stupid. Being friends with more than one person was not like cheating on your boyfriend. Cherry had Lucille, after all. But still, for some reason, Baby felt like she had to keep the friendship a secret from Cherry. To protect her. From what, Baby couldn't say.

14. *Cherry*

 "The body is the temple of the spirit. Just because the spirit has moved out and gone on to its reward, it doesn't mean that we treat the body as anything but the temple it is. No matter what procedure we have to do, we do it with solemnity and ceremony. Those are the two key words: *Solemnity* and *ceremony.* And dignity. That's another key word to remember. *Dignity.*"

———

Mr. Wilbert Wilmerding was giving me the lecture on dead people. I had pulled up at the funeral home a minute behind Lucille and Jim Floyd, and Mr. Wilmerding was standing outside by the front door waiting for me. They went on in with Tiffany LaDawn in her little carry-seat, but he wouldn't let me in the door until he had given his speech.

"Cheryl Ann, the only reason I'm letting you in the embalming room is because you're family of Lucille and Jim Floyd, and they are my family. I don't do this for everybody. We have to maintain the dignity of the departed."

"Mr. Wilmerding, I appreciate all this, but I don't need to go in the embalming room. I think I'm just going to look after Tiffany LaDawn in the grieving room."

Mr. Wilmerding was old, nearly sixty, bald and short and fat. Fat men fall into two categories—the ones who fasten their belts over their bellies, and the ones who fasten their belts under their bellies. Mr. Wilmerding was an over-belly belter—a long strap of brown cowhide buckled with a big gold Masonic lodge buckle, tightly snugged practically under his armpits, held up his giant pair of khakis. He had to buy such a big size to go around his middle that the pant legs flapped like pup tents around his skinny little ankles. The person who designs these things really should figure out that not every man who has a big paunch also has fat legs. Actually, in spite of it, Mr. Wilmerding was kind of cute, with white hair, rosy little cheeks, and twinkly blue eyes. Like ol' Santa. Only more dignified.

The funeral home was a three-story white frame house built around the turn of the century. It was set back in a big, shady yard with several large magnolia trees, loaded down with fragrant, waxy white flowers. The trees were so thick all along both sides of the street that they met and formed a canopy over the road, and it always seemed like late afternoon, even when the sun was high overhead.

Mr. Wilmerding lived alone in the private apartment on the third floor, Mrs. Wilmerding having passed away two years before. He had embalmed her, himself. She wouldn't trust anybody else to do it, which is a little weird, but then again it kind of makes sense.

Until she got sick with cancer, Mrs. Wilmerding had done all the hair and makeup on the bodies, but toward the end she got pretty weak and couldn't manage it. That's when they hired Lucille, since she was always hanging around the place on account of Jim Floyd, and had made friends with the Wilmerdings, who, unfortunately, weren't able to have any kids of their own.

When she heard that they needed somebody, even though she had never been to beauty school and didn't have a license, Lucille begged until Mr. Wilmerding gave her a tryout.

Her first trial client was a ninety-two-year-old woman, who had probably never worn lipstick in her life but sure needed something to brighten her up, having died with a severe case of liver disease, which had turned her skin duck's-foot yellow. When none of the old woman's family objected about the rosy lips and cheeks, and in fact commented on how nice and colorful she looked, Mr. Wilmerding gave Lucille the job.

And he was glad he did. Besides the fact that she livened up the place, he was real pleased at the way Lucille fixed up his wife when she passed on. But then, before she died, Mrs. Wilmerding and Lucille had spent many a long afternoon up in her bedroom, practicing hairdos and makeup until Lucille got it right. They even took some Polaroid pictures of Mrs. Wilmerding lying down in various coffins and outfits until she decided on the one she liked. At the funeral, everyone said she had never looked better.

The funeral home had a truly ingenious setup that Mr. Wilmerding designed himself and built into the wall. It was a dumbwaiter the length of a coffin. Jim Floyd and Mr. Wilmerding could just unload the body from the hearse into the basement on a roller belt, embalm it, scoot it into the dumbwaiter, hoist it on up to the second floor, dress it and fix it up, put it into the casket, roll the casket back into the dumbwaiter, and lower it to the first-floor viewing room. There, a sliding wall behind the coffin stand opened, and the coffin was slid, like a loaf of bread out of the oven, onto the platform. If they thought about it, people marveled at how Mr. Wilmerding could get those heavy coffins up and down the stairs, as fat as he was and all.

The walls of the funeral home were flocked red paper, and the floors were carpeted in thick red shag. Deep. Quiet. In the receiving room, as you came in the front door, a large, gold-framed picture of Jesus, His large blue luminescent eyes looking up at the sky, yellow beams of light coming out of His head, hung above the mantel over a candelabra of gold cherubs.

A pair of glass doors led into the viewing room, and then, separated by a screen, came the grieving room, where I planned to keep Tiffany LaDawn. It had a kitchenette and a couch, which made down into a bed for the person who stayed there all night with the bodies.

Off on the far side, a stairway went down into the cellar, where the embalming took place. I had been down there once with Lucille when no one was around, just to see what it looked like, and let me tell you, it was something right out of an old horror movie—you know, the ones where the car breaks down at night in a storm and the girl and her boyfriend go up to take shelter in an old castle that has a mad scientist at work in the cellar, cutting up people and reanimating them.

It was hard not to imagine Carlene lying on the cold marble slab table in the middle of the room. The floor was concrete, slanted toward a drain in the middle, and a deep sink and countertop ran along one wall. In the corner sat a round white machine that looked like an old-timey gas tank. It pumped the blood out and the formaldehyde in.

I got queasy just looking at the equipment with nobody on it. No amount of love nor money could entice me to go down there with a mutilated body, especially one belonging to somebody I knew. Even sitting in the grieving room would be hard, knowing what was going on just under my feet.

After he lectured me some more about proper demeanor, Mr. Wilmerding finally let me into the funeral home. Of course, Lucille and Jim Floyd had already gone down to the cellar and left me.

"Lucille! Where are you? Where is Tiffany LaDawn?"

"She's down here, Cherry!" Lucille hollered from what sounded like the bottom of a well. "Jim Floyd is setting up. He needed me to help him. Come on down."

Great.

"Bring her up here, won't you? Please?"

"Oh, Cherry, don't be silly," Lucille bellowed up the stairs. "There's nothing down here that's going to hurt you!"

Mr. Wilmerding had gone upstairs to his apartment to get ready. I took a deep breath. All right. I would just run down the stairs, grab the baby, and come right back up. I wouldn't even look at Carlene.

The light in the basement came from bald lightbulbs hanging from wires in the ceiling. They swayed and cast shadows that kept changing the shape of everything they lit. I had to make my legs go into the room.

Jim Floyd was laying out the instruments, and I tried not to look at the body, which was lying on the slab under a white sheet. The head was covered, but the toes were sticking out. Yellowish-white waxy toes, their nails painted a bright fuchsia. Seeing that pink toenail polish, it hit me like a baseball bat: Under this sheet was Carlene Moore. One night, not long ago, she had painted her toenails with bright pink polish, probably put on a pair of sandals and some dangly earrings, and gone out thinking she was going to have a good time. For the first time, her death was real. It nearly knocked the breath out of me. A person could be alive one minute and stone dead, stretched out on a marble slab, the next. One day, that would be me lying there. One day it would be every single person alive on this earth.

Tiffany LaDawn started to cry. I jumped. Lucille rushed over and picked her up.

"Oooh, is Mama's wittle baby dirl hungwy? Mama will div her a wittle snacky-wacky, wight now! Mama's wittle dirl want some tittie-pie?"

Lucille unbuttoned her shirt and unhooked her industrial-strength nursing bra. No wonder the poor little thing was so fat that she couldn't open her eyes.

"Lucille, are you crazy! Don't nurse her in here! My gosh, think about all the germs!"

Tiffany LaDawn was already guzzling and slurping, practically smothering in the billows of breast. Lucille had to pull part of it back off her nose so she could breathe.

"Eat, Tweetykins, and den Aunt Chewwy will take oo upstairs and wock oo in a wockey chair, Mama's wittle sweet patootie." Lucille talked exclusively in baby talk to Tiffany LaDawn. I didn't see how the child would ever learn the English language. No wonder most little kids can't talk plain.

I watched in fascination as the baby nursed and thin, bluish milk ran down her mouth. It didn't look anything like real milk that you get in the grocery store. A time or two, she drank too fast and started to choke. Lucille lifted her and pounded her on the back, then popped the huge pink nipple back in her mouth.

"What do I do if she gets choked? I don't think I could pound her like that."

"You just pat her. Gently but firmly. Here, you can burp her. Try it."

She plopped the baby into my arms. I was paralyzed. So far, I had managed to avoid actually picking her up. She looked up at me with big grayish eyes, the first time I had seen them. Lucille had put a stupid-looking headband around her bald little head. Pink, with a satin rosette. I was afraid it would give her a headache, it looked so tight, but she didn't seem to notice it. She waved her arms around and somehow got her little hand tangled up in my frizzy white hair. I tried to unwind the strands from her fist before she ate them but didn't make much headway. Babies have got a phenomenal grip.

Lucille came to the rescue, plucked the hair off, and put the baby up on my shoulder. Tiffany LaDawn started to sneeze; my hair tickled her nose.

"Here. Let me pull your hair back. You'll choke her with that mop."

She grabbed a piece of rubber tubing and tied my hair back with it. I was afraid to ask what it had been used for.

Tiffany LaDawn wormed around for a minute while I patted her as gently and firmly as I could, and then she let out a large burp and gushed a considerable quantity of soured milk onto my shoulder.

"Oh, I'm sorry, Cherry. Here. Let me wipe that off." It smelled really disgusting. In spite of the ponytail, my hair was full of it. Lucille wiped at me with a diaper, but it didn't do much good. I heard a loud creak, and jumped like I had been shot. Mr. Wilmerding was coming down the stairs. I really had to get ahold of myself and get out of there. "That's fine, Lucille. Let me just take her back up."

"Okay. Yell if you need me."

Upstairs, I put Tiffany LaDawn and the seat down on the table and jiggled her. She seemed to like that. As she bounced, she looked around the room with wonder. Newborns weren't supposed to be able to see much, but nobody can tell me there wasn't a real person in that tiny body, and it seemed like she liked the bright red walls.

She was cute, dressed in her little pink ruffledy dress and matching diaper cover with four rows of ruffles across the seat. I bet Lucille would never once put on the outfit I got her—teensy little blue jeans, tie-dyed T-shirt, and the cutest red tennies. I stuck the pacifier in her mouth, and she lay back, closed her eyes, and went to sleep. What a great kid. She was probably still worn-out from the birth. I couldn't imagine what it must have been like to fight to get out of a place that small.

Voices carried up the stairs. I tried to read a *Vogue* magazine that I had brought, but I couldn't concentrate, even though Goldie Hawn, who I loved on *Laugh-In*, was on the cover and there was a story about her inside. Mr. Wilmerding sounded like he was right in the room with me.

"This is a rare opportunity for you, Jim Floyd. It's not every day we have a chance to see firsthand the workings of the state homicide department." Mr. Wilmerding had an exceptionally loud, clear voice.

"Looky here—the way they sewed up this incision down her stomach. Somebody knew what he was doing, all right. Fine job. Neat stitches like my aunt Nellie used to make. We'll have to take 'em out, though, to get to the organs and embalm them. Have to inject the formaldehyde, of course. All those arteries cut during the autopsy. And we'll have to rebuild this left breast. My, my, my. Just look at this! Lordy, Lordy, Lordy. Lucille honey, get me a jar of that derma wax out of the cabinet over there. And two or three of those sponges."

It suddenly got stifling hot. I had to get out of there. Even though Tiffany LaDawn was asleep, I unstrapped her from the carry-seat and put her on my shoulder. She whimpered and squirmed, but I jigged her up and down for a minute, and she went back to sleep. She felt so warm and cuddly. Alive. We went out the front door to the porch, and I sat in a white wicker rocker, clung to Tiffany LaDawn, and rocked.

—

It was nearly four hours later when Lucille came out. I had walked and rocked and fed Tiffany LaDawn her emergency bottle and burped her gently but firmly. I felt like an old pro. Lucille perched on the porch rail and lit up a Kent. She had quit smoking while she was pregnant, but now she wanted to lose some weight, so she had started back up again.

"Are they done?" I was out in the yard, showing Tiffany LaDawn the squirrels. She wasn't really into looking at things yet, but you never know what might register in those little heads.

"Yeah. They're done. I am just wrung-out. I wish you could have seen her, Cherry. You would have just broke down and cried."

"You don't have to tell me about it, Lucille. That's all right."

She let out a big sigh. I had never seen Lucille so subdued. I didn't want her to tell me, but I knew that nothing in this world would stop her.

"For starters, there was a bad hole in her breast where he shot her. Mr. Wilmerding filled it in pretty well with derma wax."

"Lucille, it's all right. I don't really need to hear all this."

"I think she had been strangled, too. There were marks on her neck. But they are pretty sure it was the drowning that finally killed her. I just got done with the hair and makeup. They're dressing her now, so you can come in and look at her in a few minutes. Here, let me have my wittle pumpkin."

I was a little sorry to turn Tiffany LaDawn back over to her mother, in spite of the fact that she was smelling pretty ripe. I should have changed her diaper, but Lucille hadn't gotten around to giving me that lesson in baby-sitting yet. Could it be that all women have genes or something that get all fired up around babies? Not that I wanted one myself. But babies might not be the worst things. The place on my chest where Tiffany LaDawn had lain was damp and felt cool.

Jim Floyd and Mr. Wilmerding came out after a while and joined us. Lucille gave Jim Floyd the baby. "Here, Jim Floyd, take her. I've got to go and pee."

He took the baby with slow, gentle hands, laid her on his knees, and rocked her back and forth. Nobody said too much.

"Have you ever had somebody as bad as that before, Mr. Wilmerding?" I surprised myself by speaking.

"Oh, honey, I've had worse than this. Lots worse. You remember back in 'fifty-nine, when the train ran over that car right here in town at the railroad crossing and those four kids got killed?"

I nodded. I had been a little girl, but the shock of four teenagers dying tended to stick in your memory. It was the biggest wreck ever to happen on the train track, right in downtown Sweet Valley. There had been some others—it seemed like you couldn't keep people off the tracks. Once, one of the pickle trucks from Atlas was run over by a train. Three hundred bushels of cucumbers rained down all over the highway, breaking wind-shields and causing several more wrecks.

But this one was the worst. Apparently, the kids had been drinking and had all the windows rolled up and the radio blaring, so they didn't hear the train whistle. Died drunk. Daddy said he hoped they'd had a clear moment to ask forgiveness before they died and went to heaven. Though you should never count on waiting until the last minute to get saved—you might not have time to get right with the Lord, and the first person you'd see waiting for you would be the Devil. I wondered for a minute if Car-lene had had time to get right with the Lord as she was fighting for her life. It must have been hard to concentrate. I shivered.

Mr. Wilmerding continued, "You probably don't know this, but we had to go along the tracks, pick the body parts up and put them in pil-lowcases, and reconstruct them piece by piece. Like a jigsaw puzzle."

"How did you know which piece belonged to who?" Jim Floyd was all ears.

"Well now, Jim Floyd, we just had to use our best judgment. Two boys and two girls. We could more or less distinguish that much. There was a fifty-fifty chance it was going to the right one. Or at the least, one in four." Mr. Wilmerding pulled out a can of Prince Albert and rolled him-self a cigarette, long and thin, then licked it and stuck it in his mouth. We watched, mesmerized. He picked a piece of tobacco off his tongue, grunted as he reached down and struck a match on the bottom of his shoe, and lit the cigarette.

"Man, that was a challenge. That's the kind of thing they can't teach you in embalming school, Jim Floyd. You just have to have a knack for it." He took in a lungful of smoke. Blew it out.

"Take the bones, for instance. Some of the bones were missing, or too crushed into splinters to form out the limbs completely. So we got us some wooden dowels and made new bones. We got screws and hinged lit-tle pieces of dowel together to make new fingers; got wire and plaster and made new rib cages. I molded breasts out of sponges and covered them with skin made of rubber sheets. And don't ever underestimate the value of duct tape, Jim Floyd. If you don't have another thing in your tool kit, always keep you a roll of duct tape in there." He again drew in on the homemade, blew out the smoke, and diddled the ash off the end with his little finger. "Fortunately, the heads were mostly intact."

My stomach was feeling a little rocky. "Why did you go to all that trouble?" I asked. "Why didn't you just put them in the casket and shut the lid?" I had never seen anybody so into his work.

"No, sis. You can't do that. You need to see the actual body. You need the closure. The family needs to be able to look at that body and know that it is really over. Once they see the body, they are satisfied that the loved one is not going to come walking up to the doorstep. Then the grieving process can start. I try to make them look as lifelike as possible, for the sake of the family. I like to think of it as my art. You paint pictures, don't you, Cheryl Ann? We're both artists, you and me. I just work on a different kind of canvas."

Lucille came back out, the screen door slamming behind her. She stood looking out over the cool, shady yard for a minute, breathing in the good air as if she were grateful she could.

"You want to see her, Cherry? She looks real pretty."

—

Carlene's mother didn't have the money to buy a fancy casket—or probably to even pay the bill at all—so Mr. Wilmerding gave her the generic wooden kind he uses when he figures there might not be a payment forthcoming. But it was nice, lined in creamy white satin.

Lucille had done a great job on her, I must say. She had styled the hair so you couldn't see where they had sewed the top of Carlene's head back on after the autopsy. She seemed a little swollen, but Jim Floyd said that was usual for a drowning. I don't know what I was expecting, but not what I saw. She was really a pretty girl. I had never thought of her as all that pretty before. She had on pale coral lipstick and blush and a coppery eye shadow to match her hair. They had dressed her in a green velvet high-necked dress with a little cameo pin at the throat. Her breasts looked all right to me—smooth and symmetrical. Lucille had painted her long, perfect fingernails a coral color.

"I had to put on Patty-nails," Lucille whispered, as if Carlene could overhear. "She still bit her fingernails right down to the quick."

"Did you paint the toenails?" I whispered back.

She nodded. "I had to. That magenta polish she had on was awful. Redheads shouldn't try to wear pink. I couldn't let her go out with that on."

We stood for a long moment more, looking down at Carlene, sleeping so peacefully. She never had much in life, but she was going out with solemnity and ceremony. And dignity.

15. *Cherry*

 Brother Dane organized a funeral at Wilmerding's for Carlene for the Friday after she was embalmed on Wednesday. He is such a good man. I'm sure he didn't even know her, but it seemed like there was nobody else to do it. Brother Wilkins wouldn't let them have it in the Holiness Church, because Carlene hadn't been saved or baptized and had had an out-of-wedlock baby. He was probably afraid it might release a flock of demons into the good Christians sitting in the pews or something.

Jim Floyd and Lucille were working the funeral, and I had to admit that Jim Floyd looked nice in his black suit, with his mustache all combed. Lucille couldn't get into any of her regular clothes yet, so she was wearing one of her maternity dresses with one of those wide stretchy belts. A pink one.

"Lucille, don't you think you should have worn a black dress, or at least one that's a little less festive? I mean, this is a funeral." I had worn my all-purpose black sleeveless shift with black flats and a single strand of pearls. They said in *Vogue* that you could put on a black shift and some pearls— even ones from the dime store—and go anywhere, and it seemed like you could.

"I don't have a black dress. They're too depressing and hot. And anyhow, it's not what you wear but how you feel. I feel close to Carlene. Me and her went through a lot together. She knows what I'm wearing, and it's all right with her."

I had gone over early to keep Lucille company and help her with putting out the flowers that had arrived from Miss Martha's Flower Shop. There were more than I would have thought. Aunt Rubynell was watching Tiffany LaDawn, but I had talked Mama and Aunt Juanita into coming to the funeral. Uncle Jake let G. Dub take off from the Esso station for the afternoon, and he was coming. I didn't think that many people would be there, and I wanted to at least have a few people in the seats. I don't know why it seemed like my responsibility, but it did.

What I hadn't figured on was the fact that all of a sudden Carlene had become this celebrity. Already, there were cars lined up for blocks on the street, and what seemed like the whole population of Sweet Valley—plus a whole lot of people I'd never seen before in my life—was milling around in the yard waiting to get a look at the murdered girl. That is so sick. Half the people out there were the very ones who had talked about her like she was a dog or something when she got pregnant.

Actually, I shouldn't be too mad at them, because I hadn't exactly rushed to be best buddies with her myself. But it did seem a lot like a carnival, with everyone just wanting to get a look at her. Ghoulish. For some reason it made me nervous, and my hands were cold and a little shaky.

"Lucille, y'all better get on in here if you want some seats, because we're fixing to open the house," Jim Floyd called out from the viewing room.

He and Mr. Wilmerding had set up all the folding chairs they had, and when they saw what a crowd was gathering, they had taken Jim Floyd's pickup over to the school and borrowed as many from the lunchroom as they could pack in.

Lucille and I took a couple of seats in the second row and watched as Jim Floyd and Mr. Wilmerding propped up the lid of the casket and put a giant spray of orange gladioli on the top. The smell of the flowers was overpowering. There was a big wreath of yellow roses with a card from Jackie Lim, at the Water Witch, and it was signed by all the other waitresses. I didn't have time to read all the cards, but there was one from the girls she was on the basketball team with, and a big one from the class of '66—Baby had gone around and gotten donations from everybody she could locate. It looked real nice—blue and white carnations with a blue tornado in silver glitter on the ribbon. I wondered if there was one from Jerry Golden's folks.

People started filtering in, and Tripp Barlow slid into the empty seat next to me that I had been saving for Baby. I was a little surprised, but didn't want to tell him he couldn't sit there, so I put my purse on the one behind me to save for her, since the row was already filling up.

"Hi. How have you been?" he said. I had forgotten how gorgeous his eyes were.

"Okay. I didn't see you at work the other night."

"Yeah, I had some stuff I needed to do. But I'll be back tonight."

"Have you seen Carlene yet?"

We stared at the open casket, not ten feet in front of us.

"She was a beautiful girl. Just like Jerry said."

Baby came in with Bean and took the seat right behind us. She handed me my purse and pinched me on the arm, and we squeezed hands. Bean looked like he had been rode hard and put up wet. His eyes were all bloodshot, and his clothes looked like they had been slept in. I don't know how Baby put up with him looking like that. She never had a hair out of place.

"Hey, Cherry. Hey, Barlow," he said.

"Hey, Bean." Tripp turned and they shook hands, thumbs up together. "Tough night?"

"Naw. Just a little trouble sleeping. It ain't nothing new. I'm usually wound up tight as a tick after a gig out at Woody's, and sometimes it seems like I can't hardly get unwound. I'm all right."

He stopped and looked at Carlene lying there. A little catch came into his voice. "Ain't this just the worst thing that ever happened to anybody? She was a good girl, Barlow. You should have got to know her. She was a real good girl."

"She sure was," Baby said.

It felt uncomfortable chitchatting with Carlene lying right there. But it's true what they say about the body just being a shell or a vessel or whatever. There was not one spark of life in that coffin. I watched the green dress-front like I expected it to rise and lower with her breath, but it was as still as it could be. She didn't look like she was asleep. She looked dead.

Tripp had managed to take my hand without anybody noticing. He thought. I was sure Baby saw it, sitting right behind me like she was. It was hard to concentrate on the funeral.

G. Dub came in and waved at us, then sat beside Aunt Juanita in the seat she had been saving for him. She gave him a quick kiss before he could stop her. She is so crazy about that boy, and I guess seeing a girl near his age dead would make any mother kiss her kid. The rest of the seats filled up, except for some in the front row that had a black rope across them, and people kept coming in, cramming into the back and standing. There were more outside on the porch, looking in at the windows and doors, and still more on out in the yard. I saw Alfred Lynn Tucker and his old daddy, Walter, sitting in the middle, a few rows behind us. I imagined I could smell the pickles, but surely to goodness he would have cleaned up for a funeral. It was probably just in my head. They had taken seats next to Millie and Herman, the couple who owned the Freezer Fresh. I had to look at them for a minute before I knew who they were. It's funny when you see somebody out of their usual surroundings, like seeing your typing teacher at the Piggly-Wiggly pushing a grocery cart. At first you don't really recognize them, then you feel stupid that you didn't.

Jackie Lim, wearing a flashy greenish suit, sat with another Chinese man, who was dressed a little more conservatively, in dark blue. Ricky Don had found a seat over by the windows. He was still in uniform, which seemed a little like he was showing off, but I guess he couldn't get off work to change. Or maybe he just liked wearing the uniform around and making people feel uncomfortable. Why do we always feel guilty when we see a law officer? He saw me looking at him and acknowledged me with a little nod. I turned back in my seat and took my hand away from Tripp's. It just felt too wrong to be holding hands in front of Carlene. I don't think Ricky Don had anything to do with it.

I heard a voice calling in a loud whisper, "Pssst! Baby!" and twisted around to see who it was. A woman was sitting a couple of rows behind us, across the aisle. She waved at Baby, who lifted her fingers in a little wave.

"Who is that woman, Baby?" I whispered over my shoulder.

"Her name is Rita Ballard. Carlene and I used to work with her."

I pretended to lean down and get something out of my purse, so she wouldn't think I was staring, and looked at her. She was on the fat side, with the kind of thick orangeish makeup you use if you have a major case of acne scars. It ended at her jawline, making it look like she had on a mask. Her eyes were loaded with clumpy black mascara, and her hair was bleached blond, short, and ratted up high, with rhinestone barrettes nestled in it. She had a Marilyn Monroe mole on her cheek, but it didn't look real. There was something not too clean about her, kind of a dirty-underwear feeling. I looked at Baby with questioning eyes, but she just shrugged.

Brother Dane came in just then with Frannie Moore, dressed in one of her black flowered dresses, and had to push his way through the crowd to get up the aisle. She was thin and colorless, with big dark circles under her eyes. Her skin was so delicate you could see the veins popped out on the backs of her hands, like blue ropes. Holding on to her hand was a red-haired boy, who, except for his big blue eyes, was the very image of Carlene. He had a pinched little face with freckles sprinkled across his nose. He looked scared. Everyone stared at them, watching for Frannie to dissolve into tears or something, but she just hung on to Brother Dane's arm and sat down slowly on the chair on the aisle in the first row, then picked up the boy, and put him on her lap. Brother Dane patted him on the head and went up to stand at the podium set up beside the coffin.

Even though the crowd was quiet to begin with, Brother Dane stood looking out over us for a long minute, waiting for our total attention before he started to speak.

"Brethren, this a sad day for Sweet Valley, a sad day for the loved ones of Carlene Moore, but a joyous day for God. For today, God has got Carlene with Him in heaven. Amen?"

Several of the men in the back said amen. Frannie didn't, and neither did we.

"God works in mysterious ways, and although we cannot see at times why He does the things He does, or understand His reasons, we just have to put our trust in Him and believe that He is doing the best for us in accordance with His divine plan. We must never question God's divine plan."

I couldn't believe that God's plan had anything to do with some maniac murdering Carlene. In fact, it was getting harder as I got older to figure out the whole business of what God does control. I am almost scared to say it out loud, but it seems to me like either God is all-powerful or He is all good, but He can't be both. You know what I mean? How can He really be omniscient and omnipotent, like they teach us in church, and still let things happen like Carlene getting murdered or babies getting cancer or all those Jews getting killed by the Nazis? Is it the Devil that causes all of it? If God could stop it but allows it to happen, then maybe He is not all that caring about us.

I mean, for instance, look at Job. There in black and white in the Bible, God and the Devil made a bet about which one of them Job would go with. After God agreed to let the Devil kill Job's children in a tornado and take away his land and livestock and give him sores and all, it was great that he was still loyal to God, and it's true that God did give him new kids and more wealth, but what about the old kids? Nobody ever said another word about them. They were killed for a bet? Didn't they count for anything?

I was confused a fair amount of the time at church, but I knew better than to bring it up, because one time I asked Daddy about the Job thing and he got so upset that he called Brother Wilkins over to the house, who practically blistered the skin off my ears for daring to question the Bible. He made us all get down in the living room floor while he prayed over me for my lack of faith. At least it wasn't in church in front of the whole congregation. No, I learned early on that you just had faith—you didn't ask any questions.

And now here was Brother Dane, who I had thought was different, saying the same old rigmarole. I wanted to tell him to stop that old "God works in mysterious ways" business. He was starting to sound like Brother Wilkins, who, by the way—the old hypocrite—was standing in the back of the house, I noticed. Sister Wilkins stood next to him, her arms crossed as if she was hiding a sharp wooden stake in case Carlene rose up out of the coffin like Dracula or something.

What was wrong with me? I had to stop thinking mean things about them. It was their right not to allow the funeral to be in the church. They were no worse than any of the other preachers in town who didn't offer. But they—or at least he—was my preacher, and that made it worse. I felt like it somehow reflected on me. Was I beginning to lose my faith? Oh, Lord, I prayed. I believe. Help my unbelief.

I tried to stop thinking about the whole mess and listen to Brother Dane.

". . . cut down in the flower of her youth. She was not only young and beautiful, at the beginning of her life, but had a baby son to think about. A son who will now never again know the feel of his mother's arms holding him as he goes to sleep at night. Who will never again hear his mother's voice saying, 'I love you, son.' "

Dang. I got a lump in my throat. Lucille was wiping away tears, and I heard someone behind me sobbing, but I hated to turn around and look. There was sniffing and nose-blowing all around the room, and I found myself getting teary-eyed. Lucille handed me a Kleenex and I blew my nose.

Brother Dane did something then that I'd never seen a preacher do at a funeral. He stopped in the middle of speaking. He was working his mouth, but no words came out. Then he broke down, too. Tears ran down his cheeks in a stream, and his nose started to run. He fumbled in his pocket for his handkerchief and blew his nose with a loud honk, wiped his eyes with what I hoped was the clean end, and carefully put it back into his pocket—all without saying a word, like he was thinking hard about something.

"Brethren, we can talk about God's will all day and all night, but the truth is that there is no sense to any of this," he finally managed to croak out. "There is no rhyme or reason in the world to a beautiful, lively young girl having something like this done to her, and no amount of praying or trusting in God will change what happened. A man did this to her—an evil, twisted man—and it had nothing to do with God."

The room got really quiet. He went on: "Sometimes we pray and we pray for God to step in and make a miracle happen—to save our children, to cure us of disease, to get us a job, to make our husbands or wives be faithful to us, and it doesn't happen. So we shake our fists in God's face and say, 'God, why did You let this happen to me?' Well, maybe God couldn't do anything about it. Maybe He doesn't control our lives in every least little detail like we think He does. Maybe He created us and then said, 'People, you're on your own. I gave you a beautiful world and a head on your shoulders, and you do the best with it that you can. We'll sort it all out on the other side.' Sometimes I don't know anymore. I just don't know." And he stood there crying again.

Everyone in the room was shocked. I sure was. It was almost like he had been reading my mind. I don't think anybody had ever heard a preacher talk like that before, and no one knew what to make of it. The choirmaster from our church, Elvin Stokes, got up to cover the embarrassment, or maybe to keep Brother Dane from going any further, and started the choir singing "Farther Along." Brother Dane stood there for a minute, like he didn't know what was taking place, and then he got ahold of himself and started to sing along with them. Most of the crowd not already in tears broke down then. I couldn't sing, myself, for the lump in my throat. I hate that song. Why do they have to sing such sad old songs at funerals? It made you feel so lonesome—"Farther along, we'll know all about it . . . farther a-long, we'll understand why. Cheer up, my brother, live in the sunshine. We'll understand it all by and by." Like we ever would. Tripp took my hand again and squeezed it, and somehow it made me feel a little better to know that he was feeling the same things I was.

As the choir sang, Jim Floyd and Mr. Wilmerding got on each side of Frannie Moore and escorted her up to the casket to say good-bye. She stood looking at Carlene, with tears running down her face, then she reached out to touch her hair and fainted dead on the floor before Jim Floyd had time to catch her. Mama, who was sitting right behind her, jumped up, as did Aunt Juanita and a couple more women, and half carried, half dragged her out the side door to the porch, where they laid her down on a wicker couch and started chafing her wrists while somebody went and got her a glass of water.

Brother Dane stepped down from the podium and picked up little Kevin, who everyone had forgotten about in the excitement and was sitting there by himself, wailing at the top of his lungs. I'm sure he was scared half to death. He probably thought his grandma was dead, too. Brother Dane took him outside to where Frannie was, to show him she was all right.

Everyone else lined up and passed single file by the casket to get a closer look at Carlene, then craned their necks at the window as they went on around the room to see what was going on outside with Frannie. I hope they got their money's worth. I wanted to tell them to take a picture—it lasts longer.

Tripp and I filed out of our row and got into line behind a man none of us had ever seen before. It was hard to put your finger on why, exactly, but he looked rich. He was a lot older than us, probably nearly forty, and had on a midnight-blue gabardine suit that said money, and loafers made out of soft Italian leather with little tassels on the toes. He had the kind of even tan you get from lying out in the sun and basting yourself with expensive oil, and he smelled good, too, although I couldn't recognize the cologne. His hair was shot with silver, nearly white at the temples, and long enough to brush over his collar. He wore a diamond ring on the middle finger of his right hand—six rows of fairly big diamonds; it covered the whole joint, from knuckle to hand. He was carrying a single rose, and when he stopped at the casket, he reached out and put the flower between Carlene's hands, then leaned down and kissed her right on the mouth. Then he turned and walked down the aisle and out the front door, acting like he didn't notice that everyone in the room was staring at him with big eyes. I stepped up to the casket next, in my turn, and saw that the rose still had the thorns on it; they looked like they were digging into her hands. I wanted to move it, but couldn't get up the courage to touch her, so I left it there, even though it bothered me.

I would have liked to follow him to see what kind of car he got into, but it was way too crowded, and he disappeared.

I went on out and found Mama sitting on the porch with Frannie, who looked a little better. Aunt Juanita was holding the boy, letting him hunt in her purse for gum. Jim Floyd brought the limo around and they got them and Lucille in for the trip out to the graveyard. Frannie seemed so small, her ankles bony and white above her patent-leather shoes, as she climbed into the big car. It made me think of how Carlene used to look in the third grade. I hoped Frannie would hang on to her marbles for a while longer, but it didn't seem likely.

"Cherry, I'm going to go on out to the graveyard with Frannie. Y'all come on and I'll see you out there," Mama called to me as she followed Frannie into the limo.

I was so proud of her. I don't think she even knew Frannie all that well, and there she was taking care of her. I hope I can be just like that when I get older.

I got into Ramblin' Rose with Tripp and Baby and Bean, and we all headed up to the cemetery. There was a long funeral procession stretching out behind us for a mile or two. That whole crowd of people was going to the graveyard. They weren't going to miss one minute of the carnival.

16. *Carlene*

 As long as she could remember, Carlene never could do anything right as far as her daddy was concerned. If she was coloring, it was always in the place right where he needed to sit and eat. If she ate a piece of pie, it would be one he was saving for his dinner. If he tripped over anything, it was sure to be something she had left out. And the first reaction he always had was to pop her one on the butt before she even knew what was happening, and ask questions later. Sometimes he hit her for no good reason that she could figure out.

"What'd I do, Daddy? Why'd you hit me?"

"You know what you done, Ida Red. Don't think I don't know. Now, get on and let me alone."

It seemed like sometimes the very sight of her was enough to set him off on a tirade about something. She had bruises where he would stripe her legs with a hickory switch for mouthing off at him, but she couldn't seem to stop herself from doing it. It wasn't in her to take what he had to dish out, even when she was little. Even when she knew what the consequences would be.

"You're not the boss of me, and I will eat anything my mother cooks if I want to," she'd say. "It's her that makes the money to buy it."

"Don't you lip off to me, girl," he'd answer. "I'll whup you good." And then she would run and he would be after her, chasing her out the door, across the woodpile, finally catching her and blistering her legs while she kicked and tried to bite him, just making him madder.

Carl was temporarily out of work. It seemed that the boss over at the sawmill had it in for him, because Carl was a better sawyer than the boss's new son-in-law, and said something to the boy about his uneven boards. The boss didn't like Carl anyhow and was just looking for an excuse to let him go. At least that was Carl's version. Some variation of that story ended every job Carl Moore ever had.

They struggled along while Carl went from job to job until Carlene started school, then Frannie wanted to go back to work.

"Carl, I been thinking of going back to the pickle plant. It seems like we don't never have the money for nothing."

"No. You're not goin' back to the plant. I can take care of this family."

Carl was not about to let her work in the same place as Walter Tucker, who he, more than ever, suspected was Carlene's real father. Frannie still took her late-night walks in the woods after Carlene went to sleep, and Carl usually followed her, sure that she was meeting some man, doubly sure it was Walter Tucker. Sometimes she would carry on conversations, and even though Carl couldn't hear anybody reply or didn't ever see anybody, that didn't mean there wasn't somebody there. It was enough to drive a man crazy.

"Well, I got to find work somewhere, Carl. I'll lose my mind if I have to stay here in this trailer all day. Maybe I could get on as a waitress at the Town Café, or someplace."

"No, Frannie. I won't have it! You know how those men who hang out at the Town Café are—they'll be looking at you, thinking all kinds of things."

Frannie sighed. "Then how about the chicken processing plant? Carl, I swear on the Bible I'll not talk to any men. We don't even have enough money to get decent clothes for Carlene."

"Well, I don't know." He hesitated, knowing the truth of what she said. "The chicken plant might be all right. But just until I get steady work. Then you quit and stay home." The processing plant was the least of the evils, as far as Carl could see. The work was so rough that he didn't figure there would be much heart for fooling around.

So Frannie got on at the chicken processing plant. There weren't many places a woman with only an eighth-grade education could work.

The plant was kept freezing cold, for the chickens, and everyone wore as many clothes as they could move around in—layers of flannel shirts and long underwear under baggy overalls. The plant itself was a scene of carnage. After the catchers hung the chickens by the feet on a moving chain, their heads dragged through an electrified water pool that killed or stunned them and they passed by a saw that cut their heads off. The men who ran the saw wore head-to-toe rubber suits slicked over with the blood spray. The headless chickens were then dipped in boiling water to loosen the feathers and went past the pinning women, who pulled off as many feathers as they could snatch as the birds moved by. That's where Frannie started out—the pinning line. By the end of that first shift, she couldn't lift her arms, and the smell was so bad she had to go out several times and throw up; but she got used to it after a few weeks. At least she was away from Carl all day. He was driving her crazy with his jealousy. She was afraid he was becoming unhinged. She knew he sometimes sat across the street from the plant, just watching. He thought nobody noticed him, but several people asked her what her husband was doing out there sitting in the truck all day.

She considered leaving him, but she was afraid he would come after her, and hurt her or Carlene in his rage. He didn't hit her too often, but she had a feeling that if he ever let go, he could be real bad. She could stay with him, at least until Carlene got out of school. He did seem to love her, in his way. If only he could get a job, it might be all right.

"Carl," she would say, "why don't you get on at the chicken plant, too? You ain't going to get no sawmill job, it seems like."

"I'm a master sawyer, Frannie. I'll find a job in a sawmill, if you please. Don't you worry about it. You won't be working at that place long."

Deep down, he felt like he was too good to work in a factory. He wasn't cut out for that kind of work—the tedium of it, the stench. He'd wait for a sawmill job to open up.

Weeks, then months, went by and nothing came up. After a while he didn't even pretend to look. He spent most of his days spying on Frannie. Sometimes he went squirrel hunting. Or deer hunting. Or coon hunting. But there were days, increasingly, when a mood settled on him, and he would go up on the Ridge to get a quart of moonshine and then drink from the time he got up until he went to bed, and read magazines that Carlene wasn't allowed to touch. Those were the days he brushed her hair.

What was even worse than the whippings he gave her was his way of staring at her hair, touching it as she walked by him, like he couldn't keep his hands off it.

"Ida Red, go and get the hairbrush," he'd say. "Your hair is a rat's nest."

He would sit her in his lap, then, while he ripped through the curls with a fierce energy, pulling and yanking the tangles, digging the bristles into her head until the hair was smooth and shiny. If she screamed or wiggled or tried to get up, he'd clamp his legs around her and hold her there until he'd had enough of brushing it.

One night as Carlene was coming out of her bath, Frannie came in and noticed long scratches on her neck.

"Honey, what happened to your neck?"

She didn't want to tell, but couldn't think of some other reason quick enough. So she told the truth. "Daddy done it, brushing my hair."

"Your daddy brushes your hair like that?"

"Yes, ma'am, he does. He likes to brush it hard, for a long time. Sometimes it makes my head sore."

Frannie put some mercurochrome on the scratches and didn't say anything else about it, but the next Saturday she brought home a bottle of Clairol hair dye, Raven Black, and dyed the red curls.

"You have pretty hair, Carlene honey, but it seems like it's like a red rag to a bull for your daddy. Maybe he won't get so mad at you if he doesn't have to see the red all the time. Besides, you look just like I do now. We're nearly twins, don't you think? Isn't this fun?"

Carlene didn't say anything to her mother, just let her do what she wanted to. Sometimes, even at eight, she felt like she was the mother and

Frannie was the girl. When she was little, they used to sneak off from Carl together. Sometimes they would go down to the brook that ran through the woods behind the trailer and make pretend houses on the cool, wet rocks. They would pick berries and mushrooms and cook them on pretend stoves. Frannie put dolls on layaway at the five-and-dime for Carlene and paid them out a dollar a week. Every payday, they would go add another dollar, and the man would take the doll off the shelf and let Carlene hold it for a minute. Then he'd put it back up until they paid the last dollar, when she could take it home. She had a baby doll with skin that felt like real baby skin, and a Sweet Sue walking doll almost as big as she was; a Ginny doll, small and blond, with blue eyes that closed and a tiny, turned-up nose. They had to hide them from Carl, though, because he would throw a fit when he saw them.

"Frannie, you know that we can't afford play-pretties! We don't even have the money for a TV!"

Carlene protected her dolls from Carl, just like her mother tried to protect her, but she never told Frannie about the switches and the bruises. If she could avoid it, she didn't let her see them, and if she couldn't, she said she tripped and fell over a rock or something. No point in having her daddy call her a snitch, and no telling what her mama would do. It would just make things worse. She could get along all right.

———

"What do you think you've done to your hair, Ida Red? It looks like a pile of dog mess."

"Mama dyed it to look like hers. We look like twins."

Carl laughed. "You ain't ever goin' to be as pretty as your mama, Ida Red, if you took a bath in a tub of black dye."

It seemed like the dye didn't help them get along any better. He spent more and more time alone, reading his books. He hid them before Frannie got home. Carlene watched when he went out to put them away, and when he was out, she sneaked a look at them. They were all of naked women, which she knew her mother wouldn't like. But she didn't want to tell her about them. Instead, she stole a book of his, called *Peep,* and took it to school. She thought they would maybe come and arrest him or something. Instead, it just got her in trouble with the teacher, and nobody at the school ever said a word to Carl about it. The teacher kept the magazine, but Carl never even missed it, he had so many hidden in the tin box. Carlene used to crawl under the trailer when he was off hunting and look at them. The women were pretty, most of them, and looked like they were real comfortable posing in front of the camera. They didn't look like they were forced into it. She tried to make up stories about the naked women, give them reasons for doing it, like if they had a mother in the hospital and needed money for her or something. She liked looking at the magazines. It made her feel like she had a secret on her daddy. When he was mean to her, she would think of the picture books; it somehow unsettled him.

"What are you thinking, Ida Red? I know you're thinking something about me."

"I don't always think about you, Daddy." She would say with a little smile. It drove him mad.

Carlene had her own collection, too—of movie-star pictures. Frannie could always come up with the price of a matinee ticket for herself and Carlene, and they would go and get lost in the movies for hours. They went on Saturday afternoons while Carl waited for them out at the sale barn with some of his old buddies, passing around a jar of moon. Frannie had always loved the movies. She wrote to stars like Rochelle Hudson and Shirley Temple when she was a girl, and they sent her autographed pictures. She had a stack of them: Frederic March, Myrna Loy, Clark Gable, and a lot of others. Since Carlene had gotten old enough to write, they also had new ones, like Sandra Dee and Troy Donahue and Carlene's favorite, Shirley MacLaine. Most would never answer the letters, but now and again a signed photo would arrive.

"When you grow up, Carlene, you could be in the pictures. You are as pretty as Rita Hayworth. You'll get on a bus one day and go to Hollywood and then I'll write you for one of your pictures!"

It was a dream she kept secret and thought about a lot, even though she knew it probably would never happen.

———

Most of the movie stars smoked. You had to smoke if you wanted to be a star. When she was twelve, she started sneaking her daddy's Camel cigarettes. She would only take one or two at a time, so he wouldn't notice. She felt good, sitting on the big gray lichen-covered rock out behind the trailer, taking the blue smoke deep into her lungs, pretending to be on the big screen. She had watched Bette Davis do it, and she practiced French-inhaling and blowing smoke rings until she looked like a pro. She got away with it for more than a year, until he began to notice.

One afternoon, she was so taken with watching the smoke rings drift up and break apart that she didn't hear Carl come up behind her until he had grabbed the cigarette out of her hand.

"Ha! I caught you red-handed, Ida Red. You thought I wouldn't miss those cigarettes, didn't you?" He threw down the cigarette, stomped on it, and leaned close to her face. She could smell the sour liquor on his breath, and tried to pull back.

"You want to smoke? Okay. Here. I'll show you what cigarettes taste like." He took a half-filled pack out of his pocket and crammed it into her mouth. Shoved it in until she started to gag. Then, as she bent over to retch, he kicked her, and when she fell to the ground, he grabbed the pack out of her mouth and crumbled the cigarettes over her face.

"That'll teach you to smoke my cigarettes. That's the last pack of mine you'll ever get."

She lay in the dirt with the tobacco in her mouth, giving him one of her Ida Red looks that seemed to make him even madder at her. She fought as hard as she could not to cry while he looked at her.

"What are you looking at?"

"Nothing." She wiped her mouth. "I'm looking at nothing."

"Are you saying that I'm nothing?"

"You said it, I didn't."

"I'll show you who's nothing. Get up from there, girl."

He grabbed her by the arm, and she spat a mouthful of wet tobacco in his face. Then something took hold of him, like a red screen of rage had rolled down over his eyes. He twisted her arm and threw her back down on the ground, falling with her. She bit him hard on the fleshy part of his hand, drawing blood. He roared, and with the pain, it seemed like a demon entered his body. He shoved her back, and she began kicking at him, her dress riding up. He tried to hold down her legs, and at the same time he grabbed at her white cotton panties. They tore as easy as if they had been made of paper.

She was a big girl for thirteen, and the first fuzz of red hair covered her private parts. He stared for a moment, the sight hitting him like a punch in the face. He grimaced, then in a single motion thrust her legs apart, un-zipped his jeans, and released himself, falling onto her. One hard jab rup-tured the small slit covered by soft red down.

She screamed, tried to bite, tried to hit, but couldn't do anything ex-cept lie there and gasp while the weight of her father mashed her into the rocky ground.

He let out a moan, like the demon was climbing out of his throat, clawing at his voice. Then he was still. All of a sudden, he leaped up; stood and stared in horror at the girl lying at his feet, a thin trail of red laced across her white leg.

"Oh my God in heaven. Ida Red . . . what have I done?" It didn't seem like he was mad anymore. He staggered a few steps away and clutched his stomach, as if he felt sick. He heaved, several dry heaves, then zipped his jeans and leaned over, his hands on his knees, until he could get his breath. His fingers dug into his legs, like he was trying to feel if they were still there. After a long minute, he straightened and came back to where Carlene lay on the ground; reached down to help her up. She shrank from his hand.

"You don't never touch me again, Daddy. I'll kill you if you do. I swear I will."

He turned without a word and left her; walked around the side of the trailer, white-faced and numb.

Carlene lay motionless, dry-eyed, and looked up at the blue sky. It was a perfect fall day, not too cool, but with a little snap in the air. Not one cloud anywhere. A crow flew over, chased by a small purple martin. Its caw was coarse and loud, and echoed off the tops of the pine trees, the caw of a crow in trouble. Crows are bullies, but they don't have death guts. The little bird was getting the best of the old black one. She watched for a minute more until they flew into the trees, then noticed that the beige siding on the trailer was rusted and stuck out in a curl near the cor-ner, where it was starting to peel off. Everything she looked at was clear and crisp, as if it were under a magnifying glass.

She felt like she was stuck to the ground, unable to move. She lay like that for a time, waiting for her daddy to come back and say something to her, or try to get her to go into the trailer or do something, but he didn't. She reached under her back and moved a small rock that was digging into her shoulder. Finally, she sat up, and with a shaky hand wiped her legs with the tail of her dress. She wiped and wiped and still felt like there was more blood seeping from the tender red wound.

She began to cry, then, fat drops that fell onto her lap, and didn't notice when the door on the other side of the trailer opened, didn't see underneath when the feet stepped down and walked across the yard; she was too wrapped up in cleaning herself to hear the truck door shut. She was trying to think of what she would tell Frannie, how she would tell her mother that she didn't want to live in the trailer with Daddy anymore. She would have to tell her what happened, but in a way that wouldn't scare her. Frannie would move them out, she knew. They could find a new place for themselves, she was pretty sure. She was only thirteen, but she looked older. Maybe she could say she was sixteen and get a job at the chicken plant with her mother.

She had lost track somewhat, but figured it was nearly time for Frannie to get off from work. She couldn't sit in the dirt all afternoon. She had to get up off the ground and do something. She had to clean herself up before her mother got home.

Carlene didn't want to go back inside if her daddy was still there. He didn't seem mad anymore, but you never could tell. If he was still in the trailer, she'd go down to the brook and wash, stay there until Frannie got home.

She crept around the side of the trailer, holding her dress tail between her legs. The bleeding had pretty much stopped, but it stung when she walked.

The trailer door stood wide open. There was no sign of Daddy. All she heard was the ticking of the Felix the Cat clock that hung over the stove; its black rhinestone-covered tail swung back and forth, and its big white eyes looked right and left. She leaned against the door frame and peered across the yard.

The truck was parked under the big oak tree up beside the road. Her daddy was sitting in the driver's seat, just staring out the window. Carlene stood on the concrete step and watched, waited for him to put the truck in gear and leave.

But instead of starting the motor, he picked up his hunting rifle and aimed it at his head. He held it there for a long time, then put it down, rolled down the window, and called out to Carlene:

"Ida Red? Come on over here."

"My name's Carlene, Daddy. If you want me to come over there, you can call me by my name."

"Please . . . Carlene. Come over here." His voice sounded wet.

She walked over toward the truck. Carefully. She wouldn't let him see her limp.

As she came up, he stuck the butt of the rifle out the window.

"Here. Take this gun. I want you to shoot me. I never have been a daddy to you. I don't deserve to live after what I done. But before you do it, I just want to say that I'm sorry. I don't know what got into me. The Devil, I guess, and he can take me now."

He held the gun out to her. She didn't touch it.

"Why don't you do it yourself?"

"I tried to, but I couldn't. I don't guess I have the guts. You can do it. And I know it won't much bother you. You're stronger than I ever was. Just do it quick, before your mother gets home. I reckon she won't care much, either, but she might try to stop you."

He nudged her with the gun. She took it then, looked at it a minute, and pointed it between his eyes.

"You're just playing with me, aren't you? You think I won't shoot you, don't you? I should shoot you. You're right about that. I could. All I'd have to do is squeeze this trigger . . ."

She put her finger on the trigger. Lightly. She had never shot the gun before. Daddy would have switched her good if she had ever touched his gun. The trigger was smooth and cool. She looked at her hands as if they belonged to somebody else, noticed that her hands were sticky with blood, ringed dark and red around the nails that were bitten into the quick.

"Do it, Carlene. Do it quick if you're going to. It won't be like murder or nothing. I want you to do it. It ain't murder if the person wants it."

"Do it yourself. I'm not playing your game no more. For once, do one thing for yourself."

She started to lower the gun, but he reached his hand out and grabbed at it.

The gun went off.

Daddy had a surprised look on his face as the back of his head blew out and his brains hit the roof of the cab and slid down the window. Then he slowly slumped down, what was left of his head coming to gently rest on the steering wheel. There was a hole the size of a silver dollar in the middle of his forehead.

As the gun fired, Carlene screamed and jumped. She hadn't meant to do it. She just wanted to scare him, make him pay a little bit. The trigger was so easy to pull. She hadn't meant to really pull it; in fact, she couldn't tell for sure if she had pulled it or if it went off by itself.

The gun fell out of her hands, down onto the ground, but she didn't see it; she just kept staring at her daddy's face and his empty, surprised eyes.

She tried to think of what to do, but her brain was having a hard time working. She felt cold and had trouble catching her breath. It was as if the sun had stopped turning around and everything was clear and still, like in a picture, and nothing could move. A warm stream of urine went down her legs, stinging, but there was no way she could stop it.

—

The sound of gears grinding brought her back as a truck strained up the road. There was no place to hide, no way to stop whoever it was from seeing the truck with Carl at the wheel and his brains all over the cab. Carlene faced the road and waited. There was nothing else she could do.

The truck slowed down, then pulled into the yard, and Walter Tucker got out. He ran over to where she stood, unmoving, beside her dead father.

"My Lord, Carlene! What happened?"

"I shot my daddy. He wanted me to, though."

"Looks like you sure did. Where's your mama?"

"She hadn't got off work yet."

He looked at the bloodstained dress. "What'd your daddy do to you?"

"Nothing."

Walter opened the truck cab and Carl fell over. Walter caught him before he hit the ground; shoved him back in and shut the door.

"Are you going to call the sheriff?" Carlene tried to act like she didn't care one way or the other.

"I don't know. What do you reckon the sheriff would say if he saw this mess?"

Carlene looked down at her shoes and the puddle around her feet. Walter lifted up his cap and ran his hand through his hair several times, like he was trying to start his brain to working. He slapped his leg with the cap, stared out at the pine trees across the road, then at Carl, then at Carlene. He put his cap back on.

"Naw, I don't reckon we need to call the law. Go on in the house and get you on a clean dress. Bring that nasty one back out with you."

Carlene ran in and did like he said.

When she came back out, Walter was scraping what he could off the ceiling of the truck cab, slinging gobs of pink and gray brain onto the floor. He took the bloody dress she handed him and wiped his hands, then scrubbed the windshield on the inside. It would pass for clean.

Then he went into the house and found an old brown cardboard suitcase in the bottom of the closet. He raked a handful of Carl's clothes off the closet rod, stuffed them in, opened a few drawers, and emptied them into the suitcase. Carlene watched him for a minute, then ran outside and dragged the tin box full of magazines out from under the trailer. They threw it all into the truck cab.

"Come on, girl. Get in the back. We gotta take care of this before your mama gets home."

Carlene climbed in and watched through the back window as Walter shoved her daddy's body down behind the dashboard.

He got behind the wheel, turned around, and saw her face in the window.

"Sit down, Carlene. I don't need you to fall." The key was in the ignition. He turned it, and the truck hacked and jerked to life. He leaned out the window and studied Carlene for a minute.

"Better yet, you drive my truck and follow me. I don't need to leave my truck out here. You know how to drive, don't you?"

"No, sir. I never drove a truck before."

"Ain't nothing to it. Put your left foot on the clutch while you start it, then shove the gear shift up and give it a little gas with your right foot as you ease up on the clutch. You know which one's the brake and which one's the clutch, don't you?"

"I reckon. I seen my daddy drive."

"Good. When you get to going a little faster, step on the clutch and pull the gear shift down into second. Then let the clutch out slow. You probably won't need more gears than that. Follow me. Here's the keys."

He tossed the keys up to Carlene, who climbed down from the back of the pickup and got into Walter's truck. It took her a few tries to get it started, but she did, and the caravan of two set off down the road, her truck weaving from side to side while she learned, as she went, how to steer. They didn't meet a single car, which was a blessing.

Two miles from the trailer was an old rock quarry, abandoned for years, that had filled up with deep, cold water. Nobody was really sure just how deep it really was. The legend was that it was bottomless. Kids used to sometimes climb down the sheer rock walls and go swimming there in the hot summertime, but there were no ledges to speak of, the water was dark, and one time two of them drowned. The bodies were never recovered. After that, mothers were always warning their kids about the quarry, but the kids wouldn't have gone swimming there anyhow. They were too afraid the bodies of the drowned boys would pop up. There was never anybody around there.

And there wasn't anybody around there when they pulled up in the truck with Carl Moore's body and parked near the rim.

It didn't take much to shove the truck over, with both of them pushing. Carlene and Walter knelt and leaned over the side and watched it make a shadow on the rock wall on its way down, then hit the surface with a splash that sent a spray halfway up to where they were kneeling. It floated for a minute or two, then the cab filled and the dark green water of the quarry sucked it under and it sank out of sight, heading slowly to the bottom. If there was a bottom. It might have kept going all the way to the burning center of the earth.

Then the two of them, Walter and Carlene, got in his truck and drove back to the trailer together in silence.

———

Frannie was more than a little surprised to see Walter sitting in the yard when she got home. He and Carlene were drinking big glasses of ice tea.

"Well, Walter Tucker. What in the world are you doing here?"

"Hidey, Frannie. Just thought I'd drop by and visit a little while. Carlene, why don't you go on in and get your mama a glass of tea? I bet she could use one."

"Do you want me to, Mama?"

"That would hit the spot. Where's your daddy?"

"Go on, Carlene. Get your mama that tea."

Carlene went into the trailer. The window was open beside the sink, and she cracked the tray open and took out the ice as quietly and slowly as she could, so she could listen.

"That's what I need to talk to you about, Frannie. I happened to come by here just as Carl was out in the yard, loading all his clothes in the back of the truck. I thought that was a little strange, and I asked him where he was going. He said he was taking off. Said he hadn't been much of a husband and less of a father, and you and Carlene would be better off without him."

Frannie sat down on an old tire. It seemed like the wind had been knocked out of her.

"Well. I declare. That don't sound like Carl. You mean he just up and told you all that?"

"You're mighty right. It don't sound like him, but that's what happened. He might have had a bit to drink at the time."

"That part sounds like Carl."

"Men get low sometimes, Frannie. Did Carl seem low to you?"

"Lord, yes. It had just got worse and worse, come to think about it."

"Seemed like he didn't have a grip, you think?"

"I guess you could say that. It had got to where I tried to mostly stay out of his way."

"Men sometimes lose their grip, Frannie. I reckon that might have happened with Carl. He just lost his grip."

Frannie looked hard at Walter. She didn't really believe him, but Carl and the truck were both gone. What if it was true?

"You'd think he would have had the decency to at least tell it to me face-to-face."

"Naw. He'd never do that. Men like Carl ain't no good at talking face-to-face. Likely, he just took a notion all of a sudden to light out and start fresh all over again someplace else, where they don't know him. He's still a young man."

Frannie thought about that for a while. It didn't make a lot of sense, but Carl did a lot of things that didn't make much sense. Still, Walter might have misunderstood.

"Did he say where he was headed?"

"Not exactly. I think he might have mentioned something about heading out west. He did say for me to tell you he didn't want you to try to look for him, and not to worry. Just get on with your life. Take care of the girl. And that he was real sorry."

"Well, I swan. That don't sound at all like Carl." Now she was starting to worry. Walter must have got it wrong. For the life of her, she couldn't imagine Carl saying that.

Carlene came back out with a big glass squeezed full of lemons, sugar, and tea, just like Frannie liked it.

"What did your daddy say to you, Carlene? Were you here when he left?"

She looked over at Walter, who had taken out his pocketknife and was paring his fingernails.

"No, ma'am. I hadn't got home yet. When I got here, Daddy had done gone and Walter was out in the yard waiting for me."

"Walter, I just don't know what to say." The thought of Carl being gone was beginning to be exciting. She needed some time to think about it.

"You don't have to say nothing, Frannie. I think I ought to stay to supper, though, if it's all right with you. I reckon you might not want to be by yourself tonight."

"No. You go on. We'll be all right. I think Carlene and me need to be by ourselves to think this through. Thank you anyway, though. I appreciate all you've done."

———

Frannie and Carlene waved as Walter got in his truck and drove off.

"Well, your daddy will more than likely have a change of heart, so we better enjoy it while we can before he comes rolling back into the yard. What do you want for supper tonight, Carlene? You can have canned spaghetti or anything else you want. Your daddy's not here to fuss about it."

17. Cherry

 Shady Vista Cemetery was set up on a ridge of Nehi Mountain and had been there since before the Civil War. There were tombstones, in fact, that had birthdates in the 1700s, and even before that it was a place where the Indians buried their dead, because people were all the time finding pieces of pottery and arrowheads and bones and things.

There were a lot of really tall cedar trees and calycanthus bushes, making the air pungent with their rusty, spicy-smelling flowers, and it seemed like there was always a breeze blowing across the Ridge. You could stand and see across to where the Arkansas River cut through the valley and the lake ballooned off it. It was a peaceful place, like cemeteries are supposed to be.

We went through the gates right behind the hearse, but the line of cars following us jammed in, filling up the parking lot and then both sides of the road until nobody could pass. I wondered how in the world we would ever get out of there.

A little ways from the road, the grave had been dug and green artificial grass laid out over the mound of fresh dirt so people wouldn't be so aware that the loved one was going into a hole in the ground. A few rows of chairs were set up beside the grave, for the family, and Frannie and little Kevin sat down in front.

Brother Dane waited until most of the people got there, then stood by the grave and read some verses from the Bible and led us in prayer. Then he took a handful of dirt, threw it onto the casket, and said, "Ashes to ashes; dust to dust." Frannie threw in a handful, along with a few flowers, and Kevin picked up two handfuls and flung them in. He squatted down to get more, but his grandmother pulled him back. Then he started to cry, and it seemed like nothing up to that moment was as heart-wrenching as that redheaded boy standing by his mother's grave with dirty little hands and howling at the top of his lungs. They were really burying her, then, Patty-nails and all. It was final.

—

When the ceremony was over, Lucille and I sat fanning ourselves in the limo with our shoes off and the doors open, waiting for Jim Floyd and Mr. Wilmerding to finish up so the grave diggers could fill in the grave. G. Dub, Bean, and Tripp said they were going off to take a walk somewhere while they waited for the crowd to thin out and the road to open up. I had lost Baby in the shuffle, but now saw her over by the edge of the graveyard, standing next to a new-looking cream-colored Cadillac, talking to the very man who had put the rose in Carlene's hands at the funeral. He was wearing sunglasses, and they seemed to know each other real well.

"Look who Baby's talking to, Lucille."

She turned and squinted in the late-afternoon sun. "My Lord and stars! It's that guy! What is he doing with Baby? Let's go and get introduced."

We walked as nonchalantly as we could over the graves to where they were standing by the car.

"Oh! Hi, Baby. We didn't see you standing here," Lucille said, wide-eyed and innocent, like we had just been strolling by and happened to bump into them. Baby rolled her eyes at me, but the man grinned when he saw Lucille. Most men do.

"Introduce me to your friends, Baby," he said. She looked as if she really would rather not.

"Y'all, this is Franco O'Reilly. He knew Carlene from the restaurant. Franco, these are my friends Cherry Marshall and Lucille Hawkins. *Mrs.* Hawkins."

Lucille took a few steps closer, which was harder than it sounds, because she was wearing her Barbie shoes—open-backed spike heels that she ordered from Frederick's of Hollywood—and the ground was soft. She held out her hand. Franco took it and held it just a moment too long.

"Hello, Franco. It's so nice to meet you. That's an interesting name. Are you part Italian?"

He laughed. "Totally Irish. Actually, my name is Frank. When I met Baby, she understood my name as Franco Reilly. I will be Franco forever to Baby, Mrs. Hawkins."

"Call me Lucille. Can we call you Franco, too? It's cute."

"You can call me anything you want to, Lucille."

I wasn't crazy about the way this was going.

"I wish the circumstances were different for our meeting, Mr. O'Reilly," I said, with a stone face. "Did you know Carlene well?"

He stopped smiling then, and remembered where he was.

"Not too well. Of course, I saw her from time to time at the Water Witch. It's one of my favorite stops on my trips. I'm in sales. Restaurant supplies. Vending machines. Pinball machines and jukeboxes."

"Wait a minute," Baby said. "I thought you and Carlene dated. That's definitely what she told me, after I left the job. That she was dating you."

He looked really uncomfortable.

"Well, yes, you might call it dating, but it was nothing serious. She was a sweet kid, but it was more of a friendship than anything. I felt bad for her, being a single mother and all. It seemed like she never got a break."

"She sure didn't get one this time, did she?" Baby said.

"No, she didn't." He looked down at the ground, as if he couldn't meet her eyes.

We just stood there for a minute. The silence was really awkward.

"Well, it looks like the crowd is beginning to thin out," he finally said, jingling his car keys. "I had better be on the road. It was really nice meeting all of you." He looked at Lucille while he said it.

Lucille looked like she would have liked to stay, but I pinched her on the arm and we turned and left. When we had gotten a few hundred feet away, I sneaked a look back. He was still standing there, watching us as we walked back to the cars. He was smiling again.

18. Baby

 "Is Bean with you, Baby?" Manang called to her from the kitchen as she came in the front door after the funeral.

"No, Manang. He's gone."

"Come in and help me with the girls, please. It will be time for dinner soon."

Connie and Sunnie were in the backyard playing in the dirt. The late-afternoon sun rays filtered through the trees, washing the grass and the children in golden light. Baby stopped at the back door and watched them for a minute, awestruck by the beauty of the little girls, their black heads close together as they made mud pies. They seemed poignantly alive after her long afternoon with death.

They squealed and ran to her, and she gathered them up, carrying one on each hip, then took them inside and gave them their bath. After dinner, while Baby and Pilar did the dishes, Manang put the little ones to bed and sang to them, in her thin, slightly off-key voice; it was an old Filipino song she used to sing to all the children, in Tagalog. Baby had long ago forgotten what the words meant, but the song filled her heart with the sad memory of something beautiful that was lost. She would have had such a different life if they had never come to America—worse in some ways, but maybe better in others.

When Pilar finished in the kitchen, she went to her room, but Baby sat outside on the steps, smoked a cigarette, and listened to Manang sing. The song and the sweet starry night brought back half-buried memories.

Even though she had been only four when they left, pictures of the Philippines were clear—frozen in her mind, as an ancient fern in the ice of a glacier.

The house they once lived in was like a tree house, sitting up on stilts in the jungle. On one side, a long set of wooden steps led up to a porch, and latticework crisscrossed around the bottom. The sides were open to the breeze, covered only with woven mats that rolled down when it rained, and nobody had much privacy. Nobody really cared about having any. The people could sit on their porches and look at the treetops, or lean out and pick a guava or a sweet rambutan for breakfast. Baby remembered that when the floors were swept, the dirt just fell through the cracks in the boards. They would have laughed at the idea of a dustpan. Or a bathroom. Or a washing machine. Or at most of the things that everyone here took for granted and thought they couldn't live without.

The one memory that was not clear to Baby was her mother. She remembered odd things, but they were mixed up, as if they were not memories but dreams, woven with bits of old stories Manang used to tell her. Manang was the Tagalog word for "Auntie," and in truth, Manang was Baby's aunt, Auwling, the older sister of Maeling, her mother—her Nanang—who had died when Baby was three.

Auwling never tried to hide this from Baby and, as she got older, would tell her stories about her mother, making them sound like almost like fairy tales, although unlike happily-ever-after, sometimes these stories ended badly.

Auwling loved her younger sister very much. Maeling had been the most beautiful girl in the village, more beautiful even than her imposing older sister. She had an airy disposition, and her voice was clear and lovely. Maeling would sing as she washed the clothes in the stream that bubbled over rocks near their house and needed nothing much to make her laugh, while Auwling was serious and quiet and thought singing was noisy and unnecessary.

Dionisio Moreno was so in love with Maeling that he could hardly wait until her sixteenth birthday to ask for permission to marry her, which her mother was eager to give, as her own husband had died two years before and it was hard to rear the girls alone. Dionisio was a good catch—older and settled, and he owned his own fish store. Maeling was also in love with him, which was not necessary for the match but a bonus.

Since it would have been improper for them to be alone before they were married, or even to hold hands, the courtship was conducted from a distance. Somehow, that made it more exciting. Every look was filled with meaning, every chance brush against an arm a thrill. In the evenings, Dionisio would sit under Maeling's window, play his guitar, and serenade her with a *harana*. Sometimes she would join him in the song, and all the neighbors would stop whatever they were doing and listen to their beautiful harmonies. Except for Auwling, who would find some excuse to leave the house. She told everyone she thought it was too sentimental and ridiculous.

But there was another reason. She herself was in love with Dionisio, but she knew he couldn't see her for the radiance of Maeling.

Finally, on Maeling's sixteenth birthday, they were married. In nine months, a baby girl was born. They named her Maria Babilonia. She was a happy baby, and the household revolved around her every move. Auwling, despite herself, was fond of the baby, holding her for hours and even humming to her when she thought no one was listening.

Then the Japanese came. The people knew, of course, about the war, but it was far away, always happening elsewhere, in places like Manila or Bataan. And the Americans, while beaten at first, were now winning. Soon there would be no threat at all from the Japanese. Everyone knew this except the Japanese, who set up a camp not far from the village.

With the coming of the Japanese, everything changed. Women were afraid to go to the stream and wash clothes, or to go out by themselves at all, because pretty girls like Maeling and Auwling were often kidnapped and placed in Japanese "comfort camps," to service the low needs of the Japanese army. Such girls were considered dead by their families. Many of them died of disease, but even if they managed to escape, they could not become clean again and rejoin their families after suffering the debasing attentions of the Japanese soldiers. No decent man would marry such a girl. The best they could hope for was to endure the torture and hope they were allowed at least to remain in the Philippines rather than be sent to Japan to become a Japayuki, or a prostitute.

After Maeling and Auwling's mother first caught sight of the soldiers, she went to the stream and scooped up a bowl of mud, brought it into the house, and smeared it over the faces of her beautiful daughters.

"When you go out, you must wear this mud at all times, daughters. Learn to walk slowly and bend your shoulders, as an old woman does. The Japanese will think you are old and ugly and will leave you alone. And whatever you do, you must never, never, go away from the house by yourself."

When the Japanese soldiers filed by along the jungle trails, the family would lower the mats down the sides of the house and give the baby pieces of guayabana or papaya to suck to keep her quiet. No one wanted to take a chance that some soldier would come and investigate, to see to whom the baby belonged.

Then at other times, when no soldiers had been near for days, it was almost possible to believe life was normal. This was the most dangerous time, their mother would warn. "You must not let down your guard, even for a moment," she told the girls.

But Maeling was like a bright bird that hated its cage. Leaving her baby with Auwling one day, she went to get fresh water from the stream. The day was warm and her face, covered in mud, had begun to itch. She looked carefully among the thick trees of the jungle and, seeing no one, scooped handfuls of water over her face. The water felt so good! It had been such a long time since her face had felt sunlight. Seeing that she was alone, she became bolder and lowered her blouse and splashed her shoulders, under her arms, and her breasts. Then she dipped her head, washing her hair as well. And when she brought her head up from the water, long hair dripping, she looked into the face of a smiling Japanese soldier.

After Maeling was stolen away, Dionisio, in his grief, wanted to kill all the soldiers and die himself, but his friends restrained him. Then, despite the danger to himself, he joined the American army as a scout. He went out each night in stealth to do what damage he could, all the while searching for his missing wife. He learned to move through the jungle without making a sound and to decapitate soldiers with one swift blow of a machete, quickly, quietly. Before anyone knew he had been there, like a ghost, he was gone.

Night after night, Dionisio went out with the Americans, leaving the women alone. For them, the time went slowly while they waited for his return, and Grandmother—Lula—told stories to make the hours pass more quickly. As Lula spoke, Auwling would sit and pick pieces of coconut out of their shells or sew while Maria Babilonia sat on Grandmother's lap.

"Out in the depths of the jungle, far into the green dark trees where no men have dared to go, live the Aswang," Lula would begin. Babilonia listened, her chocolate-colored eyes wide.

"In the heat of the day, the Aswang sleep in boxes hidden underneath the cool ground, but at night they awaken to eat and the food they eat is the blood of human beings."

"Lula, must you tell those stories? Look at Babilonia. She is paralyzed with fear," Auwling said.

"She should know about the Aswang. So she can avoid them." Grandmother, however, drew Babilonia closer under her arm as she continued:

"In a village not too far from here, not so many years ago, lived a man who was large and handsome. He had square white teeth and a pleasing laugh and was a fisherman who, all day long, hauled in heavy nets of fish, so his back was strong and broad.

"He worked so long and hard that he had no time to take care of a wife and family, but there were times when he needed the companionship of women, and then he would go to the beer house to relax from his labors. One night while he was drinking, a female Aswang, flying over the house, heard his laugh, which was loud and healthy. It pleased something inside her. Dropping down from the sky as quietly as a bat, she crept up to the window and saw him dancing with an ugly woman. She was jealous and desired him for herself."

Lula stopped, as if listening. Only the sounds of the jungle could be heard, and after a moment, she continued:

"Later that night, just after the man had gone home to bed feeling a little light-headed from the beer and tired from dancing with the ugly woman, when he was in that moment between twilight and sleep, he heard a haunting, eerie song come floating through his window. It was beautiful and sad, and spoke of the pleasure of love, and the pain. The man raised himself up on one elbow and listened. In his drowsy state, he could not be sure if someone was really singing or if it was only part of his dream.

"But he heard it again. The song was coming from across the clearing. He got out of bed and crossed the floor to the open window. There, in the silver light on the edge of the jungle, he saw the Aswang, beautiful beyond belief. She was tall and slender, her hands long and graceful. Her jet-black hair floated in the breeze, alive to the slightest whisper of air. Her gown glowed as if it were spun from cobwebs of moonlight, shimmering with each willowy movement of her body. She sang with such a sweet, clear voice that he was hypnotized. Leaving his house, he walked across the clearing and into the jungle toward the woman, who held her arms out to him, beckoning, as she retreated into the darkness.

"Farther from the village she led the man until they were lost in a leafy bower. Then she turned to him, and he fell into her arms and embraced her. She stroked his hair tenderly, kissed his ruddy cheek, then sank her teeth into his neck, drinking all of his blood.

"As the man fell to the ground, the Aswang rose above the tops of the banana leaves and floated back to her village, rosy and happy—full of the man's good blood.

"The fisherman's friends, missing him the next morning, searched all day for him, and when they found his pale, empty body, they took it out to sea on his boat. They tossed it overboard, burying it beneath the waves, to be forever with the children of the fishes who had given themselves to be his living."

As Lula told the story, Babilonia was afraid to move. She looked down at the floor and saw something glitter between the cracks. It could have been an eye. She looked again and saw it blink. Most definitely it was an eye, and it was looking right at her. She screamed and pointed at the floor. "Aswang!"

"Lula, see what you have done! You've frightened her!" Auwling crossed the room and picked Babilonia up in her arms.

"Under the floor!" the child sobbed.

"There is nothing under the floor, Babilonia," Lula said, trying to hush the child.

"I told you, Lula! You and your Aswang! I'll go and look, Babilonia. Don't cry. It was just a story." Auwling gave the girl back to her mother and, taking a lantern, went outside.

The night was dark, without even the twinkle of stars. Auwling held the lantern low and looked closely at the ground for snakes. When she found none, she kneeled and peered between the crisscrossed slats underneath the house. The light flickered into the darkness and shone upon a crouched figure. It was a woman wrapped in a dirty cloth tied with a sash. Her hair was matted, her face bloated and bruised.

"Auwling!" the woman whispered. "It is me—your sister, Maeling! The Japanese have thrown me out to die. Don't come near me! I am filled with disease. You must not tell Dionisio I am here. I only wanted to see my little Babilonia again before I die."

"Maeling, come inside. Lula will help you." Auwling started to crawl toward her sister.

"No! Stay back! I will not have my child see me like this, or my husband. Let him remember my beauty. It is better they think I am dead than to be shamed by what I have become. You must not tell them I was here."

"Please, Maeling!" Auwling was shocked and agitated that her sister did not want to be helped. "I cannot leave you out here like this—"

"If you love me, you will do as I ask. Go now, Auwling. Let me rest for a while and I will go. Do not dishonor me. Take care of Babilonia and Dionisio. It is what I want. It is too late for me. I am dead. Your sister is dead. Say it, Auwling. Say, 'My sister is dead.' "

Auwling looked at her for a moment, torn between love and duty. Then she stood upright, tears streaming down her cheeks. She spoke to the darkness:

"My sister is dead. My sister is dead, and her husband will be my husband; her child, my child. I will take care of them. The Japanese took my sister away and she is dead." And she turned and climbed the stairs back into the house.

———

In her bed, Babilonia kissed Auwling, her Manang, good night. "It was nothing, my baby," Auwling crooned. "Only a dog. No Aswang will hurt you as long as I am here."

Manang sat on the edge of the bed and held her hand until Babilonia's eyes closed, then she tiptoed away.

But in that moment between twilight and sleep, a voice floated up into Babilonia's window. It sounded familiar, clear and sweet. It sang a lullaby that Babilonia remembered, and made her feel safe; she at last gave up and drifted off into sleep.

———

In the small hours of the morning, they were awakened by a roar that seemed to come from the bowels of the earth. It was Dionisio, who had found his beloved wife a distance into the jungle, hanging from the branches of a tree, her sash tied around her neck. Distraught, he brought her into the house and laid her on the bed as Auwling and Lula rose in alarm.

Babilonia, forgotten for the moment, heard the commotion and crept to watch from behind the bedroom door. It must be the Aswang, Babilonia thought, the one she saw in the crack of the floor. Maybe the Aswang had been bitten by a snake. Tatang had warned her about snakes. They were surely more deadly than the Aswang. Babilonia didn't know why everyone was so sad. The Aswang was dead. But she was a little sad, too. Maybe this was a good Aswang.

Dionisio was inconsolable in his grief, but Manang held him tightly and said over and over, "I will take care of you. I will take care of Babilonia. Let me take care of you."

—

Soon after the birth of her new half-brother Rosario, the baby, Tatang, Manang, and Babilonia went to America with the American army, leaving Lula behind. Babilonia remembered walking up a gangplank onto a big boat with whistles and gray colors and strange people, who were jabbering. Nothing they said made sense. Everyone was big. They smelled bad and wore too many clothes. Their hair was not straight and black and shiny. Each one had a different kind: light-colored and fuzzy, or red and wavy, or some shade of brown. Some of the men didn't have any hair at all on the tops of their heads. She stared at them, and they looked down at her and smiled, as if she were some kind of pretty puppy. Women gave her candies and patted her head.

She remembered the boat coming into the harbor in America. Tatang put her up on his shoulders, and in silence they watched the shore coming closer until they could see docks full of people. She remembered a lot of long lines, and being picked up and set down on a pile of suitcases while Manang and Tatang signed things.

She was carried onto a bus and, later, a train. They rode all through the night and stopped at many towns. Tatang would get off in the small towns and buy strange, bad-tasting food, things like pink bologna sliced from a big round tube and tiny sausages from a can; yellow cheese and white, salty crackers.

—

They were sent by the army to a base called Fort Smith, in Arkansas. Their apartment had a small concrete balcony with a fence of iron bars and it faced a big field. Babilonia would stand there and watch the soldiers march up and down the parade ground. Sometimes, when they were taking a break, they would look at her and wave. Then Manang would make her come inside, and close the door. Manang was afraid of all soldiers and afraid to go outside. So there they stayed, all of them together in one room every day while Tatang went to work. Manang didn't laugh or sing or play games with them. She sewed or ironed or read a book. She cooked their meals. Babilonia played with Rosario, as quietly as she could, and Manang didn't seem to mind.

Then Tatang left the army, but they decided to stay in Arkansas. It was beautiful, and cheap to live. Tatang had found a house to buy, near a lake, where he could fish and live much as he had done in the Philippines. They packed up their car and drove over mountains and through green fields, past little towns with redbrick storefronts and men in blue overalls sitting on benches. Finally they came to a place in the woods, on the banks of a lake. The forest was not at all like the jungle at home. The trees were different, with smaller leaves. Some didn't have leaves at all, but fine green needles that fell to the ground and made a sweet, spicy-smelling carpet. It wasn't like home, but it was peaceful and pretty. Instead of a room, there was a whole house for them, and a little store next to a boat dock.

Tatang bought Babilonia and Rosario toy trucks, red and yellow. They made mountains and roads for their trucks in the black dirt of the yard. They carried water from the lake in a tin can to make small lakes for their mountains.

One day, as Babilonia was digging in the dirt, a car pulled in and a man went inside to buy fish. Then the back door of the car opened and an angel appeared. Got out of the car and walked right over to her. Babilonia had never seen anything like it. It was a girl angel, not a whole lot bigger than she was, but pure shining white. Her hair, as white as rice, was pulled tightly into two long pigtails, with fuzzy wisps sticking out around the edges. She had skin so fine that Babilonia could see blue veins underneath. As Babilonia stared, the angel asked her a question. Babilonia still had trouble understanding English. She shook her head. The angel pointed to herself and said, "Cherry," then pointed to Babilonia. Babilonia said her name: "Babilonia."

The angel thought for a moment, then tried to say the name. "Baloney?"

Babilonia shook her head again. "Babilonia."

"That's too hard of a name to say. Can I call you Baby for short?"

Babilonia understood. She thought for a minute. She didn't really want to be called Baloney, even by an angel. She decided she liked it.

"Okay. I am Baby."

———

Manang came out onto the porch and looked a little startled when Baby stood up and gave her a hug. Manang had been a good mother to her. It had been a long time since Baby had thought about the Philippines, but because of Manang they were always there, part of her, so real that she could almost fold them up and put them into a box.

"Are you all right, Baby? Is anything the matter?"

"No, Manang. I just realized how glad I am that you are my mother."

Manang looked pleased and a little flustered. She patted Baby on the back.

"You are much like your real mother. I am happy she gave you to me. Now it is time for me to go to bed and for you to go to work. Good night, Babilonia."

Baby went into her room to change for work just as the phone rang. It was Bean, checking to see if she was all right. Since Carlene's murder, he had gotten to calling her every hour or two that they weren't together, just to check on her, like he was afraid the ground was going to open and swallow her or she that was going to put rat poison on her cereal by mistake and die or something. He was driving her nuts. It had been a trying day, with the funeral and all, and Bean had obviously been stoned when he came to pick her up. She didn't like it, but she couldn't think of anything to do about it.

She had loved Bean a lot once, when they were in high school, when they first discovered making love together. He had been tender then. He used to bring his guitar over and sing. He wrote a song, called "Baby's Eyes," that was the most beautiful love poem she had ever heard, and every time he sang it at a dance, he brought her up to the stage and sang it directly to her while the other girls watched with envy. She felt like the luckiest girl in the world.

That was then. Now it was sometimes hard to remember why she had cared for him so much. She knew, from what he told her, that he had been thorough a lot in Vietnam, and she couldn't just drop him when he needed her the most. She would have to be patient with him until he could get over the traumas he had suffered. Maybe the love would return. Maybe he would cut down on the drugs if she loved him enough.

———

"Bean, I'm fine," she said, taking a clean pair of shorts out of her drawer. "I'm just getting ready to go to work. . . . Yes, I promise I'll drive careful, and I'll lock the doors and look in the backseat before I get in . . ."

Baby held the phone between her shoulder and ear while she hopped on one foot to put on her shorts.

Bean went on for the umpteenth time about how she could protect herself if anybody tried to attack her, by sticking her fingers in their eyes and stomping on their instep, and Baby said, "Uh-huh, uh-huh, uh-huh." Truth to tell, Baby was a little nervous herself since the murder, but you can't expect a deranged killer to be hiding under every single bush. It was nearly to the point that she was trying to figure out ways to hide from Bean, just to get a little time to herself.

There were other weird things about Bean, too, since he had gotten home in March. In one batch of pictures he sent, he had included one of his hootch maid, a pretty girl named Nguyen, wearing a purple pajama-looking outfit and one of those cone-shaped straw hats. He said she was the one who washed his clothes and cleaned his hootch, and when Baby asked him if that was all she did for him, he got mad and swore he had never touched a woman over there. That made Baby feel all the more guilty for having seen Jackie while he was gone. Still, once, at an inopportune moment, Bean had called her Nguyen. It made Baby suspicious, but she pretended that she hadn't heard it. It wouldn't do for her to get all self-righteous. Especially since Bean was getting more suspicious about her.

———

"Who was that man you were talking to at the graveyard, Baby?" Bean asked while Baby tried to button her shorts with one hand.

"His name is Franco O'Reilly. He used to go out with Carlene."

"Are you sure he didn't go out with you, too? The two of you looked awful chummy out there when you didn't think I was watching."

"Bean, I swear on a stack of Bibles I never had anything to do with him other than talk to him a time or two. Not every man in the world is after me, you know." She got the phone tangled in her T-shirt and had to pull it out through the armhole.

"What about Jackie Lim?"

"He was after every woman that had a pulse. I've told you and told you there was nothing between us, Bean."

"Then why do I get the feeling you're lying?"

"Believe what you want to, then," she snapped. "I can't help what you believe."

She could kick herself for mentioning Jackie too often in her letters while Bean was in Vietnam. Somehow he had read between the lines, and now he just wouldn't let it alone; he picked at it like a scab every chance he got.

"Look, Bean honey, I have to get to the plant. You know I love you, and you're the only man for me, so let's don't talk any more about this, okay? Please, Bean?"

He hung up on her. Now she would have to sweet-talk him into a good mood again. Sometimes she wished she had never heard of Jackie Lim or the Water Witch. And sometimes she wished she had never heard of Bean.

19. *Cherry*

 I hated to go to work the night right after the graveyard and all, but there didn't seem any way out of it. At least I saw Tripp, and at the break he asked me to go to the movies with him Saturday night. I felt a little funny about going out so soon after the funeral, and I know it sounds cold, but Carlene was as dead as she would ever be. Besides, a great new movie called *Easy Rider* was playing down at the Rialto Theater. It had to be good, because Brother Wilkins had already preached three sermons about it. He said that the very Devil himself was the author of that movie, and it glorified the satanic workings of man that were taking us all one step closer to eternal damnation in these, the last days before Jesus came back on the clouds of glory and destroyed the world with fire and brimstone. I wondered, exactly, how Brother Wilkins knew so much about this movie, but I guessed he must have read a review or something.

———

Saturday afternoon, Mama was out in the backyard under the pecan trees shelling peas, and I picked up a pan from the kitchen and went out to help her. I set my lawn chair close to her so I could reach the bushel basket of peas. She leaned over and sniffed at me.

"I believe you don't smell quite as strong as you used to, honey. Are you still in the onion room, or did you get moved somewhere else?"

"No, we're still there. You're probably just getting used to it."

"Well, it will only be for a couple more weeks. I think you should quit a few days early and give yourself time to get back to normal before school starts. I'll let you soak in a hot tub with my Youth Dew bath oil after you quit. There's not much point before."

Youth Dew was Mama's signature fragrance, and was sinfully expensive. Every birthday and Christmas, either Daddy or I had to give her a big bottle of it. If she was offering it to me, I must really need it. Frankly, I had gotten so used to the smell that it didn't bother me. In fact, I could cut up a whole pot full of onions at home and never shed one tear. Isn't there always a silver lining in every cloud? But I appreciated her offer, and intended to take her up on it.

I took a double handful of peas out of the bushel, filled my pan, and started shelling.

"Mama, Tripp wants to take me to see *Easy Rider* tonight. Do you think I should go?"

Mama dumped her shelled peas into a big bowl and refilled her pan. "That's the one Brother Wilkins is so hot under the collar about, isn't it?"

"Yes, ma'am, it is."

"To hear him tell it, watching that movie will turn you into a dope fiend and Lord knows what all else. Isn't that what he said?"

"Yes, ma'am, he did say that."

"Well, I think we both should go and see what it is that is going to ruin all the kids in this town, don't you? So we'll be prepared to fight against it if we need to."

"We both? Are you saying that you want to go, too?"

"Why not? If you can see it, why can't I? Do you think I'm such an old fogey that I would be shocked?"

This was really weird. I couldn't imagine taking my mother on a date with Tripp Barlow. Who would sit in the front seat? Would we all squeeze together, or would she have to sit alone in the back? Would I have to sit in the back?

"Mama, I just don't know. Daddy won't like it."

She ripped open a pod so hard that the peas sailed across the yard. She seemed a little tense.

"I don't suspect he would. There's a lot he doesn't like. And sometimes, Cheryl Ann, I just feel like I'm turning into an old woman before I ever had a chance to be a girl."

I looked at her as if she were a little nuts. This was a side of my mother that I had never seen before. She caught my look and turned to face me.

"Think about it. Your daddy and I got married when I was seventeen. We just couldn't wait until I even graduated. I went from being under my daddy's roof to being under my husband's. Within a year, I had you. I was a mother before I even got to go to the prom. And now then, there's Lucille doing exactly what both her mother and I did—marrying the first boy that showed her what a thrill is, and having a baby. Rubynell and I tried to stop her, but you can't tell kids anything. They know it all already."

I was a little stunned. Mothers were supposed to be . . . motherly. They were not supposed to think about missed proms.

"I never knew you felt this way, Mama. I thought you and Daddy had a great marriage."

She bit her lip. "I love your daddy more than anything in this world— except you. I want you to know I have never been sorry for one minute I had you. It's just that sometimes . . . oh, I don't know . . . sometimes I just can't take his everlasting *goodness*."

To my horror, she started to cry. I set my pan down and put my arms around her, comforting her like I was the mother and she was the kid. I patted her on the back.

"It's okay. I know. I know."

That set her off. Her shoulders shook with sobs, and she hung on to me like a three-year-old. Then she started to laugh.

"Look at me! Sitting out here in the yard bawling my eyes out! I'm really something. I don't know what's the matter with me." She wiped at her eyes with the back of her hand.

I felt kind of sorry for her. She never got to go to a movie, except for *Jailhouse Rock,* which we snuck out to see when I was nine, because Daddy would no more be seen in a movie house than he would a beer joint. The only book he ever read was the Bible, and she had to hide her Harlequin Romance novels under the mattress so he wouldn't see them and burn them up, like he had a time or two, which made her as mad as an old wet hen.

She took a wadded-up tissue out of her pocket and blew her nose.

"I'm sorry. I guess I've just been feeling old lately. It won't be long until I'm forty. I have a whole new patch of gray hair, and my chin is starting to sag like my mother's did."

I stood up and looked at her hair, but I couldn't see any gray ones.

"Where, Mama?"

"Right up there on the top. Don't you see it?"

"It just looks kind of light blond to me. I don't think you should worry about it yet. And I don't see what you're talking about with your neck."

"You don't think it's a little saggy?" She stretched her chin up for me to see.

"It looks okay to me, Mama. Don't worry about it. You still look young." She did look young. Everybody always thought we were sisters, and guys were always talking about my mother and how pretty she was. "I wouldn't tell you that if I didn't think it." She gave me a hug.

"I love you to pieces, Cherry-Berry. You know I do. Maybe I feel old because you are all grown-up. I don't know what it is."

"Mama, you wouldn't want me to stay a little kid all my life, would you?"

"It's hard to believe you're twenty-one. When I was your age, you were three. I should have had more children, I guess, but they never came, no matter how hard we tried. I guess the Lord just intended me to have one."

She didn't say anything else for a long time, just sat back down to shell her peas. But I could tell that she was still upset, and it wasn't because she had never been able to have more children. She had made peace with that a long time ago.

"Mama? What is this all about? Really?" I felt like she wanted to say something that she wasn't saying. She put her hands in her lap and looked out across the yard, like she was trying to see something. I followed her eyes, but there was nothing there except our overweight neighbor, Dood Holloway, who was mowing his yard dressed in Bermuda shorts and flip-flops and no shirt. He had several rolls of fat going down his chest that looked like a row of breasts. He was an under-belly belter.

"Do you really like this long-haired boy you've been going out with? This one is different, isn't he?" She was still looking at the neighbor, not meeting my eyes. "You seem different when you talk about him. Like it might be turning into . . . love or something."

I didn't know what to say to that. I cleared my throat. "Well, it's kind of soon. I don't hardly know him. But—I don't know. To tell you the truth, I have asked myself that. He's not like anybody else I ever went out with."

"If you really love somebody, you don't have to ask yourself. You know. And it doesn't take long."

I thought about that for a minute. I was afraid to say anything. I didn't want to mess it up. She seemed to be having a really hard time with whatever it was she needed to say.

"Cherry . . . are you . . . you are still a . . . virgin . . . aren't you?"

I could feel myself start to get red. "Yes, ma'am."

In the technical sense, I was not lying. But I was a little uncomfortable with this conversation. We had never really talked much about sex before. Not many of my friends did with their mothers, either. I think all the mothers thought we would just learn about it by osmosis. And we had, it seemed. At least the important parts.

"I felt like you were, but I wasn't sure. Cheryl Ann, I want you to listen to me. Making love for the first time is something you can only do once in your life. It should be beautiful—with someone you love and trust. The trouble is, sometimes we get love confused with something else. Especially when we're young and the moon is full."

I didn't say a word. Was she able to read my mind or something?

"If you're a good girl, raised in the church, you get it hammered into your head over and over what a sin it is to have sex outside of marriage, so you get married to the first boy who sets your heart to pounding. You think it's love. You think you're all grown-up, but you're not. Even if you're twenty-one and can vote, you're still just children, playing at marriage. After a few years together, you realize it's not a game, and finally you do grow up. Sometimes you're lucky, and you grow together. You really do fall in love. And sometimes you wake up one morning wondering who that man in the bed with you is, and you realize that what you thought was love was just a raging case of hormones that has burned itself out, and there you are—you're tied to the wrong man for the rest of your life."

"Are you talking about you?" I was a little scared that she was trying to tell me she was unhappy with Daddy. Maybe she was trying to tell me they were going to get a divorce.

"No. I'm talking about you. Oh, Cherry, be a girl for a while. For as long as you can. Have some fun before you get married and saddle yourself with a baby like Lucille has done. Like her mother and I and three quarters of the women in this town did. You will be shocked to hear me say this, and your daddy would faint dead away, so don't you dare ever tell him what I said, but I would rather you . . . use a rubber and sleep with a boy and see for sure if he is the one you want to spend your life with than to marry him first and find out later that he's not the one. Do you hear what I'm saying?"

"Yes, ma'am, I think I do." But I couldn't believe what I was hearing.

"I'm not telling you to do it. You know I'd rather you didn't. But you're not a child anymore. If you're in a place where you can't help yourself . . . I don't think a God of love would send us to torment forever for doing something that He invented in the first place. And if He does, then I don't want to spend eternity with somebody like that anyhow. That's all I have to say."

She went back to her pan of peas, still not looking at me. Her face was red. All at once, I knew how hard it had been for her to say what she had. There were all kinds of questions I wanted to ask her. But I couldn't. We shelled on for a while, neither of us speaking.

"I think it would be okay if you want to go to the movies with us, Mama. I don't think Tripp would mind a bit."

"No, it's all right. Y'all go on. Your daddy and I will just spend a quiet evening at home. I don't need to go." The corner of her mouth went up. If I didn't know better, I'd think she was smiling. Somehow, I wasn't worried that she and Daddy were mismatched. I think they were among the lucky ones.

20. *Cherry*

 Easy Rider was incredible. Brother Wilkins was right, in a way, to be scared of it. The heroes were long-haired dope-smoking hippies on a motorcycle road trip across America, and the villains were ignorant rednecks, just like all the ones who drank coffee at the Town Café right here on Main Street.

One of the hippie characters, whose name was George, was played by a really adorable guy named Jack Nicholson, and in the scene when they were sitting around the campfire and he got stoned on grass and started talking about UFOs, it was just the best. I think every kid who saw that wanted to be on the road and free like that. Then later, when they stopped at that little café—which, I kid you not, was a dead ringer for the Town— and all the stupid old hicks were making nasty cracks about their long hair and all, I couldn't hardly stand it. I had seen it too many times in real life. Even G. Dub, who had lived in this town his whole life, got a lot of grief when he started to grow his hair long.

It was a big relief, in the movie, when they left the café—after realizing that they weren't going to get served—without a fight. I thought, They are smart to get out of there. They're going to be all right. Ha. In the very next scene, they were ambushed by those same rednecks from the café, and George was killed.

I just couldn't stand it. I started to cry. It was so real. I could see Tripp lying there, his head bashed in by a baseball bat, just like George.

"Don't cry, Cherry. It's just a movie." He put his arm around me.

"No it's not. It's not a movie. It's real life." He squeezed me close to him. I slunk down in the seat, making myself as small as possible, and snuzzled my shoulder into his armpit. I should have shut my eyes, too, because in the next scene, carried away by their grief, Billy and Wyatt went off to a cathouse in New Orleans, picked up two hookers, and got zonked-out on acid in a graveyard right in the middle of the daytime. The camera did all kinds of weird things—zooming in and out, getting fuzzy, distorting the picture—trying to make it look like a real acid trip, I guess, and the girls took off all their clothes and danced naked in the graveyard. You could even see their black pubic hair. That was enough, right there, to send Brother Wilkins into orbit.

"Is that what trips are really like, Tripp?" I whispered.

"Kind of. As close as you can get it on film. Not bad. Whoever made this movie knew his stuff."

By the time we got out of the theater, I was wrung-out. I couldn't believe that awful redneck with the disgusting wen on his neck just blew Dennis Hopper away like that for no good reason. I hoped the wen was cancer and his jaw would have to be amputated like poor old man Winston Coffey, who got cancer from dipping snuff and went through the last ten years of his life with no jaw, holding a handkerchief in front of his face to catch the spit and eating baby food that his daughter poured down his throat with a funnel. I know that it's a sin to wish bad things on people, and I know, of course, it was just an actor in the movie, not a real man. I mean, obviously, I didn't wish the actor to get cancer and lose his jaw, and maybe it was a fake wen anyhow, but . . . oh, I don't know what I wished. It was just all so real. Maybe I was still upset from my conversation with Mama, and the funeral and all.

We headed out to the lake after the movie. I was really glad that Mama hadn't gone with us. I don't think she's ready for something like that. Better to start her out on more Elvis movies, or Doris Day and Rock Hudson.

"Penny?" Tripp asked as we drove down the road that ran by Baby's house. Our windows were rolled down and the radio was playing "Let the Sunshine In." I loved that song and turned it up really loud, since we weren't near any railroad tracks.

"What do you mean?"

"A penny for your thoughts. You seem to be rolling some wheels in there."

"Sorry. I guess the movie got to me. It's just . . . I think that the world is full of an awful lot of hate-filled people. I mean, who were those guys hurting? Why should anybody care how long they wore their hair? It's not fair."

"Nobody ever said it had to be fair."

We had pulled up to the edge of the water, about a mile past Baby's house. It was, in fact, probably right about where they had found Carlene. Tripp killed the motor and flipped off the lights. It was real quiet. You could hear the frogs croaking and the crickets chirping.

"Why did you come out here, Tripp? It's creepy. I think it's where they found Carlene."

"Is it? Are you sure?"

"Pretty sure."

"Do you want to leave?"

What was wrong with me tonight? He was going to think I was on the verge of a nervous breakdown or something. "I don't know."

He scooted the seat back and put his arm around me. I didn't feel any easier.

"I'll tell you a story to get your mind off of the movie. Did you ever hear about the trapper and the hook?" he asked.

"What do you mean?"

"It's a true story. Once upon a time in the Ozark Mountains of Arkansas, there was a trapper who got his hand bitten clean off at the wrist by a wolf that was caught in one of his traps. He shot the wolf but was so weak from loss of blood that he couldn't get home, and he lay there in a fever, beside the body of the wolf, hallucinating for two days before they came looking and found him. He was in the hospital out of his head for months, but he lived, and they made him a hook to replace the hand he had lost.

"But the experience unhinged him, and he got crazier and crazier. He took to roaming the hills at night, and if he saw a car parked in the woods, he thought it was poachers after his traps and he would sneak up on the parkers and kill the boy and rape the girl.

"One night, a couple went parking up there, and the girl had the jitters. She just felt like something wasn't right. The guy didn't want to leave, but the feeling she had kept getting stronger and stronger, until finally, practically in a panic, she made him gun the car and take off. When they got back to her house, he got out to open the door for her, and there, hanging on the car door handle was . . . *a hook!*"

He grabbed me at that moment and I screamed.

"Tripp Barlow, I'm going to kill you!" He was laughing and dodging my fists, and then he opened the door trying to get away, and we fell out onto the ground. By then, I was laughing too.

"You really are a nut. And of course I've heard that old story before—or a version of it. My great-grandma heard that story."

"Then why did you scream?"

"Because I felt like it. Now, get me up off of this wet ground."

He pulled me up and the two of us leaned against the hood of the car, looking up at the sky and out over the dark lake.

He reached into his pocket, pulled out a cigarette, and flicked his Zippo. The smoke smelled sweet and a little like alfalfa, but different. He wouldn't . . . surely it wasn't . . . but it couldn't be anything else.

"Would you like to try a toke?" He held out the joint toward me. It was thin, and the tip glowed red in the dark. I began to tremble, but I tried not to let him see. I put my hands between my knees and pressed them together.

"Is that marijuana?"

"That's exactly what it is. Grass. Weed. Pot. Cannabis. A natural plant made by God. A gift from God to human beings. It's as natural as tobacco—grows right in the same ground. And it's probably a lot better for you."

He took another drag, inhaled it, and held it in his lungs for a long moment before he blew it out in a stream. Now I couldn't hide it. I was shaking visibly. My hands were cold. I looked out at the dark shadows on the lake. It had to be right out there where they found Carlene. I was getting a little sick to my stomach. The smell from the smoke seemed to be making me light-headed. Anyway, something was.

"Don't be scared. You know I wouldn't do anything to hurt you. I just want you to feel as good as I do right now. I promise, it is not like drugs. It's just a little wild weed. Straight from the earth."

I put my icy hands into my armpits to try and warm them up. This was crazy. I couldn't believe I was out here in the presence of an actual marijuana joint. I should run as fast as I could to Baby's house. I'd be safe there. But part of me didn't want to—the same part that hated the rednecks and loved the hippies in *Easy Rider.*

"I don't know how to smoke. I never tried it."

"Let me show you." He took a deep drag on the joint, then put his hand behind my head and pulled me into his arms. He leaned in to kiss me, and as my lips touched his, he breathed smoke into my mouth. I held my breath, then pulled away. Some of the smoke got into my mouth. I exhaled as hard as I could, so it wouldn't get in my lungs. He seemed not to notice that I hadn't actually inhaled any smoke.

"See, it's not so bad, is it?" He held out the joint toward me. "Here. You try it. You just put it between your lips and suck in. Breathe it all the way down into your lungs and then hold it for as long as you can."

There was a funny taste in my mouth. I looked up at the sky, half expecting to see a bolt of lightning coming down at my head, but it was clear. The stars hadn't moved. Tripp was still holding the glowing joint out to me. Oh well. In for a penny, in for a pound.

I took the joint from him with trembling fingers and put it to my lips. I sucked the hot smoke into my lungs. For about a second. Then my body rebelled and I started to cough. Deep, racking coughs. I couldn't catch my breath. Tripp tried to pat me on the back, but he was making it worse.

"No, get away from me!" I choked out the words and pushed him away. Leaning against the car bumper, I slowly got my wind back. I breathed several clear drafts of air, and then the strangest thing started to happen. My heart began to pound. I could feel the very blood pump through all its chambers into the veins and arteries, racing to the ends of my body, arms and legs, rounding the corners of my fingers and toes and climbing again to my heart. My whole body was beating like a giant heart. The air was so clear, the stars so bright. My heart beat faster and faster. It was going to run right out of my body. I must be dying.

"Tripp! Take me to the hospital! I think I'm having a heart attack!"

He started to laugh. He threw back his head and laughed and laughed.

"No, baby, you aren't having a heart attack."

"I'm not dying?"

"You're getting high. Like nobody I ever saw before." He put his arms around me and held me tight. He must have felt my heart pounding, because he started to rub my back in slow, firm circles. Nothing had ever felt as good as that back rub did. After a minute, I started to calm down. I did trust him. He wouldn't let anything bad happen to me.

Something new was starting. I was relaxing, my heart returning to normal. I was so relaxed that I felt dreamy. It seemed like I could float. My arms floated up and went around Tripp's neck. We kissed. A slow, warm, friendly kiss that tasted like burnt fields and moonlight.

21. Baby

The Summer of Love, they called it—1967. In Baby's mind it would forever be the summer of crabs, when she and Carlene got to be friends in the storeroom while they caught each other sneaking a scratch. They all, Jackie included, finally got rid of the lice, and Baby eventually got over the pain and shock of realizing that he slept with an appalling number of women. Not Carlene, however. She kept to her word and never went out with him again, but Baby couldn't quite give him up. She couldn't help herself. She would never let herself fall in love with him, of course, but Bean was so far away, and there was nobody more fun than Jackie.

They made love in the bushes near the edge of the lake, on top of picnic benches in the shadows of night, on the kitchen counter after the restaurant closed, and in a dozen other unlikely and thrilling places. She went home more than once with possum-grape stains on her clothes from rolling around in a patch of the berries that grew down by the edge of the water. Late one night, they even had a race to see who could take off all their clothes first as they ran from the restaurant across the parking lot to the car, and then rode around naked for an hour. Even though it was two in the morning, a few people nearly had wrecks when they saw them. It was always an adventure with Jackie. He made her feel like she was the most beautiful, the most desirable, the sexiest girl he had ever had. She knew it was a line, but she didn't care. Jackie was the best at giving a good line.

Even though she tried not to let it bother her—she did still have Bean, after all, who was writing to her from Vietnam, and that gave her guilty conscience a pang or two—it was hard for Baby not to be jealous of Jackie's other girls. She noticed every time he put his arm around one of them, and tried to read, by his smallest gesture, which one he might hook up with later each night. Baby suspected he saw a lot of Rita Ballard, because she was so sure of herself and acted like she was the boss when he wasn't around.

Jackie's brother, Park, was the chef. He had studied in the finest cooking school in Hong Kong and had come over when the Water Witch first opened to help train a chef, then liked it so much he decided to stay. His food was one reason people came from all over the state. The restaurant was always given the Best Chinese Cuisine Award from the *Arkansas Times,* and even though there were only five Chinese restaurants in the whole state, it was an honor.

Park was as quiet and serious as Jackie was loud. He seemed to like Baby, too, more than a little. Sometimes she would bring her drawings to show Park, who made much of them and told her she had the makings of a skilled artist.

As he cooked, hustling from chopping board to stove, dicing and slicing so fast that it made his fingers a blur, Baby could feel Park watching her. He sensed when Jackie had hurt or neglected her, and tried to make it up in little ways. He would give her one of his special desserts to take home, or massage her neck with a special nerve-relaxing technique when she had a hard day. Though he never said a word, Baby knew that he was aware she was sleeping with Jackie. It embarrassed her a little. She could tell from their arguments that Park and Jackie had disagreements over many things, and she sensed that she was one more.

By the following summer, 1968, she was promoted to working the dinner shift with Carlene, and her tips got bigger. The only nights that brought in more money were the special banquets, but Baby and Carlene were never included on the wait-staff list for those. It was always the older women and, oddly, several of the part-time girls. Rita Ballard was in charge of those evenings.

Rita was thirty, she said, but Baby and Carlene pegged her closer to forty. At one time she had played around with the idea of going to Las Vegas and becoming a showgirl, but she never made it out of Sweet Valley. Still, she dressed as close to her showgirl ideal as she could, with lots of gold Lurex and sequins, and her hair was ratted into a stiff cloud. Her makeup practically glowed in the dark. Jackie never would have allowed her to work in the daytime, when the lawyers' and doctors' wives came to lunch, but on banquet nights, Rita ruled the roost.

The banquets started as a thank-you party for Judge Greer, who had helped Jackie get the private club license and who had invested quite a lot of money as well, although that had to be kept secret. It was held late at night, after closing, just for men—no wives. It was such a hit that the banquets became a regular event—like the Lions Club, only with booze and friendly waitresses.

As much as a secret can be held in a small southern town, the banquets were secret, like the Masons. Rita gloried in her role as hostess, and lorded it over the younger girls.

"Doc McGuire gave me a hundred-dollar tip last night," she'd say as soon as she saw Baby or Carlene the day after a banquet, flashing the bill under their noses.

"Hmph." Carlene glanced at it. "What'd you have to do to get that?"

"Nothing. He just liked my looks," Rita would say, smirking.

She'd reel off the names of the local celebrities who'd been there the night before, too—people like Don Brandon, the weatherman from Channel 6 in Little Rock; Michael Wilson, the district attorney; and Roy Suggs, the state senator from Little Rock. According to Rita, they all were crazy for her, pushing money at her just for the pleasure of her company. Baby couldn't figure it out, but the money was real. Hundred-dollar bills didn't just pop up out of nowhere.

Carlene tried to ignore Rita, but Baby was curious.

"I wonder what Rita does. I mean, do you think there's music and dancing or what? Don't you want to go to one?"

"Look, Baby, don't get into it." Carlene said, trying to sidetrack her. "You don't want to go to those. It's just asking for headaches."

But Baby thought she did want to. She asked Jackie about them.

"Jackie, why don't you ever let me work the banquets? I can take orders and bring out the food, even if I can't serve drinks."

"No, Baby. Banquets are not the place for a young girl like you. You just learn how to be a good waitress." But he softened the words by kissing her on the ear.

She tried, but even the lunches were difficult for Baby, who was not—to say the least—a natural-born waitress. More than once, Park had to help her carry a heavy tray or rush out after her with a forgotten dish. People seemed to like her, though, and apparently they asked for her when she wasn't there.

During the lull after the rush, she often hung out with Park in the kitchen.

One day she hopped up on the counter and crossed her legs. Park sliced her a piece of Peking duck, smoking and hot.

"Sit on stool, Baby. Nobody like to eat food prepared from counter if people put their bottom on it."

Obediently, she slid down onto the tall stool. He handed her a second piece of duck and wiped the countertop where she had sat. Park was a maniac when it came to cleaning. He would have fainted and fallen over on it, Baby thought, if he knew what she and Jackie had done on that very counter.

"What do they do at those banquets, Park?"

"Nothing. Boring business dinners. It is too late for you, Baby. You have to be up early to go to class."

"It's summertime, Park. I don't have classes."

"You still should not be up so late. You young. Need sleep." He spooned creamy rice pudding into a bowl and ground fresh cinnamon onto it. "Here. Put some meat on those little bird bones."

Baby hated to be left out of anything, but she knew it was no use. Park was a Buddha when he wanted to be. She ate the pudding and vowed that sooner or later she would get to a banquet.

22. *Cherry*

 "Hold still, Cherry, and keep that towel over your eyes!" Lucille was trying to chemically straighten my hair. Over the years, we had done everything we could possibly do to get the kinks out. We rolled it on great big brush rollers, which worked not at all well—they just made it pouf out, like a hand grenade had gone off on my head. Then we tried rolling it on bigger orange juice cans, and finally we tried wrapping it all around my head and clipping it with duckbills, using my head for a giant roller. At its best, it still looked like corduroy. Then we read in *Glamour* about ironing hair, and we tried that.

It was a total disaster. Lucille evidently got the iron too hot, and the article didn't say that you needed to put the hair between layers of paper. Or at least if it did, we skipped over that part. And they didn't say anything in the article about not using hair spray.

What happened was, I kneeled on the floor in front of the ironing board and Lucille spread my hair out over it, brushing it as straight as she could. Then she sprayed it full of hair spray, to try and at least tame it down long enough to do the job, and licked her finger and sizzled it on the bottom of the iron, like you do when you iron clothes. My hair stuck to the bottom before she could make the first pass.

She jerked up the iron, burned her finger, and knocked over the iron-ing board. I fell, taking the iron with me. It was still stuck to my hair, burning it to a crisp. Finally, she got the thing unplugged, but she couldn't get my hair unstuck and had to cut a chunk out. The worst thing about it was the smell. Have you ever smelled burning hair? It's like burnt . . . I don't know . . . chicken feathers or something. Mama smelled it clear up-stairs, and ran in and flung open the window. I bet we used a gallon of Tame creme rinse to try and get the smell out of my hair.

When Mama saw what we were up to, she threw a fit. She loved my curly hair. That's easy for her. She didn't have to live with it.

I know it is stupid and shallow, but I wanted straight hair so bad. All the models in *Glamour* and *Vogue* had long, silky hair, parted in the middle, that hung in a smooth curtain down their backs. And Cher! She had the best hair in the world. It was like Baby's, long and black. She wore great big hoop earrings, and when she moved, her hair swung from side to side. I know it is not right to be that obsessed with your looks, but I wanted so much to be normal, not some pale, frizzy freak that always looms over everyone else like Frankenstein. I wanted to be glamorous.

I studied the fashion magazines every month, trying to improve my looks. I finally got the knack, after weeks of practice, of putting on false eyelashes, and I didn't even feel as bad as I used to about being so skinny, since most of the models were nearly as skinny as I was. Twiggy, in fact, might even be skinnier. Her legs were sure no better. She had those ropes-with-knots for knees, just like I did. But not a single one of the models had bushy white hair.

After the ironing disaster, in a last-ditch effort, I got one of the black girls in our class, Queen Esther McVay, to get me some of the straighten-ing cream they all used. It came in a big can with roses on the lid and smelled to high heaven of ammonia, or something else that eats out your sinuses. She thought it was funny, and I knew all the black girls would laugh about it, but I needed something heavy-duty.

Queen Esther had been a friend since we integrated in the eighth grade. Before that, the black kids in Sweet Valley had to be bused twenty miles every day to a school in Marlon County, so coming here was a whole lot better for them. She and I had a lot in common, since she was as tall and skinny as I was, and was also a good artist. Our art teacher, Miss Polly, was cool and let us do pretty much anything we wanted to. Once I sat for a whole afternoon while Queen Esther cornrowed my hair, and then I did hers. We braided clay beads into it that we had made and glazed, and Miss Polly let us photograph it and count it as an art project. It was a great profile photograph of us with our backs together; we looked like each other's positive and negative.

Now, Queen Esther was an art major at DuVall with Baby and me. She was the one who got all of us to start saying black instead of colored, like we had been taught when we were kids. She also gave me a book by a guy named Eldridge Cleaver called *Soul on Ice,* and I got a whole new insight into black people, I can tell you. The words just cracked off the page and hit me in the face while I read it. He said that a whole new movement had begun, dripping with blood, out of the ashes of Watts. He likened the police treatment of blacks in Watts to the treatment of the Viet Cong by the American army. Both were getting their heads blown off. They both were on the receiving end of what the government was dishing out.

It made a lot of sense to me, and if it made sense to me, it was likely to make sense to a lot of other people. That's what the protest movement was all about. Somewhere, the killing had to stop.

—

"I said cover your eyes! I don't want you going blind!" Lucille combed the white, thick cream through my hair with a fine-tooth comb. Every few minutes, she had to run to the door and take a few deep gulps of fresh air.

"Lucille? Where are you?" I couldn't believe she kept leaving me. "It says that you have to comb this stuff constantly for twenty minutes. You can't run off for minutes at a time like that! How long has it been?"

"Seventeen minutes. I'm right here. It only took me fifteen seconds. I have to breathe! Cut me some slack. It'll sour my milk."

She came back and kept on combing. I pulled the towel tighter around my face, and visualized myself with long straight hair. Tripp and I would be riding in Ramblin' Rose, all the windows down, the wind blowing my hair straight out like a long, silky flag. He would look at me with eyes of love.

"Cherry," he would say. "You are the most beautiful girl in the world. Your hair is magnificent. It looks like . . . a shimmering brook all iced over in winter."

—

"I think we better rinse this off. Some of your hair might be coming out."

"What!" I threw off the towel, ran to the bathtub, and stuck my head under the faucet. Great. I was going to be bald. It would serve me right for being so vain. Lucille turned on the water and it nearly scalded me.

"Put some cold in it!"

We frantically scrubbed the gookey stuff out. It took forever, and I thought I was going to turn blue and die before I got my head up out of the tub. The fumes were a killer. Then I stood up too fast, and all the blood rushed from my head. I was dizzy and lurched around the bathroom, staggered, and fell down onto the commode. Thank goodness the lid was shut.

Lucille rubbed my head with a towel, hard, and finally took it off and stood back to view the results. At least it hadn't all fallen out. But I was afraid to look in the mirror.

"Well?" I asked. "Is it straight?"

She puckered her lips and squinted. "Well . . ."

"Stop it!" I couldn't take it any longer. I looked in the mirror.

"It is! It's straight!" I started jumping up and down. "Let's dry it and see if it stays straight!"

I went and got the new blow-dryer I had bought. They had just come out with them, and it looked kind of like a gun, which you hand-held, and it blew the air directly on your hair—no hood or rollers or anything. If this thing worked, I would throw out my juice cans and all my rollers and get rid of the old hair dryer with the pink plastic bonnet that took forever and a day to dry.

The blow-dryer was incredible. It dried the whole bushel basketful of hair in only a few minutes. And it was straight! Not too much had fallen out, just a little, which would never be missed, and it hung down in a white curtain on both sides. It wasn't really shiny like Cher's, and it sort of came down in an A instead of hanging straight, but that was okay. Maybe later I could put a treatment of hot olive oil or mayonnaise on it and make it lie down and shine. For right now, I couldn't stop looking in the mirror.

"I'm going to have to cut the ends. Now that it's straight, the place where the iron took out a chunk looks really bad."

I didn't even care. Lucille got out the scissors and cut off a good four inches, but it still went down to the middle of my back, the same length as it had been when it was all kinked up.

"It looks pretty good, if I do say so myself," she said. "But to tell you the truth, I liked the old wild hair better."

"Great. Thanks, Lucille. I don't care. I've waited all my life for this moment, and I am going to enjoy it." You'd think she would at least lie and say she liked it better. I would have for her. "You're going to do great in beauty school, Luce. You might even get to like working on live people."

Mr. Wilmerding was sending Lucille to beauty school to get her license, and she had been in classes for a week already. Jim Floyd had left for morticians' school in Dallas. Although Mr. Wilmerding was paying for the schooling, he couldn't afford to pay Jim Floyd his salary as well, so he had gone a little early to take a job as an orderly in the emergency room at Baylor Hospital. Getting them coming and going, so to speak. So far, he liked it really well, although he missed Lucille and Tiffany LaDawn like crazy and wrote to them nearly every day.

"I got a letter from Jim Floyd this morning," Lucille said as she started scrubbing out the combs. "The night he wrote, they had three stabbings, a shooting, and a bad car wreck. And another one that I couldn't hardly believe. Apparently, a man caught his girlfriend in bed with this Mexican guy and pulled a gun on them. She jumped out a two-story window to get away from him and landed on a wrought-iron spiked fence. Impaled herself. The spike went up her you-know-what and out through her liver. She didn't even pass out or anything—just hung there on the fence screaming until the fire department came. There was no way they could get her off of it without killing her, so they had to cut the post off with a blowtorch. They carried her into the emergency room like that. Naked, with an iron fence post sticking out."

"Lucille! My Lord! Ooh! That makes me want to cross my legs! Did she live?"

"Oh, yeah. But they had a dickens of a time getting the spike out. It was in at such an angle that they couldn't lay her down, so they had to shove two tables close together and stretch her across the gap, and a doctor got underneath on the floor and worked it free."

"That is so gross! Lucille, you are making that up."

"No I'm not, either. You call up Jim Floyd and ask him. And the whole time they were working on her, the old boyfriend and the new boyfriend were yelling at each other and got into a fistfight, right there at the hospital. Before the law finally came and calmed them down, they wound up treating them both, too, one for a busted hand and the other for a broken nose. Jim Floyd said he would much rather work with people after they've passed on. It's a lot quieter."

I couldn't get over Jim Floyd and the jobs he picked. I'd rather sack groceries at Kroger's. It was less than a couple of weeks until Baby's and my senior year of college started, and this was my last week at the pickle plant. I couldn't wait.

After Carlene's funeral, I was a little hurt by Baby, I must say. It felt like we weren't the same old friends we had once been. I mean, there was this old guy with a Cadillac that Baby seemed to know real well, and I had no idea who he was or anything. I always felt like we told each other everything, but now it seems maybe we didn't. I guess I just get paranoid sometimes. I tell you, with everything that has happened in the last few weeks, it is enough to make anybody paranoid. Like that movie star Sharon Tate and her friends getting murdered out in California. She was pregnant, and it was a bloody slaughter. The whole thing just unnerved me, coming right after Carlene. If a whole house full of people can be butchered, who is safe anywhere?

Also, there was the writing on the walls. The killers had written in blood all over the walls of that mansion, which I think belonged to Doris Day's son, or he lived there before or something. It reminded me of the writing out at Fat Man's Squeeze. We hadn't gone back out there again. Frankly, I was afraid to, even in the daylight. I'm pretty sure it was paint, but now that I think about it, it might have been blood. It definitely was red. It has gotten to the point that I hate to pick up the paper in the morning. Between the war and the assassins and the maniacs, who is going to get slaughtered next?

The only good thing that has happened is that concert they had up north at Woodstock, a few days after the Sharon Tate murders. We saw it on TV, and it looked like so much fun, everyone rolling around in the mud and all. I wish we could have all gone up there for that. I would have loved to see all those great groups in person at once—not to mention Janis Joplin, who I loved, because she was not beautiful, with hair as uncontrollable as mine, but she had such a heart; she poured it into her songs like she cut her wrist and dripped into the microphone. Maybe we'll have one of those here in Arkansas, up at Eureka Springs. That would be a great place to have an outdoor concert.

—

While I primped in the mirror, Lucille finished cleaning up the mess and went into the living room and got the baby. Tiffany LaDawn had gained a lot of weight in the last few weeks and was just a little round butterball. She had more blond fuzz, too, although she still had to wear her pink headband, since there wasn't enough hair to hold in a ribbon.

I put down the hairbrush. "Let me hold her for a minute."

"No, you still stink of hair straightener."

"Not any more than you do." I tried to take her away from Lucille. "Look, Tiffany LaDawn. Aunt Cherry's got new hair!"

She started crying, of course, and Lucille plopped out her giant-sized breast and the baby glommed onto it. There's no way I can compete with that.

"I've been thinking—do you think it might be possible that the ones who killed Sharon Tate and them might have been the same ones that killed Carlene?" Lucille said as she settled into a chair with the baby hung for dear life on her left tit.

"I doubt it. That was all the way out in California."

"They would have had plenty of time to get out there from here. Nobody knows where they killed Carlene. Maybe they wrote on the walls here, too. What was it they said out there? 'Death to Pigs,' or something?"

"Yeah, that's what it was."

"I wonder why they said that. None of them they killed were policemen."

"They were crazy, Lucille. Obviously, they would write something crazy."

That got me thinking, though. It was true—nobody had ever said where Carlene was actually murdered. Wherever it was must have been completely covered in blood. Certainly there would have been enough to write with.

I wondered if Ricky Don knew about the writing up at Fat Man's Squeeze. Maybe I should tell him. I hadn't seen him since the funeral. I don't know why I never thought before to tell him about the writing. It just never occurred to me. I'm sure they were still working on the case, although it seems like after her funeral, most people forgot about her and went on about their business like it had never happened.

Except Mama. After the funeral, she called to see how Frannie was getting along, and had her and little Kevin over to the house for supper a few times. I always thought Frannie was unbalanced, but she isn't really; just a little eccentric, like how she dressed and all. She and Mama were the same age and had gone to high school together for nearly a year, until Frannie quit in the ninth grade. Up until then, she had attended a little one-room school up on the Ridge near Shady Vista, which only went to the eighth. It's not even there anymore. Actually, Bean Boggs would have probably gone up there if it was still going. He lived on the Ridge. Anyhow, Frannie thought she might finish high school in town, but she didn't really like the town kids. She told Mama they acted like they were better than her because she didn't have the right clothes, like sweater twinsets and pearls, so she quit and got married pretty young.

I hate to say it, and I'm not looking down on them or anything, but it still was true that the kids from up on the Ridge were different than most town kids. A lot of their mamas dipped snuff, and their daddies wore overalls without shirts in the summertime. And like everybody thinks about us here in Arkansas, some of them went barefooted in the hot months. Most of them had outhouses and drew their water from wells.

Mama told me that when Frannie was a girl, back in the thirties, most people on the Ridge didn't have cars or even electricity, but used coal-oil lamps and rode on horses or in wagons. There is not a single paved road up there yet today, just gravel. It changed a little after World War II, in the last twenty or so years, but even now you can find moonshiners up there working their stills. Ricky Don was always bringing in confiscated Mason jars full of it to the sheriff's office. One time he showed me some. It looked like clear water and didn't really smell all that bad, but he said the kick was worse than drinking rubbing alcohol. If you got ahold of a bad batch, it could kill you, or at the least blind you. Maybe eat up your liver and kidneys.

I don't think Frannie ever had too many girlfriends, and she wasn't all that close to her family since her mother died. She said her husband didn't like them and didn't encourage her to see them when they were together, and since he ran off and left, they didn't try to come and see her. I'm sure that since Carlene was gone, she was lonesome out in that ramshackle old trailer. She had a woodstove for heat, and she told us that last winter the snakes would nest under the trailer for the warmth, and one of them crawled in through a hole in the floor. She had to go out in the snow and get the hoe to kill it. I didn't know what she was doing for money, since she had to quit her job to take care of Kevin. She probably was hurting.

Usually when she left our house, she was loaded down with pies or jam or clothes or whatever stuff Mama gave her.

The phone rang. I ran to get it, my hair swinging from side to side behind me.

"Hello," I said, running my fingers casually down my straight locks. Tripp.

"Get Baby and come down to the Family Hand. I have a job for both of you. You can tell that pickle plant and Alfred Lynn Tucker to kiss your rosy behind."

"Are you kidding? What kind of job? What do you mean?"

"Something you'll like. I'll tell you when you get here."

"Wait a minute! What's the Family Hand? Where is it?"

"Down by the railroad tracks in the old train station. Baby knows. I'll be here. Come soon. 'Bye."

He hung up the phone, and left me hanging.

"What was all that?" Lucille asked, rocking the baby back and forth, trying to get a burp out of her.

"That was Tripp. I have to go." I picked up the phone and dialed Baby.

"Tripp, huh." Lucille got up and walked around the room, jiggling Tiffany LaDawn up and down. "Cherry, you shouldn't run every time a man snaps his fingers. He won't respect you. You have to play a little hard to get."

"Thanks for the advice, Lucille." I had to bite my tongue to keep from saying, "Yeah, really. Like you did." Baby answered on the third ring.

"Baby, you won't believe this, but we are quitting the onion room as of right now. We have a job at someplace called the Family Hand."

"You mean John Cool's new place?"

"John Cool McCool? He owns it?"

"Yeah. Why? Who offered the job?"

"Tripp. He just called."

"Tripp? Who died and made him God? He sure gets around, I'll say that for him."

"Well, if you're not interested . . ."

"Who said I wasn't interested? Pick me up. I'll be ready."

———

I was putting on my eyelashes when Mama came up behind me. I could see she wasn't too thrilled.

"Mama, I'm going out for a little while." I got the eyelashes on perfectly and then just stood looking in the mirror. I still couldn't believe it. I grabbed my purse and headed for the door.

"I don't know why you had to straighten your beautiful hair, Cheryl Ann. It looked so much better before. Don't you think so, David?" Daddy looked up from the paper. I don't think he had a clue what was going on. He stared at me like he didn't know who I was.

"Well? How do I look, Daddy?"

"You look like you're peeping out of a white tent. At least pull it back so we can see your pretty face. How long will it be like this?"

They just didn't understand.

But to make him happy, I picked up a green-and-orange scarf and tied it around my head, like Ali McGraw. I really liked my new hair, no matter what anybody said.

23. *Cherry*

 "What happened to your hair?!" Baby screeched when she got into the car.

"You like it?" I smirked a little, I had to admit, waiting for her to tell me how gorgeous it was.

She stared at it, not saying a word. It made me uncomfortable. "Well? What do you think?" I finally said.

"I don't know. I think I liked the old wild hair better."

"Great. You and everybody else."

"I mean, it's so different. It'll just take some getting used to."

I didn't say anything.

"Don't be mad at me, Cherry. I'm sorry. On second thought, it looks good."

"Really? You wouldn't lie?" She was lying, I could tell.

Everyone's attitude was beginning to take the bloom off, just a little. But I decided not to push it, and changed the subject.

"What kind of a place is the Family Hand, Baby? Is it a music store?" The wind was blowing my hair out the window, just like I had fantasized. I didn't care if everyone hated it. I liked it.

"Cherry, I don't quite know how to tell you this, but it's a head shop. They sell rolling papers and bongs and things that the heads use for smoking dope."

I jumped. "What! Isn't that illegal?"

"Well, they're not selling the actual marijuana. And you can get rolling papers and pipes at the Rexall. They sell other things, too. Clothes and jewelry and stuff. Hippie stuff."

I felt my face turn red, not so much from my ignorance about head shops, but because I had actually smoked a joint of marijuana myself. I wondered if Baby could tell somehow. I looked at her sideways. She was looking straight ahead. I had to find out.

"Bean smokes pot, doesn't he?" Now Baby jumped.

"Uh, well, maybe sometimes. Why do you ask?"

"Did you ever do it with him?" Baby didn't say anything. "Baby? Did you?"

"Oh, Cherry, don't ask me that!"

"You did! You did smoke it! Why didn't you tell me? What was it like?"

"Now, don't go bonkers on me here. I only did it a few times, and it was no big deal . . ."

"I thought it was a big deal. I loved it. I thought it was the best feeling I have ever had, next to kissing Tripp. In fact, when he kissed me after we smoked the joint . . ."

"You smoked pot with Tripp? Are you crazy?" I couldn't believe she was screaming at me that way.

"Quit yelling. Yes, I did."

"Stop the car right now."

We were passing the beauty school. I pulled over next to it and parked. Some of the girls looked out and waved at us.

"Why are you so upset with me? You said you did it, too."

"Yes, but I knew what I was doing!"

"Oh, so I was too stupid and ignorant to know what I was doing? Thanks, Baby." My purse had fallen, and my change was scattered all over the floor. I got busy picking it up before I said something I would be sorry for. I didn't like the way Baby was acting, and she knew it.

"I didn't mean it like that. I just think Tripp is trying to . . . I don't know what he's trying to do, but I don't trust him. How could you have let him give you a joint?"

"You don't even know him." I snapped the change purse closed. "And what about you? Here you pretend to be Miss Goody-Goody, valedictorian, straight A's and all, and you've been smoking behind my back for years, probably."

"I have not. Just since Bean got back—he made me do it!"

"Yeah, right. Like, the Devil made me do it?"

"Well, maybe he didn't hold a gun to my head, but you don't know how he is since he's been back."

"What, he was going to beat you up or something if you wouldn't smoke?"

"I don't know." She said it in a quiet voice and looked down at her hands. She was scaring me.

"Baby? What do you mean, you don't know? Has Bean hit you or something?"

"No. Not really."

"Not really? You mean he has hit you a little bit? Baby? Tell me what you're talking about. If Bean ever hurts you, he will have to go through me! I'll wring his neck. You better tell me the truth."

"No, Bean has never hurt me. He just gets in these bad moods, but I can handle Bean. It'll get better. I just have to give him time to get used to being back home. But we're not talking about Bean and me, we're talking about you and Tripp, and you are right about one thing—I don't know Tripp, but then neither do you. I mean, don't you think it's weird that he would come to little old DuVall University when he could be at Berkeley? What's wrong with this picture, Cherry?"

"I told you. He wanted to go where Jerry would have gone. You're just trying to change the subject. Why didn't you trust me enough to tell me about you and Bean? What all else don't I know, Baby? Maybe I don't know you any better than I know Tripp."

I felt like crying. A minute ago I was so happy, and now . . . is nothing what you think it is?

"Let's don't fight, Cherry. We've never had a real fight, and I don't want to start now. I didn't tell you because I just didn't want you to think I was getting into drugs or something, because I'm not. I'm really not. You know how you are with the church and all . . ."

That really got to me. I knew she didn't especially like the church, but I never thought she was serious when she would kid me about it. I thought she understood how I felt.

"No, tell me. How am I with the church and all? Do you think because I belong to the Holiness Church that you can't trust me? Did you think I'd turn you in or something? I'm not Ricky Don, Baby. I don't work for the sheriff. And as far as the church goes . . . I'm not all that sure what I believe anymore, anyhow."

"What do you mean you don't know what you believe anymore? You mean about God? Don't you believe in God anymore?" She was shocked, I could tell. I'm not even sure why I said that. It just popped out.

"Well, I mean, yeah, I believe in God. Of course I believe in God. It's just that . . . oh, I don't know."

Now I was really confused. I don't think I even understood myself. How could Baby possibly understand me? I tried to make sense out of what I was feeling.

"All of them at church are so smug and self-righteous and think they have all the answers when they won't even ask themselves the questions. They think if they ignore everything and pray, it'll go away. I just don't believe that anymore, I guess."

"So what are you saying? Are you going to quit the church and become a pothead?"

"Don't make fun of me." It seemed like everything was changing and I didn't have a clue how to make it stop. Things that I had always taken for granted, like Baby's friendship, were all of a sudden not like they used to be. Tears started coming into my eyes. I couldn't help it.

Baby knew that I was really hurt. She turned her head and looked out the window. I rummaged around in my purse for a Kleenex. Baby handed me one, and put her hand on my arm.

"I'm sorry, Cherry. I didn't mean to make fun of you. I'd like to understand. Please give me a chance." I blew my nose and wiped my eyes.

"It's just not like how it was when we were kids, Baby. Back then, right and wrong were so clear, and when we used to ride our bikes at night and go to Little League ball games, the only thing our folks worried about was if we had a wreck and skinned our knees. It's not that simple anymore."

"You got that right. But it never was simple for me like it was for you."

"What do you mean? We had exactly the same childhood. We were in the same classes since first grade. We did everything together."

"We may have done everything together, but we didn't have exactly the same childhood. You were always the golden girl. You were the only child of parents who loved you and were part of the community, and I . . ."

"What?"

"I am a Filipino."

"Well, I know that. So what? You're the most beautiful girl in school. Everybody is crazy about you."

"That's just you, Cherry. Not everyone thinks that. I'm trying to tell you something here, and you don't get it. I mean, I'm an Arkansas red-neck, just like you are. I hang out with you, I think like you, I talk like you, and I can even believe I look like you until I pass a mirror. Then I stop in surprise and wonder who the girl in the mirror is, because she has nothing to do with the way I feel. Once, I was standing at the movie theater waiting for Bean, and I heard somebody say something about an Oriental girl, and I looked around to see who they were talking about. You don't know what it is like to not even know who you are."

This was nuts. I never knew she felt that way. She was the most to-gether person I knew.

"Baby, that's crazy. So you're different. I am, too. How many six-foot-tall albinos are there around here? You think because you are Filipino that makes it okay to smoke pot and sleep with boys, and because my father works at the post office and I go to the Holiness Church that I can't? What would you like me to do, Baby, while you go to dances and drink beer and have fun? Just sing in the choir the rest of my life and die an old-maid virgin? Maybe I want to have some fun, too!"

We had been raising our voices pretty loud. The girls in the beauty school were looking out the window, trying to figure out what was going on. Lucille would be there soon, and I'm sure they would fill her in on the fight we had. You can't do anything in this town without everybody tak-ing a front-row seat.

"Stop it, Cherry. Just stop it! So we're both different. You can do any-thing you want to do, and so can I. I'm not trying to boss you around. I don't want to fight anymore. Just forget what I said."

"I don't want to fight anymore, either."

We sat for a minute, not knowing what to say next. A time or two I started to say something, but stopped. I felt like if I said the wrong thing, our friendship would be lost forever. Maybe she was right and I didn't un-derstand how she felt. I had never really thought about her being Filipino before. I mean, I didn't think it was something that bothered her. I felt like I obsessed over my looks a lot more than she did. She didn't have anything to obsess over. She was perfect. I guess we are never perfect to ourselves, are we?

I knew what they meant when they talk about a heavy heart. It felt like there was a lump the size of a bowling ball in there. Baby finally spoke.

"Leaving everything else aside, let me just say this, and I promise I won't mention it again—take it slow with Tripp. That's all. People sometimes aren't what they seem like."

"Why . . ." I began, then stopped. I was beginning to get the feeling that nobody was what they seemed like. "Okay. I promise. I'll take it slow."

"Have you done anything yet?"

"What do you mean by anything?"

"You know what I mean. Have you done *it*?"

"No. Not yet."

"Are you going to?"

"Baby, how should I know?"

"Just think about it long and hard before you do anything, okay?"

"Long and hard. Yeah. I'll think about that."

She realized what she had said. I started to laugh. She smacked me on the arm.

"I didn't mean *that* way . . ."

"I know what you meant. But if you are going to tend to your own rat-killing, I'll tend to mine. I never said anything to you about Bean, did I? Even thought I thought you could do better."

"No. You never did. Is that what you thought all this time, that I could do better?"

"I think you could do better. I know he is cute and sexy and can sing and all, but he doesn't have a brain, Baby. You have to know that by this time. All he cares about is that stupid band. He probably has never even read a book all the way through. He's just not your equal, and he's not even that great to you."

"Now who's stepping over the line?"

"You're right." I said. "That's the last thing I'll say about it. I'm sorry."

Although I wasn't, really. I had wanted to say that to her ever since she started going out with Bean. Back in school, he wasn't much of a student and made C's and D's. Then, when he started going out with Baby, he got a little more cocksure, like he thought he was so cool because he had the band and the smartest girl in class. Since he got back from Vietnam and became the star out at Woody's, it seemed like he expected Baby to ask, "How high?" when he said, "Jump." It had gotten to the point that she had to check in with him before we could even go out shopping together.

Maybe I was just jealous. I guess when you fall in love, the guy always takes first place over the friend. That might be why she wasn't all that crazy about Tripp. I would just have to try to accept it, and so would she. She was right. Whatever she did with Bean was not my business.

"I'm sorry. I love you, Baby."

"I love you too, Cherry."

"You're not mad at me?"

"Are you mad at me?"

"Not anymore," we both said at once. We laughed, which relaxed things a little, and hugged and kissed. The girls in the window of the beauty school practically had their noses mashed against the glass. Now word would be out that we were queer. I didn't care. Everything was beginning to change, and it was a little scary. But maybe that's the way it should be. Everyone had to grow up, and it couldn't be 1956 forever.

I started the car again and headed across the railroad tracks to the Family Hand, and the new job, whatever it would be.

24. *Cherry*

 On the way over, we were trying hard to get back together from the fight, and I think Baby really wanted to fill me in on everything. She had known about the plans for the head shop for a while but didn't tell me because she thought it would upset me or something. I was beginning to see that there was a lot I didn't know.

The depot had sat empty since the trains stopped carrying passengers back in 1957, and it was pretty dilapidated when John Cool and his girlfriend, Rainy Day Jones, rented it and started fixing it up. They had painted the outside dark green with lavender and blue trim and had already put a big sign up above the door. It was shaped like a giant hand, and every finger was a different color—red, white, brown, yellow, and black—to represent, obviously, all the races. The palm was colored to look like the earth. Across the wrist, in psychedelic letters like a lace cuff, it said THE FAMILY HAND.

I loved the way the place smelled when we walked in the door—like art: the acrid aroma of new-fired pottery, the musty scent of Indian batik, and the deep satisfying odor of handmade leather all mixed on top of incense, patchouli oil, and clean new wood.

The shop wasn't supposed to open for a couple of weeks, but it looked like it was starting to come together. Although half-unpacked boxes sat around everywhere, a lot of things were already on the shelves. There were handwoven ponchos, peacock-feather earrings, and Indian baskets stacked in the corner near a table full of Rainy Day's Raku pots—smoky and delicate, like dinosaur eggs that have just hatched. If her skin ever cleared up, Rainy Day would be a really pretty girl, even though she didn't wear makeup. She had nice long straight brown hair, cornflower-blue eyes, and good big teeth, a little bucked, which gave her a cute pouty look. She wore earth shoes and was what you might classify as a granola eater. She had that calm self-assurance they all seem to have, like if you put them out in the woods with only a Swiss Army knife and a piece of string, they could build a shelter, catch fish, dig up roots, and survive quite nicely.

I think before I had smoked that joint the other night, I might have been nervous about coming into a place like this, but somehow now I wasn't. I felt like part of the club. To my surprise, I didn't even feel guilty about smoking it. It was not the big, awful thing that everyone makes it out to be. It just makes you feel good. Maybe I will feel guilty later.

I did kind of feel guilty for was what almost happened on the hood of Tripp's car. It had been a crazy night, starting with Mama saying all that about the rubbers. It might have gone further than I meant it to, but the zipper on my skirt scraped the hood with a loud *skreek,* and Tripp freaked out about the paint job. By the time he had inspected the damage, spit on it, and polished it with his sleeve, I had gotten a case of the simples. It wasn't nice to laugh at him, but you would have thought that the car was a baby or something. It was only a tiny scratch, and before it was too late, he turned it into a joke, apologized, and laughed at himself.

I really liked him so much. For some strange reason, I wasn't uptight around Tripp like I usually was with boys, maybe because he liked *me* a lot and didn't act like I was a freak or something. He was the first one since Ricky Don that I really felt comfortable with.

———

Now, Tripp came down the stairs when he heard us come in. He had on his muscle shirt, and a blue bandanna wrapped around his head. I went up to him and gave him a sweet kiss hello. Baby just stood there looking at the ceiling, her hands on her hips.

"So what's all this about a job, Tripp?" she said. "Where's John Cool and Rainy Day? Are you taking over the shop or what?"

That was blunt enough. I wished she liked Tripp more.

"They went out to get a water bed. And I'm a partner in the shop—put some of my inherited wealth into it. I think it will be a good investment."

"I didn't know you were a rich boy, Tripp," Baby said. "Most rich boys don't work at the pickle plant."

"Rich is all relative, Baby. I expect to make money on this venture. And what better way to get to know the masses than to work among them, right? I'm interested in all kinds of experiences."

"Baby, leave Tripp alone. What's the matter with you?"

"It's all right," Tripp said. "We're just kidding around, aren't we, Baby?"

It didn't sound to me like they were kidding. I hoped I wouldn't have to start choosing between Tripp and Baby.

Tripp had been looking at me funny, then it finally dawned on him that something was different. "What happened to your hair?"

"Don't you like it?" I took off the scarf and turned around so he could get the whole effect. He studied it, hand on his chin.

"I think I liked the old wild curls better. This isn't permanent, is it?"

I just couldn't stand it. I thought I was going to scream. He was the third person to say that. Why couldn't anybody see how wonderful my hair was?

"It might be. I don't know," I said through tight lips. "Why are they getting a water bed?"

"We're installing a black-light room upstairs, where you can lie back and groove to some sounds. We'll be selling records up there, and putting in a juice bar. You can relax, have a carrot-and-apple juice, and try the discs out before you buy. Nice, huh?"

"Sounds groovy to me."

I wandered around looking at all the things and finally saw the case with the pipes, papers, and bongs tucked in the corner. It made me a little nervous, I have to say.

"What is it that Baby and I are supposed to do?" I asked him. "I don't think I could work selling pot pipes. My parents would flip out." Maybe I wasn't as comfortable in all this as I thought I would be.

"We want you and Baby to paint murals on the walls. You can do anything you want to do, use any kind of paint you want. You design the whole thing—the crazier, the better. We'll pay you each fifty dollars."

"Fifty dollars! That's incredible! That's as much as we make in a week at the pickle plant!" I couldn't believe it. Getting paid for what you love to do. I didn't tell him, but I would have done it for free. I looked at Baby.

"What do you think?"

I would have died if she had said no, but she just shrugged and said, "Okay. Fine by me."

I think she was more excited than she let on. I already had an idea of what I wanted to do, and I could tell Baby was thinking, too. It would be almost like we had our own gallery! I couldn't wait to get started.

"Tell John Cool y'all have a deal. We'll go over to the pickle plant right now and tell Alfred Lynn where he can put his onions."

25. Cherry

 Let me put it this way: Alfred Lynn wasn't exactly all choked up with grief when we told him we were quitting a week early. I can't believe how free it felt to come out of that steamy, sticky, smelly, hot pickle plant and know that we would never have to go back in there again as long as we lived.

We went directly from the plant to the art-supply store and bought a bunch of cans of high-gloss enamel in bright colors—orange, red, electric blue, yellow, and green—and black. I had already worked out a design for the murals in my head. I wanted to transform the Family Hand into a jungle, with tigers and lions and likenesses of John Cool, Rainy Day, us, and all of our friends. It wouldn't be corny, though. More like the Impressionists.

Tripp, on the other hand, had brought some posters with him from San Francisco of the Grateful Dead's concerts at the Fillmore. Baby saw those and thought the murals should be like that—song lyrics and names of rock groups crazily winding into and around each other. So we compromised. Baby would paint the upstairs record store and juice bar with the psychedelic lettering; the black-light room would be solid black, with posters of Jimi Hendrix, Janis Joplin, the Grateful Dead, and all; and the downstairs would be my jungle.

As we pulled into the parking lot of the Family Hand with the paint, John Cool and Rainy Day were dragging a frame for the water bed up the steps. This was really going to be some place—like nothing Sweet Valley had seen before. I felt an excitement like the pioneers must have felt, knowing they were starting a whole new way of life.

———

It took me nearly a week to draw it all out on the walls, and I was up on a ladder, starting to put green on the leaves, when I heard a familiar voice behind me.

"Hello, Highpockets. I didn't expect to find you here. What are you doing up there?"

"What does it look like, Ricky Don? I'm baking bread."

"Same old smart mouth, aren't you? I meant, what are you doing in this hippie store? And what happened to your hair?"

"I straightened my hair, and don't say you liked the old wild hair better, or I'll cram this brush down your throat. I'm painting a mural. The hippies hired me and Baby to do it. Is that against the law?"

"That depends."

"Yeah? On what?"

"Where they got the money to pay you."

"Where do you think they got it?"

"That's what I intend to find out."

"Oh come on, Ricky Don. Do you think they are going to sell drugs here?"

"No. Not here. And I'm not accusing them of selling them at all. But there's a whole lot of that going on in this town. Places like this don't help it any. I don't think you should be hanging out here. People might get the wrong idea."

"I'm not hanging out here. I am working on a job." I put down my paintbrush and wiped my hands. I couldn't work with him standing there staring at me. "You've changed a lot, you know? You used to be more fun."

"Yeah, well, if you had seen all I've seen, it might take away a little of your fun, too. In Nam, I saw a lot of guys I liked die from overdoses. That, to me, was worse than if they had been shot, because they did it to themselves. I don't think you realize that this is not something to play with. They always started out with marijuana and then went on to speed and then the hard stuff."

"Ricky Don, how long have you known me?"

"You know how long. Since the first grade."

"Do you think I am going to become a drug addict?"

"Don't be ignorant, Cherry. I just think you're hanging out with the wrong crowd."

"I told you, I'm not hanging out. I'm working." I was looking down at the top of his head, and he was getting a crick in his neck, so I climbed down off the ladder. He had become so heavy and serious since he took this job.

"What is happening with the investigation about Carlene?" I asked him just to get off the subject of me and drugs. "Any leads?"

"Not any I can discuss. You know I can't talk about my work."

"I don't know any such of a thing. Who am I going to tell? Your boss? Like I'm really going to call up that fat old geezer and say, 'Oh, Mr. Sheriff, Ricky Don's telling secrets!' Please. You know you can trust me."

He crammed his hands into his pockets and sighed. He never could resist me when I really wanted something from him, and I was pleased to see I still had a little control.

"The honest to God truth is that they don't tell us a lot of what is going on. The state police has come in here like they're Perry Mason or something. They've taken over the office. They treat us like the Junior Woodchucks, and I don't mind telling you it is beginning to get to me. Half of those guys don't even know zip-all about the people or the country around here, and they won't ask us a thing. They've interviewed everyone out where she used to work and done some more things, but I don't really think they've found out much. They still don't know where the killing actually took place or who had a motive. Her truck was parked near the restaurant, but nobody out that way saw anything that night."

"What if I was to tell you something that is all yours? Something that they don't know?"

"What are you talking about?"

I told him about the writing up at Fat Man's Squeeze. He didn't say anything.

"Well, don't you think that might be a clue?" I asked after a minute. I thought he'd leap on this piece of information. "I mean, Baby said that Carlene's nickname was Ida Red, and then it shows up on the rocks? Don't you think that might mean something?"

"I'll check it out. It probably was just kids, though. I wouldn't get too excited about it. Kids are always writing stuff on the rocks up there. We did it ourselves, remember?"

Of course I remembered. A bunch of us climbed the rocks and wrote SENIORS '66 in silver paint on a big bald outcropping called Sweet Rock, the one by Fat Man's Squeeze. There were SENIORS OF written on it every year in every color since 1904, when the high school was built. It was tradition. The rock was a landmark for people passing by on the highway below.

"I painted your shoes silver, remember?" I said. "You nearly killed me!"

"And I grabbed the paintbrush out of your hand and put a big X on your butt!"

"My mama was so mad at you—those were brand-new jeans!"

I guess we must have looked a little chummy. It was the first real conversation we'd had in years, and unfortunately, at just that moment, Tripp walked in the door. He looked a little surprised, to say the least, to see Ricky Don standing there in his uniform, his big gun on his hip, laughing and talking with me. For the first time ever, I must have looked disappointed to see him. What bad timing.

"Ricky Don just stopped by to say hi. Ricky Don, you know Tripp, don't you?"

"I know of him. Never had the pleasure to meet him."

"Well then, Ricky Don Sweet, meet Randall Tripp Barlow."

Tripp stuck out his hand; Ricky Don shook it.

I probably was wrong, but Tripp seemed a little nervous. He fumbled in his pocket for a pack of cigarettes, shook one out, and put it in his mouth.

"The store isn't open for business yet, Sweet."

"I'm not here to buy anything. Just checking it out."

"We have the permits. Everything is in order."

"I'm sure it is."

Before he could get his lighter out, Ricky Don pulled his and lit the cigarette. Tripp drew in until the tip glowed red, then blew out the smoke and looked close at the lighter.

"Can I see your lighter?" he asked Ricky Don.

"Be my guest."

It was a silver-colored Zippo, more or less like the one I had seen Tripp use. There was an inscription, and I craned my neck to read it, over Tripp's shoulder. It said: "Yea though I walk through the Valley of the Shadow of Death, I will fear no evil—because I am the meanest son of a bitch in the Valley."

Tripp laughed a little and handed it back. "I saw that one a few times. That's a good one."

Ricky Don put it back in his pocket. "You got yours?"

Tripp reached in his jeans pocket and pulled out a Zippo just like Ricky Don's. I saw now that it, too, had an inscription. Ricky Don took it and read out loud: " 'Let Me Win Your Heart and Mind or I'll Burn Your Hut Down. Charlie Company, 1/20th Quang Ngai, 1968.'

"Quang Ngai. Charlie Company." Ricky Don seemed to be trying to remember something. "Wasn't that Jerry Golden's outfit?"

"It was indeed. He was my friend."

"What happened to him, again?"

"Booby trap. A Bouncing Betty."

"Right. Where'd it happen?"

"Around Son My."

"Son My. Seems like I heard something about that place. Didn't they call it Pinkville?"

"Yeah. They did."

"I was at Chu Lai at the time. It happened around the first part of 'sixty-eight, didn't it?"

"Right about then."

"March or April, wasn't it?"

"Yeah, right about then. Why do you ask? What did you hear?"

"Nothing. Just that it was a rough place."

"That it was, my friend. That it was."

Ricky Don and Tripp locked eyes for a minute too long. I was beginning to get a little uncomfortable, like they forgot I was standing there or something. Then Ricky Don spoke, still looking at Tripp.

"Well. I got to be going. See you around, Barlow."

"'Bye, Ricky Don." I said. "Be good."

"Oh, I'm always good. At whatever I do." He was talking to me, but his eyes were on Tripp. "I like your hair, Highpockets. Take it easy. Remember what we said."

He took his time as he walked toward the door, stopping to look at some of the baskets and things, as if he were thinking about buying them. Tripp seemed a little tense. After Ricky Don left, Tripp stood in the door watching his car drive away.

"What did he mean?" Tripp asked. " 'Remember what we said'?"

"I don't know. We were just talking about high school and stuff. Nothing big." He looked like he didn't believe me. "Really. He's just trying to get to you. Are you going to let him?"

"He could mess up the whole thing if he sets his mind to it."

"Oh, Tripp, he's not going to do anything. What can he do?"

He looked like his mind was not with me there for a minute. Then he came back.

"Oh. Well, he could harass the customers—park across the street to see who comes in and out, that kind of thing."

"He won't have time for that. He has real crooks to chase."

But I knew that was exactly the kind of thing Ricky Don would do. And then what? Would he follow them home and search them to see if they had pot? Didn't you have to have warrants and things to search somebody's house or car? I had never had to think about this stuff before. Everything I learned was from TV—*Perry Mason* and *Dragnet*. Well, there was nothing I could do, so I might as well not worry about it. I went on with the painting, and Tripp got back to work upstairs.

26. *Vietnam*

 Until he enlisted in the army, Jerry Golden, like Ricky Don and Bean, had never been on an airplane. The first time it left the ground and started to climb, his stomach lurched, and every time it banked for a turn he popped out in a sweat, clung to the armrest, and prayed it would not go on over and plummet to the ground; but by the time he landed in Hawaii, twenty hours later, he was a seasoned flyer. Soaring above the clouds in the clear blue sunshine gave him some idea how the angels his Church of Christ preacher father was always talking about must have felt.

His mother was devastated when her only son joined the army, and would have snatched Carlene bald-headed if she could have. In spite of her faith that God would watch over him, she was sick with worry about Jerry going to Vietnam. His father, on the other hand, had been in Okinawa in World War II and knew what combat was like. Having gotten through it, he had no doubt his son would as well. Besides, after God, you owed allegiance to your country, and no Golden had ever shirked his duty—going back to Great-Grandpa John Ben Golden, who fought for the Confederates in the Civil War even though he had never owned a slave. It didn't matter if you believed in the cause or not; you had a duty to fight for your country.

Of course, Reverend Golden wished his only son had gone to college instead, but he was young. There would be time enough when he got back for that. The army was a good place to learn discipline, get his head on straight. Then he would come home a man and get serious about his studies. And forget about that little girl who had caused him such aggravation.

—

Carlene. High up in the sky on his way to Hawaii, Jerry didn't want to think about Carlene, but he couldn't help himself. She haunted his dreams at night, with her tornado-colored eyes and big pregnant belly. He hadn't said good-bye before he left, and it bothered him a little. But surely she understood that he couldn't—not after everything that had happened. She would be fine. She was a fighter, full of whatever it took to make a better life for herself. He hoped she would. In spite of everything, he couldn't wish anything bad for her.

As he stared out at the cotton-ball clouds, he went over for the umpteenth time how it had gone wrong for them. He still didn't understand. Before the night he asked her out for the first time, he had never thought much about her. She was just one of the girls who he might say hello to in the hallway. Everyone said hello to him. She was kind of quiet—almost invisible. Then one night at a basketball game, she came alive for him. She played with such fever and spirit that even though they were behind by twenty points, she alone seemed to will the team to win. She scored twenty points that night. Bumping into her in the parking lot afterward, he told her what a great game she had played; asked if she would let him buy her a Coke. It was a spur-of-the-moment thing, and he didn't really expect her to say yes. But they had a good time, and he asked her out again. Before they knew it, to all of his friends' surprise, they became a couple.

She wasn't like the cheerleaders and the giggly sorority-type girls with their headbands and Weejuns, their candy-pink mouths and drive-in kisses. She was wise beyond her years in a lot of ways, but unworldly in others. She could cuss like a man or be funny and warm. He never knew what she was going to do or say next. He had the feeling there was something dark in her, but whenever he tried to ask her about her life, she just said, "I had a perfect childhood. Perfect in every way." Given the little he knew about her past, he thought he knew better, but how could he argue? If he had any reservation at all about her, it was how little she confided in him. But maybe that was the attraction. He never could figure her out, which made her forever interesting.

Heartbreak was only a word in a song until he found out she was pregnant. He felt like he had been standing there minding his own business and she had kicked him in the gut. How could someone so close to you be such a stranger? It hurt, too, when his friends didn't believe it wasn't his. His parents believed him, but that didn't make him feel any better. They couldn't resist saying, "I told you so."

"You should have known what kind of girl she was when you first went out with her," his mother said, "living out in that nasty old trailer and all, with no father. Girls like that will do anything with anybody. It doesn't make you look good. She just wanted to get her hooks into you because you are going to be a lawyer, and she knew a good thing when she saw it."

He didn't want to believe it, but the evidence was right there in front of him. While he didn't consider himself a goody-goody, he was a Christian, and believed you should save yourself for marriage—at least the important part. The rest, he rationalized, didn't really qualify as a sin.

Carlene didn't seem to have any hesitation about sin. Sometimes she had tried to get him to go all the way—really make love to her. It took all the willpower he could muster to resist. Now, looking back, he realized that it was because she was pregnant and she wanted him to believe it was his so that he would marry her. When she started to show, she had to break down and tell him the truth. He couldn't believe how much it hurt. Men aren't supposed to cry, even when their hearts are broken. Their hearts shouldn't be broken at all—they are supposed to be the ones doing the breaking. But that redhead had dug her bald little fingers into him, and even though he tried to forget about her, he still felt them there.

He hadn't been in touch with her for nearly two years, since he had left and joined the army, but when she heard he was in Hawaii, getting ready for Vietnam, she sent him a letter, enclosing a picture of her and the baby. He carried it around for two weeks, read it a hundred times before he answered it, but finally he did. Then she began writing to him. He looked forward to the letters a lot more than he wanted to. On the page she opened up to him in a way she never had when she was with him.

In that first letter, she wrote:

Dear Jerry,

Don't get mad at her, but Baby got your address from your mother and gave it to me. You don't have to answer this letter if you don't want to, but please don't throw it away until you read it. I know you will never forgive me for not being honest with you and telling you about the baby until I did, but I just couldn't. I really loved—No, Jerry, I still love you—and I hoped for the longest time I was wrong about the baby. It will do no good to tell you it wasn't my fault, because I guess it was my fault, but it had nothing to do with you and me, or my feelings for you. There is nobody else that I love, and there never has been. Anyhow, I am not sorry now that I have Kevin, because he is the sweetest, best, most beautiful little thing you ever saw, and I am trying to be a good mother to him. I know you will never want to be with us or maybe even to see me again, but is it possible for us to be friends, a little? Can I write to you? Will you write back? Maybe you will be so lonesome in Vietnam that you will be happy to get a letter from even me. I hope so. I pray so. I mean, I pray not that you will be lonesome, but that you will be happy to get a letter from me.

Your friend,
Carlene

He read the letter, then studied the picture—a smiling freckle-faced redhead, her hair falling down over her shoulders. The baby she was holding looked like any other—bald and fat. He couldn't see a resemblance to anybody he knew, even its mother. Instead of returning the picture to the envelope, he put it in his helmet. He answered:

Dear Carlene,

Sure, you can write to me. A lot of my friends are writing to me. Mail from home is important to us over here. I will write you back. For the record, I'm no longer mad at you, and in fact, it probably all happened for the best. Like my father says, God has a plan for each of us, and whether we like it or not, what we think we do on our own is really what He wants us to do in order to fulfill His plan. Maybe Kevin needed to come to you just when he did and couldn't be my baby because I wasn't ready to be a daddy. We don't know. But it no longer matters. We can be friends if you want to.

It is beautiful here in Hawaii, but I haven't seen much of the island yet. We are training hard, learning to use weapons, bayonets, hand-to-hand combat, and close-order fighting in preparation to head to Vietnam. The American army has the most concentrated firepower in the world, and the VC don't stand a chance against it—but we have to be prepared just in case. I got my GED, and figure I'll breeze through this year and start DuVall in the spring of '69. I haven't given up my dream of being a lawyer. I hope you don't give up your dream, either. You can still be a great actress. Maybe your mother will keep the baby until you go out to Hollywood and get your break.

Don't worry about me. Our unit, Charlie Company, was voted Company of the Month. We're a good, tough unit. I've made some great friends, one who is a real cool guy from San Francisco, who has actually been to the Fillmore to see the Grateful Dead in person, and hung out at Haight Ashbury, plus he went to Berkeley! We are taught to appreciate the importance of friends, since they say that once we get to Nam you can't trust anybody over there but your buddies. We won't be heading for Nam until sometime in December. Most of the guys will have had their eighteenth birthday by then, and I will be nineteen. I don't think they like sending seventeen-year-olds over there, although I don't know what big deal difference a day makes—

one day you're seventeen and a kid and the next you're eighteen and a man!

I'm glad you are still my friend, Carlene. Write again, if you want to.

Your friend,
Jerry

27. Carlene and Frannie

 For a year or more after she had killed her daddy, Carlene thought about him all the time, and wondered and worried every day if Walter had done the right thing and whether, somehow, somebody would find out. She played the scene over and over in her head, tried to be honest and know in her heart if she had meant to pull that trigger or not. She honestly didn't think so, but at that moment she had been so full of hate for him. She had never really hated him before. Not that he had ever given her any love. He was just her daddy—a fact of life.

She dreamed about him a lot, dreamed that he would come driving up in the yard, all wet from the quarry, gun in hand, looking for her. She would be trying to lock all the doors and windows and find a place to hide when, all of a sudden, the window would fly open and he would stick the rifle in, dripping water over her bed, and shoot her. She always woke up in a sweat, heart pounding, trying to scream but able to manage only small whimpers down in her throat.

They were just dreams, she told herself, and in spite of them, she had one thing her mother didn't: She knew he was gone for good and would never be back. No matter how many times Carlene was tempted to tell her mother, she couldn't find the words.

At first, Frannie expected him come back without any warning, and she was so on edge waiting for the door to bust open that she put a chair under the knob at night. She waited for him to write a letter explaining himself, but one never came.

"Reckon we ought to call the sheriff and see if they can't find out what's happened to your daddy, Carlene? File a missing-persons report? He might have got in a wreck and been hurt or something." Privately, she watched and listened in town, to see if she could find out something he might have done to make him have to leave. But she didn't hear about anybody being beaten up or anything being stolen or even any gossip at all about him. It was like nobody cared enough about him to talk about it.

"They would have got ahold of us if he had been in a wreck, Mama. He had his address on his driver's license, didn't he? I think he just wanted to go off and leave us. If we found him, he might not like it." Carlene tried not to show how scared she was of going to the law.

Finally, Frannie stopped haunting the mailbox and propping the chair up against the door. If anything, life without Carl was a lot better, with one less mouth to feed and fill with whiskey, and nobody to fuss or get mad at every last little thing they did. Plus, there was nobody to spy on her every move, nobody to mess up the trailer and leave nasty-smelling socks and underwear lying around for her to take to the Laundromat. She didn't even miss losing her bed partner, since Carl wasn't too fond of bathing; there hadn't been much going on there for years anyhow. One morning she realized that she was actually happy.

Since Frannie worked all day, Carlene stayed by herself a lot. On nice afternoons, she got into the habit of going to the rock quarry and sitting on the rim, dangling her feet over the edge, smoking and tossing the butts into the water down below. She half thought she might see her daddy looking up at her, see him float up to the surface and spit water at her, but of course he never did. She looked as hard as she could to see if she could see some sign of the truck, but all she saw was black water. She knew he was there, though; felt him down there, like he was parked, watching, waiting for something. She tried to talk to him and find out if he was sorry or mad or what, but she never got an answer. She tried a time or two to talk to God, and never got an answer from Him, either.

More than once, as she walked up the path toward the quarry, she saw Walter Tucker's truck, and then she would turn back before he saw her. It seemed he went out there a lot too, but she didn't like the idea of the old man knowing that she went there. She didn't want to make light conversation with him at the place where they had pushed her father's truck over. In fact, if she never had to see Walter Tucker again, it would be a day too soon. But that was impossible, because he had taken to stopping by the house and sweet-talking her mother. They went out together on what would have to be called dates.

"Hidey, Carlene," he'd say, coming in the door without even knocking, like it was his house. "Is your mama ready? I'm taking her out to eat catfish. You're welcome to come with us."

"No thank you, Walter. I need to do some homework."

"Okay then." He'd plop down on the couch, flip on the TV, and make himself at home until Frannie came out from the bedroom. Then he'd get up, hat in hand.

"Well, looky here," he'd gush. "Who is this movie star? You look good enough to eat with a spoon, Frannie."

"Walter Tucker, you silly old thing!" Frannie would giggle as she put her sweater around her shoulders and picked up her purse. "We won't be out late, Carlene. I'll bring you home a piece or two of fish for your supper."

Carlene wished her mama had another boyfriend. She was so young and pretty—she could have gotten somebody better. Besides the fact that he was old and shaped like a pear and combed his peach-colored hair into a cock's-comb, there was something about Walter that she didn't like. It had nothing to do with the fact that he knew all about her daddy. He just seemed fake, like he was wearing a fake, smiling Walter face and underneath was the real Walter, an ugly monster with warts and welts. It was probably just her imagination, but she got nervous around him. And what was worse, she couldn't say anything to her mother about it. So, mostly, she just tried to be gone when he was there.

———

It went on like that for a couple of years, Carlene keeping so much to herself that Frannie began to worry why she didn't have any friends. Thankfully, when she was fifteen, one of the young coaches watched Carlene play in PE class, saw she had potential, and began to get her interested in basketball. She did real well at it, even though she couldn't give up her cigarettes.

Frannie finally let her smoke in the trailer. "I would rather see you not smoke, but if you have to, there's no sense in your sneaking around like some outlaw," she said.

When Carlene started basketball practice, she at least stopped spending so much time alone, but she never brought any of the girls home. She didn't want to have to explain Walter, who practically lived there now.

She had always had a lot of nervous energy, which was probably one reason she was so good at basketball. It had at least gotten her a boyfriend—the best boyfriend in the whole school. Jerry could have had any girl he wanted, and he liked *her.* She had his picture beside her bed, and at night she would stare at it for a long time and then kiss it before she turned out the light. He had dark hair, nearly as black as her mother's, and amber-brown bedroom eyes, the whitest teeth you ever saw, and a small brown mole above the right corner of his mouth. In the picture he was smiling a crooked little half smile. Just looking at the picture made her heart pound. He was a great kisser—soft, warm lips; sweet breath. And he was going to be somebody important one day—a lawyer or, maybe down the road, a congressman or senator. She dreamed that they would get married after they got out of school. *Carlene Golden,* she wrote in her notebook. *Mrs. Jerald Anthony Golden.* She loved his name, so shiny and bright. She would work while Jerry went to college and law school, then she could quit because he would make lots of money, and they could go to Little Rock or Hot Springs for dinner at fancy restaurants every night if they wanted to. Maybe take the Baths or go to Oaklawn and watch the horses run. He would play golf out at the country club while she swam in the pool. They would get a brick house with a room for her mother, and she could quit the chicken plant. They would burn down the trailer if they wanted to, roast weenies in the fire of the hateful thing.

She liked to think about a life like that. It was her second-best day-dream. The best was that she would go to Hollywood and make some movies and become a star, then get married to Jerry. Either way, it was going to be so perfect. There was only one problem. No way could she forget where her daddy was while she had to look at Walter Tucker every day.

28. *Cherry*

There was going to be a big party, kind of a housewarming or shopwarming or whatever, at the Family Hand. Baby and I had finished the murals, the black-light room was done, and we had registered at Du U for our senior year. Tripp enrolled there, too, and the three of us were taking the same drawing class. I usually had to get some kind of job during the school year for pocket money, and last year it was being the model for this same class—figure drawing. It paid five dollars an hour, four hours a week, more than any other job on campus, which is the main reason I took it. That, plus my secret ambition to be a model, which I have never before told anybody about, because it is embarrassing. I mean, I know I am too weird-looking to be a model like Maud Adams or Colleen Corby, and there is no way I could ever go to New York City, which you would have to do if you wanted to be in the magazines, but I could at least model for figure-drawing class. That was a start.

Of course, we weren't allowed to draw nudes—thank goodness. I certainly wouldn't have done it if I had to be naked. I did have to wear a bikini, though, which was bad enough. If you think sitting still is an easy way to make money, think again; it is not. Besides the fact that you are every minute worrying that your pubic hair might be showing in spite of shaving it around the edges, you have to hold the same position for anywhere from two or three minutes to sometimes as long as an hour without moving, or at least moving very much. Never in your life has your nose itched like it does when you are posing for figure drawing and can't scratch it. I felt like I earned every penny.

But this year, I would be on the other end of the pencil. Besides figure drawing, Baby and I had third-year oil painting, second-year ceramics, advanced studio, which included copper enameling, weaving, printmaking, and stuff like that, and a course in the English poets, just for some variety. Next semester would be our practice teaching, and then we would be out. Out in the world, as they say. It was scary and exciting at the same time.

But all that would be later. The big thing right now was the party. The Family Hand looked phenomenal, if I do say so myself. To tell you the honest truth, I didn't know which I liked better, my own jungle or Baby's psychedelic room upstairs with the black-light room, which was separated from the juice bar by a heavy red velvet curtain. Jimi Hendrix and the Grateful Dead seemed to float on the black walls in the eerie light, and the water bed took up most of the room. Baby had painted stars and planets on the ceiling with special black-light paint and looking up, you almost felt like you were in outer space. It was so cool. I love the way a black light makes your teeth look white and your skin, black. If you have on a white shirt, it glows like it is electric. My hair looked like I had stuck my finger in a light socket. It freaked everyone out.

The shop had been open for less than a week, and already it was the favorite hangout of the college kids. A lot of stuff had been sold, and they had to buy a second juicer. It was packed all evening, and kids lounged under big signs that said alcoholic beverages and drugs were not allowed. Ricky Don hadn't come back in, and as far as I knew, he wasn't hanging around across the street.

I spent a fair amount of time there just admiring my own work, which is a little conceited, I know, but everyone else seemed to like it a lot, too. I had used my fifty dollars from painting the murals to buy a robin's egg–blue turquoise and silver squash-blossom necklace. I shouldn't have done it, but it just kept staring at me from the case every day as I worked, calling out my name: "Cherrrrrrrry! Come and get meeee!" I just had to have it. It went with everything I owned, whether it was jeans and a white shirt, miniskirts and poor-boy sweaters, or long Indian-print dresses. Mama said it was a good investment and I would have it as long as I lived, so I didn't feel too bad about it, even though it was the most money I had ever spent on anything.

—

The night of the party was clear and full of stars, not as hot as it had been—you could almost catch a whiff of fall in the air. The tables and clothes racks had been pushed against the walls to make a dance floor, and of course Bean and John Cool and the Draggons were playing. The word was out that if anybody brought beer or liquor, they would not be allowed back. Ever. This was an unspoken effort to show the law and everyone else that the Family Hand was just a clean-cut place for the youth of Sweet Valley to hang out in.

I even brought Mama and the aunts to see the murals. G. Dub and some of his friends were coming, but the uncles and Daddy weren't too interested.

"I know you do nice work, Cheryl Ann. I'll see it sometime," Daddy said, and gave me a little pat on the arm. I wish he thought more of my art. Sometimes I feel like he thinks I am just playing, like if a job doesn't have something to do with sick people, it isn't real work.

Mama was excited to be coming with me to a party. She hesitated at first, because she thought she would be the oldest one there, but I told her all kinds of people would be coming. It was an open house, and everyone was curious. We had never gone to a party or anything like this together without Daddy, and I think she felt like a naughty little girl. He was going to a revival that Brother Dane was preaching over at Salem's Crossing, so he was happy. I think he would go to church every single day if he could.

—

"I don't know what to wear to one of these things, Cherry," Mama said as I sat on her bed and she riffled through her closet.

"Anything you have will be fine, Mama. You always look nice."

She dug around in the back and pulled out an old peasant blouse, the ones that have embroidery and elastic around the neck, and a full red skirt. She buckled on a black leather cincher belt and tugged the blouse shoulders down, just a little. She looked really sexy, with her blond hair down around her shoulders.

"What do you think?"

"Uh, are you sure you want to wear that, Mama? I mean, it's kind of . . . you know."

"You think it's too much?"

"It's not really a mom dress."

"Oh. Well, what do you want me to wear?"

"Maybe your dark-brown shirtwaist or something."

She took off the skirt and blouse and put on her shirtwaist. I think she was a little disappointed, but I was not going to be responsible if somebody said something to her that she didn't like. I didn't want her to be embarrassed. She did wear a pair of spike-heeled pumps, though, and I let that go.

We got there early, so she could see the work without the crowds. She and the aunts weren't going to stay for the dancing, of course; they just wanted to see our work.

Mama and the aunts went through the racks, picking out things they might want to try on sometime later. Lucille and I walked around the room, looking at the mural.

"Which one is you?"

I showed her me, dressed in a You-Tarzan-Me-Jane leopard skin, swinging on a vine. My hair was, of course, straight in the painting, flying out behind me as I swung, and I had fudged the size of my feet. Artist's prerogative. Tripp was hanging out of a tree house by one hand like a monkey, and Rainy Day was a mermaid lying on a rock, with her tail languidly floating among lily pads (sort of borrowed from Monet and John William Waterhouse). John Cool perched in a tree, eating a banana, and Baby was in a tiger skin, swinging on a vine that would collide with mine at any minute. Bean sat under a thatched hut, playing bongos, while Rocky danced; he was wearing his yellow aviator sunglasses.

Lucille laughed. "These are great, Cherry. They really look like all of you. Who are those other ones peeping out of the grass and all? Is that Ricky Don?"

"Yeah. He has to keep his eye on things." I had snuck Ricky Don in, hiding in the bushes, watching all of us. I don't know why I did it. It just seemed right. Nobody had said anything about it, although I was afraid Tripp might ask me to paint him out.

We looked some more, then Lucille took me aside and whispered, "Okay. So where are the bongs?"

"The what?"

"Don't give me that. The bongs. The pipes. The pot stuff. I know what kind of a place this is."

"It's legal, Lucille. They don't sell drugs here."

"Did they hide them? I want to see what they look like." She had that glow in her eyes.

I sighed. "They are right over here."

We went around the counter to the case of bongs and pipes. They weren't exactly hidden, but they were well out of the traffic pattern. An Indian shawl was draped over the case. It was locked, as Lucille found out when she tried to open it.

"Wow. How do they work?"

"What makes you think I know how they work?"

"Oh, come on. You are going out with a head. Everyone knows that. You must have done it."

"Everyone knows that? Who's everyone?"

"All the girls at the beauty school. Tripp Barlow is a most interesting new boy in town. Word gets around."

My face got numb. It sure doesn't take long in this town for everybody to know your business.

"Well?" She poked me in the ribs. "Have you smoked pot or not? Don't lie."

"All right! I did. But just once. I really don't want to talk about it."

"Don't be that way! You know I can't do it because of the nursing, but if I could I would. Maybe when Jim Floyd gets back we'll try it. Do you think Tripp would get us some?"

"Lucille! No, Tripp is not going to get you any pot! And you have to swear you won't tell anybody what I just told you. Especially those loud-mouths at the beauty school."

"You know I won't tell . . ."

"Swear! Pinkie swear."

"All right! Pinkie swear."

We licked our right pinkies and hooked them around each other. I knew she would never tell on a pinkie swear. But I had to talk to Tripp. I wished he would hurry and get here.

She was too much, that Lucille. I had a bad feeling that she was an accident waiting to happen. But then I had always felt that way about her, and it had never much come to anything yet. She was more settled-down than I was.

Mama and them had gone upstairs to look at Baby's painting and see the black-light room. We heard a baby squealing and found them behind the red velvet curtain. They had Tiffany LaDawn on the water bed, bouncing her up and down. She was having a great time. I sat down beside her and helped bounce. I wondered what she thought about all of us looking so weird under the black light.

"Ooh, oopsie daisy! Widdle dirl is having a ride!" Up and down Lucille went, sloshing the water. The bed rolled and rocked. I started to get a little queasy.

"Y'all go on and play with her awhile. I'm going to get something to drink." I weaved out, leaving them there.

Downstairs, more people were beginning to arrive. Baby came in with her brothers and her sister Pilar, who was fourteen but looked like twenty-five with all the makeup she was wearing. She either had developed overnight or was stuffing her bra with Kleenex. I suspected Kleenex. She was chewing gum, popping pink bubbles, and trying not to act like she was excited. G. Dub followed them in, and Pilar almost swallowed her gum. The girl obviously had a crush on my cousin. She was growing up in a hurry.

"Hey, y'all. This is some crowd, huh?" I said as they came over to me. "I guess this is our first two-woman show, Baby. What do y'all think?"

"Well, it's colorful, that's for sure," G. Dub said. "I like it, Cherry. You did real good."

Pilar came over and stood next to him. She put her arm through his and looked up at him with adoring eyes.

"G. Dub, the part Baby did is upstairs. Do you want me to take you up there and see it?" she said. "There is a really cool black-light room, too. With a water bed."

"After a while, little girl." He tousled her hair, and she blushed. She was so cute. G. Dub didn't have a clue that she liked him. Men are so dense sometimes.

Rocky went over to help Bean, who was setting up the amplifiers. The band wasn't going to start playing until a little later, around ten, when the older curiosity seekers would probably be gone. Most people in this town eat supper at five and are sound asleep by nine or ten.

Rainy Day scurried around putting out bowls of Fritos and bean dip. There wasn't going to be a whole lot of food and people had to buy the drinks at the juice bar, but that didn't matter. There was still going to be a big crowd.

Tripp came up behind and grabbed me. "Hey, gorgeous. Everybody loves your jungle." He nearly made me jump out of my skin.

"Don't scare me like that!" I just hate to be startled.

"You better watch yourself," G. Dub said. "One time I did that to Cherry, and she swung around and clocked me!"

"And you deserved it, too, sneaking up on me like that! You have to learn how to make noise when you walk, G. Dub, or clear your throat or something."

"Thanks for the warning, G. Dub. Cherry looks like a girl who could pack a punch."

I gave him a tap on the chin, not too gently, and then took him by the hand. "Y'all excuse us for a minute, okay? I need to show Tripp something."

I took him over to the corner and pretended to point out the picture of him, even though he had seen it a zillion times before.

"Lucille said that everyone knows we smoked pot, Tripp."

"What? Who did she say knew?"

"The girls at the beauty school were talking about it. If Ricky Don hears this, there's no telling what he might do."

"Cherry sweetness, you worry too much about Ricky Don. Cops can't go around arresting people for gossip. They have to have evidence. Those girls don't know anything. They just want to cause trouble. They're jealous of you."

"Jealous of me?"

"Sure."

"For what?"

"You have me, don't you?"

"Oh. Right. Boy, there's no conceit in your family, is there? You have it all."

He laughed and hugged me. "Stop worrying. I'm careful. I would never let anything happen to you. You're my girl."

Tripp's girl. It had been a long time since anybody really wanted me to be his girl. I got shy all of a sudden, and started toward the stairs.

"Come on upstairs and meet the rest of my family."

They were sitting at the bar drinking apple juice. Lucille had Tiffany LaDawn up on her shoulder, jiggling her up and down, patting her on the back. I wondered if the kid ever spent a minute perfectly still. She obviously hadn't inherited my motion-sickness tendencies, thank goodness.

"Mama, Aunt Juanita, Aunt Rubynell, Lucille—y'all, this is Tripp Barlow. I might have mentioned him."

"Just once or twice. Hello, Tripp. It's real nice to see you," Mama said.

"I knew your mother looked like your sister, but you didn't tell me you had such young and beautiful aunts and this gorgeous cousin. If I didn't know better, I would think you all were sisters."

"He sure knows how to do it, doesn't he?" Lucille said. "But that's okay, Tripp. You can call me gorgeous anytime you want to."

"I wouldn't say it if I didn't mean it. And look at this little beauty-in-training." He reached out and took Tiffany LaDawn from Lucille, like he was used to babies. I waited for her to scream, but she didn't. She gave him a big gummy smile. She was Lucille, Jr., all right. In fact, they were all smiling. When a whole family of women, from youngest to oldest, is in love with somebody, he must be some kind of guy. He gave the baby back to her mother, and got us some juice. Rainy Day was struggling up the stairs with a big bowl of Hawaiian Punch, and I went over to help her.

"I decided to put out some punch. It wasn't right for everyone to have to buy the drinks," she said. The two of us carried it as steadily as we could over to the table she had set up. Only a little sloshed out.

"We did a great week's business, Cherry. Sold nearly all my Raku. I am going to have to work overtime to make more pots. I've been thinking. Would you like to work here a few hours a week? I didn't realize how much time running this place was going to take."

I did need a job. Since I was taking the drawing class, I couldn't pose for it. I looked over at Mama. Tripp was sure entertaining the women. They were laughing their heads off about something. She wouldn't mind if I worked here, now that she saw what a great place it was. I had to get over this reflex of mine to always ask Mama and Daddy's permission for everything, like I was a little kid.

"Sure. I'd love to."

"Great! Now that you're an official employee, help me with these cups."

Mama and the aunts and Lucille left soon after that. Lucille would have probably liked to stay and dance, but she was a mother now and had to go home and take care of her baby. I began to see what Mama was talking about when she said all that stuff about tying yourself down. I kind of felt sorry for Lucille, but there was nothing I could do about it.

"I'll probably spend the night at Baby's, Mama. Don't worry about me." I kissed her good-bye. Tripp kissed her, too, and she got a little flustered.

Most of the older people had come and gone, and more and more kids were coming in. The band tuned up, then blasted out the first song, "Light My Fire." Tripp grabbed me by the hand, and we were off, dancing like maniacs.

Tripp was a really good dancer, of course. I hadn't found anything yet that he wasn't good at. I am okay, but only in a crowd, so nobody can really see what I am doing. I try to keep my elbows in and not go too wild with my arms, because a time or two I have hit somebody in the head. I once even crunched a girl's high heel and broke it, which really made her mad. But if I stand in one spot and just sort of wiggle around, I can get by.

We must have danced more than an hour without stopping, but then I had to take a break.

"I gotta sit down for a minute, Tripp. I need something to drink."

I was about ready to pass out, it was so hot in there. There must have been over two hundred kids packed in. You could hardly move, and the air was full of smoke.

Tripp went and got us two great big cups full of Hawaiian Punch. I gulped the whole thing down without taking a breath. He did the same.

"Fill 'er up again?" he asked.

"Please."

He got us two more. It was good punch. Had kind of a funny aftertaste, though. Something made it a little whangy. I drank the second cup a little slower, and then Tripp went and got us a third. It was so hot in there. My stomach was feeling a little rocky.

"I'm going outside for some air, Tripp."

"I'll go with you."

———

It was cooler outside. We stood in the parking lot for a minute, but I wasn't feeling much better. I had a bad feeling that I was going to be sick at my stomach. Now I started to worry that the punch had gone bad. Maybe it was botulism, which we learned about in Home Ec class. What was it the teacher had said? You should test the ends of cans by pressing them to see if they bumped, and if they did, it was full of botulism. Maybe Rainy Day had never taken Home Ec and didn't bump the cans.

"Go on back in, Tripp. I want to be by myself for a minute."

"What's wrong? Are you okay?"

"I think I'm going to throw up. I think the punch was bad."

"It wasn't bad. Just a little spiked. Bean snuck in a quart of cherry moonshine."

Oh. Of course. I wondered for a minute if Tripp was making fun of my name or if the moonshine was made out of cherries. I looked up at the stars, and they were going around and around, like I was on a merry-go-round. My head was swimmy. Now I knew I was going to throw up. I remembered what all Ricky Don had said about moonshine, how it ate up your kidneys and all. Trust me, Tripp had said. Boy, was I a fool. If I died tonight, I would definitely drop right down the chute into hell. I tried to worry about it, but it was too hard. The parking lot was doing some crazy dips and swirls. I had to lay down before I fell.

"I'm just going to lay down here and rest for a minute, Tripp." My tongue seemed like it was thick. "You go on back in."

"Here? On the gravel? I don't think so. Come on, I'll take you for a ride."

"I don't want to go for a ride, Tripp. I'll get carsick and ruin your car . . . let me lay down just for a minute. Please. I'll go to the grass. I need to take a nap."

I tried to walk over to the grass, but my legs wouldn't work right. Just as my knees started to buckle, Tripp picked me up and threw me over his shoulder. He carried me across the parking lot to where Ramblin' Rose was parked. With every step, his shoulder dug into my stomach. He opened the door, which was not easy with me draped across him, and just before he put me in, the entire contents of my stomach came up and cascaded down his back, then onto the ground. I should have been horrified, but I really didn't care. He shouldn't have jostled me around like that.

I slid off his shoulder and he threw me into the front seat. I slumped over and immediately fell asleep. At least, I thought I was asleep, because I remember thinking, How silly. I'm falling asleep. In reality, I had passed out, and was too stupid to know.

———

The next thing I knew, I was lying on a bed. It was a room I'd never seen before, and the bed felt odd and lumpy. There was an open window right above the bed. It was soft and gray outside, the first light of morning. I started to sit up, but the top of my head felt like it was going to blow out. I grabbed it to hold it on, lay back down, and realized that next to me was a body, and it wasn't Baby. I reached out and felt of it. A naked body. The head that stuck out from under the blanket was covered in long wheat-colored hair. And then I realized that I was naked, too.

"Tripp Barlow! What have you done?" He moved a little, like he was going to wake up, but just fixed his pillow under his head and fell back asleep. I shook him. Hard.

"Tripp, wake up! What happened? What am I doing here?"

He turned over, put his arm around me, and pulled me under the covers. I was touching every inch of his naked body.

"No! Stop it! Let me out!" I tried to throw off the blankets and get out of bed, but they were in such a tangle that I only succeeded in wrapping them around my legs. I fell onto the floor. By this time, he was awake, watching me with a sleepy grin.

"Good morning, sunshine. How did you sleep?"

"Like the dead. Ow! My head! You poisoned me! Where are my clothes? Did you undress me? What else did you do?"

"In the closet. Yes. Nothing. What do you think I'd do to a woman who was passed out? What kind of man do you take me for?"

I managed to get up off the floor and wrap the blanket around me. Then I realized that I had left Tripp lying there uncovered. Naked. He was tanned except where his bathing suit had been, and that part was pearly white. He lay on his back, put his hands under his head, and grinned as I stood looking at him, horrified, and tried to figure it all out. The first thing I noticed, of course, was his penis, rosy and pink, jutting straight out of a nest of honey-colored hair. I realized he knew what I was looking at, but I couldn't help it. It was the first one I had ever seen, in the daylight. Or in the dark, for that matter. So that was what they looked like. They were a lot bigger than I thought.

Then my attention was taken by a long red scar that seemed to be growing from the hair above his penis, up across the whiteness, into the tan of his belly, and on up until it tapered off just under his rib cage. It was like a big red rope, raised and shiny, about two inches wide. It obviously had healed, but was still angry-looking. For a minute there, I wanted to reach out and touch it, but I pulled my hand back almost before the gesture was begun. I didn't know what to do, whether to turn away, where to look, what to say. So I did nothing. Just stood by the bed and gaped.

"Come here," he said in a gentle voice, holding out his hand like you would to a dog. "Come on. Don't be scared. Just sit and talk with me for a minute. We won't do anything you don't want to do. I'm not going to hurt you."

He seemed real comfortable, naked like that. Not at all self-conscious about his scar or anything, like I would have been. For some reason, the fact that he wasn't ashamed of his scar relaxed me a little, and I sat down on the edge of the bed. I was still clutching the blanket, though.

"What happened to your stomach?"

"I fell into a pit that the VC dug and embedded with punji sticks. It was my ticket home from Nam. I just wish it had happened a few months earlier. I was short—only had two months left."

"Does it still hurt?"

"Not anymore. I just can't eat as much at once as I used to. The body has a whole lot of intestines, thank goodness. The red will fade with time. Do you want to touch it?"

I reached out my hand and touched it then. Delicately. It felt smooth and hard, like a tube running under the skin. There was no hair on it. My middle finger traced the scar from the top to the bottom. When I reached the soft hair, I stopped. But I didn't take back my hand. Tripp lay unmoving, watching me. It felt like time stood still. The air was thick. A shaft of light crept over the potted red begonia on the windowsill and lit up thousands of motes that boiled in the early-morning sunbeam, then spread like melted butter across a patch of dim worn rug, bringing out shades of coral and rust and lemon and blue. A clock ticked somewhere.

He put his hand over mine and brought it gently down onto his penis. I had never felt one uncovered before. It was hard and warm, the skin like soft pink velvet, like the belly of a week-old kitten. I held it without moving, and it was alive in my hand, like a small animal.

He reached up and took the blanket away from my body, and I was as naked as he was. The sun was warm on my back.

"You look like you were made on the moon." There was awe in his voice.

I had always imagined the first time I made love would be in the dark. But there was no more perfect place than here, in the morning light. I was glad for the sunshine. I wanted to see all of him, and I wanted him to see all of me. I forgot about my flat chest and pale nipples that stuck out like pink jelly beans. It didn't matter if I was skinny and my legs were too long, my feet too big. I saw myself in Tripp's eyes, and I was beautiful.

I leaned down and we kissed, one of those kisses that made my heart and stomach melt and pour into my you-know-what, and he lay me down beside him on the bed, stretched his body against mine from our toes to our mouths, and kissed me again. I thought I would pass out.

Then he licked my neck until the skin was covered with chill bumps, and he worked his way south, over my nipples—sucking them and making them stand out even higher—down my belly, and finally into the white Brillo patch between my legs; pushed them wide apart and comfortably settled in. I didn't even know you could do what he was doing, but it seemed natural and not nasty at all. After a few minutes it started to feel really good, and at the edge of my consciousness, it was like a volcano began to bubble, far away. My body tensed, every muscle straining. My breath was ragged. My fingers dug into his arms, and it must have hurt, but he didn't notice or stop what he was doing. It seemed like I was hanging on the edge of a high rock cliff by the tips of my fingers. Then I let go and fell through the air; hot lava gushed from deep inside and melted over my body, and I think I started to scream.

He raised himself over me then, and I felt the hard pink velvet touch me once, then plunge as I raised myself up to meet him. There was a sharp pain. Then the lava flowed again and swallowed everything up, and the sun burned red in my eyes.

——

"I didn't know you were a virgin."

"I don't go around advertising it. I mean, *didn't* go around advertising it. Most girls my age are not. It's kind of embarrassing."

He kissed me on my forehead, both eyes, my nose, and my mouth. Almost like a blessing.

"Thank you." There were tears in his eyes, and also in mine. One ran down across my cheek. He licked it off, and we both laughed.

"I had no idea it was going to be like this." I snuggled in his arms.

"It's not, usually."

"Why? What is it usually like?"

"Hmm. Let's just say a lot less . . . everything. I don't think I ever met anyone quite like you."

"Is that good?"

"Oh, yes. That is good."

I could tell by his voice that he meant it. I felt like I was glowing like a lightbulb. I had never felt this relaxed in my life.

"Have you had a lot of girls?" As soon as the words were out of my mouth, I knew I shouldn't have asked him that. I really didn't want to know, and besides, it was none of my business. But I waited to hear what he would say.

"None until now." He kissed me again, lightly. "Are you thirsty?" he asked.

"I could drink the Arkansas River, mud and all."

He got out of bed and went to a fridge in the corner, poured me a glass of orange juice. Nothing had ever tasted as good as that thick, sweet juice. Or maybe it was him. It was like I had been crawling in the desert and he was a cold drink of water. He lay down beside me and watched me gulp.

Then he took the empty glass out of my hand, put it on the table, and it started all over again.

So this was what love was like.

29. Baby and Carlene

By the early spring of 1968, Baby had nearly forgotten what Bean looked like. She had a lot of pictures of him that he had sent to her from Nam, but the GI with a tan and a mustache, wearing aviator sunglasses and squatting next to a pile of captured VC weapons, didn't look like the Bean she remembered. His letters weren't much in the love department, either. They were mostly about the war, filled with language she only half understood, like diddy-bopping, loach and lurps, gooks and dinks, boo koos of this and boo koos of that, klicks and grunts and zips. He didn't even explain; just figured that it was normal language everyone would know. Sometimes she only half read them. If she had had more of a romance with Jackie, she might have written Bean and told him she couldn't wait for him any longer, but with Jackie, it was never a question of love, and it was comforting to know that Bean was there on the back burner, so to speak.

However, she wrote to him faithfully every few days, and she was the one who told him about Jerry Golden getting killed. She heard it from Carlene, who came in one evening for her shift with her eyes all red and swollen from crying and said Jerry's mother had called her that afternoon to tell her the news. She thought it was decent of Mrs. Golden to call, knowing how much she hated her. Or maybe it was because Mrs. Golden blamed her for his going to Nam and wanted Carlene to hurt like she was hurting. If she did, it worked; Carlene was in pain.

Jackie offered to let her take the night off and go back home. She shook her head.

"It's all right. I'd rather stay and be here with y'all, if y'all don't mind."

"Okay, beauty," he said, putting his arm around her. "But take your time. You don't have to start work right away. Go out and sit on the patio for a little while. Meditate. Rita and Baby can take care of the early birds."

"I'm not much in the meditation department, Jackie. Maybe Baby could go out and sit with me, if she doesn't mind."

"Sure. Take all the time you want. Go to the kitchen, get Park to give you something to eat."

Park gave them thick mugs of coffee with cream and packed a basket with sweet rolls, hot from the oven. They carried it down the path to the end of the promontory where the lake branched off from the river, and settled themselves on a rock. It was the second week of April, but as the sun dropped behind the mountain, there was still a chill in the air. The river was the same color as the coffee, and it swirled around a sandbar, making café-au-lait ripples. Down further, the dam stretched across to the far bank, cutting the river in half. From their perch, they could hear the water rushing through the locks. Years before, when it hadn't rained for a long time and the river was low, some teenagers thought they would wade out to the sandbar right near this very spot, but the water was deeper than it looked and they stepped into a sinkhole and drowned—two brothers and a sister. The river was treacherous. You didn't fool with the river.

Three or four old beer cans floated by. People were such pigs, using the river for a dumping ground, Baby thought. The rock was icy on her behind, and the cold seeped into her bones through the thin material of her uniform. She wished she had her sweater.

They got as comfortable as they could, sipping their coffee in silence. In her head, Baby went over all kinds of things she might say to offer comfort, but none of them seemed right. She couldn't say, "I know how you feel," because she didn't. She couldn't say, "Don't think about it," or, "Time will heal," or, "It was God's will," or any of the other stupid things people always say when somebody has died, because there was no way you could *not* think about it. So Baby didn't say anything. Finally, Carlene blew her nose and cleared her throat. "We were going to get back together. Did you know that?" she said.

"No. You didn't tell me that."

"We would have, when he came home. We'd gotten real close again, in the letters. Sometimes you get to know a person better from letters than if you were with them every day. Jerry changed in Nam; grew up a lot, in those four short months." She wiped her eyes, which, it seemed, couldn't stop leaking. "I just knew he was going to make it back home. I never thought for one minute he would get killed, not even when he told me all the horrible things that were happening over there. I felt like he had a guardian angel or something. But I guess there's no such of a thing. Do you think there is?"

Baby took a drink of her coffee and thought about it.

"I don't know if I think there is or not," she finally said. "It sure would be nice if there was. I've read a lot of stories about people being saved by what they thought were angels."

"That's just to sell magazines. If that was true, then why are so many people not saved? In this world, you have to take care of yourself. If you won't, nobody else will."

"Ain't it the truth." Baby nudged a loose rock with her toe. It bounced down the bank and plunked into the water.

"I just wish I could have seen him one more time to say good-bye. The last time I saw him, he was so mad and hurt he wouldn't even speak to me. I tried to get him to talk to me, but he just turned away, got in the car, and drove on off to go enlist. I never even got to say good-bye when he went in the service. The last thing I saw of him was the back of his head and his taillights."

Baby put her arm around Carlene and let her sob. Held her and smoothed down her hair, like she did her little sisters' when they were hurt.

"I'm sorry," Carlene said. She sat back up and pressed her fingers into her eyes, hard. "I've got to get ahold of myself. This is silly. It's just that I had already given up on Jerry, and then he started writing to me and I got my hopes back up. But he's gone forever, and I've got to think about Kevin now. I have to figure out a way to make a better life for him. I don't always want to be just a waitress, us living out in that old trailer house with Mama, Kevin not even having his own bed."

"Maybe you could go part-time to DuVall. Get some kind of a degree. What would you like to do if you could do anything you wanted to?"

Carlene pulled a crumpled pack of Camels out of her pocket and offered one to Baby. They lit up.

"If I could do anything I wanted to? Don't laugh. I'd like to be an actress. A movie star. Move out to L.A. and get me one of those little pink houses on a curved street with palm trees in the yard. Swimming pool out in the back. Take Kevin and Mama out there, so she could get out of that stinking chicken plant. Do you think I'm crazy?"

"Not if that's what you want to do more than anything in the world. A lot of girls make it in the movies, and most of them didn't come from money or anything. Look at Marilyn Monroe. She was an orphan. You're good-looking enough, that's for sure. You have one of those cute little turned-up noses that a lot of girls pay good money to get—except theirs never look real. And you sure have the body for it. In fact, you're built a little bit like Marilyn. I bet you would make it."

"You really think so?"

"I really think so."

"It would be nice to be close to the ocean, wouldn't it? Just lay out on the sand in a bathing suit and wait for a producer to discover you." She took a long drag on the cigarette; flicked off the ash. "Did you ever see the ocean, Baby?"

"I was born on the ocean, in the Philippines, but I don't remember too much about it. They never let me go in swimming. Lula—my grandmother—was scared I'd drown, or afraid the Aswang mermaid would get me." She gave a half laugh.

"What's an Aswang mermaid? Is that how you say it?"

"I think so. Aswangs are like a vampire. It's been a long time since I heard the stories, but there's two kinds, one that lives in the banana trees and flies through the air and one that lives in the ocean and is a mermaid. I don't know the name of the one that flies, but I think the mermaid one is called Seriena. She would come out every year at Lent, as the priest led the procession for the Stations of the Cross through the streets at twilight. Everyone in the village held a candle and walked along the seashore to the church for mass."

Baby saw that Carlene was listening, so she went on as she remembered her grandmother doing.

"The Seriena, who could grow legs instead of fins when she came on land, would join the procession as it passed by the edge of the sea near her lair. She was the most beautiful thing you ever saw, with long, flowing black hair, opalescent skin that shone in the moonlight like mother-of-pearl. She would come out of the sea, bone-dry, wearing a black silk dress, with her hair and face covered by a fine lace mantilla, so nobody could see the sea-green glow of her eyes and know she was a creature of the water.

"Grandmothers always warned their granddaughters never to lag behind in the procession, because the Seriena would find a girl who was alone and walk along beside her, singing with the most incredibly lovely, haunting voice, until the girl practically swooned with the beauty of the song and got weak enough for the Seriena to put her arm around her. Then she would lift her veil and hypnotize the girl with the green pulsating light of her eyes, turn, and walk into the sea, and the girl—her will completely gone—would follow out into the deep water, where she would drown, and the Seriena would take her and swim with her to the bottom and drink her blood from a goblet made from a seashell."

Carlene shivered. "Great bedtime stories your grandma told."

"Yeah. I had nightmares for years."

Carlene picked up Baby's hand and looked at the ring she always wore, an elaborate cameo carved into a shell. "Is this little pink ring made out of a seashell?"

"It sure is. In fact, it was a present from Lula that she sent me for my thirteenth birthday. She's still over there, but I never saw her after we left the Philippines. I can't say I really knew her. She doesn't speak English, so we don't really even write. Isn't that weird? I don't remember the language, but I do remember her stories."

"That is weird. I never knew my grandmas, either one of them, because they died young. I wish I had known them."

"What about your daddy? You never talk about him."

"Me and him didn't get along. He used to call me Ida Red, just to aggravate me. He took off and left us one day, and I can't say I miss him much."

Carlene gazed out over the river, and Baby knew not to ask any more questions.

"Here, you want to try this ring on?" Baby twisted the ring off her middle finger and handed it to Carlene, who tried but couldn't get it on her ring finger. She put it on the little one.

"You sure do have small fingers. It only fits my pinkie."

Carlene admired the seashell ring a minute more, then took it off and handed it back to Baby.

"That's a real pretty ring. I can see you diving to the bottom of the sea and breaking it off a big seashell, sticking out your tongue at that old Aswang. No Aswang would dare mess with you."

Baby took the ring, put it back on. She had worn it for so long that it had left a pale groove around her finger. Carlene glanced at it one more time.

"Maybe I can get me one like that when I get to the beach in California. Give me a reason to quit biting my nails."

The sun had gone down, and a fingernail moon hung right over Sweet Rock, high above the river, in a Maxfield Parrish sky. The trees were cool and green in the dusk. A catfish, or something big, splashed on the other side of the sandbar. They could see a dark tail flick out of the water, then disappear.

"Whoa! Looky at that, would you!" Carlene said. "There you go! The mermaid!"

"You don't think there might really be such a thing as a mermaid, do you?" Baby tried to act like she was kidding, but she half thought there might be.

"Sure there are. The river's full of them. Real bloodsuckers. But around here they call them water moccasins." They laughed, too loud. Like they were trying to find something—anything—funny. Baby gathered up the cups and uneaten rolls.

"Maybe I should go on back in. Rita might need some help. Will you be all right?"

"I'll go with you. I think I can work now. Thanks, Baby. You're the best friend I ever had. I mean that." They hugged, and Baby started down the path. If she was the best friend Carlene ever had, she thought, that was a sad fact.

"Baby? Can I ask you to do something for me?" Baby turned around and walked the few steps back to where Carlene was standing.

"Sure. If I can."

"I have a whole stack of letters from Jerry that he sent me from Vietnam. Some of them are pretty rough—you know, about the fighting and all."

"Yeah. Okay."

"If anything was ever to happen to me, I wish you'd get hold of those letters and not let my mama read them. I'd appreciate it if you didn't read them, either. Just put them in the fire or something, okay? Would you?"

"Well, sure, Carlene. You can trust me. But you are going live to be an old woman with fifty grandkids and still have those letters to read, so stop all of this. You're making me nervous."

"Thank you, Baby."

"He really told you a lot of bad stuff that was going on, huh? Like what?"

"Baby—you have no idea. There's no way I could describe it."

"That bad?"

Carlene looked Baby in the eyes. There was something in her gaze that was ancient; raw and frightening, like a high, piercing wind was blowing through her head. The look almost made Baby stagger.

"It blows your mind, Baby. It really blows your mind."

Carlene put her arm around Baby, and the moment passed. She must have been imagining things. After all, what could Jerry have said that was that bad? They went back into the Water Witch with their arms around each other's waists. Carlene would be all right. She had no choice.

But even though she would pretend she was fine, Carlene knew she would never get over Jerry. He was a part of her. He would never age, and he would forever be her love. No matter what happened.

30. *Vietnam*

Dear Carlene,

We're here. Vietnam at last. I hate to brag, but the honor of being the advance party for the 11th Brigade went to none other than our own Charlie Company. I think that means we were the best in the 1/20th.

Vietnam is, in a lot of ways, nothing like I thought but everything I was afraid it might be. You are going to think I'm crazy, but it's funny—the closer I got to coming, the more I really wanted to get here. I had heard so much about it, been trained so long in what to do—how to kill, really—that I wasn't scared at all. In fact, I was afraid I'd draw some dumb office job and spend my days typing orders or something, and never get to see the action. I can't believe how ignorant I was.

The action started from the minute we got near the country in the airplane. We came in at Quang Ngai province, up in the northern part of South Vietnam. Looking down, you fly in over the South China Sea, a stretch of blue that has the prettiest white sandy beaches you ever saw. Then to the west you see the deep green of the Annam Mountains. Most of Vietnam is jungle or green rice paddies, and real pretty. At least from the air. The plane we were on had stewardesses and everything, and there were some nurses with us, all dressed in their class-A uniforms, tight skirts, high heels and stockings, like they were going to a party or something. We were having a high old time until we started to land, and the pilot announced, kind of casually, that there was some incoming and we would circle for a while. I mean, right down below us, there was a firefight going on! We could see the smoke and hear the gunfire. It didn't seem real, like it was a movie or something. This was a big base. It was supposed to be secure. I didn't realize then that there was no secure place in the whole country, not even down at Saigon.

Before we landed, they handed out flak jackets and told us to hit the ground running. One of the nurses said, "How the h*** am I supposed to run in these high heels?" The army is so stupid, sometimes. If they send women to where there is fighting, they should at least give them the right gear.

The stewardesses stood by the door crying as we got off the plane. They had made this run a lot of times before, both ways. They knew already, better than us, what we were getting into. I heard one of them say to another one, "We bring in boys and take back old men." Not the greatest thing to hear as you arrive, that's for sure.

Anyhow, we jumped out the door, and all of us took off running across the field, our heads hunkered down into our shoulders, like that would do any good, bullets whizzing all around us. Only one guy took a bad hit, in the leg. I figure that was it for him—forty-five seconds in-country, and then turn around back home. Still, I was glad it wasn't me.

The nurses all made it, but they looked kind of funny running, taking short, hobbled steps in the tight skirts, their little heels going Tic! Tic! Tic! Tic! on the tarmac. They were cussing like sailors, every step they took. I bet that is the last time they wear that outfit if they can help it.

We all ran into this building made out of tin, and collapsed, exhausted, just from that short run. Even coming from Hawaii, where it is hot and humid, the heat of Nam literally slaps you in the face and saps your strength. The minute I got out of the plane, my uniform was soaked to the skin. Whether it was from fear or the heat, I couldn't say.

The smell of Vietnam is like no other place in the world—at times it smells like hothouse flowers and at times it is worse than old Stink Creek that the pickle plant drains into. It is a mix of this pungent fish sauce they eat on everything, called *nuoc mam,* and fuel and gas and latrines and a sweetish, rotten smell—death, I guess. That was our welcome to Nam.

The very next day, our first assignment was to gather and burn the bodies from the firefight. I think they did it to us on purpose, because we're the FNGs (that's f***ing new guys, you fill in the blanks) and we should get a taste in a hurry of what death was like. Break us in right away, so to speak, almost like a fraternity initiation.

This was the famous body count we had heard so much about. Before, back in the world, you didn't think about it much, it was just numbers: high was good and low was bad. But when you saw it, you realized the body count was real actual dead bodies—a bunch of VC laying on the ground and hanging on the perimeter fence, already bloated and stinking in the heat. I couldn't imagine how anybody would be so crazy as to try to get through the barb wire and fight a force that had all the firepower we do, but they do it all the time, and they somehow manage to get through the wire and kill a few GIs before they buy it themselves. I guess that's why they have lasted so long—sheer crazy determination.

We had to drag them and throw them into a pile, like cordwood, pour gasoline over them, and set them on fire. They used to just throw the bodies in the river, but the ship captains complained that they were getting tangled up in the propellers, so they started burning them.

At first, when we got out there, we just stood gaping. None of us wanted to touch them, but we had no choice. Some of the bodies were in pieces, and we gathered up arms and legs and tossed them on the pile; feet with calluses on the bottom like slabs of butterscotch, heads with white bones sticking out of the necks. All of us were throwing up, but we had to do it anyhow. After a while, we didn't have anything in our stomachs, so we drank water, just to have something to throw up besides bile.

The sky turned black with greasy smoke from those burning bodies. I still can't get the smell out of my nose. I can hold my breath and the smell comes right out of my head, like it's lodged up in the far corners of my brain.

It is so weird to watch a face burn. First it gets black and the eyes go dead white, like boiled eggs, before they pop open, and then black stuff runs out. Then the face looks like it's grinning, but it's just the skin shrinking back and burning off the teeth. I tried not to look at the faces, but for some reason I couldn't help myself. I still see them in my nightmares.

The old-timers (some of whom had been here a whole month or more) laughed at us and thought it was the biggest joke. Yeah. Some joke. I can't wait to get our assignment and get the heck out of here. Wherever it is, it can't be any worse than this is. But even if it is, I am determined to be a man, do what I have to do, and get through it.

Write and tell me how you are, how the baby is, and what is happening in Sweet Valley. It seems very far away from this place.

Your friend,
Jerry

P.S. If you don't want me to tell you all this stuff, just let me know. I don't want to sugarcoat anything, but I know it is kind of rough, so I will do what you say. Needless to say, if you see my mother or father, don't say anything to them about what I have told you. Somehow, it does help if I can tell somebody about it, though. Maybe just to get it down on paper takes some of the curse away. Let me know. J.

31. *Carlene*

Dear Jerry,

 You can tell me anything you want to. I am not in the least bit squeamish, and I would like to know the truth of what is happening over there. I can't even imagine what it must be like to see so many dead bodies like that. I saw one once, and will never forget it. It does stay with you, all the time. I hope you get to a nicer place soon. But please don't think you have to keep anything from me. You could always tell me anything and it would go no further, you know that. Or I hope you do. I'm the close-mouth type, as you ought to know.

I am fine, working at the Water Witch a lot. Kevin is walking now, and getting into everything. He toddled over and put his little hand on the stove before I could stop him, and burned blisters on the palm. Thank goodness we had a pitcher of ice tea in the fridge, and stuck his hand in that until he quit screaming. Tea is the best thing for burns, did you know that? Don't ever use butter, because that just fries it. If you get a burn, grab you a tea bag, wet it, and wrap it over an ice cube, then put it on the burn and hold it there. It will stop the pain right away, I guarantee. It works with sunburn, too. Kevin was playing not thirty minutes after he did it. But he's getting to be a handful. You have to watch him every minute. We went right out then and there and got some of those folding gates to put around the stove. My mother keeps him at night while I work, and I stay with him in the daytime. It works out fine for both of us. She loves him like he is her own.

The Water Witch is a pretty good place to waitress. Baby Moreno has been working there since the summer, but now because school started, she's just there on the weekends. We have gotten to be pretty good friends. I always thought she was the nicest one of the girls from our class, not stuck-up and self-centered like some of them. Her boyfriend, Bean Boggs, is over there in Vietnam, too, I think someplace called Cu Chi. Is that near you? Do you ever get a chance to see each other? Ricky Don Sweet is there also, but I'm not sure where. I'll ask Baby. She might know. Wouldn't it be neat if all of y'all ran into each other?

It may be too soon to get into anything like this, but I want to be aboveboard from the beginning if we are going to keep on writing to each other. I won't ask you for an answer right now, but when you get back home, do you think we might get together, face to face, and just sit down and talk? I owe you a lot of explaining, I know, and I have a lot to tell you. Maybe it won't make it all right, but at least you will know the truth. I have held things bottled up inside of me for so long that it is going to be hard to tell anybody, even you. But maybe by the time you get back, I will be ready. Think about it. I will understand if you don't want to see me in person. Take care of yourself, Jerry.

Your friend,
Carlene

32. *Cherry*

 "Brethren, the Lord took ahold of Joshua and said, 'Joshua, look down there at Jericho. It's a fine city, and I'm going to give it to you as a city for your people, the children of Israel. But you have to do your part. What you have to do is take it away from the heathen that is already there, and it won't be easy.'

"And Joshua said to the Lord, 'Lord, how can we take this big city away from these people? They have a thick old high wall around it that we can't climb over.'

"The Lord said, 'Joshua, do you doubt Me now? After I brought you out of Egypt and got you this far, would I let you down now?'

"And Joshua said, 'Forgive me, Lord. I wasn't thinking. What do I do?'

"And the Lord said, 'You and your people go and march around the walls of that city seven times, and on the seventh go-around, all of y'all shout with a loud voice, and the walls will come tumbling down. I guarantee. Then what I want you to do is go in there and kill every single living thing. I mean, I don't want one chicken or donkey or child or old lady of those heathen left living. Then I want you to take all the silver and gold and iron and brass and put it in the temple of the Lord, and Jericho will be yours.'

"So, brethren, the people marched around the wall seven times, and they shouted, and the wall fell down flat. The people went up into the city . . . and they took the city.

"And they utterly destroyed all that was in the city, both man and woman, young and old, and ox, and sheep, and ass, with the edge of the sword. And they burnt the whole city with fire, and all that was therein."

———

Brother Wilkins was preaching from the Old Testament again. It was my least favorite part of his sermons, except for the one on hell. I really hated that one. "Tonight, we are going to talk about . . . *hell,*" he would say in this voice like doom, and then go on for an hour about all the ways to sizzle and fry and all the things you can do that will send you there. Those hell sermons always give me nightmares—I'd dream I was out in a pretty field or someplace and all of a sudden the clouds would open up and there God would be, pointing His finger at me for something I had done and forgot to ask forgiveness for, and the ground would open up and I would drop into the fiery pit. I'd wake up screaming and Daddy would come in to see what was the matter. Somehow, he never put two and two together that it was Brother Wilkins's hell sermons doing it to me.

The Old Testament sermons were a close second in the nightmare category. I mean, don't get me wrong—some of the stories were interesting, and of course it is all in the Holy Bible, but to tell you the honest truth, a lot of it really upset me. You know, think about it—God gave the children of Israel the promised land for their own, but there was one little problem: It was already settled with a whole country full of other people. So what did He tell them to do? Wipe out everyone and take it over. I just couldn't reconcile myself to the fact that even if they were heathen, babies and women and old men were getting their heads lopped off and guts ripped out, and people were moving right into their houses and taking their jewelry and stuff and in fact God told them to do it. I mean, really. There must have been someplace else the children of Israel could have gone.

But then you start thinking about all the wars and killing that have happened down through history from the beginning of time, when there were only four people on earth and one of them killed another one—Cain and Abel—and right on down through the Second World War, which was not all that long ago.

My daddy was over in Germany during that war, and while he didn't talk much about it to me, he was with the American troops who liberated the concentration camps.

I don't think Daddy was ever the same after the war, although obviously I didn't know him before, but Mama said that's when he got real religious. Once, she said he told her that when they came and opened those gates, the people were so starved that they looked like walking skeletons. He could put his finger and thumb around their arms and legs and still have room left. He actually saw piles of skinny bodies waiting to go into ovens, like you'd burn garbage in an incinerator. Before they put them in, the Nazis knocked out their gold teeth and cut off their hair to stuff mattresses with. He told her that a buddy of his found this box of leather wallets and each one of them had a tag that said *Made from the skin of a Jew.*

The two of them took the box and buried it outside the barbed wire of the camp and said a little prayer over it, which might have helped in some way. At least it made him and Daddy feel like they had done some little something, but the whole thing just boggles the mind.

And now, right at this very minute, there is Vietnam, with body counts and our boys getting killed and crippled when they ought to be playing basketball and going to the drive-in.

Maybe by the time Jesus came with His message of love, it was already too late, because man had developed a dark and evil side that was so ingrained in the genes that it would never be erased, no matter how much love he was given.

It was a scary subject, and if I thought too much about it, it made me anxious, like you get at three in the morning when you wake up from a nightmare with your heart pounding and realize that one of these days you are going to die.

Better to just daydream when the preachers preached and then sing gospel hymns, which at least was a lot more fun.

—

Anyhow, I was sorry that Tripp was sitting beside me at church during this sermon. I had convinced him to come with me, maybe because I was feeling guilty about what we were doing. Daddy was thrilled that I had a boyfriend who was interested in the church. I'm not going to get into it, but we had seen each other a lot since that first time, and each time was better than the last. He gave me a real crash course, so to speak, in lovemaking, which I seemed to take to without much urging. My face burned when I thought about the things we were doing. (At least we took Mama's advice and used some protection after that first time, so I wouldn't get pregnant.) I had no idea I would be like this. Most of the time I felt like I was walking on air several inches off the ground. Mama noticed it right away, of course. I kept singing around the house, and couldn't seem to wipe the smile off my face.

"What are you so happy about, Cherry? You're lit up like a Christmas tree," Mama said as she brought in a basket of clean laundry from the clothesline.

"I think I'm in love, Mama. I really do."

"Well. I figured that was coming. Are you sure you know enough about this Barlow boy? You haven't known him but a little over a month. We don't know anything at all about his family." She dumped out the clothes on the bed, and I helped her sort them.

"How long was it that you and Daddy went out before you got married?"

"We're not talking about your daddy and me."

"Two months? Was that it? Or was it six weeks?"

"It was seven weeks, but that's different."

"How is it different? You weren't even as old as I am. You were seventeen. You got your Mrs. degree before you got your high school diploma."

"We had gone to school together, even if he was a few years older than me. He was from here. We knew his people. Don't change the subject. Are you saying you're getting married?"

"No. I don't want to get married right now. I'm just in love. That's all. Remember what you said? You'd rather I . . ."

"I remember. You don't have to remind me."

She got busy folding clothes. She didn't want to look at me.

"I don't think I meant for you to run right out that minute, though, and . . . do anything. I was thinking maybe a few months down the road, if you got to know him, and the two of you talked about getting married and . . ." She sat down on the edge of the bed. "Do you want to tell me about it?"

"Mama . . . I don't think so. I don't think I can."

"That's all right. I don't think I really want to know, either."

"Keep a little mystery in the relationship, right?"

"Right."

That was an old joke with us. Mama never would let Daddy or me in the bathroom with her or walk around undressed, and I was the same way. "Let's keep a little mystery in the relationship," she'd say. It worked for me. We all need a few things that belong to ourselves alone.

This way, she knew, but she didn't know for sure, so she didn't really have to face what I was doing. And although I kept waiting for the mighty hand of God to strike me down, it didn't seem to. I didn't even feel all that guilty. Maybe the Devil had so completely taken me over that I was unaware he had done it. That was another danger of growing up in the Holiness Church. You found yourself thinking of everything as either being done by God or the Devil. In truth, if they spent as much time messing in our lives as we thought, they would never get another thing accomplished.

Brother Wilkins was not the greatest of speakers, as I may have already said, bless his heart. He was from the old school of preacher that danced around on the stage, slapped his hands together a lot, and spoke in a loud singsong voice with a lot of gasping and saying "Ah" between each word or two, like, "Brethren, ah, as we gather together here tonight, ah, hallelujah, ah, to praise Jesus, ah, we come with humble hearts, ah, and . . ." You get the picture. I counted once, and he said *ah* 133 times during the message. He let fly with spit, too, as he spoke, and if you were sitting on the front row, you had to watch it. Seeing him through Tripp's eyes, I wished it was Brother Dane up there instead. There was just something about Brother Dane that caught you up, made you want some of whatever it was he had: life; enthusiasm; charisma.

Brother Wilkins was going into great and gory detail about the Israelites killing every baby, old lady, dog, and chicken and not daring to leave anything breathing, because that would have gone against what God had said. Tripp started to fidget.

"I'm going to go out and have a smoke," he whispered.

I didn't blame him. I wished I could go with him, but Daddy would have killed me. We were sitting in the back row, though, so Tripp didn't cause too much of a commotion when he left. He stayed outside until after the altar call, and when everyone closed their eyes for prayer, I sneaked out and found him sitting in the car out under the trees at the edge of the parking lot, with the windows rolled down, smoking.

"Are you okay?"

"I'm fine. Sorry about that. I don't know what happened. I all of a sudden got a flashback or something when the preacher started talking about what happened in Jericho. I had to get out of there."

"You mean about Vietnam?"

"Yeah. That is not something you can just get on a plane and leave behind, you know? I'm afraid it might be with me the rest of my life. I never know when it will hit. Sometimes I'll be doing the most mundane things—drinking a beer and reading a book, or cleaning the carburetor in the car—and I have to stop in my tracks because it all comes back; the enormity of it takes my breath away, and I can't move."

I wasn't sure he wanted to talk about it, but given what I saw on the news every night and what he had told me about Jerry, he must have seen some killing.

"So, you actually saw a lot of killing? I mean, did you ever . . ."

"Did I see a lot of killing? Yes. There was a lot of killing in Vietnam."

The way he said it let me know he wasn't interested in answering any questions about who all he had killed any more than he wanted to tell me about the other girls he had slept with.

"But I really don't want to talk about it. If I talk about it, it will grow and get stronger. If I keep it tight inside my head, maybe it will finally shrivel and dry up."

"Okay. We don't have to talk about it. I'm sorry. I wish Brother Wilkins hadn't picked that subject. I didn't like it much, myself."

"Are all his sermons like that? I kind of enjoyed the other preacher, you know, the night you washed feet. Brother . . . what's his name?"

"Brother Dane."

"Yeah. That was a guy I could relate to."

"I bet. You seem a lot like him. Well, who knows? Maybe you'll be a preacher one day."

He laughed. "I don't think you would like that. In my religion, to be a preacher means you have to give up women."

"You mean become a priest? You're a Catholic?"

"I was raised a Catholic. I'm not anymore."

"You're the first Catholic—ex-Catholic—I ever went out with. What were the services like at your church? I bet at least you didn't have the sermons about hell and Jericho, did you?"

"No, but we had the saints crammed down our throats from the time we were infants. Pretty bloody and vicious, the way they killed most of them. Like Saint Apollonia, the healer of toothaches. They tortured her by pulling all her teeth out and then burned her at the stake. Becoming a saint was not a great career choice. It seems like every religion is full of killing, doesn't it?"

He lit another cigarette off the butt of the one he was smoking. This sure wasn't the time to mention it, but that was the one thing about him

I could have done without, the amount he smoked. At least the windows were rolled down.

Church had let out and people were standing around on the porch, talking and smoking. A lot of Holiness men smoked, and even a few women. If I was going to pick something that was a sin, I would pick smoking over a lot of other things, but most of them didn't feel that way, probably because they liked to smoke.

Mama came out and stood on the steps looking around for us. Then she saw us and waved, came on out to the car, and leaned down to look in the window.

"Cherry, is everything all right? Tripp's not sick, is he? You're not sick, are you, Tripp?"

"No, I'm all right, Mrs. Marshall. I wasn't feeling too well, but I'm better now. It was probably just too hot in there."

"Is there anything I can do, or get you?"

"No, Mama. Maybe we'll go get a Coke at the Freezer Fresh. That might make him feel better. Don't worry. I'll be home after while."

We waved to her as we took off. Neither of us mentioned the war again, and it seemed like, at least for now, I left God and the Devil back at the church.

33. *Vietnam*

Christmas Night, 1967

Dear Carlene,

 You know we can see each other and talk when I get back. I don't think things will ever be like they once were, but who knows? Don't worry about it. We have a lot of time until then. It is eleven months until I get home. We don't have to decide anything now.

How was your Christmas? We're here in a place called Gilligan's Island, just for a few days. (A lot of jokes about the Skipper and company, of course.) It is a small island that is a fishing village on the South China Sea, still in Quang Ngai.

Our captain somehow managed to get us a Christmas tree, and we had a big dinner tonight, but it sure wasn't anything like I would have gotten at home. We sat around singing carols, though. Old favorites like "O Little Town of Ban Me Thuot," "God Rest Ye General Westmoreland," "Deck the Halls with Victor Charlie," and a few others I can't mention in mixed company.

As far as contact with the enemy goes, there hasn't been much. The guys before us pretty well searched and destroyed everything around this area. I would estimate that ninety percent of the houses were burned, and most of the people have relocated. What we have been mostly doing is guarding bridges and practicing our search-and-destroy in the deserted villages that are left. A lot of the guys are real unhappy that they haven't had any gooks to kill, but I'm not. In fact, I'm not so sure I could kill a man, gook or not, if it came right down to it. I mean, I think I could if he was coming at me and it was self-defense, but what if I just saw one minding his own business? Could I shoot him in cold blood? That, I don't know.

The hardest thing to get used to over here is the living conditions of the people. They have nothing—I mean literally nothing—and live almost like prehistoric people. They squat by the fire and eat their little bowls of rice, scooping it into their mouths with their fingers, but to them it is as good as steak and potatoes. When they need to go to the bathroom, they just drop their drawers and squat right wherever they are—on the trail, in the field, anywhere—in front of God and everybody, and don't even wipe. I dread like heck to step in a pile of it, but you can't avoid it. A lot of the guys hate the Vietnamese, but I feel sorry for them. The kids are the most pitiful. They are wormy little beggars, all the time wanting gum or candy or C rations. "Numbah-one GI!" They have learned to say. "Numbah-ten VC!" Our lieutenant hates it when we give them anything and runs them off, but I sneak them something once in a while. It's funny, this attitude most GIs have about the Vietnamese, like they are all worrisome dogs or something. The whole purpose of this war is supposed to be to save them from the Communists. They are supposed to be our allies, but the lieutenant is scared of all of them—even the kids—because there's no way to tell where their loyalties lie. The Cong use them to set booby traps. The kid you give a Hershey bar to today might be the one who sets a trap that gets you killed tomorrow. This area around here is supposed to be a bad booby-trap area, but so far, so good. It won't be long, I think, until we go out on patrol for real. Then we'll see what we are made of. I am almost looking forward to it.

Take care of yourself. Say hi to Baby, and tell her and everyone else to write to me. Letters from home mean a lot.

Your friend,
Jerry

P.S. It is now two in the morning, and I couldn't sleep. I've been thinking about what you said, about wanting to tell me some things. Maybe you should write me the big secret. Nobody will read it, and I will burn the letter if you say to. It might be easier than saying it in person. Then we will know for sure what the score is before we see each other. But only if you really want me to know. I do think we have to have no secrets between us if we see each other again. And if we can't deal with it, we'll know that, too. Think about it. J.

34. Baby

 Sometime after Jerry died, in the spring of 1968, Carlene started working the banquets. She tried to keep it from Baby, but Rita let it slip.

"Carlene was working there?" Baby asked after Rita mentioned Carlene had burned her arm on a candle at a banquet. "How long has she been doing that?"

"Oh, nearly six months now. You mean you didn't know?" Rita said, her eyes wide.

It hurt Baby's feelings that Carlene hadn't told her, but more than that, it really ate at her that she was being left out. Why should everyone but her get the big tips? By now, Baby knew that the banquets were pretty much an excuse for men to go out with girls they weren't married to. And Rita made no bones about what she did with those men. She showed Baby some pictures of herself taken in a motel room.

"Hey, Baby. Take a gander at these." Rita handed her a stack of black-

and-white photos. In them, she was wearing a black bra and G-string, black garter belt, and white fishnet stockings. She had darkened up the Marilyn Monroe mole on her left cheek with an eyebrow pencil and had on her usual pound and a half of makeup.

Baby's eyes bugged out. In one of the pictures, Rita was lying on a bed with her legs in the air, and the only thing hiding the whole works was the thin crotch of her black panties. Her boobs were pulled out of the top of the bra and squashed together in the middle of her chest. She had the biggest nipples Baby had ever seen—they almost covered her enormous breasts. Rolls of fat pooched out around the tight elastic of the garter belt. She was biting a string of dime-store pearls and looking at the camera through half-closed eyelids. It was gross.

All the pictures were pretty much like that, except they were in different poses. Looking at them one after another, Baby couldn't help but giggle.

"Oh, Rita, these are the funniest things I've ever seen!"

"Funny? What do you mean, Baby?" Rita said, snatching them out of her hand. "Can't you see they're very sexy? I was paid a lot of money to pose for these pictures." She carefully slid them into an envelope and put them away in her purse.

"I'm sorry, Rita. I didn't mean it that way. I've just never seen any-thing . . . like that. You're right. They *are* sexy. Who took them?"

"I can't tell you, but he knows somebody who makes porno movies and he thinks I can be a big star."

"Are you serious? You want to be in porno movies? Why?"

"Why do you think? I've been giving it away for free, so why not get something out of it? Besides, they aren't even shown in America. They send them to Europe and Sweden and places like that. He says I definitely have the body for it. They appreciate big-boned women in Europe and Sweden."

"Does Jackie know about this?"

"What? So he can take a piece of the action? I think not. And you bet-ter not tell him either."

"Oh, right. You know I'm going to rush right up and tell him. But what about the guy who took them? Where did you meet him?"

"At a banquet. He's an old friend of Jackie's. And now he's an old friend of mine."

"Is that what you do at the banquets?"

Rita laughed. "No, you silly thing. What do you think—I get up on the table with my clothes off? It's just drinking and eating, with a little music and dancing. What people do afterwards is their own business."

"Well, if it's all so innocent, why won't Jackie let me work at one?"

"Sweetheart, have you looked in the mirror lately? Jackie and Park think you're the Oriental Ivory Snowflake queen. You must remind them of their sister or something.

"Now, you better not tell anybody I told you all this, or you and me will both be in big trouble. I mean it, now."

"I'd still like to go, just once. If Carlene can do it, I can too. You could get me in. Please, Rita. Pretty please, with sugar on it."

It was exciting and scary, the thought of being in the same room with so many famous people—and wicked ones, who had dealings with porno. But mainly, Baby wanted to go just to show Jackie that he wasn't the boss of her. His letting Carlene work the banquets but not her was one more in a long string of slights, and she was getting sick of it.

Bean would be home in a couple of months, and although she probably would have to stop seeing Jackie anyhow, he had told her that if she went back to Bean, it was over between them. As if Jackie would ever be true to *her*! She knew she should quit working at the Water Witch, but it wasn't so easy to just walk away like nothing had ever happened, as if none of it meant anything.

"Please, Rita. Will you get me in?"

Rita narrowed her eyes. Baby could almost see the wheels turning in her head, and knew she was probably up to no good, but it didn't matter if she could get to a banquet.

Rita sighed, as if Baby had worn her down. "Oh, all right. There's one a week from Tuesday. Jackie will be in Little Rock, so I'll be in charge. I'll leave the kitchen door unlocked, and you can sneak in. Park always fixes the food earlier, so the kitchen will be empty. But you better watch your tail, because if you get caught, I'll lie and say I had nothing to do with it— and you know Jackie will believe me."

———

Tuesday night finally came. Baby changed clothes three times, but in the end she decided to wear her waitress uniform. That way, she could just tell everyone she was working.

Baby switched off her car lights as she eased into the long gravel driveway of the Water Witch. Her glow-in-the-dark watch said it was one o'clock.

The dining room was dark, but the back room was lit up like a lantern. She left the green Volkswagen down by the marina and went up the walk around the back. Music and laughter boomed out across the long lawn. The kitchen door was unlocked, as Rita had promised.

Baby stumbled over the dirty linen bags waiting for early laundry pickup and sat down on the pile, hard, with a small *"Oof."* She listened for a minute, but nobody seemed to have heard. Her wrist stung where she had scraped it on the counter.

In the dark kitchen, a skinny ray of colored light squeezed out between the double doors to the banquet room. Hearing Rita's screech of a laugh above the noise, Baby opened the doors a crack. She had never even been in the back room before. It was kept locked.

There didn't seem to be anyone near this entrance, and Baby slipped inside and moved to the corner. It took a few seconds for her eyes to adjust to the lights. The back room was nothing like the elegant restaurant; it had the feeling of a gaudy Gypsy tent. Loud music blasted from a stereo. Suspended from the ceiling, a faceted mirrored globe spun above a small dance floor. As it turned, it picked up light from red, green, amber, and blue lamps and candles scattered around the room and flung it back against the walls, which were covered in silver-colored paper. The air shimmered. There were lush Oriental rugs on the floor and low red velvet banquettes against the walls. Little round tables were everywhere.

Rita was draped over a barstool. She was wearing a gold lamé hostess gown with a neckline that plunged nearly to her waist. Her breasts were clearly visible when she leaned over, as she was doing now.

The man sitting next to her on the barstool handed her the tube to a water pipe. Rita inhaled a cloud of smoke as bubbles formed inside the globe, then leaned over and blew smoke into his mouth. Everywhere Baby looked, men were kissing and fondling girls—on the dance floor, in the booths. Some were stretched out on the rugs. The air was hazy with pungent smoke. It brought to life a painting by Hieronymus Bosch. Before coming here, Baby had tried to imagine what it would be like, but she was still shocked to see it all out in the open like this.

Carlene passed by with a tray of drinks and caught sight of Baby, who was trying to blend into the woodwork.

"Baby! What are you doing here?"

"Sh! I just wanted to see what went on. I'll only stay a minute."

"Oh, Baby, I wish you hadn't come."

"Why didn't you tell me you were working the banquets, Carlene? What did you think I'd do?"

"I don't know. I just didn't want you to know. I thought you'd think less of me, I guess."

"Why would I think less of you?"

"The girls who work here are party girls, Baby. You know what that means?"

"Not exactly."

"It means that they're here to drink and dance, and if they want to, they sleep with the guys."

"You mean for money?"

"Money. Presents, favors—whatever. Nobody has to do anything they don't want to, but yeah. That's what the banquets are. There's a hefty cover charge for the drinks and drugs, which Jackie provides, along with the company of all these girls."

"Are you serious? Wow." Looking more closely, Baby could see that she knew a lot of the girls from around the county. "Carlene—you don't . . . I mean . . ."

"No, I don't." Her voice was small.

"I'm sorry. I shouldn't have asked you that."

"It's all right. I don't blame you for asking. I do have a boyfriend, though, who helps me out a little. I'm saving up to get to California, like we talked about. I hope you're not mad at me, Baby."

"Why would I be mad at you, Carlene? I just wish you had told me, though. I wouldn't have thought less of you. You're doing it for a reason."

Just then, Rita caught sight of Baby and came over, giving her friend with the pipe a pat on his backside as she got up.

"Hello, dollface. I see you made it."

"I should have known you were behind this, Rita," Carlene said stiffly. She turned to Baby. "Okay. You're a big girl, Baby. Have fun. I'm working." Carlene left with her tray and started delivering drinks. Rita put her arm around Baby. She smelled like smoke—a pungent tang that wasn't like any smoke Baby had smelled before.

"Look at this crowd. Isn't it exciting? That was Weston Bartlett I was talking to. He owns TV and radio stations, advertising agencies—you name it, he owns it. Over there is Don Brandon, the weatherman on

Channel Six, and Merle Ferguson, a big lawyer from Little Rock. That's Judge Greer in the corner with Brenda." Baby squinted to see the gray-haired judge nestled into a banquette with one of the girls. They were smoking from a water pipe, too.

"Rita, there's marijuana here," Baby whispered. "That's against the law!"

"Sure it is."

"Well, aren't they afraid they will get caught?"

"Who's going to catch them? The judge is right here, and so are the lawyers. You don't think they would rat on each other, do you? How could they do that without incriminating themselves?"

Baby stared. Rita was right. Who were they going to tell? The judge who was sitting there smoking had sentenced a guy she knew from Du-Vall to twenty years in the pen for possession of marijuana. He was famous for being tough on kids who were caught with even one joint. A lot of them were sitting in prison right now. Baby had a sick feeling in the pit of her stomach. The hypocrisy of it all was alarming. If you couldn't trust the judges and the lawyers, who could you trust?

She jumped when she felt a hand nudge her on the shoulder.

"Can a guy get a scotch around here?" The voice was deep, as if it had been cured in cigarette smoke for years. He was back-lit, from the mirrored globe, and Baby squinted, trying to see his face. He thought she was a waitress. Well, why not? She had on her uniform.

"I'm not supposed to tend bar," Baby answered.

The man stepped back and looked hard at Baby. "You work here?"

"Well, usually I work the dinner shift on weekends, but tonight I'm helping Rita."

"I don't think Rita needs any help," the man said, laughing. Rita was back at the bar.

The kitchen door swung open then and Jackie came in. One of the part-time cashiers was draped around him. He was staggering a little, drunk, and the woman's hot-pink lipstick was smeared all over her mouth and chin. A pang of jealousy hit Baby hard. She was used to Jackie's flirting, but she had never had it thrown in her face like this before. She should have known that Rita was lying about him being in Little Rock.

He waved and called out greetings, then spotted Baby, who tried to hide behind her companion. The man put his arm around her waist as Jackie came up to them. His eyes were liquid red, a little unfocused.

"I like your new girl, Jackie. You're bringing them in younger and younger. This one looks about fourteen."

Jackie looked straight at Baby and flashed a smile. "Well, Frank O'Reilly, you old son-a-ma-gun! When did you get back in town? How the hell are you? This is Baby. She's not regular banquet help. In fact, I'm not sure what she is doing here, but she *is* twenty-one."

His voice was smooth but hard as he turned toward Baby. "Did you miss your ride home tonight, Baby?"

"No, I'm here with Franco," she lied.

"In your uniform?"

"I didn't have time to change." Baby took Franco's other arm and put it around her shoulders. He was tall, and the top of her head only came to the middle of his chest. He felt like a wall behind her, helping her face Jackie's anger.

Franco's eyebrows lifted slightly, and he almost smiled, but didn't. Baby could feel his breath blowing her hair; the warm scent of scotch wafted around her.

"Franco needs a scotch, Jackie."

"Park can make it. He's behind the bar."

Baby's heart froze. She hadn't noticed Park, but he had noticed her. Now, looking at him, she could see that his jaw was clenched. Baby felt his fury and disappointment burn a hole in her chest.

Franco took Baby by the arm, and they walked to the bar. "Cutty, neat," Franco ordered.

"Nothing for me, Park, thanks," Baby said, as if he had asked. Park picked up the bottle of Cutty Sark, poured it without taking his eyes off Baby, and set it on the bar. As Franco reached for the glass, Park's hand went around his wrist. The drink spilled. Franco looked at him, surprised, and tried to pull away, but Park had the advantage. A silent game of arm wrestling began, each man rigid, fixed in an arm lock.

Baby stood rooted at the bar, watching the struggle, afraid to move or speak. Franco was bigger than Park, but Park was all wiry muscle. Jackie ambled over, as if he were coming to watch an amusing game. He laughed, slapped Park on the back, and said something in Chinese. Without taking his eyes off Franco, Park spoke.

"Baby has an early class tomorrow. She has to leave." Then he let go of Franco's wrist.

Franco rubbed the wrist and straightened his sleeve. "I'll walk her to her car."

"See you on Saturday, Baby," Jackie said as she and Franco started toward the door. His words were calm, but his voice was strained. A large vein was throbbing in his temple. "Drop by the office before you start the shift."

Baby looked over her shoulder at Park. He was busy wiping the bar with angry swipes and didn't watch her leave.

Franco put his arm around Baby's shoulders as they walked toward the VW. She caught another whiff of scotch as he leaned down to kiss her. She turned her head, and his lips brushed her cheek.

"I get the picture," he said. "Jackie's a lucky guy and is too stupid to know it. If he gives you any trouble, give me a call."

He stepped back and opened the car door for her. She got in and shut the door. He leaned down and spoke through the open window.

"You smell like fresh jasmine. I bet you taste like moonlight." He ran the back of his finger down her cheek, gently, like a butterfly wing. Then he walked away.

———

Too keyed up to go home, Baby drove into town, around the sleeping streets of Sweet Valley. Most of the houses were dark. Inside, babies were asleep in their cribs; men and women were deep in the last hours of good sleep before they had to get up for their seven o'clock shift. They were all so normal, and decent.

After a while, Baby found herself in front of Cherry's house. It was an older two-story house with a wide porch and a dark green swing. At the side of the house was a big empty lot they called the clover patch. When they were kids, they used to search every inch of that patch on their hands and knees, looking for four-leaf clovers, waving away the bees that lit on the sweet-smelling purple flowers. They almost never got stung, because the bees were too busy taking the nectar to notice them, but once Cherry sat smack down on top of one. It had scared Baby to death when Cherry jumped up screaming and pulled down her pants, right out there in the daytime.

Baby smiled, remembering, then looked up at the dark windowpanes of Cherry's room on the top floor. Baby imagined her asleep under the orange-and-yellow coverlet, stuffed animals tossed onto the floor, a soft cool breeze from the attic fan blowing across the bed.

She sat for a long time, looking at the clover patch and the Marshalls' house in the fading moonlight and wondered about Carlene. Maybe after Jerry was killed, she had just given up and decided to get some money any way she could, just to get out of town, start over fresh where nobody knew her. Goodness knows that the people in this town never gave her anything but the rough side of their tongue when she was down. Why she had kept it a secret from Baby was obvious: Carlene was ashamed.

Baby felt so tired. Dirty. She wanted to be a little girl again, her and Cherry, wanted to play in the clover patch with no worries except being stung by bees—no wars; no boys dying; nobody doing drugs or selling their body.

She would call Cherry tomorrow and tell her they'd work together at the pickle plant this summer. Bean would be home soon, and she would tell Jackie Lim where he could put his banquets. She was through with the Water Witch. Let Carlene do what she had to. Baby wouldn't be part of it anymore.

It made her sick that she had cared so much for Jackie. He had so little character. If he wasn't a pimp and a drug dealer, he was the closest thing to it. She vowed then that she would be true to Bean and make it up to him when he got back. And hope he never found out what she had done while he was away.

Then she started the car and went back toward the lake and home.

35. *Vietnam*

Feb. 2, 1968

Dear Carlene,

If I ever wished for some action, I got my wish, because we sure had it the last two days. We're up at a place called LZ Dottie, about 12 miles north of Quang Ngai City, which I may have told you is a pretty big town, and is the headquarters for the 2nd ARVN division—that's the South Vietnamese army. We hadn't had much in the way of action for a while, just setting the base up. It was getting ready to be a truce, because of a holiday they have over here called Tet. That's kind of like the Fourth of July and Christmas and Thanksgiving all rolled into one, and we were supposed to have thirty-six hours off while everyone—Viet Cong and ARVN, both—partied, like they do every year. We were going to have our own party, as you can imagine.

Anyhow, we had the party, and just after four o'clock in the morning on January 31, all h*** broke loose and the VC launched an all-out attack. We were all in bed, most of us having had a little to drink the night before—yes, even me, I hate to tell you—not thinking there was going to be any action, and we were lifted out of our beds by a mortar attack that sounded like it was right on top of us. I never got my boots on so fast in my life. The adrenaline shot through my body like it was high-test straight from the pump.

They were hitting everything at QN City—the airfield, the headquarters of the ARVN, hospitals, churches—everything was sitting there like ducks in the water. Even more scary than that was we could see the munitions dumps going up sixty miles away at Chu Lai. If they were hitting a big city like Chu Lai, then we were dog meat. We were out there in this little old firebase and there was no place to go or nothing we could do. If they wanted to take us out they could, without breaking a sweat.

Finally we got it together and started firing back, and the big guns came rolling in. Charlie Co. was moved out a few miles to a place called Hill 102 to try and block the enemy's line of retreat, but it was strictly out of our area of operations, and the ARVNs should have been the ones sent to where we were, not us. They have these rules about where they fight and where we fight, but it was so disorganized and nobody knew what they were doing, so they sent us there anyhow.

We found out that it was the 48th Local Force Battalion of the VC that overran the training center of Quang Ngai, and it took until early yesterday morning for them to finally fold under all the firepower we threw at them, and they started their retreat—right in front of us. You won't believe it, but we were ordered not to fire on them, that it was not our jurisdiction but the ARVN's, which we knew already, but if they weren't going to let us fire at them, then why the heck did they send us out there in the first place? We were all really frustrated, I can tell you.

We watched those suckers, in their black pajamas, walk out right under

224 · *Norris Church Mailer*

our noses, and there was nothing we could do. They were heading up toward Pinkville, which is a group of villages not too far from here. The captain did his best to cut through the red tape and let us fire, but by the time he got the word, they were long gone. I will tell you this—we are going to get those gooks if it's the last thing we do.

We heard today that they attacked not only us up here but all over South Vietnam—even Saigon was hit hard. I don't think all the talk about the war nearly being won means anything if they can mount an attack like this one. I would bet we are in for a long haul. I just hope I can do my time and get out of here in one piece.

Sorry to go on so about this. I know you probably aren't interested in the war, but it seems like that's all I have to talk about.

One funny thing, though. Or really it's not so funny. Did I tell you about the rats over here? You have never seen rats like the ones in Vietnam. They are as big as cats, and a lot of them carry rabies. When you dig a bunker, the first thing you do is look for rats, because you can be sure they will be right down in there with you. I have to admit I'm as scared of the rats as I am of the VC. Anyhow, the other night, we were in bed, all covered up in spite of the heat, with our blankets tucked tight around us, even over our heads, so the rats wouldn't get in, when Barlow—I think I told you about him, my buddy from San Francisco—jumped straight up, grabbed his gun, and started blasting away. We thought we were being attacked, and of course all of us grabbed our weapons and started firing, too. It turns out that a rat had gotten in bed with Barlow, and Barlow blew the rat all to pieces. Unfortunately, he shot up his bed, too, and it was just a miracle that we didn't all kill each other in the process, or that he didn't get bit. One of the guys was not so lucky. He couldn't sleep with his head under the covers and a rat bit him in the face. Took a chunk out, the size of a half dollar, if you can believe it. He had to have those shots that they give you in the stomach that hurt like heck, and plastic surgery. It got all infected and turned out to be his ticket home, but he will have a hole in his face the rest of his life, and have to tell everyone that his Purple Heart came from a rat bite. If it is not one thing over here, it's something else.

We are going on patrol tomorrow. If we see the 48th, permission or not, we are going to stitch their butts. Write soon and tell me what all is going on. What is Kevin up to? Did you ever find out where Ricky Don is? If

Bean is in Cu Chi, that is not very close to here. Anybody else we know over here? I miss everyone. I miss you. And I really wish you would tell me what the secret is.

Love,
Jerry

36. Carlene

Dear Jerry,

 We heard all about the Tet offensive, they're calling it over here. It is the biggest thing that has happened in a long time. Walter Cronkite said that the war is going to end in a stalemate. Do you think that is true? The worst thing is that it is giving them a reason to escalate the war even more. I can't believe you were right in the middle of it. I watch TV every night, thinking I might see you. Do you ever see any TV crews where you are? Those guys are pretty brave to follow the soldiers around right in the middle of battle and all, with no guns to defend themselves.

I wish there was something I could say to help you make it easier, but things like "Take care of yourself" are useless. I know you will do the best you can, and all we can do is trust in God to take care of you. I always thought you had a guardian angel, so maybe she went to Nam with you. I know your mama and daddy and probably his whole church are praying for you, and I do believe that prayer works.

There is nothing new, really, to tell you since the last time I wrote. Work and taking care of Kevin. That's my life. I am not seeing anybody right now. Not that I don't want to, but there just isn't anybody I'm interested in. I guess I'm still carrying a torch for a tall, good-looking guy who is in the boonies of Vietnam.

Oh, Jerry, I cried when you signed your last letter "Love." Even if you don't mean it, no fooling, I do still love you so much. I try not to, but I can't help myself. I always will, and if you can't forgive me, I will survive, but I will never be happy again. Not like I was when we were together.

I have thought and thought and worried about telling you everything, and I still don't know if I will mail this letter or not after I write it, but I know in my heart I have to if we are going to ever have anything together. We have to start all over if we can, and the only way to do that is to be honest with each other and vow to always tell each other the truth from this minute on. This will be long, but I have to start at the beginning so you understand everything that went on later. So here goes. Buckle your seat belt. You're in for a rocky ride.

There is no way to ease into this, so here it is: I shot and killed my daddy when I was thirteen. He was trying to kill himself and couldn't do it, so he put the gun in my hands and tried to make me do it. I don't think I meant to pull the trigger, but I'm not sure. Maybe I did mean to. I was young, but I can't hide behind that. We never got along all that great, and it ended up with him attacking me pretty bad, but I don't need to get into that right now. The point is, he's dead, so there it is. Everyone thought he ran out on Mama and me, but he is down at the bottom of the quarry in his pickup truck. I was afraid for years that somebody would find out and the law would come knocking on our door and take me away, but I guess nobody cared enough to find out what happened to him.

Walter Tucker knows, though, because he helped me push the truck off into the quarry. In fact, it was his idea, and that has been part of the problem. Afterward, he started coming over a lot, and before long he was like a ghost haunting our house. I guess in a way he had a good heart for trying to help me, but sometimes I wished he would have just called the law and got it all over with. When you have to keep a secret like that, it takes over everything in your life. I hated to even see Walter's face; every time I looked at him I saw my daddy, but there was nothing I could do about it because he sweet-talked my mother and for a long time was almost like a part of our family. I couldn't have a minute's privacy, because he was always there, eating out of our refrigerator, sitting on our couch, watching TV, making a mess for us to clean up all the time. He got to be as bad as my daddy was, and I didn't feel like I could say anything to my mother about him because I was scared he'd tell her what we had done. It got to where I found reasons not to go home. At least they didn't get married, but, Jerry, I swear sometimes I felt like I couldn't stand being around him one more minute. I just wanted to die.

When I met you and we started going out, it was like I had a new chance. I was really, almost, like the girls in our class who had boyfriends and necked at the drive-in. Even though I could never undo what I had done, I wanted to be clean, for you, and although I could never be a virgin again after what my daddy did, I could be washed in the blood of Jesus Christ and start a whole new page in my life.

At least that's what I found out when I went to a revival. It was one of those funny things that happen to you—one of those little things you don't think anything about at the time but changes your life forever, you know? After you and I had been going out for a few months, I went into the post office one day to get some stamps, and Mr. Marshall, Cherry Marshall's daddy, waited on me, and we started talking and he asked if I had a church to go to. I said no, and he invited me out to the Holiness, where he was a deacon, and then he told me about this revival that Brother Dane Harkness was holding in a little church up on the Ridge and said I might like to go to that, since a lot of young people went to hear him. I never knew Brother Dane to talk to, but everyone said he was the best preacher around here, and, Jerry, I felt like my soul was so black with sin that I needed the best to help me, so that same night I went up there all by myself.

It seemed like everything he said was meant right for me when he talked about his rough experiences and how he used to be headed straight for hell until he gave his life to Jesus. I have felt like I was already in hell ever since the day I pulled that trigger and became partners with Walter Tucker.

I went up to the altar that night and accepted Jesus as my Lord and Savior. Brother Dane and all the ladies in the church prayed with me, and I felt a load lift off my spirit like I hadn't had in years. I never told you about all this at the time, because I knew what a good Christian you were, and I guess I felt like if you knew I had just gotten saved you would somehow know that I had been an awful sinner or something, and there was no way I could ever tell you what I had done. It was best to just pretend that I had always been a Christian, like I told your daddy when he asked me.

Anyhow, that night I stayed and talked to Brother Dane for a long time after the service, and he seemed to understand a lot about sin and forgiveness. I knew in my heart that I had been forgiven, but I needed to tell somebody all about it, in detail, not just say, "Forgive me of all my sins," and leave it at that. I guess I wanted somebody to help me get over it, because I knew I couldn't do it by myself. I said that I needed to tell him some things in private, and he agreed to come out to the trailer and talk to me one afternoon. He was the nicest man I had ever met. The love and the power just flowed out of him when he looked at me, and I really needed some love at that point—not like the love you and I had, but a love from God that would wash away my sins. I had been trying to carry the whole burden too long.

Oh, Jerry, I can't tell you why what happened that day did—I don't even know myself—but I'll try.

It was a hot afternoon, and Mama was off at work when he drove up in the yard a couple of days later. I thanked him for coming, asked him if he'd like to have a cold drink, and we went into the trailer to get some ice tea. Then we sat in the living room drinking our tea, and I told him everything—I mean everything—about Daddy and Walter and how much I loved you. I cried, and it was like Jesus Himself was listening to my troubles. It felt so good to finally let somebody know the horrible truth, to not care what happened, because I knew that it was going to be all right, that I wasn't a bad person and Jesus loved me and forgave me.

And then he talked. He told me some things about himself, how he still struggled every day of his life with sin and temptation, that he understood what I had gone through, and that there was nothing that you couldn't get over and go on from, with the help of Jesus. I felt so close to him, Jerry, like I never had to anybody else, because I was finally free of the secret.

We got down on our knees to pray, and he put his arm around me, and the feeling of his sweaty arm on my back and shoulders made me so warm and light-headed, and before I knew what was happening, we were in each other's arms hugging, and then we were kissing and our clothes were all over the floor and we were tearing at each other like two cats in heat, and it was glorious. Even if it hurts you, Jerry, I can't pretend it wasn't. Maybe all those nights of you and me necking and holding ourselves back built up a dam inside of me, and Brother Dane just happened to be there to open the floodgates, but when they opened, the heavens washed down, and right there on the floor of the trailer, Kevin was conceived.

I don't know what you are thinking about me right now, but I want you to know that it never happened between us again. Brother Dane got dressed and went outside and sat on the steps and put his head in his hands and sobbed like a baby. He is such a good man and has tried so hard to overcome his wild past, but there was no way in this world that either one of us could have stopped what happened that afternoon.

I swore I would never tell anybody, and up to now, I kept my word. When I knew I was pregnant, I never told Brother Dane the baby was his, even though he found out about it and came and asked me. I didn't want for him to think he had to marry me, and I didn't want to marry him, because I was in love with you. I let him and some other people think it was yours, and that was my biggest sin, because you were so good and so innocent that I guess I hoped somehow you would love me anyhow, and yes, I did try to get you to go all the way and then you would think the baby was yours, and that might be the thing you can never forgive me for. But I felt like I was punished when you broke up with me. All I had then was my pride, and let me tell you it was a job to try and keep any pride with the way this town is and all.

But, Jerry, if I'm honest, I can't, even now, after all that has happened, say I'm sorry for getting pregnant, because when I look at Kevin, I feel like he is a gift from God. I don't know what plan God has for me, or for you, or for Kevin, but I know in my heart that he will be somebody someday. And if you can still talk to me after all this, then you are, in truth, a big person with a big heart, and I swear I will work my fingers to the bone for you as long as I live. If you can't, then I understand. If I was in your shoes, I don't know what I would do. I really don't. The only good thing is that Mama finally broke up with Walter. I don't know what she ever saw in him in the first place, but I guess she was lonesome, and I sure know now what that is like.

After I found out that I was going to have the baby, I told my mama everything, about what Daddy did and about what Walter and I did with him. Everything except who the father of the baby was. I let her think it was you, and that was wrong, but I couldn't betray Brother Dane, even to my mother.

Not long after that, Walter made the mistake of driving up in our yard. Mama was out working in the garden, and when he got out of the truck, she went after him, yelling like you never heard the like, about how could he do what he did and let a child carry the load of believing all these years that she had killed her miserable daddy, afraid that she was going to be hauled off to jail any minute, and not even be able to tell her mama when she needed her the most, who—on top of it all—he had lied to and made believe that her husband was off somewhere and was just too sorry to write or call and tell her why he'd left.

He kept saying that he thought it was for the best, and she said the only thing that he thought was for the best is all the free food he had got at our house, and free laundry, and free loving, while she bought the groceries and paid the bills, and him not asking her to marry him because she already had a husband who was off somewhere.

She got so worked up that she finally went after him with a pitchfork. He jumped in the truck and locked the doors while she pounded and broke the windshield, yelling that if he ever set foot in our yard again, he would have a bullet between his eyes and a home in the quarry, and she didn't mean maybe.

She'd do it, too. I should have told her everything years ago. I should have told her the day it happened. But I was scared, and thought she would never forgive me, that she was not strong enough to stand it. I should have known that anybody who could work eight hours in the chicken plant every day and sell Avon to the women in the break room could do anything. She is my best friend, now, and my rock. I just wish I hadn't lost all those years when we could have been leaning on each other instead of her leaning on Walter. Everything might have turned out different.

So now you know it all. I will wait to hear from you. If you don't want to keep on writing, please let me know that, too, so I won't wait for a letter and have false hopes. Even if you can never love me, I love you, Jerry.

> Still and forever, throughout all eternity,
> your Carlene

———

She folded the letter, put it into an envelope, and carefully laid it in the bottom of her box, under the pictures of Shirley MacLaine and Sandra Dee. She would mail it when she could.

37. *Cherry*

 "Lucille, are you really, really, really sure you know what you're doing? I would dearly hate to have all my hair fall out."

"Cherry, who do you think you are talking to? I took the curl out of your hair, didn't I? I can surely put it back in. You forget I have done numerous permanents on every single old woman out at the nursing home, and I think I know how to do them by now."

———

My head was leaned back in the shampoo bowl at the beauty school, and Lucille was scrubbing my hair between her hands like she was washing out a sheet. It filled up the whole bowl. She had already sprayed me in the face with the sprayer and gotten water down my neck, soaking me to the skin, so it didn't seem to me unreasonable to think maybe she was not all that familiar with the proceedings. Either that, or she was just her usual clumsy self, and I couldn't get mad at her for that.

I didn't mean to hurt Lucille's feelings, but it was pretty scary, having two harsh processes done on your hair so close together. People got bald-headed like that. And it didn't make me feel any better to hear about all the old women she worked on. I'd seen them leaving the beauty school. The owners of the old folks' home loaded them on a bus and brought them all to the school once every two or three weeks to get their heads washed and set, and perms when they needed it. They only paid a dollar each for the shampoo and sets, since it was students doing it, and three-fifty for the perms. Dye was an additional seventy-five cents. You could always tell when they had just come from the beauty school, in the Haven of Rest bus that was painted white, with a big gold cross that went across the top and down the back bumper. Each little face peering out of the windows was engulfed by an enormous helmet of ratted-up bouffant hair, dyed blond or purple or blue or red or whatever color the girls felt like putting on them. They needed the practice, and the old women didn't seem to mind. They thought they were getting a bargain, which they were, and they liked the attention. But I sure wouldn't have trusted anybody that was there at that school with my hair, unless they were blood kin. I might have gone to the Kwik Kurl, but Miss Dottie was so old now that I didn't trust her. Nobody under thirty went there anymore. Besides, it would have hurt Lucille's feelings.

———

The girls looked at my hair like they were starved and it was a fresh piece of meat when I walked in. Most hairdressers were scissors-happy— students more than most.

I wouldn't have been at the beauty school at all, since I really loved my straight hair, except that it had started to grow out, and the roots, of course, were curly and made it stick out and look weird. Plus, nobody else liked it, and after a while I got tired of defending it. To tell you the honest truth, it never looked like Cher's anyhow. It was too coarse and thick.

Lucille's short-term solution was to put a perm in the straight part so it would match the curly part. Frankly, I was a little dubious, but I had to do something. I couldn't wear a scarf to moosh it down all the time.

—

Lucille finally got all the soap rinsed out, toweled off my hair—I don't know why they use such skimpy little towels in beauty shops; she had to use four—and brought me over to her workstation.

On her dresser was a mannequin head whose hair had been curled and straightened and ratted so many times that it was just wisps. I looked at it with pity, like an old friend who had been too many times around the block. I had a bad feeling that if I wasn't careful, I would look just like it.

Lucille dragged over the tray with the pink and green perm rods and poured the permanent-wave solution into a bowl. It smelled like ammonia and rotten eggs. Then she started combing me out, which looked like it was going to take a while.

"Your hair is just rats. I wish you'd let me cut some of this off. You would look so cute with a little poodle cut."

"Forget it, Lucille. You know I'm too tall and my head is too little for short hair. It would look like a fuzzy white peanut on top of football-pad shoulders. Just put the perm in and make it like it used to be."

Even with what all I just told you, I probably wouldn't have been doing this at all, except Tripp had mentioned more that once how he missed the curls. I never thought I'd say it, but I would have done almost anything he wanted me to. I'd always had contempt for women who were slaves to men, but now was a different story.

"You and Tripp finally did it, didn't you? I can tell. It was about time. I thought it was never going to happen. You were the oldest virgin in this town."

"What do you mean, you can tell?" I whispered. "Is it stamped on my forehead or something?"

"You're loose as a goose. And you've been avoiding me because you knew I'd know. A woman can always tell. Well? How was it?"

"Lucille!"

"Oh, come on. Who do you think you're talking to? Tell."

"It was incredible. Fantastic. I can't describe it. So I won't."

"Good girl! I sure envy you. Jim Floyd won't be coming back until Christmas, and I'm as tight as a wound-up spring. I have to take a cold bath every night. Doing it to yourself just isn't the same thing."

"Lucille!" I shrieked in a whisper. She has no judgment whatsoever about what she says or who might hear her.

I don't know why I was so uncomfortable talking about this with Lucille. I had never had much trouble before, but then I had never had much to tell before. I needed to change the subject before she started to go into details about her and Jim Floyd, which she loved to do. I had heard it all before, and each time was more lurid than the last. It was hard not to picture poor Jim Floyd hanging on for dear life, feet flapping.

"What's happening in the land of Dallas dead people?" I couldn't think of anything else that might interest her enough to throw her off the subject. "Is he getting to embalm them by himself yet?"

"Yeah. But not fresh ones. The school has these unclaimed bodies of transients, plus a few who decided to leave their bodies to science and save the price of a funeral—or their families decided for them—and they can't use them for a year, in case somebody comes forward and claims them, or the family changes its mind or something, so they just let them sit in a vat and soak."

"Are you serious? That is so grody! How can Jim Floyd stand to embalm a year-old body? The smell must be horrible."

"It is, but you get used to it. The thing that is killing him, though, is the class work. Jim Floyd didn't know he'd have to take stuff like organic chemistry, and he's not all that great at math in the first place. He is studying like crazy, which is not easy with his job at the hospital and all, but he's afraid he might flunk out. I may try to go down there for Thanksgiving and cheer him up. I don't think I can wait until Christmas."

It was almost impossible for me to see Lucille's attraction to Jim Floyd, especially now that I knew he had his hands in year-old bodies. But whatever rings her chimes, I guess, is fine with me. At least I finally knew how she felt. I would die if I had to be separated from Tripp for half a year. We saw each other every day now that school had started, and most nights, too. The drawing class was the highlight of the school week, because I got to sit next to him for four hours and work, which in an odd way was a turn-on, just casually brushing his leg or his arm, heat radiating out and enclosing him and me in our own little world, right in the middle of the rest of the class, while we both drew the same model.

He was an incredible artist, on top of everything else. He had the most unusual way of drawing the figure I had ever seen. He started with the pupil of the eye, then the rest of the eye, then the face, and finally the head and whole body. It was so perfect, too. He didn't use the loose, broad strokes like most of us had to, to get the proportion first and then gradually fine it up. He hardly ever used his kneaded eraser, and the drawing was neat and tidy and perfect from the first stroke on—meticulous, just like everything else about him. I should have known from the way he took care of his car he would be like that.

The house he rented, while a little old and shabby, was spotless too. His underwear drawers were immaculate; each pair of Jockey shorts was folded into a little square and put in perfect rows. So were his socks; he rolled them into round balls, toes tucked into the tops. His shirts were starched and ironed and hung exactly an inch apart on the rod, all facing the same way, and he had special pants hangers neatly set apart from the shirts. The cans in his kitchen cabinets were alphabetized, with the labels all facing out. There was not the smallest piece of crud behind the faucets in his bathroom. I had always thought of myself as being pretty neat, but next to Tripp, I was a slob. I guess it was his army training, but the army hadn't made Bean any neater. Baby was always complaining that he hardly ever changed his socks or underwear. He wore the same pair of leather pants every night when they performed, and I'm sure they were funky beyond belief. If I was her, I don't think I could stand it. Since we had had that fight, I wasn't about to tell her to break up with him, but I think she would be happier without him.

It took Lucille forever to roll the long hair onto the rods, and then she dribbled the solution all over my head with a cotton ball. I had a towel over my eyes, but the thin, cold liquid ran into my ears and down my neck, and the fumes seeped through the cheap, skinny towel. It smelled almost as bad as the straightener had.

"How much longer till you take it down?"

"I have to let it set for thirty minutes. Cool your jets. Tell me about the job at the Family Hand. Who all have you sold bongs to?"

"Just kids from the college, mostly. Nobody you really know. Rainy Day made some crazy clay pipes, though, that are best-sellers. The bowls are little men's heads, and they have big bloodshot eyes and mustaches and beards. They are real works of art."

"Does your mama know what it is you sell?"

"No, and she won't. I take her things home, though—jewelry and stuff. I get a discount. If you want anything, just let me know."

"I don't think there's anything much that is my style. The colors are not really right for me."

"Not much pink."

"No, not much pink. I might get one of those pipes, though. They sound real cute."

"What would you do with it? Smoke grass? Come on."

"I might. Why not? Have you smoked it again?" Lucille dropped her voice, which was good, since a girl came over to the next booth and brought along a woman with a towel around her head.

"Not yet," I whispered.

Actually, that was a lie. We had smoked pot several more times, and the sex was outrageous on it. I tried to describe to Tripp the things I saw, and he thought it sounded almost like I was hallucinating on acid. I hated to lie to Lucille, but we were in the beauty school, and even though we were whispering, you never know who could be listening. I wasn't sure I would tell her different later, though. It was almost too personal, like inviting someone into the bathroom with you. Like I said, everyone needs to keep things to themselves that nobody else knows.

It was scary how good I was getting at sin and breaking the law. Every time I went to church, I expected the roof to cave in. I felt like I had been sprayed with glow-in-the-dark paint that would flash like a neon sign— SINNER, SINNER, SINNER—but everyone just treated me like they always had. I began to wonder if some of them might be hiding things, too. The whole business of good and evil seemed completely turned around to what I had always been taught. How could something so good as loving Tripp be considered so bad?

Tripp had gone back with me a few times, in spite of the hell and Old Testament sermons, and thought it was fascinating, especially the shouting and talking in tongues and the healing services, where Brother Wilkins lined people up and said, "In the name of the Father, the Son, and the Holy Ghost, BE HEALED," and slapped them on the forehead whereupon they fell down in a faint. It must be really different from the Catholics.

Speaking of Catholics, I couldn't believe it, but I had found out that my practice teaching next semester would be at St. Juniper's Catholic Boys' Academy, up near Buchanan in the Ozark Mountains, about seventy-five miles from here. It was the best of all the assignments, because the supervising teacher, Father Leo, was known as a really cool priest. He had long hair and played rock-music tapes in class and smoked cigars, and they had a great art department.

The school was deep in the mountains, up high by itself, and looked like a medieval castle. At the center of the campus was a stone church, with huge windows of brilliant stained glass portraying St. Juniper and Jesus and Mary and a lot of other saints, which I would ask Tripp about. It had turrets with round red-peaked roofs and, I kid you not, a moat around the church that you had to cross on a wooden bridge, which was guarded by stone gargoyles on either side. When I went for my interview, Father Leo said they threw the bad boys in there for the alligators to eat. I stopped and stared, trying to see the alligators, until Father Leo laughed and I felt really stupid.

Even so, I guess Father Leo liked me, because I was the one he picked. The art department was off in a building by itself, across a creek with another wooden bridge, and had several pottery wheels, kilns, pedal sinks, and a lot of other great art facilities. It would be so much fun. The only thing that was going to be weird was that I would be the only woman in the whole school, except for the lunchroom ladies and the secretaries. They had no women teachers and no girl students. That part was a little daunting, but after all, they were only high school boys, and I would be twenty-one. A grown-up. Their teacher. I would start right after Christmas vacation—only three months away. I couldn't believe it. I was almost out of college.

———

Lucille started to take down the perm. "Uh-oh."

"What do you mean, uh-oh? What's wrong?"

"Uh-oh, my gosh. Cherry, I think your hair is breaking."

"Breaking? Lucille, what do you mean, breaking?" I could hear a little hysterical note come into my voice.

"Calm down and let me think! It may not be so bad. Come on, let's wash the solution off." There was definitely a little hysterical note in Lucille's voice. My heart started to race.

We went back to the shampoo bowl and she took all the rods out and poured shampoo on my hair. It felt really funny. Lighter.

"Cherry, I don't know how to tell you this, but you have short hair."

"What!" I jumped up, slinging water everywhere, and looked in the bowl. There was a big wad of white hair at the bottom. I felt my head, and my hair was really short in some places. I started to yell.

"LUCILLE, HOW COULD YOU DO THIS TO ME! I'M BALD!"

"Shhh, stop that howling! No you're not! Come back over and let's see what we can do."

By this time, all the girls had heard the ruckus and were standing around staring.

"WOULD Y'ALL PLEASE GO ON BACK TO YOUR OWN BUSINESS? I NEED ROOM TO THINK!" Lucille screamed at them, and they scurried away, sneaking looks over their shoulders.

I stared at myself in the mirror. It was a poodle cut, or at least some of it was. The rest was still long and curly. I looked like a sheep in the middle of shearing.

"Oh my Lord, Lucille! Do something," I wailed, tears starting to stream.

"All I can do is even it out. Stop crying, Cherry. It will look really cute. Please stop crying. It doesn't make it any easier for me to cut your hair with you bawling like that!"

"You'd bawl, too, if it was your hair!"

I wiped my hand across my eyes. My eyelashes were coming unglued. I peeled them off and put them in a Kleenex, then tried to pick off the glue, gobs of which were sticking my eyelids together. Tears dripped down my cheeks as Lucille went to work cutting the rest of my hair off. Big piles lay on the floor, like white wool. I never realized before how big my ears were. They were kind of pointed, like an elf's. Mr. Spock ears, that's what I had, and I never even knew it. The girls started to come back. They couldn't help themselves.

"Ooh, it's really cute! I love it!" one of them said. The others all agreed, and oohed and aahed some more, but what did they know? They were student hairdressers. Obviously, they would all love hair that was cut down to the scalp.

"No, really, Cherry, it's adorable. You will be really happy this happened. You'll see." Lucille was getting more and more excited as the girls carried on about what a great cut it was.

It was a short Afro, just long enough to pull a little in front of my ears to half hide them, and a fringe of curly bangs, a few corkscrew tendrils down my neck.

"Go and fix your makeup, put on these hoop earrings, and every girl in this town will want a haircut just like yours. I promise."

Lucille took her own gold hoops out of her ears, real ten-carat ones that Jim Floyd had given her for her birthday, and handed them to me. I went to the bathroom, fixed my lashes and makeup, put in the earrings, and stared at myself. It was different, I'll say that for it. I did have a little head, though. My neck was as long as a goose's, and my head seemed to bob around like a dandelion on a stalk. I had no idea what everyone would say, but there was nothing to do about it at this late date. Maybe I could get a wig or a fall or something until it grew out. Maybe this was my punishment for being vain and for all the stuff with Tripp and for lying to Lucille and for the pot and for everything else. It sure seemed like punishment to me.

———

"There! Don't you love it?" Lucille gushed when I came out. "It is so . . . fresh! So . . . kicky."

"You've been reading too much *Glamour* magazine, Lucille. How long will it take to grow out?"

"Like it used to be? Five years, more or less. Two years down to your shoulders."

"Two years. And I have to practice-teach." I sighed and resigned myself. If it was really punishment, then I would accept it and try to make the best of things.

"How much do I owe you?"

"Three-fifty for the perm. I won't charge you for the haircut."

I nearly bit through my tongue.

She took my five and handed me change. "I'm through for the day. Do you want to go across the street to the Rexall and get a tuna-fish sandwich or something?"

"No, thanks. I have to get over to the Family Hand to work."

"You're not mad at me, are you? I mean it—it really looks good. You'll get used to it."

"No, I'm not mad at you. I mean it, too. It was time for a change." There I was, lying again.

She hugged me. "Let's go to the show or something this week, okay? I miss hanging out with you. *Midnight Cowboy* is playing, and that's supposed to be good. I'll get Mama or Aunt Juanita to keep Tiffany LaDawn, and Tripp can live without you for one night."

"Sure. That would be fun."

We went on out, after all the girls had told me again how wonderful my new hairdo was, said good-bye, and Lucille started walking up the street. I got into the Green Bug and had just started the engine when a cream-colored Cadillac slid by me and pulled up and stopped right beside Lucille, a block away. It had to be that guy from Carlene's funeral—Franco, or something. The one Baby knew. Nobody else in this town had a car like that.

Lucille stepped over to the car and leaned in the window. It made me nervous, since she had on a low-cut dress. I sent her a mental message to stand up straight, but she obviously didn't get it. They talked for a minute, then she opened the door and got inside and they took off down the street. I didn't like the look of this one little bit. What was she doing getting in the car with some guy she hardly knew? She was a married woman, for Pete's sake. They were nearly out of sight before I had the presence of mind to follow them. I hated to be a snoop, but I had to see where they went.

After a mile or two, I realized they were heading for the road that led to the lake. A cold chill went up my back. The lake. Where they found Carlene's body. My cousin was in the car with a total stranger who had kissed a dead girl on the mouth and might be a murderer, and they were headed for the lake.

I thought about stopping at the Esso station and picking up G. Dub for protection, but it was at the other end of town and I would lose them if I did that. I had to keep them in sight. At least it was broad daylight. Even if he was the killer, he surely wouldn't do anything. They turned the corner, and I followed, at a discreet distance.

38. *Baby*

 Auwling liked to take walks down by the lake after the little girls were in bed and Dionisio was deep into some television show. The older ones seldom were at home anymore, and she had no idea where they went or what they were doing. When she asked them, they just said, "Out with my friends." She tried to keep Pilar home more, but it was no use. She couldn't tie the girl to the bedpost, and punishment seemed to do no good. Their Manang couldn't be angry at them all the time, and in truth, anger never came easily to Auwling. It was better to just let them do as they pleased. She had allowed all of her own children to call her Manang, as Baby did, even though the correct name for "Mother" was Nanang.

She didn't know how she had gotten to be like this. Important things didn't seem to matter in America. When she was a girl in the Philippines, she dreamed that when she had a family, she would be the calm center and all her children would love and respect her; her husband would honor and take care of her. Instead, the children hardly talked to her anymore. They didn't have the time or inclination to hear stories of their homeland. They were foreigners—Americans. Southerners. They drove pickup trucks and ate fried chicken and got into fistfights. They couldn't speak Tagalog, even though she had tried to teach them when they were little. Sometimes she had a hard time understanding them, with all the American slang they used.

She never again saw her own mother after they left the Philippines. A few times, Auwling and Dionisio made the effort to bring her over to live with them, but Lula didn't want leave her friends and home.

Auwling had no friends except her husband. She knew that Dionisio cared for her, but he would never love her as he had loved Maeling. He had only married her because she was Maeling's sister and it made him feel close to his lost love. Auwling knew this, even though Dionisio would never admit it. There were times, even in the middle of the night when they had just made love, that Auwling felt more alone than if she had been by herself in the bed. Dionisio would pat her on the hand—two quick pats—turn his back, and leave her—to go into his dreams of Maeling, she suspected, running through the fields, singing as she used to do.

Auwling, of course, never mentioned her fears. She swallowed them, as she swallowed the small hurts and insults from her children, until, over the years, they had made an indigestible ball in the pit of her stomach.

—

At night, though, the moist lake air was like a balm to her spirit, and she would sometimes sit, outside of time, on a log at the edge of the water and watch the frogs leap and the catfish splash. This night, Maeling was once again on her mind, a strong presence, as if she was out there waiting for something. Auwling wondered if her sister's spirit would ever find rest. Since her death, Maeling had visited her older sister many times—not only in dreams, but in the waking hours of the night. When Auwling was alone in the dark, she would only have to sit quietly, empty her mind, and Maeling would appear as if through fine silver gauze, her eyes liquid brown and sad.

Maeling spoke to her mind, not with words, exactly, but with whole thoughts. She asked her sister to forgive her for taking her own life. She assured Auwling that she had done the right thing by leaving her under the house. It was what she had wanted. There was nothing else to be done with one so unclean. She was full of sorrow that she didn't live to be a mother to Babilonia and a wife to her husband, but she was grateful to her sister for taking her place. There was also something else Maeling wanted to say that Auwling could not understand. She tried, because she knew that if she could understand, then perhaps Maeling would let go and rise to the next world, but the message eluded her. More and more often, Maeling appeared with an urgency not felt before.

Even now, Auwling could see her sister's spirit out over the water, in a silver cloud, hovering above the surface of the still lake as wisps of fog began to rise.

It was the same now as it had been the night the girl Carlene died. That night in July, Auwling remembered, was also damp with summer fog. The tops of the trees disappeared into the mist, which gave its own light and made the woods closer—sinister, as though they were hiding the Aswang in their branches.

Almost, she hadn't gone for her stroll that night, but then decided not to be silly and afraid. Even so, as she walked through the woods near the lake, the feeling of danger persisted, and she decided to listen to her senses and return home. She had just turned toward the house when she heard an unfamiliar noise and stopped, frozen.

Behind the honeysuckle vines near the edge of the lake, she squatted and listened. She heard the sound of paddles, then the low moan of a woman and the curse of a man. There was a splash, as if a fisherman were throwing a large fish back into the water. There were no more moans then, only the sound of the paddles slapping against the surface of the lake.

As the sound moved farther away, Auwling parted the vines and saw the silhouette of a man sitting in a small rowboat. He continued rowing and was soon swallowed up in the mist. The surface of the lake was calm and there was no sign of a woman, but over the water the silver form of Maeling hovered. Perhaps the Aswang mermaid Seriena had already taken the woman to the bottom to feed on her blood and the spirit of Maeling watched.

Afraid, hidden on the bank, Auwling appealed to her sister.

"Maeling, tell me what to do. Tell me what it is you want. Who is this woman? What should I do?" But the ghost of Maeling rose higher and then faded, leaving nothing behind, not even a cleft in the fog.

Auwling went home and told her husband what she had seen.

"Should we call the police, Dionisio?" she said. "I don't like to think about the woman alone in the lake with the Aswang."

"She is dead, you say?"

"Now, most certainly."

"And you are sure you don't know who the man was?"

"No. It was dark, and I could not see him clearly. I have never heard the voice before."

"Then there is nothing you can tell the police. They would only question you and disrupt our lives. They wouldn't trust us, because they think we are like the Vietnamese. They will find out about her soon enough. It has nothing to do with us."

"As you say, Dionisio. I will tell no one."

And I will tell no one about the ghost of Maeling, either, she thought. Especially not you, my beloved husband. She is enough a part of you as it is.

39. *Vietnam*

February 15, 1968

Dear Carlene,

 A lot has happened since I wrote you last. We got our first kill. I should be really happy, but for some reason I'm not. I don't even know if they were Viet Cong or not. Some of our guys were keeping watch on a bridge here in Son My, and there were a couple of Vietnamese out in a little boat fishing. I was back a ways, and it seemed like they were just minding their own business when I heard shots, and they slumped over and fell into the water. I guess they must have been VC, though. We didn't recover any weapons, because the boat was shot full of holes and sank. Anyhow, we have our first body count.

It has been a horrible few weeks. We have been on constant patrol, which means you get up in the morning after only half sleeping for a few hours, put on a pack that weighs nearly a hundred pounds, and walk through the jungle in the muggiest heat you can imagine, looking for the enemy. All you hope is that you can get enough air in your lungs so that you won't pass out, and have the strength to keep putting one foot in front of the other. Nobody ever feels good.

That, plus there's the constant tension of looking for booby traps and waiting for somebody to shoot at you, like what happened three or four days ago, when we were attacked near the Diem Diem River and several of our guys were wounded. We never even saw the VC, but got the heck out of there after calling in some support. Then the next day, our a★★hole lieutenant leads us right back to the same spot and lo and behold, they're still there and they hit us again, hard. Nobody knew what they were doing, and we were all running around in circles like chickens with our heads cut off. We called in for support and withdrew from the riverbank, but the lieutenant, with his unerring sense of direction, led us in a circle right back to where we started, right back into the fire, and our radio operator took a hit that ripped out his kidney. It shook us all up—our first to be killed.

It seems real now, Carlene. Before, death was just something we talked about, but this was a healthy eighteen-year-old kid, not some sick old lady that my father preaches over at church. He was a buddy of ours. His life just ran out on the ground in big gouts of blood, and we were helpless to do anything about it. It's real to me for the first time that I might not make it back home. You can't think in those terms or you'd go crazy, but you have to be realistic.

Through all of this, we haven't seen any actual VC, but the guys who hit us are part of the 48th we let escape during Tet. I know they are. I mean I think I know. We don't even know half the time where the shots come from. It seems like these guys are ghosts or something. They are most likely concentrated a few miles from here in Pinkville, but they slip away every time we try to pin them down. And you can bet the villagers know nothing about anything. It is so frustrating sometimes to try to get information out of them when they always play dumb. *"No bic! No bic!"* they say, which means "I don't understand," and we know good and well that they know exactly where the VC are. Sometimes a shot will come right out of a village, and then when we go and check, there will be nobody there and nobody knows nothing.

A time or two, some of the guys and even the captain have roughed up some villagers, which isn't pretty to watch, but it is just so d★★★ frustrating that they won't help us. In fact, they seem like they despise us, staring at us with hatred in their eyes when we come by. It's hard to keep going, I tell you. I guess I'm used to being the good guy. We feel like we are all alone out here, just us guys against the world.

The rest of the time, it's like we are walking around in circles for nothing—no destination, just walking and looking, making camp, eating K rations and sleeping in our clothes. Some of the guys haven't had their boots off in three weeks. You can't imagine what we smell like.

To give us a treat, the colonel came out on an APC and brought us ice cream. Can you believe it? Got out in his starched fatigues, with his spit-shined boots, and handed out this stuff that was half melted and ran down our hands and elbows and made everything sticky and even worse than it was. Then he saluted us, went on back to base to his steaks and clean sheets, and left us out here with the snakes and the booby traps and the mud and the heat.

Some of the guys are getting a little crazy, I think. You can do that over here in a hurry with no trouble. We met up with a renegade bunch of grunts that would make your hair stand on end, Carlene. They were like wild Indians, living in the bush so long that they weren't even remotely civilized anymore. They had Mohawk haircuts and earrings, and wore necklaces of ears around their necks. That's right. Ears. They cut the ears off the gooks they kill and string them like dried apricots around their necks. Most of them have already done two tours of duty and are on their third. The army only lets you do three, thinking that if you want to do more than that, you are really one sick puppy. One of those guys told me he had gone home after two and just couldn't relate to anything back there in the world. He wore his uniform at the airport, and mothers pulled their kids back from him like he had TB or something. His family asked him how many people he had killed, then kept staring at him like they were afraid he was going to murder them or something. He couldn't hold down any kind of a job, so he went to the recruiting office and begged until they sent him back to Nam. He said he was going to stay until he was killed or they locked him up. Said that all his friends had been killed, and he wasn't going to leave them out here in the jungle. I don't know what he will do when this tour is over. The only thing he knows is killing, but he's very good at that. He must have a hundred ears on his string.

They hate us back in the States, I guess, for doing our duty, because our duty is to kill people. The protesters are right in a way, but they shouldn't blame us for the mess of this war. I don't think half the guys want to be here, or believe in the war. Less. Maybe not a quarter. Surely not the way they are doing things at the top.

Like this whole business of the search-and-destroy policy. What kind of stupid logic is it to destroy something in order to save it from Communism? I mean, every day we take out our Zippos and burn to the ground what little shelter these people have, run them off their land, poison their wells, kill them, rape them, and what the heck are we saving them from? Would the Communists kill them any deader?

I know it is not patriotic to say all this, but I am so dispirited sometimes. Our lieutenant doesn't know his butt from a hole in the ground. I don't know how he ever made it through OCS. Nobody likes him. We are all afraid he is going to get us killed doing something stupid one of these days, like that firefight. He is only five-foot-four, and constantly has to throw his weight around to make himself seem like a big guy. Even the captain calls him Lt. S★★★head. Makes us really confident in him, I tell you.

All in all, I hate to be so depressing, but there is not much I can say that will cheer you up. Maybe part of it is because I haven't heard from you in a while. You don't have to tell me the secret if you don't want to. But please write. I need to hear from you. I still have the picture of you and Kevin in my helmet. It is my good-luck charm. Please write soon.

Love,
Jerry

40. Cherry

 I let the cream-colored Cadillac get a good distance ahead, then followed it out to the lake road that led to the Water Witch. I had no idea what I was going to do when I got there. It would really be embarrassing for everyone. I mean, what was I doing checking up on Lucille like I was some kind of detective or something? I wondered what Nancy Drew would do in this situation. Not confront them and look stupid, that's for sure. "Hi, y'all," I'd say. "Nice day for a drive, huh? Fancy meeting you here. By the way, I thought you might be about to murder my cousin, so I thought I'd come out and try to stop you."

So I drove slow and gave them a lot of time to get all the way to the end before I made the turn. I had never been out to the restaurant, even though Baby worked there for a couple of years. I can't really explain why, except for the obvious reason about them serving alcoholic drinks, but it belonged to a part of Baby's life that had nothing to do with me—just like she had never gone with me to church. It didn't mean we loved each other less, but we just couldn't be everything to each other, I guess.

Seeing the place was strange. I don't know what I was expecting, but it was a really beautiful restaurant. The views were incredible, and there were flower beds full of deep red and purple velvety flowers. The bushes that lined the turnaround driveway were cut in round shapes that reminded me of fancy poodles. Like my haircut. A striped awning shaded the entrance.

I didn't see the Cadillac, but this was the end of the road and there was no place else for it to go that I could see, so I parked in the parking lot and got out. It didn't look like the restaurant was open. There was only one other car.

I tried to think of what I would say to them if I saw them. Maybe I could say I had a message for Lucille from her mother or something. I had to try. I didn't think Franco, or whatever his name was—even if he wasn't the murderer—had anything good in mind in relation to my cousin. Poor little Jim Floyd was slaving away on pickled corpses down in Dallas, and his overripe wife didn't need any more temptation than she already had.

I crept around the side of the restaurant as nonchalantly as I could, butterflies in my stomach. Funny, but my short hair made me feel really vulnerable and exposed, as if I'd lost my security blanket.

Down in the marina was a good-size houseboat, and the Caddy was parked near it by the dock. Lucille and Franco were standing out on the deck of the boat, drinking something pink. Of course he would have a pink drink for Lucille—he was no amateur. I hugged the corner of the building so they wouldn't see me.

— ⸺

"Are you looking for something?" I jumped about three feet into the air.

"Uh, are you open for supper yet?"

"We open at five."

"Oh. What time is it now?"

"Three."

The guy doing the talking was Chinese, short, and wiry. He squinted up at me with the sun in his eyes.

"You are a tall one."

"Yes. I know that already." People can be so rude if you are tall. He wouldn't have said "You are a fat one" if I was fat.

"I am Park, the chef of this restaurant. What is your name?"

"Cherry Marshall. I'm a friend of Baby Moreno's. She used to talk about what good food you had out here, and I was in the neighborhood, so I thought I might stop in and have a bite."

I sneaked a peek at the houseboat. Lucille and Franco were laughing about something. They hadn't noticed us.

"Baby! You are a friend of Baby! How is Baby? She has not been here for months. We miss her." It was amazing how fast his tune changed when I mentioned Baby's name. He was smiling all over the place now. "What is she doing?"

"Well, she is in college at DuVall University with me. We worked at the pickle plant this summer. I never understood why she would give up a great job out here to work at the plant, but she said she needed the change."

"Perhaps she did. Why don't you come in and I will give you something cool to drink. You can wait until the restaurant opens, and you can tell me all about Baby. Okay?"

"Uh, okay. Sure."

There was nothing else I could do, unless I wanted to bust in on them down at the houseboat. At least I would finally see the inside of a bar.

It was sort of scary to see the rows of liquor bottles lined up on shelves in front of the mirror. I had always been taught in church that every one of the beautiful gold and amber colors was poison and that drinking even one glass of alcohol would send you straight to hell. After being nearly poisoned by the moonshine I had a bad feeling they might have a point, but the bottles sure were pretty. There was a funny smell in the bar, too, like . . . I don't know what. A rich, old, brown kind of smell, not unpleasant.

"Would you like a drink?"

"I don't really know all that much about drinks, Park. You pick out something that is good. And not too strong."

"How about one that tastes like a milk shake? Kahlúa and cream? It will put meat on those bones."

"Sure. That would be nice." I didn't have to drink it if I didn't want to. I would only take a small sip, to be polite. I couldn't just sit there like a nitwit and watch for Lucille. One little sip couldn't hurt anything.

"This is a really beautiful restaurant," I said while Park took down the brown bottle of Kahlúa. I was a little nervous, I have to admit, but I tried not to let him know. "Who built it?"

"My brother, Jackie. The bar was shipped from Hong Kong, as well as the rugs and the tables and chairs. They were part of a famous old restaurant that was torn down."

This bar was not like the ones I had seen in the movies. It was elegant, with deep vermilion walls, wet-looking, like the burnt-orange reflection of the sun setting on the lake. It felt like I was in China. I half expected to look out the window and see one of those little boats they called junks, with its fanlike sail, tied up at the dock.

He handed me the drink, which looked like milk with dark brown coffee swirled into it, over ice.

"Cheers."

"Cheers." I drank a tiny sip. Oh my gosh. It was wonderful. Rich and creamy, like a coffee milk shake. It clung to the back of my tongue. I took a bigger sip.

"You like it?"

"I like it. Is there alcohol in it?"

"Little. Not much. Good afternoon drink. Gives energy. Builds bones and teeth." He had fixed himself one, too, and took a deep swallow.

"You have a car like Baby. I came outside because I thought it was her, for a moment."

"People are always mistaking us for each other. At least our cars. We don't look much like each other in person."

"No. I would say not. So how is Baby? Did her boy come home again from Vietnam?"

"Yeah, he did. He sings out at Woody's. Have you ever been out there?"

"No. But maybe I will go one night. I should get out more. It is hard, when you have to cook all the time. Does Baby go a lot to this Woody's?"

"Uh, I think so."

"Is she happy?"

"Yes. I think she is."

I felt a little uncomfortable discussing Bean and Baby with Park. Although she had never spelled it out, I suspected she'd had a thing with Jackie, but she never said much about Park. Maybe he just liked her. I took my drink and walked over to the window that faced the river. I needed to see what my cousin was up to, and I wanted to try and change the subject.

"Really nice view. Do a lot of people keep boats down there?"

"Some. More in the summer than now."

I couldn't see Lucille and Franco anymore. They must have gone inside.

"Does somebody really live on that houseboat?"

"Yes. Some of the time."

"Who is it?"

"Why are you so interested?"

"I just thought it would be neat to live on a boat. I wondered what kind of person would do that."

Nancy Drew would have been proud of my cool.

"A single man with no family. Takes his home with him, like a trailer, but without wheels. He is the salesman for the company of the restaurant machines. He leaves the boat here much of the time while he travels, because it is a good location and he likes the beauty."

"I can see why. No family, huh? I guess it would be hard to drag around a wife and kids. School and all. Better to be footloose, I reckon."

"I reckon."

"Do you have a wife and kids, Park?"

"No, I was not so lucky. What would you like for dinner? I can make you something now."

"Dinner? Uh, I don't know. You decide."

"Leave it to me. You sit. You will like it, I promise."

—

An hour later, Lucille still was in the houseboat. I had eaten moo shoo pork, garlic shrimp, shredded beef with orange sauce, and lemon chicken.

It was the best food I had ever put in my mouth. Park and I were old friends by the last course, and he brought me a fresh orange cut in wedges for dessert, and a fortune cookie. "You will renew an old acquaintance," it said. I had also had two more Kahlúa and creams, and was feeling pretty relaxed. At this rate, I would get some meat on my bones in a hurry. He had tried to pump me some more about Baby, but I didn't give him much information, beyond the fact that I didn't think she was going to marry Bean. It was obvious that Park had a major unrequited crush on her. I felt kind of sorry for him.

The last scrap had been eaten, and the empty plate stared at me. I couldn't sit there much longer without him getting suspicious. A couple of the waitresses came in for their evening shift and looked at me like they couldn't figure out what I was doing there.

"What do I owe you, Park?" I tried to remember how much money I had with me.

"The first meal at the Water Witch is always on the house, Cherry. Next time you pay. Don't be a stranger. Bring Baby back. Tell her Park misses her."

Park was really nice. Baby would probably be better off with somebody like him than Bean, especially now that I knew how he had been treating her since he got back. On top of everything else, she said, he had started making her sit and rub his feet to relax him while he lay on the couch, and I couldn't imagine they were always that clean. And the two of them always had to do what *he* wanted to. She would have liked to do something else once in a while besides watch him play the guitar, I bet. If he ever got to be a rock star, he would be impossible. I decided to talk to her about Park.

The girls were setting up the tables for dinner, and Park had gone back to the kitchen. I had no choice but to leave. I walked to my car as slowly as I could, looking at the houseboat all the while. I pretended my shoe was untied, and bent down to tie it, trying to see into the windows. Whatever Lucille and Franco were going to do, they had probably done it by now. I didn't know whether to be aggravated at her or scared for her, but I leaned toward aggravation. I had decided to wait five more minutes and then go down and knock on the door and just take my chances when the door opened and they came out. She looked up and saw me, said something to Franco, and left him down there alone on the boat. He watched her walk up to the restaurant. Nobody could climb stairs like Lucille.

"Why, hello, cuz. Fancy meeting you here," I said as she came up to the car.

"All right, Cheryl Ann. What do you think you're doing following me out here?"

"What do you mean? I just had a hankering for Chinese food. Were you here, too? I didn't see you."

"Let me in the car right now."

"Nobody's stopping you. Get in."

She got in and I started the car.

"Let's get out of here. Go down the lake road." I pulled out and headed back down the gravel road.

"Okay, Lucille. What is going on? You better have a good story to tell, and I want to know the truth. Why did you get in the car with that man? He didn't do anything to you, did he? You didn't do anything with him, did you?"

"What's he going to do in the middle of the day right in full view of the restaurant? And how can you think I'd cheat on Jim Floyd, anyhow? He just asked me if I wanted to go out to the houseboat, have a drink, and talk over a business proposition. It didn't seem dangerous, right out in broad daylight. He's kind of cute."

We got to the turnoff and I drove down the lake shore for a couple of miles, then pulled up by the edge of the water and stopped.

"So? Tell. What kind of business did he want with you? Besides the obvious."

"He wanted to put me in the movies."

"Right. Sure. He's a salesman, Lucille. He sells cigarette machines. Park told me. He can't put you in the movies. He just wants to get in your pants, and thinks you are a ditzy blonde who would believe he was a movie producer."

"Well, he might sell cigarette machines, but he has friends in Memphis who make movies, and since he travels a lot, he is always on the lookout for new stars for them."

"What kind of movies do they make in Memphis? I never heard of any."

"Low-budget films. Not like they make in Hollywood, but real films."

"What did you say when he said that?"

"I laughed at him and asked him if he was aware I was a new mother. He said that was no problem, that a lot of movie stars had kids, and that even now I had the perfect body for the low-budget film industry. Low-budget audiences like full-figured women. He did seem to like my body a lot."

"Lucille, every man likes your body a lot. I don't want to be mean, but the way you dress might have something to do with it."

"What's wrong with the way I dress? I can't help it if men have dirty minds."

"Most men do have dirty minds. It's a fact of life. Did he say what kind of films these were?"

"Not really."

"What do you mean, not really?"

"Well, maybe that there might be some partial nudity involved."

"I knew it! He was trying to get you to do dirty movies, Lucille. So did he try to kiss you or anything?"

"No, he was a perfect gentleman."

"Did he know I was up at the restaurant?"

"Of course he did. He's not blind, and you were standing there in full view staring right at us. It was hard to miss you. I told him you'd give me a ride home, so he wouldn't have to. He said to tell you that you should go to New York and be a model, that you were too skinny for the low-budget movies but perfect for the fashion world."

"Did he really say that?"

"He really did."

I grinned, then had second thoughts and smacked my forehead with the heel of my hand.

"What am I saying? Here is a guy trying to get you to do dirty movies, and I'm thrilled he thinks I can be a model! Lucille, he is a sleazebag!"

"You don't know the half of it. I said I had to go to the bathroom, and while I was in there, I snooped in a cabinet and found an album with a little lock that only took a minute to open with a bobby pin. It was full of pictures of naked women, and you won't believe who one of them was."

"Who?"

"Baby."

"Baby? Maria Babilonia Moreno? That Baby?"

"Yes. That Baby."

"I don't believe it."

"I told you, you wouldn't believe it."

"Are you sure about this?"

"Well, if I had to bet my life on it, I wouldn't, since most of the face was in shadow, but it really looked just like her. She seemed to know him awfully well at the funeral."

"I would be as shocked if it was Baby as if it was Mama. Did you steal the picture?"

"No, I was afraid to. They were pasted to the page, and there was no way to get it out without tearing it. I didn't want him to get suspicious."

"I have to get a look at those pictures, Lucille. I just don't believe it could be her."

"Now, how do you think we are going to accomplish that? Knock on the door and ask him for them?"

"We'll figure something out."

———

I was starting to see that the part of Baby's life that had nothing to do with me was much bigger than I had thought. And the more I found out about it, the less sure I was about anything. Baby was becoming a stranger, and it scared me.

41. Bean

 The road down by the river was hard-packed dirt, and a stretch of it went stone-straight for a quarter of a mile before it took a curve. It was a perfect place for racing, and during the warm months, a gang of guys would take their old cars and trucks down there nearly every night and have drag races that went on so late that sometimes the sun rose on them. The ringleaders of the bunch were J.C. and Denny Moreno, and in spite of the danger of Sheriff Melvyn Arbus driving by once in a while and trying to catch them with beer, there wasn't much the law could do to them. He tried one time, when they were particularly rowdy—took their car keys away and made them all walk home, then had their parents come to the courthouse and claim the keys—but it backfired, because the parents were all so mad at him that he got afraid he would lose their votes and so he pretty much left the boys alone after that.

Bean had taken to dropping by after he got through at Woody's and after Baby was safe in bed—just to smoke a last joint or two and hang out with whoever was crazy enough to try his luck against the Moreno brothers. Bean never raced, himself, because his old truck didn't have the juice, but he usually had a bag or two of grass stashed under the seat and there was always somebody who wanted to buy. This was where he did the bulk of his business.

It was the dark of the moon when Bean pulled up, and warm for October. Frogs were croaking and a breeze blew across the river, stirring up the smell of murky water and dead fish. Five or six cars were lined up along the side of the road, parked about ten feet apart, with their headlights on, lighting up the race course.

Bean was a little surprised to see Ramblin' Rose at the starting line, going up against Denny, who was driving a '59 turquoise Ford Thunderbird with oversize wheels and the back end jacked up. They were revving their motors, waiting for J.C. to come out and give the signal to start.

"Hey, Barlow! You better watch yourself! That boy knows how to drive!" Bean yelled, and Tripp turned and stuck his head out the window.

"So does this boy, Bean! Put your money on Ramblin' Rose!"

G. Dub stood beside his car, a '64 white Mustang, smoking a cigarette. He waved at Bean, crushed out the butt, and ambled over. He had on jeans and a white T-shirt; a leather headband held down his long hair. He looked like the very incarnation of Sam Muskrat, his Cherokee grandpa.

"Hey, Bean! How's it going, buddy?"

"Not too bad, G. Dub. How did they rope Barlow into this?"

"Aw, them boys have been after him to race ever since they first seen his car, and just finally wore him down. I got a couple of dollars on him, just to make it interesting. You putting anything down?"

"I think I'll sit this one out. I don't want to bet against my bud, but he ain't going to beat Denny in that T-bird." They hopped up and sat on the tailgate of Bean's truck.

"Got Mary Jane with you tonight?"

Bean looked around, then pulled a joint out of his pocket. He handed it to G. Dub, who lit up, sucked the good smoke down into his lungs, holding it as long as he could, and passed it back to Bean.

"Thanks, Bean. Whoo, boy, that's primo stuff. Put hair on your chest."

Bean took a toke and handed the joint back. "What are you talking about?" he said in a strained voice as the smoke leaked out of his mouth. "You know you don't have no hair on your chest, G. Dub."

"Naw, I don't on the Indian part, that's a fact, but I'm fixing to sprout me some right now on the white part, it feels like." He took another deep toke.

J.C. went out to the middle of the road in front of the two cars, holding the white rag he used for a flag in his upraised hands. He stood there for a moment lit by the headlights, as if poised on the end of a diving board, then brought the flag down. The two cars squealed tires and flung dirt as they blasted down the road, one on either side of him.

"Look at old Barlow! That thing is sweet as a baby's butt, ain't it? I bet it is cleaner now than it was when it rolled off the line of the Chevy factory. Whooee! That was a close one! They nearly touched bumpers! Lordy, Lordy!" G. Dub stepped up into the truck bed to get a better look.

The cars ran neck and neck until the last minute, when Denny gunned the motor and swerved out in front of Tripp. It was crazy, but it worked; Tripp hit his brakes and slowed down.

"Ha! I could've told Barlow he didn't have no business racing that car if he was afraid to get a little scratch on it! Dang. I lost my two bucks."

Tripp turned around and drove back to where the boys were waiting, and another two cars took their place.

"Hey, Barlow! Don't feel bad," Bean called out as Tripp got out of the car. "Denny's been racing since he had to sit on a cushion to see out over the steering wheel. He don't care if he wrecks his car, just as long as he wins. How much did he get off of you?"

"Ten bucks. But it was cheaper than a new paint job would have been. How you doing, boys?"

"Fine as frog hair." Bean passed the joint to Tripp. "How'd you get roped into racing the Moreno boys?"

"Just lucky, I guess. I get a lot of people trying to race with me when I'm stopped at red lights and things. It goes with the 'fifty-seven Chevy."

"Well, those gooks are pretty sneaky, and they're not afraid of nothing, so don't feel bad that he beat you," Bean said.

"Gooks?" G. Dub looked at Bean in shock. Tripp stopped and stared at him, too. "Are you calling Denny and J.C. gooks, Bean?"

Bean looked at them in surprise. "What are you talking about, G. Dub? Why would I do that?"

"You just said, 'those gooks'—didn't he, Barlow?"

"That's what I thought you said, Bean. Maybe I misheard."

"Maybe you did," Bean said in a tight voice. "You know I would never call them that! Denny and J.C. are practically my family!" He looked at them with narrowed eyes. "I think you better apologize right now, G. Dub. You too, Barlow." Bean had a look on his face that didn't ask for argument.

"Okay, okay. I'm sorry. I guess I need to get my hearing checked," G. Dub said.

"Yeah, me too, Bean. I'm sorry."

There was an awkward silence. Then G. Dub pulled out his wallet and took out a card.

"Well, my bad hearing can't save me now. Look at what I got in the mail today, boys. I'm 1-A. My number finally came up."

"Let me see that, G. Dub," Bean said. His tone had changed back to normal, as if nothing had happened. He looked at the card, then handed it back. "Looks like they got you. They're taking anybody that can see out of one eye and hear out of one ear. You'll be heading to Nam for sure."

"Nope. I ain't going. No siree, bob."

"Now, just how do you think you'll get out of it? Wear lace panties to your physical?"

"Ha. No, Canada has said they would welcome anybody who doesn't want to go to the war. I'm thinking about just heading up there. I know how to work on cars, so I should be able to get me a job."

"What will your mama say? She ain't going to like it."

"She knows all about it. It was her that put me up to it in the first place. She don't feel like our people ought to have to fight in this war. We done fought the army and lost, back in her great-grandpa's time. Those old feelings die hard with us. If I go to Canada, I can't never come back here to the States, but at least she knows I'll be alive, and she can come up there and visit."

"I don't know, G. Dub. Are you sure you know what you're doing? I mean, it's only for a couple of years, and the thought of not ever getting to come back home . . . I don't know." Bean shook his head.

"Barlow, you been over there. What would you do if you was me? Would you go back to Nam if you had it to do all over again?"

"No, I wouldn't," Tripp said with no hesitation. "I would be in Canada in a heartbeat."

"What about you, Bean? Think about it hard and tell me the truth. I got to make a big decision. Would you do it all over? Would you go back to Nam if you could?"

Bean looked out over the river. Somewhere in his mind he was standing by another river, on a hot, muggy night in Vietnam. He could almost hear the water buffalo bellow, and the high silver laughter of slender girls as they paddled wooden boats down the narrow canals that branched like fingers off the river. He took a deep breath of the thick, damp air, then turned back to his friends.

"G. Dub, knowing everything I know now . . ." He hesitated for another minute. Tripp and G. Dub waited for him to finish the sentence. "No, I wouldn't. It's not something you want to get into. Maybe you would do better to just take off."

"Well, I have thought hard about it. It ain't going to be easy. I'll miss all of y'all, and it goes without saying I'll miss my family. It's scary, not knowing where I'll be or if I'll have the money to last until I can get a job. I just don't know."

Bean reached into his pocket and pulled out a wad of money. "If you need a little help, I can loan you a couple hundred."

G. Dub stood for a minute deciding, then reached out and took it.

"Thanks, Bean. I appreciate it. I'll send this back to you as soon as I can. I'm going to miss you, my friend."

"You going to miss me or Mary Jane?" They laughed.

"Both of you."

"When you plan on taking off?"

"Soon. They'll be coming after me if I don't report in ten days."

"Let me see that draft card, G. Dub," Tripp said. He took out his lighter and lit the corner of the card. "You won't be needing this anymore."

The three of them watched it burn until it scorched Tripp's fingers and he dropped the curled black ash on the ground and stepped on it.

"You're doing the right thing, G. Dub. I would give anything in this world if I could turn back the clock and not go, myself," Tripp said. "You write and let us know how you're doing,"

G. Dub shook his hand and then Bean laid his hand on top of theirs. The three of them stood gripping hands as the drag race went on behind them.

42. Carlene

Carlene read Jerry's last letter for the third time, folded it, and put it into the box with the rest, under the movie-star pictures. Then she got out the letter she had written to him with her confession, read it a time or two, changed a word here and there, and added on the bottom: BURN THIS AFTER YOU READ IT. She put it in an envelope and then carried Kevin out and buckled him into his car seat. He was a big boy, nearly three, and didn't like to be strapped in the baby seat.

"Stop that crying, Kevin. I'm not having you get thrown through the windshield if I have to slam on the brakes. We're going to the post office. I'll stop and get you an ice cream if you don't make a fuss, okay?" A tear slid down his cheek, but he stopped crying. He liked ice cream.

Carlene pulled into the post office parking lot and dropped the letter into the drive-by mailbox. She didn't like to go inside, because she was sure to see Mr. Marshall. Even though it all happened over three years ago, she had never been able to speak to Mr. Marshall since the day he suggested she go to the revival and she met Brother Dane. If she hadn't gone in that day to buy stamps, she might never have gone to the revival or gotten pregnant, and both her life and Jerry's would have been a lot different. He would be in college right now instead of Vietnam. They might even be married. She didn't blame Mr. Marshall for any of it, because he was trying to do something good for her—and it sure wasn't his fault about what happened between her and Brother Dane—but it was hard for her to see him and make conversation. So she always put her letters in the drive-by box, and asked Mama to pick up stamps for her from time to time.

Even the thought of Mr. Marshall handling the letter with the confession she was sending to Jerry was a little scary. Too late—after she had already dropped it in—she thought that maybe there might be censors who read the letters. But surely there weren't. Jerry had already said a lot of things that a censor would have cut out. Still, she was half sorry she had sent it, and went home with a weight on her chest. Jerry would never understand, and probably would stop writing to her. But no matter what happened, she couldn't live a lie anymore.

Now there were four people besides herself who knew the truth. Brother Dane would never tell, because he was bound to her by what they did. Her mother would never tell, either, because she was bound to her by love. Walter couldn't afford to tell, so that left Jerry. She was putting her life on the line by trusting Jerry, but there was nothing else she could do. The letter was gone.

She went back home, to wait until she heard from him again.

43. *Vietnam*

March 15, 1968

Dear Carlene,

 I can't believe I am sitting here calmly writing you a letter. These last three or four days have been the worst days since we got here. First, I just want to say that I got your letter, and I don't even know how to start to talk about what you told me. If you had told me all this stuff when I was back in Sweet Valley, I know for sure that I couldn't have handled it, but the guy who lived back there was a different person than the one who is writing you right now. The first thing I want to tell you is that *it is not your fault*. None of it. You were thirteen years old, for Pete's sake. There was no way you could have meant to kill your father, although it sounds like he needed killing, and that SOB Walter should have taken care of it the right way and treated it like the suicide it was instead of saddling you with that guilt all these years. It wasn't even your fault for getting pregnant, although I sure don't think much of that preacher. He took advantage of you when you were in a bad place, and I don't think he should be preaching to other people. I can't believe what you had to go through all by yourself, honey, and I wish there was some way I could change it, but I can't.

I have learned one thing over here, and that is there are times when a person will sometimes do things he wouldn't think about doing in his wildest dreams under normal circumstances, but it doesn't mean he is not a good person down under it all. I guess the same holds true for you or anybody else who has their back against the wall.

The U.S. Army has proved that you can take anybody and turn him into a killer. They brought us over here to kill dinks. That's our job. And once you kill one, it is easier to kill the next one, then the next one, until finally it doesn't mean anything at all, like swatting flies. It's like things you would be sent to the pen for back in the States are commonplace occurrences every day here. I don't think any eighteen-year-old over here left the United States with the idea of, "Oh, boy. I'm going to become a rapist and killer," but somehow, when you get out in the jungle, somebody flicks a switch and turns off the old you and a new you takes over. Torture and rape have become everyday facts. Some of the guys have gotten to like it too much, and some of us who don't—me, for example—don't have the guts to stop them.

For instance, not too many of the guys know I'm still a virgin—yes, it's true, believe it or not, I still am. But my buddy Tripp Barlow knows, and ever since he found out, he has been bound and determined to get me to lose it one way or the other, and in the process, a few of the other guys have found out. They have made it their project. There are always a lot of girls around who will take on ten or twenty guys for a couple of bucks each, but you know me—if I wouldn't make love to you, I'm not about to go down that slippery slope, so to speak.

In spite of the easy women, a few of the guys in this company, not all, are known for just raping any woman they feel like, and nobody much says anything. They think of it more or less like going to the toilet. A few days ago, they had one in a hootch and there must have been a dozen guys lined up waiting to go in. I was trying to ignore the whole thing when one of them came over and said, "Golden, we decided it's time you lost your cherry. This is a prime piece of meat, and clean. Never been touched. You can have the honor of being the first."

I said thanks but no thanks, and after most of the guys took their turn, they all came over and dragged me to the hut and shoved me in. They thought it was a big joke. The hut was dark and this little girl—she couldn't have been more than twelve or thirteen—was lying on the bed with her legs spread open, half out of it. She looked at me with terror in her eyes, and I tried to tell her that I wasn't going to do anything, but she started to shake and take on. I got some water and tried to wash her off, but she curled up in a little ball and I couldn't touch her. I looked back outside and there were a whole gang of more guys from another company waiting to get their turn. I tried to tell her to climb out the window and run for it, but if you have had thirteen guys and you were a virgin, you can't exactly run too well.

I picked her up—she hardly weighed anything—and went outside myself, then, and tried to talk some sense into the men, but they took her away from me and put her back in the hootch.

Carlene, as much as I hate to tell you, I walked away. I left her with them, because I wasn't ready to shoot my own friends, and I wasn't ready to fight them all. You never know what a man with a weapon will do, and it doesn't pay to tick some of these guys off. It's too easy to get hit by friendly fire out in the bush. It's so common, there's even a name for it— fragging.

I think all of us are beginning to go a little nuts. In the last few weeks, we have taken a lot of losses by booby traps. We wandered into a field of them yesterday, and every single one of us managed to get right in the middle of it before anyone tripped a wire. Then all of a sudden, there was an explosion and then another one and another one. Captain yelled for us to freeze, but people were running around trying to help each other and in the process setting off more and more of them. One guy got split from top to bottom, intestines hanging out and all, but miraculously was still alive, and when the medics went to put him on a poncho to move him, they set him down on top of another mine and blew the poor guy into a thousand bits. Parts of him rained down and landed all over us. We looked like we'd been hosed down with blood. There was a big gob of liver or something on my boot that I kicked off.

Guys were crying and screaming, crawling around on the ground and going to pieces. Captain had to slap a couple of them who were in hysterics. He had a job getting all of us out of there, I can tell you. We had thirty-two either killed or wounded, out of about ninety of us. When you see your buddies blown to bits, legs blown off, blinded, right in front of you, there is no way you are ever the same again.

We were all practically in the Twilight Zone when we went back through the village. The people just squatted and watched us with sulled-up eyes. They knew exactly what we had marched into. They didn't warn us, because they had probably laid the traps themselves.

This wasn't the first time this has happened. The 48th is still around this area. Not long ago, we encountered a lot of fire from some villages north of here, called My Lai 4 and My Lai 6—there's a bunch of little hamlets that make up what we call Pinkville, I may have told you that—and we had one man killed and fifteen injured. By the time we got reinforcements and went in, the enemy had just melted away down their tunnels or mixed in with the civilians. We never know how many of them there are, or where they are. You can't imagine what it is like to fight a phantom army, to see your friends dying one by one, getting their guts ripped out, and be helpless to do anything about it.

Another horrible thing happened, too. I hate to even tell you this one, but it will show you what we are up against. One of our guys was captured by the VC, and we didn't even know it. All night long we heard screams from seven klicks away. We thought the VC had amplifiers and were playing a tape to make us crazy, but they weren't. They had skinned him alive, taking their sweet time, then soaked him in saltwater and tore off his . . . I can't even say it in a letter without getting sick at my stomach. They're not human, Carlene. They are worse than animals, because animals at least only kill to survive. But I guess that makes us worse than animals, too.

We had a memorial service this afternoon for our dead buddies, which was pretty tough, I can tell you. Tonight, we had a pep talk from the new colonel, and tomorrow, we are going to clean out that nest once and for all. We're going to be dropped into My Lai 4, which we think is the 48th's stronghold. We have known for a long time that the villages were basically sympathetic to the VC, but there was never any concrete proof. This time, though, our intelligence said they are definitely there, two hundred or more strong.

By seven in the morning, all of the civilians leave the village and go to the market, so whoever is left behind is bound to be Viet Cong. But this is one trip to the market that will be different for them. When they get back, they're in for a big surprise: We are going to level that VC pus pocket and turn it into a parking lot. We'll see where the Cong get their support from then. Our orders are to neutralize the area. That means not to leave one thing the enemy could use, not one hootch or chicken or duck or cow or rice cache. There are some expert tunnel rats coming in to join us, too, so if those suckers try to get away down the tunnels, they'll know what to do.

It is going to be our first big battle, and I don't have to tell you I am scared. If you don't hear from me again, Carlene, let these be my last words to you: I love you, and if I make it out of here alive and back home, we will be together and try to make some kind of a life together, I promise you. You have been through your own war, too, I can see it now, and you are a braver soldier than I am. Take care of that boy. I pray that I can be a daddy to him after all.

All my love forever,
Jerry

44. Cherry

 In all the excitement of following Lucille out to the Water Witch, not to mention me getting practically scalped and the upsetting news about Baby and those pictures, I completely forgot to go to work. I was supposed to be there at four and work until eight, but it didn't even enter my head until I pulled into our yard after dropping Lucille off and heard the phone ringing. It turned out to be Rainy Day, wanting to know where I was.

"Omigosh! I'll be right over. I'll explain when I get there."

Rainy Day was waiting at the door when I came in.

"Are you all right? I was worried when you didn't show up and nobody answered at your house, and . . ." She stopped in midsentence. "Wow, you cut your hair! It looks really cute!"

"Thank you. I'm so sorry, Rainy Day. Lucille gave me an accidental haircut, and then I had to go someplace kind of unexpectedly, and to tell you the truth, I just plain forgot that I was coming in today. I hope I didn't mess anything up for you."

"You seem a little strung out. Your aura is kind of jagged around the edges. What's the matter?"

Rainy Day was into psychic stuff. She read tarot cards for people, did astrological charts, and could see auras. I should have known I couldn't hide anything from her.

"Come on upstairs and I'll mix you a juice cocktail. You can tell me all about it."

She put the CLOSED sign on the door and locked it, even though it was still more than an hour until closing time.

We went into the black-light room, sank down into the beanbag chairs, and drank our carrot/beet/honey drinks—a beautiful Persian melon color—while I poured out my heart to her. I didn't mean to say anything to her about any of it, but somehow she got it out of me.

"It just seems like everything is getting out of control, Rainy Day. What really freaks me out is that Franco character coming to Carlene's funeral with that rose and kissing her on the mouth. It makes you feel like he is somehow involved in her death. I wish we could find out what happened to her. It seems like the police aren't going to."

"Why don't we ask her?"

"What do you mean?"

"There are ways. I sometimes have this knack of speaking to people who have crossed over."

"You're not serious."

"Oh yes I am. Even when I was a child, I saw people that nobody else could. We had this elderly neighbor named Goldie, who used to give me sticks of horehound candy, and I would help her dig in her garden. She passed on when I was about five, but every afternoon after she died, she'd still be out there working in the backyard, and I'd go out and we'd talk, just like we always did."

A cold chill ran down my spine. "Rainy Day, don't take this the wrong way, but is this witchcraft or anything?"

"No, Cherry. It is not black magick, if that's what you're worried about. I only practice white magick. You can only use it for good, for protection, not to do evil against anybody. Satan, if he even exists, has absolutely nothing to do with it.

"And I'm not sure the power I have has anything to do with magick anyhow. My great-grandma came from Wales, and she was tuned into things not of this world too. She was always seeing little people everywhere. I think it is just a Jones thing. Aunt Frannie has a bit of it."

"Aunt Frannie?"

"Frannie Moore. Used to be Frannie Jones. Carlene's mother."

"Carlene was your cousin?"

"Didn't you know that? My daddy is Frannie's big brother."

"Well, I'll be dog. Did Carlene ever, well, how do you say it? Appear to you after she died?"

"No, she didn't. There is no telling which plane she is on or what she is doing. It's a big place over there. You don't always see everyone you

want to, and sometimes ones you don't even know at all will barge in, trying to take over. You have to be tough with them. All kinds of low-life
trashy spirits try to come through from the lower plane. It's like a stadium
full of fans at a Rolling Stones concert over there."

She was talking in this calm voice, like what she said made perfect
sense, and I tried to listen in the same way. Who's to say that what she was
saying wasn't real? We believe in angels, and they aren't so easy to prove,
either. I decided to keep an open mind.

"Okay. If we were going to, how would we call up Carlene?"

"Well, ideally, we could have a séance, but since it's just you and me,
we could try to reach her on the Ouija board."

"You mean those things really work? I thought they were toys."

"If you know what you're doing. Are you game?"

I swallowed hard. I only half believed in that stuff, but the half that believed, really believed.

"What do we have to do?"

"The first thing is to get some salt."

She went to the juice bar and came back with a box of Morton's.

"Sea salt is better, but this will work." She started sprinkling it in a circle around a little table in the black-light room. "You need to sprinkle the
salt in the deasil—that's sun-wise, east to south to west to north. If you
were going to do something bad, you'd sprinkle it in the widdershins,
which is the opposite direction."

"I thought you couldn't do bad stuff."

"Not couldn't. Wouldn't."

She laid down a light circle of salt around the low table, then lit a candle in the middle of it. "This is a white candle, which represents purity and
the life force. Here, sit down by the table and I'll get the Ouija board."

I sat down cross-legged on the floor. The candle took away most of the
effects of the black light, but not entirely. It seemed like the air was vi-
brating neon outside the circle of salt. I was beginning to get a little nervous.

Rainy Day came back in with the board and put it on the table. "Okay.
Here it is. Now, what we have to do is say a little prayer to my spirit guide,
so he will not let any evil spirits in, and see if he can find Carlene for us.
Then it would be helpful if we sang a song. Spirits like that."

I nodded, ready to strip off naked if she said to. She had tied a crystal
on a black velvet ribbon around her head, and it hung right between her

eyes and sparkled in the light. It was a Hot Springs diamond. We had some of those for sale out front. I thought I might get one, now that I saw how pretty it looked. I think I was half hypnotized by the reflected sparks of the candle flame. She raised her arms, closed her eyes, and prayed:

"Oh, Abilar, my most dedicated spirit guide, please hear our reverent pleas in this hour of time on earth. Protect us from evil spirits. Do not allow them to enter the sacred circle of salt. We come to you, Abilar, because we seek Carlene Ida Moore, recently murdered, in order to shed some light on the events that caused her death. Help us speak to her, Abilar, and we will be now and for eternity most grateful." She opened her eyes. They had never looked bluer. "Now it helps if we sing a song. Do you know the words to 'Hey, Jude'?"

"Spirits like the Beatles?"

"A lot."

We sang the whole song of "Hey, Jude," and really got down on the part that goes, "Da, da, da, dadadada—dadadada." Rainy Day had a really nice, mellow voice. Her cat, Florentine, a long-haired smoky blue with amber-colored eyes, came in to see what was going on and climbed right up into my lap.

"Is it okay for Florentine to be here?"

"It's a good sign. Cats are sensitive to spirits. They like to be in the middle of whatever is going on. It means we are making contact. I think it's time." I jumped as her voice changed—boomed out, full of authority.

"Carlene, if you hear us, give us a sign."

Florentine arched up and yowled at that point, a hair-raising sound, and dug her claws into my leg. I thought I was going to have a heart attack.

"That is a good enough sign. Thanks, Carlene." I said out loud, then I leaned down and whispered to Rainy Day, "Do you think it's her?"

"There is something at your left shoulder. I can't tell if it is her or not."

I turned around but didn't see or feel anybody there. I guess I am just not sensitive to spirits.

"She is trying to say something, but I can't understand. Maybe she will speak through the board."

Rainy Day put her fingers on the pointer, as if she were touching a fragile flower.

"Now, you put your fingers on the other side of the planchette. Lightly."

I did.

"Carlene, who killed you? Tell us, please."

The planchette didn't move at all. It was like she either didn't hear us or didn't want to tell us. The silence made a ringing noise in my ears.

"Maybe she doesn't know. Ask her again, Rainy Day."

"If you can't name the killer, is there anything else you want to tell us?"

The pointer moved and formed the word B-A-B-Y-L-E-T-T-E-R-S.

"What letters? Is it Baby Moreno or a baby? What is she talking about?" I asked in a whisper.

"Carlene, is it the letters of a word or letters like you send to somebody? Is it something to do with Baby Moreno?"

The planchette didn't move.

"She is getting fainter. Maybe she doesn't want to tell about the letters."

"Maybe we should ask her something else, Rainy Day. Is it okay to ask personal things? Can they see into the future over there?"

"Sometimes." Rainy Day was whispering now. "They don't always tell us, though. Most things that happen to us here on the earth plane are tests we have to pass before we can get to a higher plane. Spirits can get into trouble if they help us too much. But you can try."

"Carlene," I said as loudly as I could, feeling really stupid. "I have a boyfriend named Tripp Barlow. Can you see into the future? Is he the one I ought to marry?"

The planchette began to move. It spelled out A-S-K-F-A-Y-E.

" 'Ask Faye.' Do you know somebody named Faye, Cherry?"

"There was Faye Dean Murphy, but she moved to Texas in the fourth grade. I don't know any other Fayes."

"Maybe there's one you can't think of."

"Or maybe it isn't Carlene at all who is talking to us but one of those low-rent spooks. It looks like she would have told us the name of the killer if it was her."

Just then Florentine jumped down out of my lap and skidded across the board, knocking over the candle. The room was bathed in black light again; the melted white candle wax glowed in a neon blue puddle on the table where the cat had knocked it over and spilled it.

It came over me then we might have been talking to an actual dead person. The room seemed too close, like the walls were moving in.

—

Rainy Day walked me outside to the car. It had come a little shower, and the air felt clean, like it had been rinsed off. Somewhere, somebody was burning leaves. It was comforting, that smell; it brought you back to the world of moms cooking fried potatoes and dads raking leaves in the early fall.

"Well, that was something, Rainy Day. Do you think it was really Carlene?"

"Maybe. She was so faint I couldn't be sure. We can have a real séance, if you want to—get some of the kids together and do it right: John Cool, Bean, Tripp, Baby. That is, if you and Baby get back on the same wavelength."

"I need to talk to her, I guess, but I don't know what to say. What if it's true that she posed for those pictures? Do you think she'd tell me the truth?"

"What do you feel in your heart?"

"She would never do anything like that."

"Then trust your heart. Our senses never lie to us. Like if you are hungry for some particular kind of food, it means your body needs the nutrients it provides. If you feel like something is the truth, or something is wrong, then it usually is."

I nodded. That went along with what Mama had said—if you have to ask yourself if you are in love, you're not. Trouble was, my own senses had been going haywire ever since I met Tripp Barlow. Things that I would have once sworn on the Bible were wrong now didn't seem so bad. Can we ever trust our own senses? I didn't know anymore.

"Maybe I'll go see Baby right now. Should I say anything to her about the séance?"

"If you want to. Ask her if she knows anything about any letters. I feel like Carlene wants to tell us something, if we can only make contact."

45. *Cherry*

 Baby wasn't at home. Her car was there, but Manang said that Bean had picked her up and she didn't know where they went. I should have called before I came out, but I didn't trust my voice on the phone. Baby knows me too well.

"Come in, Cherry. We haven't seen you in a while."

The little girls were playing Barbie in the living room, tiny high heels and clothes scattered everywhere, and Pilar was right in the middle of it, down on the floor with them. She seemed embarrassed that I had seen her playing dolls, and got up. She didn't have on her makeup, and looked a lot younger than she had at the party.

"Hey, Pilar, how's it going?"

"Okay. I was just helping Sunnie and Connie. Some of those little zippers and buttons are hard for them to fix."

"I remember. I have all my old Barbies. I still take them out once in a while and dress them. They sit on my dresser, kind of like a room decoration." I said that because I didn't want her to feel bad that I had caught her playing. In fact, it was true, but I normally wouldn't have told anyone. She smiled like she appreciated it.

"So, Pilar, are you excited about being in high school this year?"

"I guess."

"Think you might try out for cheerleader? You should."

"You think so?"

"Oh yeah. You'd be great at splits and jumps. You have the body for it."

She did, too. She was built a lot like Baby, but was even more slender and graceful, if that was possible, and her legs were longer. I took a hard look at her and realized that she hadn't stuffed Kleenex in her bra like I thought she did that night at the opening of the Family Hand. She had just sprouted a pair of really nice breasts in the last year. She must be nearly fifteen now. I couldn't believe it. I still thought of her as a little girl.

"I really like your haircut, Cherry. I've been thinking about cutting my own, but I'm scared I won't like it. I've never cut my hair in my life."

Pilar's hair was longer, even, than Baby's.

"You would look really cute with a pixie, Pilar, like Audrey Hepburn wears. You have that great long neck like she does. I wanted to cut my hair for a long time, too, and now I am so glad I did," I lied. No sense in telling her how much I hated it if she was going to do the same thing.

"Maybe I'll do it, then." She gave me a big smile. This was the first conversation the two of us had ever had without Baby being there. I could tell she was happy I was talking to her like an equal. The kid was growing up.

"I can give you something to eat, Cherry?" Manang asked. "I have some nice egg rolls made tonight."

"Okay, sure. I'd love one, Manang." Manang's egg rolls were actually pretty tasty. In spite of the big meal I had eaten earlier, I scarfed down three almost without breathing. Pilar and Manang hung out around the kitchen table with me while I ate.

"I think Baby is with Bean out at Woody's," Pilar said. "I would love to go with you, but they wouldn't let me in. I'm not twenty-one." She seemed a little wistful.

I could go to Woody's, though. I had been to a bar just this afternoon and drunk liquor. As long as I was at it, I might as well visit the gateway to hell, as Brother Wilkins called it, and add that to the growing list of sinful things I had done today.

"Thanks, Pilar. Maybe I'll run on out there right now before it gets too late. Let me know if you decide to cut your hair. I wouldn't advise you to go to the beauty school to get it done, though."

She and the little girls stood in the yard waving as I left. I still didn't know how I was going to bring up the subject of the pictures with Baby; I would have to play it by ear. I hoped we could talk without Bean being right there in the middle of it. He had gotten funny about leaving Baby alone, and between him and my job and school and Tripp, there was hardly any time for Baby and me to do anything together anymore, just the two of us. I guess that was part of growing up, but I felt farther from her than I ever had.

46. *Baby, Bean, and Nguyen*

 In spite of the angry way Bean denied it, Baby knew down deep that he must have had something to do with other women while he was away. He was a young, healthy man, and she knew there probably were willing women all over the place in Vietnam.

There was something about the way he had said that strange name, Nguyen, while he was making love to her, like he was in pain or something. When she asked him to tell her about the hootch maid in the picture, he pretended not to know who she was talking about. Then, when she showed him the picture, he just said that she had disappeared and he didn't know what happened to her. Another girl came and took her place, he said, and then another, and he couldn't really remember their names. Hootch maids came and went all the time.

Baby finally had to let it drop. Bean got mad every time she brought it up. Whoever the girl was, Baby tried to tell herself, she was long gone now. Still, it hurt. That may not have been rational, in light of her affair with Jackie, but nobody said you had to be rational.

———

In fact, Baby's instincts were right on the money. Nguyen had been more than just Bean's hootch maid. She not only washed and ironed his clothes; she gave him baths and massaged his feet for hours. She knew all the fine points of acupressure: She could press a spot on his foot, and his neck would go limp. She could make him relax like no one else. It felt so good, after wearing the hot, heavy boots all day, to be fussed over by a pretty girl.

Baby was so far away, and there were times she didn't seem real to him, times he had to look at her picture to really remember her features. Life back home was becoming like a dream that fades as the day wears on. Real, vivid life was the army base and the endless crawl through the tunnels. And Nguyen. He hated to admit it, even to himself, but she was, in a lot of ways, more agreeable than Baby, and she didn't ask for much in return. Baby always liked to be in charge. He was proud of her, but she made him feel like she was smarter than him. She tried to help him, but he would rather take a D or F in algebra than let her know he didn't understand it. A man had his pride. He was even afraid that his music, the one thing he was better than anybody at, bored her. She sometimes read a book during rehearsal. There were so many girls who loved bands and would gladly have taken her place, but they were too easy. They bored him. Bean only wanted Baby, who didn't seem to realize how important he was.

But in Vietnam there was no question of his value. He was the toughest Rat in the pack, and everybody treated him accordingly. On his door, someone had painted a cartoon of a rat smoking a cigarette and wearing a crown, with the words KING RAT underneath. He went down tunnels where nobody else could go, stayed down longer, and made more kills that anyone. He was almost happier underground than above. He felt alive down there, adrenaline feeding him like dope. It was a high like nothing else to come out of the tunnels and breathe sweet air. It got his juices flowing, and the only way he could get release from the rush was with a woman.

Nguyen, graceful in her purple silk ao dai, a garment designed to cover everything and hide nothing, was there to do whatever he wanted and do it gladly, without question or hesitation; and it was good. Not as good as with Baby, at least as Bean remembered it, but if it had been, Bean might have fallen in love with Nguyen, and that would have caused real trouble.

There were always enthusiastic prostitutes smuggled in to service the men, but women of class—no matter how poor or desperate—didn't mix with the Americans. A girlfriend of Nguyen's, who worked in the PX, had tried to marry a GI and wound up with her head on a pike outside the main gate of the base. A note pinned to it said, "This is what happens to Vietnamese people who go around with the enemy." As long as money or espionage was involved, the VC let women fraternize with the Americans—but not for love.

Bean never thought once about marrying Nguyen. She was, after all, a gook and could hardly speak any English. It was her job to make him comfortable, nothing more. But in the middle of the night, when he awakened from his worst recurring nightmare—that the VC had captured Baby and he was underground searching for her, could hear her screaming but kept taking the wrong turn—it was Nguyen who would hold him while he shook and cried and said Baby's name over and over; Nguyen who would wipe the sweat from his eyes and kiss him until he relaxed and tucked her into the crook of his body; Nguyen whose skin felt like soft cream and was a balm to his spirit; Nguyen whose smile he thought of as he fell asleep again.

Then one day Nguyen didn't come to work. Days went by. When Bean tried to find out where she was, nobody seemed to know. At first he was angry. How dare she leave without a word? She was young and too pretty to stay for long in such a menial job, he decided. But he was not prepared for how much it hurt to know she had no feelings for him, how much he missed her. Then he worried that something bad had happened. He tried to find her, but realized he knew nothing about her—not where she lived or what she had done before the war or if she had any brothers and sisters. He didn't even know her last name. She couldn't speak enough English to tell him these things, and it had been enough that she was there for him, the way she was. She was a fact of his life. But when she was gone, he realized he needed her as much as he needed nourishment. He found himself scanning the crowds, looking into the face of every Vietnamese woman he met, looking for Nguyen.

To forget her, he threw himself into his work with even more passion.

———

Bean was right: Nguyen was more than a washerwoman. She was a classically trained actress who belonged to a troupe of fervent Viet Cong. She sang and danced to keep up the spirits of the underground army in the tunnels, and also passed on information she learned while on the American base.

In fact, most of her friends who worked for the Americans were Viet Cong as well. It was amazing how stupidly lax the Americans were about talking in front of the people who cut their hair and served them drinks. They thought the "gooks" couldn't understand, but in fact a great many Vietnamese spoke passable English, including Nguyen. It got harder with each day to keep up the charade with Bean of not speaking English. She had come to respect him, even though he had killed several of her friends in the tunnels. Any American who could navigate the tunnels deserved respect. They were soft, the Americans, and if they had had to live for long underground, among snakes and scorpions and bats, on a diet of half-cooked rice and roasted rat, she knew the war would have soon been over and they would all go home.

Bean was not soft, though. She knew he was a worthy adversary. More than an enemy soldier, she was beginning to see him as a man. He played his guitar for her and sang in a voice that stirred something inside her. She looked forward to their lovemaking and did not have to pretend her passion.

But the day Nguyen bicycled to work and stopped, horror-struck, beneath the head of her friend from the PX, she pushed aside any feelings of love she might have had for Bean. He was the enemy. She would pretend to care for him as part of her job, but she hardened her heart. At least she tried. On dark nights, when Bean sang the strange songs to her and kissed her with soft lips, she sometimes forgot it was merely her duty to be with him. At those times, the line between duty and the heart was smudged.

The leader of her troupe could see she was gaining too much regard for the small American, and decided to send her full-time to the theater in the tunnels. Before Nguyen had a chance to let Bean know, she was moved to a village not far from Cu Chi, to spend her days beneath the earth. There, she performed a play about a poor girl who is captured by the Americans but saved in the end by her brave comrades.

After a few weeks, she realized that she had in truth been captured by an American. She was pregnant. Her leader surmised who the father might be but was kind enough to allow her to lighten her workload. Soon, she became too big to navigate the narrow tunnels that led down to the second level, and so was able to remain on the first, where at least the air was a little better.

———

Nguyen was resting in a hammock in her sleeping nook when she heard the rumble of big guns, felt them vibrate the ground. Anxious, she raised herself up, but she couldn't tell how far away they were. The nook, only two meters high, was carved out beneath many feet of earth, but you could never tell, when a shell hit, if the dirt would protect you or cave in and bury you alive.

She felt the baby move. He was strong, like his father. She could picture him curled inside and was secretly glad for the mix of his blood—American and Vietnamese. He would be a fiery soldier, like both his mother and his father, but perhaps he also would have soft brown eyes and a voice like burnt sugar. With this baby, she would be allowed to keep a part of her American, even if he never knew he had a son. But who could tell? Perhaps she would find a way for them to see each other again. He would be so surprised. She liked to imagine the meeting and his first look at his baby, but tried not to think past it. There could be no future with Bean—not for her, and not for her child.

The baby moved again. A lump appeared, moving across her belly, and Nguyen put her hand on it. She thought it might be a foot, the baby stretching out to make more room for itself. She was happy to feel movement. The baby had been quiet for a few days, and she poked it from to time to time just to make sure it was still alive. The little one was resting for the big ordeal of being born. Nguyen smiled at the thought of the baby working so hard and finally coming out, only to look around and find itself still inside a tunnel. But there was nothing to do for it. If she surfaced in the middle of a fight, she would surely be killed and give away the position of the tunnel, endangering everyone inside.

A gush of water flooded from her, pooling in the hammock and dripping down onto the earthen floor. The baby was trying to get out now. A dull pain hit in the lower part of her back, and Nguyen knew she had to get to a bigger place soon. The connecting tunnel to the nearest large room—called the cool room, because it was eight meters square and had many airholes—was only half a meter wide, and she was afraid she might not be able to squeeze through, but she had to try. The cool room was draped with parachute silk to screen the ever-falling dirt. There was water there. But even though she had been taught how to deliver the baby herself, she was afraid. She listened but could hear no movement ahead, no voices anywhere. The next sleeping chamber was empty, as was the cooking chamber. Everyone had gone down deeper to get away from the attack.

The blasts were getting closer. Small pieces of earth crumbled onto her face as the ground shook from the bombs. She started through the connecting tunnel to the cool room, squeezing her belly gently. The baby lay still, as though it knew it must be quiet and help her.

She dropped into the cool room as a contraction seized her and sat breathing hard for a moment, exhausted from the effort. Then she put her candle down and found an oil lamp and a straw mat to lie on as the next pain hit. She bit her lip so as not to cry out in case anyone was near the vent holes. Maybe a friend would come soon. But time passed and no one came. She heard only the sound of the guns and the rumble of the earth.

Hours went by. Her throat became raw with the cries she held in. A long whistle sounded directly overhead, and the cool room shook as part of the exit tunnel filled with earth. Nguyen screamed with the screaming of the bomb. She dug her fingernails into the floor and scratched until fat crescents of dirt were packed under the nails. One more blast that close would cause the ceiling to crumble. A fine dust hung in the air, and the candle flame flickered. Nguyen could feel dust catch in her nose, and it was hard to draw a deep breath.

She steeled her nerves and focused her concentration on breathing, attempting to slow her racing heart as her belly hardened with each contraction and the baby inched toward life. She tried to remember Cu Chi as the lush jungle it had been when she was a little girl, before the Americans came. She tried to hear again the sound the bright birds made as they called from the tops of high green trees, and to see the clear water flow over stones in the stream. She remembered how her orange cat would paw a ball of string in the packed earth of her hut and how the rooster would puff out his chest and strut across the yard, king of the hens, his red cock's-comb bobbing atop his russet head, his green and black tail feathers shimmering in the sun. She pictured her mother, graceful as she stirred a pot on the stove, then bent to put a piece of wood into the firebox underneath. She saw her father as he came in from the fields and picked up her little brother, lifting him onto his shoulders in one fluid motion, as easily as he lifted baskets of rice. In the distance behind him, the sun glinted off the shrine containing the bodies of her grandparents, a little white stone house in the middle of the watery rice field, there to bless the crop and keep the ancestors near the family. She had thought one day her own parents would have their shrine there, too, but it was all gone now: her house, her field, her parents, her brother, her shrine, her life.

Now Cu Chi was burned and barren. As far as the eye could see, there was no green, only black sticks, broken and sharp, sticking out of the earth like silent hands reaching in supplication to the sky. No animals ran through the charred skeleton of the jungle; no men and women worked the blackened fields. If there was no jungle, reasoned the Americans, there could be no hiding place for the Viet Cong.

But we do not need trees to hide among, Nguyen reminded herself as her belly grew soft, preparing for the next contraction. Mother Earth hides us. She is old and patient. The Americans, with their bombs, their Agent Orange and napalm, will not be here forever. Inside her belly, Mother Earth stores the seeds of a new jungle, a new life: green, shady trees and vines that will cover the ground once again live inside the earth, alongside the people who hide below and wait, beneath the burned-out jungles of Cu Chi.

———

The contractions fused into one long pain, giving Nguyen time only to dig her heels into the ground before the urge to push took her over. She reached between her legs and felt something round and hard and wet. The baby's head emerged for a moment, then retreated back into its sheath. With each push, the head came out farther, and then a terrible pain seized her like none she had experienced before. It felt like her body was being ripped from bottom to top. She screamed then through her swollen lips, unable to stop herself, and grunted like a beast as she pushed hard and felt the baby, warm and slippery, slide from between her legs. The pain ceased, as though it had never happened, and she reached down to pick up the girl; slipped her up and across her belly and held her tightly. The baby squirmed, making sounds like a mewling kitten, and Nguyen laughed and cried at the same time as she wiped the little one's eyes and nose free of blood and mucus. She had been so sure it was a boy! The baby's little arms and legs trembled while with one hand her mother held her tightly and with the other tied the cord with a piece of parachute string, then cut it, using a small knife she had taped to her leg. Another contraction brought out the afterbirth.

There was no cloth to wrap the baby in, so Nguyen ripped off a piece of parachute drape and cleaned her as best she could, then tore another and stuffed it between her legs, to staunch the bleeding. Then she lay back and stared at her daughter. She was beautiful—pale, not red as most newborns, with dark hair and eyes that looked around the room in wonder, as if to say, "Where have I come to? What is this? Who are you?" Nguyen laughed at the funny little face, so much like Bean's, and put the rosebud mouth to her breast, engorged already.

———

Time is meaningless underground, but it seemed to Nguyen that hours had passed and still the bombing had not stopped. There was some rice and salt in a pot, and she ate a big bite before realizing it had gone bad. She knew she couldn't stay here much longer, but there was nowhere to go. The exit tunnel was damaged, and she didn't have the stamina to crawl through the connecting tunnel with the baby. She would have to rest and regain her strength.

She must have dozed, because she was awakened by a noise, faint, like the swish of fabric against dirt. Someone was coming through the connecting tunnel. It must be a friend, since the tunnel was heavily protected with poisonous bamboo vipers, hidden in tubes set along the way, as well as cleverly concealed mines. Nguyen called out quietly, in a hoarse whisper.

There was no answer, and she realized too late that it must be an American. A flashlight beam flickered and then blinded her as she pushed the baby to the back of the room and lunged with her knife toward the hand emerging cautiously from the tunnel. She cut the arm, deeply, and blood spurted as the flashlight fell to the floor. She picked it up just as the soldier fired his gun at point-blank range. The beam swung wildly before it dropped from her hand.

She never saw the shock on Bean's face as he recognized who she was. "Nguyen!" Bean blinked to clear the sweat from his eyes, and looked again. It was her. She was a VC. She had played him for a fool, and left without a word to join those subhumans who took pleasure in torturing and killing his buddies and then hiding in stinking holes.

Just outside this very tunnel, they had nailed an American's arm to a tree with a skull and crossbones carved on it. It was a miracle that Bean had even seen the entrance. Everyone else was too put off by the grisly sight, but Bean noticed that the charred foliage was a little too perfect over the spot underneath the tree, and sure enough, it hid a trapdoor.

Nguyen lay dead, staring. A whimpering came from the corner, and Bean whirled and shot twice into the darkness. He stopped still and listened but heard only his own heavy breathing. He crawled over, lifted a stained scrap of parachute, and shone his light on a newborn baby girl, still and unmoving.

In a moment of hopeless clarity, he understood that she was his, and something in his soul cracked and shattered. In anguish, he backed out of the tunnel, then tossed a grenade, blowing up the cool room, leaving the pretty Viet Cong actress in a grave she had created for herself and her half-American baby, who never got to see the blue sky.

47. Cherry

 Pickups and cars crowded the gravel parking lot at Woody's. Thank goodness I drive a Bug. I found a little space by the trash barrels out back, and squeezed in.

Woody's was a low building painted barn-red. A blue-and-red neon sign that shouted BUDWEISER and a green one that said HEINEKEN glowed like Christmas lights in the front window. Bean's pickup was there, and as my feet crunched the gravel, I could hear him singing "I'm a Long Gone Daddy," an old Hank Williams song, in a voice that wasn't all that far off from Williams's. I was a little surprised, but I should have known that Bean could sing any kind of music. Besides which, the crowd that hung out at Woody's wasn't exactly your typical rock 'n' roll hippie gang.

He was really good—had that little catch in the voice down pat—if you like that kind of music. Mama did, and she played records by Hank Williams, Ernest Tubb, and Bob Wells and the Texas Playboys all the time, so I kind of liked it, too, although I'd never mention it to my friends.

I peeped in at the window and all the good ol' boys in cowboy boots and their girlfriends with teased-up hair and circle-tail skirts were dancing up a storm. Bean was wearing his leather pants and a tight flower-power shirt, but he had on a black cowboy hat, too. This was a side of him I didn't know. Come to think of it, I don't think I really knew a whole lot about Bean at all. Like with Manang and Pilar, I had never had a conversation with Bean where Baby wasn't there too, and when we were all together, Baby and I mostly talked to each other.

Somehow, seeing Bean sing something so out of the norm for him impressed me more than when he sang like Mick Jagger, although he was great at that, too. I guess, like me, he hadn't found his own style of art, either.

I watched through the window for a little while longer. Everyone seemed to be having a fun time, laughing and dancing and drinking. A waitress hustled by with a tray full of beers. After hearing about this place my whole life, it was going to take all the courage I could get together to go in. In fact, if a couple hadn't come up behind me just then and held the door open, I might have chickened out. I smiled and thanked them and hoped to goodness I would see Baby and wouldn't have to talk to anybody on my own or order a drink or anything.

Luckily I spotted her right away. She was at a table by the bandstand, talking to a woman about Mama's age, who was wearing a turquoise cowboy shirt with pearl snap buttons and purple piping, and a pair of tight jeans tucked into red cowboy boots. Baby had on a white miniskirt and black turtleneck sweater and black patent-leather knee-high boots. She looked fantastic, but kind of too chic, like she should have been at a nightclub instead of a roadhouse. They were both drinking beer.

I hung by the door, trying to decide the best way to get by the dancers without being elbowed to death. The floor was covered with roasted-peanut shells; buckets of them sat on all the tables. People were popping them into their mouths and tossing the shells on the floor as fast as they could crack them open, and the dancers stomped around, grinding them to powder. I hoped I wouldn't slip and fall, which would be all I needed. I'd be trampled to death in three seconds flat.

Several lonesome guys leaning against the bar already were eyeing me. I thought one of them might be fixing to make a move, so I made mine first and cut across the dance floor, scootching between the dancers, and plopped down in a chair at Baby's table. I thought she was going to pop her eyeballs into her beer.

"Cherry! What are you doing here?"

"I just thought I'd stop by and see what this great place you go to all the time was like."

The woman with Baby stuck out her hand.

"Hidey, darlin'. I'm Maureen. Me and my old man, Woody, that big-bellied old geezer standing over yonder behind the bar, own the joint. You a friend of Baby's?"

"Yes, ma'am. I'm Cherry Marshall. Me and Baby go way back. I'm pleased to meet you."

"Well, welcome to Woody's, Cherry. We think a lot of Baby around here. Can I get you something to drink?"

"What are you having, Baby?"

"A Bud."

"I'll have one of those."

"You twenty-one?"

"She's twenty-one. Barely. She was the baby of the class," Baby said. Maureen got up and went over to the bar to get me a Bud.

"It doesn't seem like you're glad to see me."

"If I had known you wanted to come out here, Cherry, you could have come with me anytime. You didn't have to sneak in like that and scare me half to death. And when did you start drinking beer?"

"I haven't actually started drinking beer yet."

Maureen brought over a thick mug, frosted white from the freezer. It was full of foamy beer and had a lime wedge stuck on the side.

"Thank you, Maureen. That looks real good."

"You're just welcome. I have to go out to the kitchen and see how those pizzas are coming. You girls like a pizza?"

"That would be great. Pepperoni and black olives with extra cheese?"

"You got it." She sashayed into the kitchen through the swinging doors, the kind that all the saloons in the western movies have.

Baby just sat and stared at me. "If you'll tell me the name of the spaceship that kidnapped my friend Cheryl Ann Marshall, I'll be happy to pay a ransom for her."

"Hardy-har-har."

"What happened to your hair?"

"Lucille sort of cut it all off by accident."

"What, her hand slipped while she was shearing a sheep and your head got in the way?"

"Not exactly, but close."

"I really like it. In fact, it's adorable. You should have done it years ago."

"Well, I hate it, and it has already started to grow out as we speak. But I didn't come out here to chitchat about my hair, Baby. There is something really serious going on, and if you were ever straight with me in your life, you have to tell me the truth about something tonight. Swear you won't lie to me."

"What's the matter with you? You know I won't lie to you. What is it? You're scaring me."

"Swear. On your friendship for me."

"I swear. On my love for you. Now, what is it?"

I took a big swig of the beer. It made me gag. "How can you drink this stuff? It's awful!"

"Cherry, I am going to reach across this table and strangle you if you don't tell me what you're talking about!"

As the band played so loudly that nobody else could hear, I leaned in and told her about Lucille going out to the houseboat with Franco—but not about his wanting Lucille to make dirty movies and not the part where Lucille found the pictures. I wanted to see what Baby would say about him first. I had to be cool about this, even though what I really wanted to do was grab her and shake her and ask her why our world was coming apart.

"How well did you know Franco, Baby? You seemed pretty friendly with each other out at the cemetery."

"No, I didn't know him all that well. I met him at a party at the Water Witch back in the spring, just before Bean got back home. We talked a little, but you remember I quit when school was out and went to work with you at the pickle plant, so I didn't see Franco at all after that. He just didn't know anybody else at the funeral. Then he saw me and asked how I was doing. That's it. Really. I swear."

I really wanted to believe her, but it sounded too simple.

"You don't think Lucille is going to do anything with him, do you?" she asked.

"Do anything?"

"You know, sleep with him or anything."

"I don't think so." It was hard to make the move, but I had to find out what she knew. "Did you do anything with him, Baby?"

"No, I did not! What's the matter with you?"

She was really getting angry. I had to stop beating around the bush and cut to the chase. I couldn't stand it any longer. She might lie, but I would know it if she did. I could always tell.

"Well, if you didn't sleep with him, did you ever . . . I mean, like, did he ever take any pictures of you? Or get somebody to take pictures of you?"

"No, he didn't. What are you trying to say?"

"Lucille said he tried to get her to do dirty pictures. Dirty movies, actually. He has some friends in Memphis who make movies, and from the way he talked, they aren't what you would take your kids to see at the drive-in."

"I don't know anything about that, and I really resent the fact that you think I would do something like that. Why are you questioning me like this?"

It seemed like she was on the verge of blowing up. I crumbled.

"Oh, Baby! Because Lucille snooped and saw a book with a lot of dirty pictures in it, and she said there were some of you. So if it is true, just tell me. I'll understand. Or I'll try to, if you tell me there was a good reason. I have been just sick with worry about you ever since she found it."

"Are you serious? No. No way! That's not possible! I never posed for any pictures! Rita Ballard did, and she showed them to me, but I didn't know it was Franco who took them, and I would never, never, never do that! Oh, Cherry, I can't believe you'd believe it was me! Wait until I get my hands on that Lucille! How dare she say it was me!"

"Here's your pizza, girls! Having a nice girl-talk?"

Maureen set the plate down on the table. We thanked her and I tried to smile, but it never got as far as my mouth. Baby was tearing up. She took a swig of her beer, and I could see her lips tremble. Maureen went back to the kitchen, pretending not to notice anything wrong.

"Well, if it's not you, then it must be some girl who looks like you. He has probably been taking them of girls from a lot of different places."

"Yeah. You know all us gooks look alike."

"That's not funny."

"No, it's not." Baby wiped her eyes, took another swig from her mug. "We have to find a way to get a look at those pictures," she continued. "You know who else I'm afraid might be in them?"

"Who?"

"Carlene. I have a hunch she was getting into something over her head, and since you say all this, I wouldn't be surprised if Franco did have something to do with it. She said she was dating him, and he tried to deny it at the funeral, remember?"

"Oh, Baby. Do you think *he* might be the one who killed her?"

"I don't know. There was a time I wouldn't believe that anybody in this town was capable of something like that, but now I just don't know."

"Let's tell Ricky Don, Baby. I'm scared. We don't want to get into something over our heads, either."

"*No!* Are you serious? We can't get the law involved until we know something for sure, and maybe not even then. There's a lot of things you don't know, Cherry, but now that you're in this far, I might as well tell you all of it. There was a reason I quit the Water Witch, and it wasn't because I had a burning desire to peel onions. Let's eat this pizza before it gets cold. You won't believe what I have to tell you."

She was right. I would never have thought in my wildest dreams that a judge and lawyers and TV weathermen would get together and act like that, right out in public. Not to mention that smoking pot was against the law, which they very well knew. I mean, I know Baby and Bean smoke it, and so do Tripp and I, but . . . I don't know. Somehow, kids doing it wasn't the same as those older, important men doing it right out in the open like that and making out with women who weren't their wives. That was sleazy.

And Baby was right not to want to go to the law, because they were probably in on it, too. I couldn't believe Ricky Don was, but the sheriff, Melvyn Arbus, might be. He was a corrupt fat old guy who had been the sheriff for thirty years and had built a big house with a swimming pool from the money he got off of motorists for speeding. Everyone knew you just handed him your driver's license wrapped in a ten-dollar bill if he stopped you.

I felt like I was in one of those movies where the good guys turn out to be the bad guys and you couldn't trust anybody. But at least Baby and I were close again—probably even closer than we had ever been, because we didn't have secrets from each other anymore. She even told me about sleeping with Jackie, which I had sort of suspected anyhow. If it took a few beers for us to get back together, then I guess it was worth it. Two months ago, I would have sworn on my life that I would never ever do even one of the things I was doing right now. If this was what growing up was, then I guess I had finally done it, but it wasn't at all like what I thought it would be. I thought of Pilar and Connie and Sunnie playing dolls. It made me a little sad.

The beer got to taste not quite so foul when you ate pizza with it. Woody's had great pizza. I'd come back again just for that, and order a Coke. Unfortunately, it seemed like the best places to eat around here were the ones that served liquor.

Bean and John Cool and Rocky came over at their break. If they were surprised to see me there, they didn't act like it. We all went outside and sat on the hood of somebody's car while they smoked and got some fresh air. By this time it was nearly eleven, and while Mama and Daddy never said too much about me staying out this late, I hated to make them worry. It had gotten to where I was spending a lot of nights with Tripp, and they thought I was practically living at Baby's. They weren't too happy about it—like, why did I prefer Baby's house to my own? It was just one more thing I had to lie and feel guilty about.

"I better get on home, Baby. Y'all have fun, and let's talk tomorrow some more, okay?"

"Yeah. Definitely. We have to figure out what we are going to do."

"Do about what?" Bean asked.

"About shopping for some new clothes, Bean-Boy. Don't you think we need some?" Baby tweaked his nose.

"I think you have more clothes now than any three women can wear. You don't see me or John Cool or Rocky changing clothes every five minutes, and we do all right, don't we, boys?"

"Yeah, we should just get us a pair of leather pants, Cherry. That'll last us for the next ten years."

"Aw, you women," Bean said. "You never give a guy a break, do you?" We laughed. "Say good-bye to Cherry, Baby," he went on. "We have to get on in and start the second set."

"Y'all go on in. I'll just walk Cherry to her car, Bean. I won't be a minute."

"I don't think you will. She knows the way to her car. You come in with us. Now. I mean it."

We all looked at him like he was crazy. There was an ugly edge to his voice all of a sudden. I mean, what did he think we were going to do in the parking lot?

"Bean, I promise, I will be right in after Cherry leaves. What's the matter with you?"

"Yeah, Bean. Come on. Let the girls talk," Rocky said.

He and John Cool took Bean by the arms and walked him in. He didn't like it, but there was nothing he could do, short of yanking away to follow us and getting in a fistfight with them.

Baby and I walked around back, to where my car was parked.

"Boy, Bean sure doesn't want to let you out of his sight, does he? What does he think—that Jackie Lim is out here behind the garbage cans, waiting to grab you and run off or something?"

"I don't know what he thinks, but it's beginning to get to me. I feel like I'm smothering to death sometimes. I've mentioned a time or two that maybe we shouldn't spend so much time together, but he either gets mad and pouts or acts like he doesn't hear me. He won't even talk about it."

"If you want to break up with him, you don't need his permission— just do it. You know I'll be right there with you. Don't let him push you around, Baby. You could have anybody in this town you wanted. Park Lim is crazy about you."

"Park is sweet, but he just doesn't have that . . . I don't know . . . fire or something. I guess when it comes down to it, I'd rather be with somebody who is a little crazy and exciting than somebody who is safe and boring."

"Well, I hope Bean doesn't get too exciting. You're not afraid he'll do something to you, are you?"

"No. He would never hurt me. That, I'm sure about. It'll be all right. He's getting better. It'll work itself out."

I wasn't so sure that he was getting better, but I couldn't make her break up with him. We hugged for a minute, and I had already opened the door and started to get in when I remembered about Rainy Day and the Ouija board. I couldn't believe I had forgotten it, but in the excitement of everything else, it had just left my mind.

"Oh, one more thing, Baby. I know it sounds crazy, but Rainy Day and I were playing on the Ouija board, and it spelled out the words *Baby Letters*. Does that mean anything to you? Like, did Carlene ever say anything about any letters?"

"Letters. I can't think of what . . . oh my gosh. Wait a minute. Right after Jerry got killed, Carlene asked me to get his letters and burn them up if anything ever happened to her. I totally forgot about it."

"Maybe we should go out to her trailer and ask her mother about them."

"Oh, Cherry, you don't believe that it was really Carlene moving that thing around the board, do you?"

"I don't know what I believe."

"Did the board say who killed her or anything?"

"No, it didn't say that, but it told me to 'ask Faye' if I wanted to know if Tripp was the one I should marry. Do you know any Faye?"

"There was Faye Dean Murphy, but I don't know anybody else named Faye. Do you?"

"No. I don't really think that Ouija board is for real, Baby. Milton Bradley makes it."

"Probably not. But maybe we should go out to her mother's and check out the letters, just in case. I better get on in now. Bean will be getting nervous."

Before Baby had a chance to move, G. Dub pulled up in his white Mustang. His car was piled high with duffel bags and suitcases.

"Hey, cuz, I been looking all over for you!" he said as he got out of the car. "Pilar said y'all were out here at Woody's. I wanted to say good-bye."

"Good-bye? Where are you going, G. Dub? It looks like you crammed all your earthly possessions in there."

"As much of them as I could. I'm leaving out for Canada. I ain't coming back, Cherry, so you'll have to come up and see me once in a while."

"Canada! Why are you going way off up there?"

"It's that or Vietnam. I got my draft papers."

"Oh no, G. Dub! Don't tell me that! What do Aunt Juanita and Uncle Ray have to say?"

"Daddy don't know. He would throw a fit, him being in Korea and all. Mama will tell him tomorrow, so don't say anything to your mama and daddy or anybody else about it yet. I've already seen Lucille and given her a letter to hand to Uncle Jake and Aunt Rubynell. I know it seems like maybe I'm a coward, running off at night like this, but I can't help it. I've wrestled in my mind for two days about it, and I know it is the best thing for me. I'll miss y'all, but at least we'll see each other once in a while. Which is a whole lot more than Jerry Golden and Bobby Richmond can say."

"Well, there's no way anybody could argue that one," Baby said. "I bet their mamas would give anything in this world now if they had gone to Canada. Nobody will think you are a coward, G. Dub. It takes a lot of guts to leave your home and take this kind of gamble. You take care of yourself, now. Do you want me to get Bean so you can say good-bye?"

"He knows. I talked it over with him and Barlow both. They was all for me doing it."

I had a taste in my mouth like cold ashes. The closest thing I had to a brother was being forced to leave his home and family.

"I can't believe you're leaving out tonight just like that, G. Dub!" I grabbed him and hugged him tight. "I'm going to miss you like crazy."

Things were happening too fast all of a sudden. It felt like my whole world had done a 180 in the past few weeks, like a car spinning out on an icy road. I had a bad feeling it wasn't over yet.

"I'll miss you too, Cherry-Berry." He was trying hard not to cry. "You write to me, now, you promise?"

"You know I will. Call collect and let us know where you are when you get there. And drive careful. Don't get any speeding tickets. Oh, G. Dub, I hate this stupid old war!"

I didn't want to break down and sob, but tears ran down my cheeks, and I kept wiping them with the back of my hand. It took everything I had to keep from hanging on his leg and begging him not to go. I felt so helpless. But when I thought about Jerry and Bobby, and Tripp's long red scar, I knew I would do anything to just know G. Dub was alive somewhere on the earth.

We hugged some more and kissed, and he and Baby hugged, then he got in the car and waved as he drove away, leaving us feeling empty. I was thankful, not for the first time, that I was a girl and didn't have to make this decision or to worry about going to Vietnam.

48. *Vietnam*

March 18, 1968

Dear Carlene,

I'm still here. Although I'm not sure if I want to be or not. I might as well tell you the whole sorry story of what happened in the last few days. I don't know how much longer I will be around, and somebody back in the world needs to know about it. I haven't slept in nearly three days. I don't know how anybody else has. It's like my brain is grinding its gears and I am moving in slow motion, so if this letter doesn't make any sense, then I guess it is just one more thing in this life that doesn't.

I don't know if you got my last letter or not, but I said we were going to go in and clean out a nest of VC on Saturday, and we went in to do that, all right, but it didn't go exactly like I thought it would. I'll start from the beginning. If I can. My head is pretty jumbled up right now. Just be patient, because I need to tell it all, if only for myself, to try and make some sense out of it.

—

It was cloudy, quite a bit of hot wind when we got up at 5:30 that next morning after I wrote you. It was the kind of weather that unsettles you, not that we weren't unsettled enough anyhow. By seven, our two platoons were boarding the line of slicks, choking on the cloud of dust their propellers kick up, and getting ready to go up the eleven miles to the target, My Lai 4. We were taking an extra load of ammunition and supplies, because it was going to be the biggest battle we had ever faced. I can't tell you how scared I was, Carlene. It was like my whole body was quivering. My teeth were chattering, and from the looks on their faces, so were a lot of the other guys', although they joked around and tried to act tough.

We climbed up in the slicks, two gunners on either side of the open doors, and took off over the most beautiful land you will ever see anywhere. Beautiful and deadly. Under those thick green trees were tunnels full of VC, living like rattlers underground, waiting to pop out and strike at us.

We were as prepared as we could be, though. The artillery was all set to clear out a drop zone for us, and the brown-water swift boats were in position to give us support. We had the whole battle mapped out, with plenty of choppers for scouting and for backup.

We passed right over the field where we were booby-trapped, and on a little farther was the Diem Diem River, where we were hit that time and lost our radioman.

As we got close to the LZ, our machine gunner poured a trail of tracer fire down to clear out anybody who might be waiting for us. We were six feet above the ground when Lieutenant Calley said, "Let's go!" and we all jumped out and hit the ground running. There was a lot of smoke from the tracer blast, and we couldn't really see much, but a machine gun off to the right let loose and we saw a man running with a bunch of cows. He was too far away, though, and escaped. Another one stopped and held up his arms to show he wanted to surrender, and he was cut down.

A couple of the Warlord aero scouts took off after two dinks in black pajamas carrying weapons. I didn't see if they got them or not. All of us spread out and secured defensive positions along the dikes. The rest of our guys landed, and we moved forward "on line," firing our weapons. Our job was to sweep through the village and take out any enemy opposition. Then the third platoon was supposed to follow and mop up, kill the livestock, and torch the hootches. Search and destroy, emphasis on destroy.

I was braced, waiting for return fire, but there didn't seem to be any. There were a lot of people in the village who still hadn't gone off to the market, and most of them were racing around trying to get out of the way, jumping down into their dugouts or hunkering in their huts. A man popped up out of a trench, and I fired off a round at him, but missed, and somebody else got him.

One of the guys shot at a woman running with a baby, and I yelled at him, but he didn't seem to hear me and kept right on shooting. The two of them fell stone dead, blood pouring out of a dozen wounds. I ran over to see if I could help them, but they were past help. Their eyes were already fixed and staring. It had to be a mistake. I mean, there was so much chaos that you sometimes just reacted when you saw movement and shot before you thought, but it seemed like he would have known they weren't the enemy after the first shot.

The village was pretty dense with bamboo and banana trees, and you couldn't always see what was going on fifty feet away. From the minute we landed, there was a constant din of gunfire. Everyone all around me was shooting as hard and fast as they could, at anything that moved—people, pigs, chickens, cows, anything. Guys would yell for people to come out of a hootch, and if they didn't, they threw a grenade in. Sometimes they didn't even yell, but just threw one in anyhow. A woman crawled out with a bad chest wound, and one of the guys blew her brains out. It didn't take long until I realized that they were killing all of the people, not just the men, and there was not one thing I could do about it.

I couldn't believe what I was seeing, Carlene. As far as I could tell, there were no men of fighting age who could be VC there, and the villagers were offering no resistance. They were mostly old men and women and children. If there had been any VC, they were long gone down the tunnels, but I'm sure they weren't there, or they would have tried to defend the village. I stood right in the middle of what I can only describe as a slaughterhouse.

It was like they had all gone into some kind of insane frenzy. They pushed gangs of women and children into bunkers, then threw grenades in on them. Pieces of flesh rained down like hail.

It was one big mess of confusion. People were crying and yelling and screaming. I don't see how we kept from killing each other with all the bullets flying. Anybody that stuck their head out of a tunnel or a hootch was shot down, even if they had their hands up. A woman ran by me with her arm dangling off by a thread of skin, and somebody soon shot her. The ground was churned up in sticky red mud. I had never been so sick in my life, not even when we were burning the bodies.

Three little girls ran by me into a hootch, with my pal Tripp Barlow chasing right behind them. That was too much, and I started to go in after him, until I heard him yelling, *"Di di mau, di di mau!"* Which means, "Run! Run!" They were scared of him, but he dragged them out and ran with them toward the rice paddy. At the edge of the field, he pushed them, still yelling, *"Di di mau,"* and they took off. I think they made it, which at least is something. I don't know what I would have done if Barlow had hurt them. At least he hadn't gone crazy like some of the rest of the guys.

I followed them to the edge of the rice paddy, where I nearly stepped on a girl about eight or ten laying there with a hole in her chest, white blouse soaked red. She looked up at me and said, "*Chop chop,*" which was what the kids used to say when they begged for candy. I took my canteen and poured some water into her mouth, but she couldn't swallow, and it ran out. Carlene, I have never felt more helpless in my life. I didn't know what to do. I just turned and walked away, and when I did I heard a shot and didn't even turn back around because I knew somebody had killed her.

A sergeant ran by, one who had always been a pretty good guy, and I grabbed him by the arm and asked him what the hell was going on. He said he didn't like it, but he had to carry out orders. I said, "Who gave us insane orders to murder all these women and babies?" He said, "Pal, this is war, and war is no place for pussies. If you can't do it, then don't get in the way."

Barlow saw me and came over to where I was, just as the lieutenant yelled and said he needed us to go take care of some prisoners. I was ready to go do that—if they were taking prisoners, at least some of the people were going to be all right. He told us to go over to a ditch where eighty or a hundred people—mostly mothers with kids, and old men and women—were squatting on the ground, and we sat down with a couple of other guys to watch them. After a few minutes, Lieutenant Calley came up and asked us what we thought we were doing. I said we were doing what he said; we were taking care of the people.

He cussed at me and said that what he meant was to kill them. No way, I said. If you want them killed, you can do it yourself. He barked at Barlow and the other guys to start shooting, and Barlow wouldn't, either, but stood up to him and said, "You can send me to jail or kill me, but you can't make me do it." Calley pulled his M-16 on us and I thought for a minute he was going to blow Barlow and me away right then and there, but instead he swung around and turned it on the people in the ditch and started blasting away at them. All of them jerked and danced as the bullets ripped them to pieces. It felt like the whole world had lost its mind. I didn't know where to put myself.

Carlene, it was the most pitiful thing I have ever seen. One little kid about two years old tried to climb out of the ditch and the lieutenant kicked him back in and shot him in the face. Mothers were throwing themselves on top of their kids, trying to save them. Calley yelled for the two other guys to shoot, and they joined in, firing and kicking people back in when they tried to get out, and in a short time nobody was moving in the ditch. It looked like chopped meat stuck to the edges of the ditch. There was nothing human about it.

Then Barlow and I just walked on off and left it, helpless to do anything. We wandered around the village, looking at the piles of bodies laying around. Some of them were still alive, but most wouldn't be for long. A little boy about five came out of a hootch with both of his hands and wrists blown off, blood was pouring out of the stumps, and there was a hole in the middle of his face where his nose had been shot off. He looked like some monster from a horror show, like a zombie in a movie. He kept coming toward us with blood dripping off his chin, and just before he got to us, Barlow aimed his gun at him and shot him right in the chest. He fell not five feet in front of us.

"What did you do that for, Barlow?" I asked him. Barlow said, "It was a mercy killing." I guess it was, because even if somebody else hadn't killed him, he would have bled to death. Without his hands and nose, he never would have had much of a life.

"We need to help these people out of their misery," Barlow said, with a fire in his eyes. "That's the least we can do for them."

The two of us went around then, like angels of death, him finishing off with a quick shot to the head the ones that were still alive, the ones we judged to be grievously, mortally wounded and were only going to lay there and suffer and die anyhow. I was right there with him, helping him, even though I couldn't bring myself to pull my own trigger.

Carlene, I felt like I had floated out of my body and was watching someone else down there. This must have been what it was like when the Nazis killed all those millions of Jews back in Germany. It couldn't have been any worse than this, and this was us doing the killing. Americans. The good guys. We are supposed to be the saviors of these people. Guys I had laughed and played cards with, guys I had been through hell and back with in the booby-trapped fields, guys who had risked their lives for each other were raping and slaughtering unarmed people who were offering no resistance.

After a while, I guess Barlow had all he could stand. I know I had. He threw down his gun and we took our helmets off and sat by a tree. Barlow took out a cigarette and lit up; gave me one. The sun came out, then, hot and sticky. We were covered in blood. Gnats buzzed around us, whining in our ears and noses, lighting on our arms. We sat and smoked and listened to the screams and the gunfire.

—

Not far from us, a bubble ship lit down over by the ditch where the lieutenant and them had killed all those people. The pilot got out, and I recognized Hugh Thompson, a good old boy from Georgia, who I had talked to a time or two, and who I knew was a Baptist. He had a reputation as being tough in battle, but fair. By that I mean he never fired a shot until he saw the man had a weapon, and he always tried to get a clean kill and not leave him wounded.

Barlow and I got up and went on over. I thought I might talk to him and find out if he knew why we had been given the orders to kill all these civilians. He had always been a straight shooter, and if anybody could make sense out of it for us, it would be him.

Before we could get to him, though, a sergeant came up, and I heard Thompson ask him why all those people were dead and if there was anything he could do to help them. The sergeant said the only thing that would help them was to put them out of their misery.

Then Lieutenant Calley came over to see what was going on, and Thompson started asking him questions. The lieutenant said that it was none of Thompson's business, and that he, Calley, was in charge of the operation.

You could tell Thompson didn't like it, but he got back in the chopper and they lifted off, and almost immediately, some guys ran by chasing a bunch of people, mostly kids, that were running toward a homemade bomb shelter.

Thompson set the bubble ship down again, between the soldiers and the civilians, and ordered his gunner to turn his guns on the soldiers. We thought for a minute they were going to shoot each other, but the soldiers didn't fire, and Thompson got out and coaxed the kids out of the bunker while the gunner held the soldiers off and radioed for help to get the civilians airlifted out.

Before too long, some more choppers came and took the people away. Thompson got back in his bubble, and as he made a pass over the ditch, I guess he saw something moving, because he landed for a third time, and covered two of his men while they waded into the knee-deep blood and gore of a hundred or more bodies and pulled out a little boy.

He was covered in filth, but didn't seem to be hurt at all, although he was in shock, as you might expect. Thompson started to cry then. One boy alive out of a hundred people. One ragged scrap of life. He took the boy up in the bubble ship, holding him in his lap, and left.

Thompson, at least, saved a few of the people. What did I do? Maybe some of the ones Barlow shot could have been saved. Who were we to judge that it was mercy to kill them? My knees almost buckled with the enormity of what we had done, and I laid down in the grass and tried to pray.

I don't know how long I lay there, but finally somebody came over and nudged me with their foot and said they were bringing out chow.

We stopped and had lunch, just like on any other day. Guys sat right next to piles of corpses, didn't even wash their hands, and ate, joking around about what they had done, how many they had got, how those little bastards wouldn't grow up to set mines now.

I began to wonder if I was the weirdo and they were all the sane ones, because I thought the whole thing was so horrifying. This sounds really sick, Carlene, but I wondered if they knew I hadn't killed any myself, and hoped they didn't.

I wasn't hungry, but Barlow came and brought me a plate and, to my surprise, I dug into it like I was starved. I ate until I couldn't lift my fork, like I was trying to fill up a hole in my gut that wouldn't be filled.

—

Then it seemed like it was more or less over. Maybe Thompson called in to the brass what was going on and they stopped it, or maybe Captain Medina thought it was enough. Maybe there wasn't anybody left to shoot. Whatever, it pretty much stopped. I would estimate that there were between four and five hundred people killed, and countless animals. None of us were even fired on. The only one hurt was a guy who got too excited and shot himself in his own foot. He was medevaced out, and will more than likely get a Purple Heart.

After we ate, Barlow went around with his camera and took pictures of a lot of it. I'm not really sure why. There was also a man from some news outfit taking pictures, and nobody acted like they cared. Guys even posed, like with trophies, and somebody took the camera from Barlow and got a shot of me and him together. For a lot of them, it seemed like they thought of it as just one more day, one more search and destroy, a high body count. But for me, I feel like my life is over. The Jerry Golden who suffered so when you got pregnant seems like somebody else, a long time ago. I can't even remember those feelings.

The Zippo squad came in to burn the hootches, and we left to make camp a ways away from My Lai, in another abandoned village; dug foxholes and settled in for the night.

After supper, Barlow and I sat for a long time talking about what had happened. It shouldn't have been any worse, I guess, than it is for the pilots to fry women and children with napalm, but killing them like this was different. It was intimate, and left a mark on your soul like dropping a bomb on a faceless crowd never would.

I still don't know if what happened was because it was ordered or if the men just went into some kind of mass hysteria. Seeing something like this, you understand how genocide can take place—after a while, you aren't killing people, just things. Something in you just snaps. I was part of it. I didn't have the guts to help any of them. I saw girls with their vaginas torn open, breasts cut off, ears cut off, people scalped, throats cut, and all I did was stand there and watch. I hope they are in heaven now, because they had their hell today.

—

I took a roll of Barlow's film. He doesn't know it, so I guess it's stealing, but I am enclosing it with this letter. I want you to get the pictures developed and hang on to them for me. I don't know if anything will be done about this massacre—you can't call it anything else—or if even anybody cares, but I want proof in case there is. I don't think I can do anything about it myself, at least not while I'm here, because it would be easy for somebody to "accidentally" shoot me, and I am not ready to take on the whole platoon, plus the brass, assuming the brass really did order it. But these pictures need to be seen, if for nothing else than to let the world know what this war has done to the kids they sent over here—what it has turned them into.

I hate to lay all this on you, Carlene, but I have to. Don't say anything to anybody about it. Not now. When I get home around Christmastime, we can figure out then if there is anything to be done. I am ready to take my punishment, too, if it comes to that.

——

We just got word that the VC 48th wasn't anywhere near Pinkville. They were forty miles away. I need to go to bed, but I don't know if I will ever be able to sleep again. We are not all that far from My Lai, and I can hear the sound of an old woman keening; a high-pitched wail that cuts through the night and slices your brain. She is mourning for her lost loved ones, I guess. She has been doing it for two days straight. Or maybe it is not an old woman at all; maybe it is the ghosts of all those people still screaming in my head. I don't know anymore.

I love you, Carlene. It almost seems obscene to use that word right now, but I do.

Jerry

49. Cherry

Leaving Woody's, I felt sleepy, and it seemed like I was having a hard time focusing on the road. A time or two, my wheels went off the pavement. My head was feeling a little buzzy. I didn't think one beer would get you drunk like that.

I rolled down the window and stuck my head out for some air, to wake myself up. The only good thing I had found so far about my haircut was that the wind didn't blow the hair into my eyes.

There is a hill on Route 66 that is really a booger, because you can't see what's coming over it until you are right on top. There had been more than a few head-on collisions there from ignorant daredevil people passing over the double yellow line. I was just topping that hill when a dog came out of the brush and ran right out in front of me. Hot on his heels was another dog, and another one, and one more. Four dogs strung out across the highway, and the only choice I had was which dog to hit, or which ditch. I figured the smallest dog would cause the least damage, and swerved to the right to avoid the others. Fortunately, the little guy managed to jump out of the way, but I skidded into the ditch, went for twenty feet or so, and then bumped back up onto the highway. My guardian angel must have grabbed the steering wheel, because I don't know how it happened that I didn't wreck.

I was pretty shaken up, and driving slow, when a car pulled up right on my bumper with his brights on. I slowed on down to twenty miles an hour, hoping he would pass me. I just hate tailgaters. He didn't pass, but slowed down, too, and the lights in the rearview mirror were killing my eyes, so I tapped my brake a couple of times to show that I didn't like him being so close, and when I did, a set of red lights went off. My heart sank into my shoes. I could figure out who it was. I pulled over and cut the motor.

"Good evening, Highpockets. That was some fancy driving you did just now. Are you all right?"

"Ricky Don, why did you scare the life out of me riding my tail like that? You knew it was me. Why didn't you just throw on the red lights when you saw me?"

"I thought it was either you or Baby, but I couldn't be sure. I didn't recognize you without your hair. Sorry." He leaned his arms on the top of the car and looked down at me. "I saw those dogs. You're just lucky you didn't crash."

"I know I am. Thanks for stopping, but I'm all right, so I better get on home."

He leaned in close to me, like he was going to kiss me. I pulled my head back.

"If I didn't know better, I'd say you had been drinking beer. Here, let me smell your breath."

"I will not! And what if I do have a little beer on my breath? I'm not drunk. I only had one. I'm legal age, you know."

"Get out of the car."

"I will not! Stop acting like a cop, Ricky Don! Who do you think you're talking to?"

By this time, if I had ever been a little drunk, the adrenaline had sobered me up.

"I don't care how well you know me, Cherry. My first duty is to my job. Now, I want to see if you are driving drunk. Get out."

I opened the door and got out, boiling mad. I threw my arms up in the air. "All right. I'm out. Want to frisk me?"

"Hold your arms straight out to the side and close your eyes."

I did.

"Now, touch your nose with your right hand."

I did.

"Now the left one."

"See, I'm not drunk!"

"Fine. Now, walk that white line, one foot in front of the other, heel to toe."

I walked it without wobbling too much. A little.

"You know how uncoordinated I am, Ricky Don. I couldn't walk that line straight even if I had been drinking milk all night."

"All right. You're not drunk. But what were you doing at Woody's?"

"Have you been following me all night? I went to hear Bean sing. It's not against the law to go to Woody's, you know. It's in a wet county, in case you forgot."

"Don't get smart. I go there sometimes myself. They have the best pizza around. But knowing how you are, and how your folks are, I just thought . . ."

"Stop right there. I'm not the same girl you used to know in high school. I'm a grown-up now, not a little girl who has to report her every move to her daddy, and sure not to her ex-boyfriend. It's a free country."

"All right, all right. Cool out. I'm sorry. I really am."

He leaned back on the hood of the cruiser, took his hat off, and threw it in through the open window; ran his hands through his hair. It didn't seem like he had as much Wildroot in it as he usually did.

"Can I go now?"

"If you want to. I'm not stopping you."

There was hardly any traffic on Route 66 this time of night. The sky was overcast and the only light was from the cruiser's red lights, still circling on top of the car. One of the pack of dogs across the road howled, and a couple of the others joined in barking, chasing after a coon, probably. Nehi Mountain loomed up solid and black off to the right. The leaves on the trees were beginning to turn, and they rustled like paper in the breeze. It was a lonesome stretch of road.

"Could you at least kill the lights, please? They make me nervous."

He reached in the window and flipped them off.

"Do you want to sit and talk for a minute?" he asked.

"Are you allowed to? Aren't you working?"

"I'm allowed to do anything I want to do. Like you said, it's a free country."

"Well . . . okay. I'll sit for a minute."

I took the keys out of the VW, and we got into the cruiser.

"Wow. Look at all this radio stuff. I guess you're plugged into the whole state, huh?"

The radio crackled with voices, speaking a code language I only half understood.

"Can you turn it down?" I would go crazy with that racket if I had to drive around and listen to it all night. He turned it down, but you could still hear it.

Sitting next to him was so familiar—the way he scooted his body down in the seat of the car, the heat that radiated out from him, his smell. He still wore English Leather. I didn't know what I was doing there. I couldn't think of anything to say.

"I like your haircut, Highpockets. It makes you look . . . I don't know . . . really cute."

"Not ugly like before, huh?"

"You know I always thought you were the most beautiful girl in the class."

"Oh? So who was more beautiful than me in the class ahead of us?"

"Let me try that again: the most beautiful girl in the world. Always was. Always will be."

Then he leaned over and kissed me, and by golly the old familiar hot streak went through me and I kissed him back. More than kissed him back. I put my arms around his neck, he pulled me to him, and we lay down on the seat, just like the old days. It didn't seem to matter that we were in a police cruiser and he had a gun on his hip, or that I was madly in love with Tripp Barlow. In that moment, we were the old Cherry and Ricky Don, and it was 1965, not 1969.

The radio crackled and he tried to ignore it, but they were clearly calling him.

"Dang." He straightened up and picked up the handset.

I opened the door and got out. I didn't want to sit there while he talked, and I didn't want to keep on with what we were doing. It was crazy. What was the matter with me?

I had never needed to pee so badly in my life. Since I had on a denim miniskirt, all it would take would be to pull down my panties, squat, and do it. But not close to the cars or the highway. As best I could remember, the field next to the road was a potato patch. I'd just go out there a little ways and get it over with quick.

It was hard to see in the dark, and I bumped right into the fence and scraped my leg. I spread apart the barb wire and crawled through—ripping a big hole in the sleeve of my shirt—went several rows out, and did my business. It sounded really loud, like a cow peeing on a flat rock. I hoped Ricky Don couldn't hear it.

By this time, he was yelling my name, but understandably, I didn't want him to find me. I couldn't squat in the potato patch all night until I dripped dry, though. I was getting a cramp in my thigh and finally had to stand up. Thank goodness I wear cotton panties, because I didn't have any paper.

When I stood up he saw me, since I had on a white blouse and practically glow in the dark anyhow. He came out across the field. I guess I got scared at the feelings that were coming back or something, but I ran from him, and when I did, he chased me, both of us hopping and stumbling over the plants until I fell, and then he was on top of me.

I'm not proud of what happened next, but let's just say his equipment had not been permanently disabled in the freak accident of our last date. We threw ourselves hard at each other, scratching and clawing, buttons popping, zippers ripping. It was frantic and deep; unfinished business that apparently had been smoldering down inside us for three years and finally caught fire. It was nothing like what Tripp and I had, but more like two hogs squealing and rutting in a wallow. We tore up half a row of potatoes, both of us covered in loamy black earth before we'd had enough and it was all over. We flung ourselves apart and lay back panting.

"I'm sorry, Ricky Don. I didn't mean for that to happen. I don't know what got into me."

"Me neither. It was kind of a surprise."

"You know I'm not that kind of girl." I gulped air, trying to catch my breath. "And before this goes any further . . ."

"How much further do you think it can go?"

"Ricky Don, I'm trying to tell you that I'm in love with Tripp Barlow."

"Are you, now?" he gasped, trying to catch his breath. "Is he in love with you?"

"Of course he is."

"You're sure?"

"I'd stake my life on it."

"That's something I never do, Cherry, stake my life on anything. Not even as a figure of speech. It's bad luck."

"You're right. I take it back. But I'm sure he is." We were both breathing a little easier.

"Are you okay?"

"Oh yeah. I think so. Are you?"

"What do you think?"

We finally calmed down and just lay there, not knowing what to say. I couldn't quite believe what had just happened, but it had to be the capper on this long, crazy day. It seemed like three days ago since I got up and ate breakfast.

I leaned up on my elbow and tried to see Ricky Don's face. It was too dark to see, but it felt like he was thinking really hard.

"What are you thinking right now?"

"Whether to tell you something or not."

"Tell me what?"

"I did follow you to Woody's. I saw your car go by on the highway and pull in, and I kept driving by and checking until you left. I was going to stop you anyhow, for another reason."

"Ricky Don, you just love to torture me. What are you talking about?"

"We got a call today from somebody looking for Barlow. The person who called the sheriff knew Barlow was in town here but didn't know how to get in touch with him."

He paused, like he was trying to figure out how to tell me something.

"Is he in trouble? Ricky Don? What is this all about? Who called him?"

"I don't know if he's in trouble or not. As far as I know, he's not. I told them I needed to know what it was all about before I spent a lot of valuable time trying to find him. They said a Colonel Wilson in the army has been calling them and trying to track Barlow down to talk about some things that happened while he was in Vietnam; they wouldn't say what. The person who called said that they didn't want to tell the colonel where he was until they talked to him."

"Well, who was calling? One of his soldier buddies?"

"No. It was a woman. She was his . . ."

"What? His aunt? His cousin?"

"His wife. Faye Barlow."

It felt like somebody had punched me in the stomach.

"Cherry? Are you all right?"

"Yeah. I'm fine. Faye Barlow. Is that what you said?"

"Did you know he was married?"

"No."

We lay there, not saying anything for a really long time, not touching.

"Have you talked to him?" I couldn't believe how normal my voice was.

"Not yet. I couldn't find him today."

"Will you wait until I get a chance to see him?"

"Do you think you'll see him tomorrow?"

"I'll make a point of it. But right now I need to go home."

"I'll follow you to make sure you make it, okay?"

"Sure. Fine."

"You sure you're all right?"

"Oh yeah. I'm fine."

We brushed ourselves off and walked across the field. He held the wire up for me and I ducked under. I was calm, almost floating over the ground. Was this what shock was like?

I started the VW and headed toward home. Ricky Don pulled out behind me and followed, but not too close. In the quiet of the car, it hit me. All of it. I started to yell, big loud screams, and pound the steering wheel. I'm surprised Ricky Don didn't hear me and pull me over again. How could Tripp have done this to me? How could I have just had a roll in the potato patch with Ricky Don? I was disgusted at myself, and furious at Tripp. It took nearly fifteen minutes to get home, me screaming at the top of my lungs all the way, but it sure felt good to let out all that steam. When I did, I was feeling better—washed out, but better, even though my throat hurt. All I wanted to do was to take a shower and crawl into bed and worry about the whole mess some other time.

—

Ricky Don flashed his brights to say good-bye, and I slipped upstairs and took a quick shower. My whole rear end was black with dirt, and my white shirt was completely ruined. I'd have to sneak out and burn it in the trash barrel before Mama saw it.

As the hot water stung my skin, I thought about Tripp and the weird, spooky Faye business. I should have been bawling my eyes out, but for some reason I didn't. It was like I had always known it was inevitable that something like this was going to happen with him. Sooner or later, I knew in my heart, it was going to fall apart. It was just too much too soon. I had been flirting with the Devil, and I knew it.

I got out and dried off and felt the fatigue that comes over you after a tornado has passed by and you are still alive.

I put on my pajamas, and heard somebody downstairs. Daddy was in the kitchen. When he can't sleep, he gets up and pours milk over the cornbread left over from supper and eats it like a soppy cereal. It looks kind of unappetizing, but he says it makes him sleepy. I went into the kitchen, and there he was at the table in his maroon robe, his hair standing up in all directions.

"Hi, Daddy. You can't sleep?"

"Hi, punkin. Naw, I guess I couldn't. Can I fix you some milk and bread?"

"Sure. That would be nice." I didn't really want it, but I needed to be near somebody normal and safe.

"Where you been, out this late?"

"I was at the shop, then I went out to Baby's. I ate out there." At least it wasn't a total lie.

"You're spending a lot of time at Baby's."

"I guess so."

"It won't be long before you'll be out of school and on your own, away from us for good."

"No. It won't be long."

"I just want you to know you don't have to move out when you graduate. You can live here as long as you want to. This will always be your home."

"Thank you, Daddy. I don't know what's going to happen yet. I might have to get a job in some other town if they don't need an art teacher here at the school."

"I'd hate for you to move off. All our kids would be leaving us at once."

"You should have had ten. Then there'd still be nine left."

"You're all the girl I need. I couldn't have had a better one if I'd hand-picked you." I got a little lump in my throat; swallowed it down.

He patted me on the cheek. We ate our milk and cornbread. I was feeling pretty low, and nowhere near worthy to be his daughter. He looked at me then, like he had finally figured out what was different.

"What did you do to your hair? It looks real good."

"Lucille cut it all off."

"Well, you should have done it a long time ago. Now you can see your pretty face. Keep it like that."

"I might."

I wanted to ask him a lot of things, like if he thought there were ghosts that could come back and talk to you, and what it was like to fight in a war, and how he felt when he saw all those starved Jews, and if he ever had any other girlfriends or slept with anybody besides Mama, and if he thought you could be in love with one boy and do what I just did with another one. I wanted to tell him about G. Dub, but I had promised to wait. I wanted to tell him about Tripp and everything that had happened, but I knew if I did, he would be shocked and disappointed in me. I was shocked and disappointed in myself. But all I said was: "When you were my age, were you always sure what was right, Daddy, like you seem to be now? Sometimes I don't think I know what's right and what's wrong anymore."

"About what?"

"I don't know. A whole lot of things. How do you always know what is the right thing to do?"

"I don't always know, Cheryl Ann. I have made a lot of mistakes in my life, like anybody else. I learned a long time ago that there is not a lot we can do to help ourselves sometimes, and things just get away from us. That's why we have to trust in the good Lord. He will show us what's right at the time we need to know, and guide us to make the right decisions. You can tell by a feeling in your heart when a decision is the right one."

"What if He doesn't tell me?"

"He'll tell you. You just have to know how to listen." I spooned in some more milk and bread, not saying anything else. I should have known he would put it all back in the Lord's lap. I guess he was just as uncomfortable about telling me anything bad he had done as I was telling him, and going back to the Lord was the only thing he could do. Safe. Neutral ground. It was just the way he was, and I loved him no matter what he had done, and he probably did me, too, so it didn't really matter. But I did wonder what, if anything, had made him feel like things had gotten away from him. They sure had gotten away from me.

"I'll tell you something you don't know," he said in a lighter voice, trying to change the mood. "There's going to be a wedding at the church next month. Guess who's getting married."

"I don't know. Who?"

"Brother Dane and Frannie Moore."

"You're kidding me. I didn't even know they were going out."

"I don't think a whole lot of other people knew they were, either, but Brother Wilkins is marrying them. Frannie told your mama she had to go to court and get a paper saying her husband had abandoned her and she hadn't heard from him in seven years. She'll get it in a few weeks, and they're getting married. Brother Dane's going to adopt little Kevin. Seems like he took a real shine to the boy."

"Oh, that is so great." I was really happy to hear that. Frannie needed somebody right now to help her raise the boy. She was still young enough to have kids herself. Maybe they would have one together. That would be funny if they did—Kevin's uncle or aunt would be younger than him. Wouldn't it be wonderful if Brother Dane would settle down now and take a church instead of traveling all the time as an evangelist? I'd love to fire Brother Wilkins and get him to be our preacher.

I'd call Baby in the morning and tell her about the wedding. We could take Frannie out a gift of some kind, and Baby could ask about the letters. That would be a natural way to do it. Since finding out about the Faye business, I took the letters more seriously.

Somehow, the news about Brother Dane and Frannie made me feel better. At least there was somebody in the world having some happiness. All of a sudden, I couldn't keep my eyes open.

"I'm going up to bed, Daddy. I have to go to class early in the morning. I love you."

"I love you too, punkin."

I leaned down and kissed him, and hugged him close for a really long time. I wished every man could be like my daddy, even with all his hang-ups, but it seemed like he was the only one like him that I knew of.

Then I went upstairs and fell right asleep.

50. *Carlene*

Kevin—or Superman, as he was known in his secret life—ran as fast as he could around the yard of the trailer, his red hair standing straight up like a lit match in the wind. A blue-and-white-striped towel, safety-pinned to the shoulders of his shirt, flew out behind him like a cape. Brother Dane chased after him with an exaggerated swagger, much like a gorilla, holding a lump of coal in his outstretched hand.

"I've got you at last, Superman! I have a big old chunk of kryptonite in my hands, and it will make you weak if it touches you!"

"No you won't, Lex Luthor! I am just as strong as a train, and I can leap tall buildings with a single bounce!" He jumped up on an upside-down tin washtub and held out his hand, palm up, like a traffic cop. "Halt! In the name of the law! My X-ray vision will burn you!"

Brother Dane fell onto the ground and the lump of coal rolled from his hand.

"You got me, Superman! Turn off your X rays! You got me." He closed his eyes, then doubled up with an *oof!* as Superman giggled and dived onto his stomach.

"You boys come on in! I just took some cookies out of the oven, and I need somebody to eat them while they're hot!" Frannie called out across the yard. Brother Dane picked Kevin up, put him on his shoulders, and they went inside.

"I swan, the two of you run me ragged, scrubbing all the grass stains out of your clothes. Can't you play something that don't include rolling around on the ground?"

"Aw, Grandma, Superman can't keep his clothes clean. He has to chase crooks!"

Brother Dane sat with Kevin in his lap as they ate the hot chocolate chip cookies and drank big glasses of milk. He hadn't known it was possible to be this happy.

Ever since Carlene's funeral, it seemed like he couldn't get the boy off his mind. He stopped by every day or two to see how Kevin and Frannie were doing, and before long he was taking them out to eat and for long drives up the mountain.

Women were his weakness, and he had been with a lot of them in his life—the thorn in his side, as St. Paul said—but somehow he never found one he wanted to settle down with. He liked the life of an evangelist, traveling around the countryside and preaching at a different church every week; liked the admiration of women and the freedom to take off and go where he wanted to go without having to feel guilty about neglecting a wife and family. But he was thirty-nine now, and traveling had lost a lot of its appeal. He got lonesome. It might not be so bad to have a family.

The first time he looked hard at Kevin's diamond-blue eyes, watched him walk with his little hand on his hip in a strangely familiar way, saw him stick out his chin and cock his head to the side when he listened, Brother Dane knew that the boy was his child. Carlene had told him the father was Jerry Golden, but he didn't believe her for a minute. When she said it, she wouldn't look him in the eye.

That crazy afternoon out here at the trailer—it was as if he had felt life leave his body and go all the way in; felt it take hold somewhere else. And once he saw that Carlene was pregnant, he knew the baby couldn't be anybody else's, no matter what she said. He would have married her right then and there, but she wouldn't do it. She was in love with that Church of Christ preacher's son, and there was no way he could force her. When Jerry went off into the army, Dane tried to talk to her. She was polite, but she clearly didn't want to have anything else to do with him. Not that he could blame her. He had grown calluses on his knees from asking God for forgiveness, but short of confessing in front of the congregation—which wouldn't have accomplished anything but wreck both their lives and give the gossips something else to wag about—he didn't know what else to do. He had to let it go.

Then when Carlene was murdered, he just about lost his mind. Two people had paid with their lives for his one moment of weakness, and several other lives had been ruined. God was taking out on that poor girl something that *he* was responsible for. If he ever wrestled the Devil in the hog pen, he wrestled God then. He still wasn't sure who had won.

He felt an overpowering need to go out to her house, to comfort her mother; to see if in her comfort he could find some relief for himself. The night after the funeral, he and Frannie sat for the better part of the night and talked. As the night wore on, Frannie finally broke down and poured out her heart to him about Carl, and about what Walter and Carlene had done. It took everything he had, but he listened, never letting on that he had heard it all before.

In the small hours of the morning, as they sat near each other on the couch, when he could feel the pain and fatigue and the regret and the love seep out of her as she relaxed through the telling, when her soul touched his and burned him like a hot poker, he was tempted to confess to her everything, himself, about what had happened between her daughter and the black-hearted preacher she was talking to right that minute.

But something held him back. He knew then, with a clarity that hit like a lightning bolt, if it was the last thing he ever did, he would marry this woman and raise his boy—and if there had to be a lie between them to accomplish it, then so be it. Worse lies were kept between husbands and wives.

He set out with a passion to win Frannie, and when he concentrated all his power, there were few women alive who could stand up under the on-slaught. The night he went swimming in the lake with her in the full of the moon, she knew he was the man for her, and as they lay on a bed of leaves deep in the woods, he promised her that if she married him, he would always love and take care of her and the boy, and nothing would ever hurt them again. And he meant it with all his heart.

———

"I sure do hate to box all of Carlene's things up, Dane, but I guess it has to be done. I'll keep some of her nice clothes, and give the rest to the church for the rummage sale."

They were in Carlene's old bedroom, emptying out the drawers and closets. The trailer was piled high with boxes, ready to move to the new house that Dane had bought in town. It would be nearly a month until they could actually get married, but the house was ready now. Frannie and Kevin would stay in it alone until after the wedding, when Dane could move in.

They were excited to live in a real house, built on the ground, not on wheels. It was redbrick, with dark green trim and a wide border of marigolds running down both sides of the front walk. There was a big oak tree in the backyard that was made to order for a tree house and a swing. It seemed like a palace to them.

Frannie pulled a tin box from under the bed, opened it, and set it down on the dresser.

"Oh, look at this, Dane. Here's Carlene's movie-star pictures, and I guess these are her letters from Jerry."

She picked up two or three letters and looked at the handwriting. She started to take one out of the envelope, but changed her mind. She put them back in the box.

"Did you know they were in here? Have you read any of them?" Dane tried to sound casual and not let on that his heart had leaped into his throat.

"Oh, I knew, but I wouldn't do that. They're too personal, I guess. They're from Kevin's daddy. Maybe we should keep them and give them to him when he grows up."

It was all Dane could do to keep from laying hands on those letters. If there were this many, Carlene and Jerry would have gotten close again; they must have talked about how Kevin was conceived. There was no telling what Carlene had told Jerry. The one thing Dane knew was that Frannie must never read them.

"Jerry wrote those letters to Carlene, Frannie. Like you said, they were personal. I'm not so sure he would have wanted the boy to read them. Maybe we should send them back to her."

"What do you mean?"

"I think we should just burn them up, don't you? They were hers. It wouldn't be right for us to keep them." He tried to keep his voice even, like he was just making conversation.

"Well, maybe you're right. But we can at least keep these pictures. Kevin might like to look at them one day." She took out the photos of Troy Donahue and Sandra Dee, along with a stack of others. Underneath was a manila envelope marked FOR CALIFORNIA.

"What is this? Oh my Lord, Dane! It's a pile of money! There must be well over a thousand dollars here!"

The money was all in hundred-dollar bills, bound by a rubber band.

"I knew she was saving up to go and try her luck in the movies, but I didn't know she had this much. I guess her tips were a lot bigger than I thought over at that restaurant. Well, this, at least, we can save for Kevin."

They put the money away and took the box of letters out to the backyard, to the old oil barrel they used for burning trash. Dane lit a fire, and one by one, Frannie put the white onionskin letters with their red-and-blue borders into the flames. They curled into ash as the smoke drifted up, pearl gray, into the blue October sky, where it spread out thin and faded away.

Dane watched it disappear and said a little prayer of thanks to God. He would always carry guilt about Carlene, but now he knew that God did, indeed, work in mysterious ways.

51. *Vietnam*

Dear Carlene,

I hope you got my last letter. There is a big investigation going on right now. They came around and questioned some of us, but everyone lied and said they thought there might have been a few civilians killed in the battle at My Lai, but they didn't know much about it. I wasn't here when the investigators came around, and for some reason, Captain Medina thinks I might be likely to spill the beans. He told me in no uncertain terms that I better keep my mouth shut. Maybe somebody told him I didn't kill anyone, or maybe I just don't fit in with the guys anymore and he knows it. If they really pin me down, I'm not going to lie and protect him or Calley or anybody else—including myself. I won't run to tell everything I know, but I won't lie.

Everyone is scared now. We could be facing twenty years to life in the pen if this thing is found out.

—

I didn't finish this letter before, and now it looks like things have been turned around. They're going to do a cover-up. Colonel Henderson isn't about to have the murder of five hundred civilians at his doorstep the day after he takes command if he can help it, and none of the other top brass wants it on their records, either. In fact, the whole My Lai thing is being turned into a victory against the Communists. There was a big story in *Stars and Stripes* about it, and General Westmoreland himself sent a letter of congratulation to Col. Henderson and Captain Medina. Colonel Barker got the Silver Star, and believe it or not, Hugh Thompson got the Distinguished Flying Cross for rescuing Vietnamese civilians. They didn't specify who he saved them *from,* though. He took it, but I heard he threw it away later.

They sent in a body count of 128, which anybody who saw the place will agree was ridiculously low, but everyone just wants to make it go away, I think. They will probably give us all a lot of medals for it. They give out medals for just about anything over here. A commander whose company has a lot of medals is seen as an effective commander and has more of a chance for advancement. If you get your leg blown off, you get a Purple Heart. If you get a case of jungle rot or an infected pimple on your butt, you get a Purple Heart. Since the whole purpose of this be-nighted war is to kill people, everyone gets Bronze and Silver Stars for killing people; shiny medals to make heroes out of boys for inflicting pain and suffering on their fellow man. How else can you get boys to kill one another day after day but by giving them rewards and throwing around glory words like *hero, duty, honor,* and *valor?* The real secret of war is that evil is the gasoline that runs a war.

Anyhow, we all can relax for the moment. If you can call it relaxing.

—

We're still humping the boonies with our a★★hole lieutenant, Calley. He is even worse than he was before, as far as throwing his weight around. He took us up a hill against orders, and one of our men got his foot blown off. The guy was moaning and saying it was God's punishment. I'm waiting for God to give me mine. Morale is the lowest it has ever been with us. No-body gives a s★★★ about anything anymore. We're all just marking time.

I'm sorry I have nothing good to say in these letters, Carlene. There just isn't anything good happening in my life, or the life of anybody over here. I don't know what we are doing in this country at all. I hope you are having a good life. I hope I see you again, but if I do, it won't be for an-other eight or nine months. It seems like a long time off.

If something does happen to me, don't feel too bad. I'm ready to go. The people we killed haunt me day and night. I still see that little boy without any nose every time I close my eyes. Maybe if I die, too, I can do something to make it up to them in the next life. I've asked God to forgive me, and don't know if He has or not. But there's nothing I can do to change what happened, and I am ready to take whatever comes my way. I love you.

Jerry

52. Carlene

 After they had the big memorial service at the high school for Jerry, people went back to their lives, got up and had breakfast in the morning just like they always did, and said less about him all the time. Once in a while, somebody might remember something he had done or the touchdown pass he had made that won some game or be talking about the war and speak about how sad and awful it was he was killed, but outside of his parents, who totally ignored her at the service, no one grieved like Carlene did.

Jerry was never coming home. She would never be his wife. That dream was gone forever. Now she had to make herself think of Kevin and what was going to happen to him. Somehow, she had to get together enough money to move them out to California. The narrow-minded, sanctimonious hypocrites in this town would always think of Kevin as a bastard, and that was one thing she would not stand for—anybody saying mean things to her boy or thinking less of him for the way he was born.

Jackie was a little surprised when she asked him if she could start working the banquets, but he said yes. The second night she worked, she met Frank O'Reilly, who flirted with her and, after everyone else had gone home, drank one more scotch and listened to her pour her heart out about her boyfriend, who had just been killed in Nam. He understood how she felt, he said, because he had a wife who had died of a hemorrhage from a tubal pregnancy, and he never got married again.

He told her what she needed was to get away for a few days and go down to Hot Springs to get her mind off of things, stop dwelling on the past and start a new chapter in her life. He had money, he said, and he would be happy to give her a free trip. It would be good for him, too, to be with a beautiful young girl who needed him to cheer her up. It was selfishness on his part, he said, because it would cheer him up at the same time.

Her first reaction was to say no, but he promised they would have separate rooms and that he would be a perfect gentleman. He liked her and wanted to get to know her better. She talked it over with her mother, who thought it was a bad idea.

"What would people say, Carlene, you going off with an older man you don't hardly know like that? Him spending all that money on you?"

"Mama, I have a bad reputation in this town anyhow. No matter what I do, I'm branded a tramp forever, so I might as well do what I want to. I'm not going to sleep with him. He's a nice guy and just wants to do something good for me. I didn't promise him anything. I've got to find a way to pull myself together and move on."

Frannie got a little tight around the mouth, but she understood what Carlene was saying. Once people put you in a box, there was precious little you could do to get out of it.

"Well, I guess you might be right. I don't have much to say about it anyhow, do I? You're a grown woman with a baby. You go on. Have a good time. Me and Kevin will be all right."

They drove down in Frank's Cadillac and stayed at the Majestic Hotel, in the Lanai Towers—in two rooms, just like he said. They swam in the heated pool and took the baths on Bathhouse Row, hot soaks and salt scrubs and massages that made their skin tingle and feel like fresh peeled eggs.

At night, he took her to a restaurant where they wouldn't let you in without a coat and tie, and ordered lobster for her. She got to pick out her own lobster from a glass tank, and then cried when it came out boiled and red on her plate. They drank champagne, which made her sneeze, toasted the future, and he gave her a sweet kiss at the door to her room and said good night. Then he went into his own room. She slept all night long, for the first time in years, without one nightmare.

The second day, they passed a jewelry store. A ring of pink coral that reminded her of Baby's ring caught Carlene's eye. Frank walked right in and bought it for her—eighty dollars, and he didn't blink at the price. She had never known anyone like him before, who had the money to spend and who spent it without begrudging it.

He didn't push her to sleep with him, but she wanted to, and the second night when he kissed her good night, she opened the door and he came into her room. He was amazing. It seemed like he got his pleasure from giving her pleasure. She was a girl who had never had much, and it all went right to her head; later, she realized that she hadn't thought of Jerry for twenty-four hours.

Sunday night the coach turned into a pumpkin, and on Monday she was back in the real world of the trailer, Kevin, and work. It was too soon to think of more with Frank, but she knew something was starting. He traveled a lot, but he called every few days, and whenever he was in town he would take her out or make dinner for her on the houseboat, make love to her, and put a hundred dollars in her purse, which she found when she went home. She never asked him too many questions—where he went, or if he had any other girlfriends. For now, it was enough just to be with him when she could and to look forward to the next time he came to town.

He brought up the pictures one night as a new game. He loved to dress her in costumes, and each time she came over he gave her a gift, like a set of black lace underwear in a box with a red ribbon, or a gold-sequined G-string. After she told him she wanted to be an actress, they always played like they were characters in a movie, meeting somehow and of course winding up in bed. He bought a Polaroid camera and came up with the game that he was a photographer for *Playboy* doing a test shoot for the Playmate of the Month. The pictures were sexy and cute. He said she was extremely photogenic, a good actress, and would do well in the movies. Of course she got the pretend job of Playmate. It became his favorite game.

The pictures really turned him on. She wanted to tear them up, but he promised he would lock them in a drawer and nobody else would ever see them. He didn't want to share them with anyone; he wanted to keep her all for himself. He would have the pictures to look at when he was away from her.

The picture-taking got to be almost as important to Frank as the love-making. Sometimes Carlene was almost jealous of her own self as he pored over the pictures while she sat and watched, waiting for him to come to bed. Every time they did it, the camera equipment became more elaborate—more lights and tripods—and the pictures got more and more raw. Then he suggested making a home movie.

"Frank, I don't think this is something I want to do. What if somebody was to see it?"

"Who's going to see it? It's just for you and me. It will be a turn-on. Do it for me, sweetheart. If you don't like it, we'll burn it up." But she said no.

At Christmas, he gave her a diamond ring—not an engagement ring, exactly, but a cluster of small diamonds in a leaf shape. He put it on her left hand.

"What does this mean, Frank? Are we engaged or something?" She tried to tease him, but it sounded serious when she said it.

"It's a little pre-engagement ring, honey. The real one will be as big as a goose egg."

———

They made the movie. When she got home that night, there were three hundred-dollar bills in her purse. Her stack of money in the tin box under the movie-star pictures and Jerry's letters was growing. She bought a map of Hollywood, and that went into the box as well. At this rate, they might be able to move by the summer. Where Frank would fit in, she didn't know. She didn't really want to marry Frank, but then he hadn't actually asked her, either. She appreciated the money, but sometimes she felt like he enjoyed giving her the money, like he was paying for the sex or something, and it made her feel funny. At first, she tried to give it back to him, but he insisted.

"A hundred dollars to me is like ten to you, Carlene. Let me help you and your family out. It's the least I can do."

He knew about her son, of course, but she still hadn't let him meet Kevin or her mother. Frank didn't strike her as the daddy type. There was something too slick about him that nagged at her sometimes. He never talked about his life or family, and he seemed not to have any friends. She didn't even know if he had a home besides the houseboat. He mentioned once that he didn't want children, and for Carlene, that was reason enough not to marry him. But she would cross that bridge when she came to it. For now, California was getting closer, and that was all that mattered.

53. Cherry

 I woke up at four with Tripp and Faye and Ricky Don on my mind, tossed and turned for an hour, and finally got up at five. I had to see Tripp and find out what was true and what wasn't.

Ramblin' Rose was not in the driveway at Tripp's house, but I got out and knocked anyhow and waited on the porch while the silence seeped around the door. I hoped to goodness he hadn't somehow found out about Ricky Don. Maybe he had driven by when we were out in the potato patch and seen our cars or something, but I couldn't remember any car lights passing while we were out there. Then again, I probably wouldn't have noticed if there were any.

I knocked again, but he didn't answer. I couldn't imagine where he would have been all night, but he obviously wasn't at home. It wasn't like him to get up this early and go off with somebody. I didn't want to think he might have another girlfriend. Maybe he had spent the night with Bean or something.

As often as I had come to Tripp's house, it felt like a strange place to me now. I tried the door, and it was open. If he came back, I'd just say I had dropped by and was waiting to surprise him. I hesitated for about ten seconds, then went in.

There was no sign of him. I went into the living room and the bathroom, calling out his name, but he wasn't there. The house was as neat as it always was. The bed hadn't been slept in. I had never thought about going through his drawers and things before, but now I needed to see if there was something that would tell me what his secret life was like, if there was a picture of Faye or letters from her, even though it seemed like if she had written him letters, she would have known his address and phone number and not had to call the sheriff's office. Maybe he had left her and he hadn't told me about her because they were getting a divorce. Surely to goodness he wouldn't have started up with me, or even come here at all, if he was happily married. I didn't look forward to telling Daddy that I was dating a married man, or a divorced one, either. I still couldn't believe that he had fooled me so completely, although I guess no woman who is fooled ever believes it until it slaps her in the face. It's not hard to fool somebody who loves you and trusts you. Look at me fooling Mama and Daddy. I got a guilt pang, but it didn't stop me from searching.

There was nothing in the closets or drawers but clothes, all clean and tidy. I felt under the stack of undershirts and in between the underwear. Nothing.

On the top shelf of his closet there were three guns. Not too unusual around here, but one was a pistol, which I had never seen up close in person before. Daddy had never had a gun, and I was a little afraid of them, so I didn't touch these.

The desk drawers in the room he used as a studio were empty, with not even a stamp or an envelope. There was an easel set up by the window, and he had started a big oil painting of me. It was a nude, and although I really liked how I looked in it, I had told him he should put a bathing suit on it if he was going to show it to anybody. So far he hadn't.

Beside the desk was a small bookcase nearly filled with books. They were mostly schoolbooks, history books, art books—he liked Edward Hopper a lot, and Andrew Wyeth—a few novels, a dictionary, and two or three cookbooks. One had a red-and-white-checked cover, and I picked it up to see if it looked like he had used it much. Cookbooks always have flour or vanilla stains on the pages of the recipes used the most. He had made dinner for me a time or two, and his puttanesca sauce was incredible. I wondered what all else he had made.

A letter fell out. It was a pink envelope with a woman's handwriting, the round kind that girls have, with little circles for dots on the *i*'s. It wasn't addressed to Tripp but to Jerry Golden, to some army post office number. In the corner the return address was Carlene Moore, Rt. 3, Sweet Valley, Arkansas.

I got weak in the knees, and sat down to read it. It took me a couple of minutes before I could take it out of the envelope. She had sprayed perfume on it, Revlon's Intimate. I wore that myself sometimes.

Dear Jerry,

I don't know how to answer your last two letters. It was hard to believe what all you told me at first, although I know you wouldn't lie about something like that or make it up, but I went and had the film you sent developed at the drugstore. Thankfully it was busy and the girl who worked there had too much to do to riffle through the pictures like she usually does. I worried that the guys at the developing place looked at them, but maybe it is a machine that does it. I hope it is a machine.

Even with them right in front of me, I couldn't hardly accept what was in the pictures, but everything you wrote in the letter is there, and pictures don't lie. I don't know if you know what all was on the roll, but there are pictures of guys posing beside piles of corpses like you would hunting trophies, just like you said. One of

318 · Norris Church Mailer

them had what looked like a hank of black hair stuck in his helmet like a plume. There is one of you and some blond, good-looking guy who must be the Tripp Barlow you took the roll of film from. You have your arms around each other, and in the background a soldier is holding a Zippo to the straw roof of a burning hut.

There is a picture of the ditch full of people you talked about, with fat little baby legs sticking out of the pile of dead bodies. The pictures are in color, and that makes it even worse.

Oh, Jerry, I wish I could come and snatch you up out of that awful place and bring you home. Please don't talk about not coming back and getting ready to die and all. Please try to hang in there. You didn't do anything wrong. It was Tripp Barlow who shot those people, and even if you and him thought in some twisted way it was mercy, it was him and not you who pulled the trigger. They can't send you to jail for just being there.

I think we ought to at least try to do something about it when you get home. Maybe send a letter to Senator Fulbright or Congressman Wilbur Mills to let them know what they are handing out medals over there for. I'll wait to hear from you, though, and we can do it together when you get home. In the meantime, I'll hide the pictures and not say anything to anybody about all this. I don't think anybody would believe me, anyhow. You have to hang in, Jerry, and come back home. You just have to. I love you, and we will get through this together.

> All my love forever,
> Carlene

——

I read it a few more times. It was hard to know what she was talking about, but obviously there had been some kind of a massacre over there, and Tripp was somehow involved and had killed some people. What was Tripp doing with a letter addressed to Jerry, though? I needed to know what was going on. I went through every book on the shelf, shaking them out and flipping the pages. Several twenty-dollar bills fell out of one, but the rest were all empty, except for a copy of Joseph Heller's book *Catch-22*. Stuck between the pages were pictures—color pictures just like the ones Carlene described in her letter. My ears started to ring, and the room began to get black around the edges and dwindle down to a pinpoint. I sat down and put my head between my knees before I passed out. After a few minutes I was all right, but the room with its tidy air felt like it was smothering me. I had to find Baby and tell her we wouldn't have to go out to Carlene's and get the letters. I had found one already.

54. *Carlene*

 "Telephone, Carlene! It's some guy with a sexy voice, and he don't sound like he's from around here!" Rita yelled out across the dining room.

"Thanks, Rita. Everyone in the restaurant appreciates that information." Carlene took the phone, not too gently, from Rita's hand. Rita grinned and pretended to get busy filling salt shakers so she could listen.

"Hello?"

"Carlene, you don't know me, but I was a good friend of Jerry Golden's in Vietnam. My name is Tripp Barlow."

Her heart nearly froze. She had been afraid this might happen one day. Rita had her big ears pointed toward the phone. Carlene turned her back, so she could at least feel like she had a little privacy.

"Yes?"

"I'm here in town. I came to see you, really. Do you think we could get together for a little while tonight? There's something I need to talk to you about."

"What is it?"

"I don't want to get into it over the phone. Will you meet me?"

"All right. I get off work at ten. Do you want to pick me up here at the restaurant?"

"Why don't you meet me at the Ramada? I'm in room twenty-six."

"All right. Sure. I can do that. I'll be there between ten and ten-thirty." She hung up. Her hands were trembling.

"New boyfriend?" Rita screwed on a salt-shaker top and dusted salt off her hands.

"Who knows? Might be."

"Can I have the old one? I always did think Frank was cute."

"If you think you can get him, Rita, go for it. Do your worst."

"Thanks. I always do."

———

The Ramada Inn was out of town, a few miles east on Route 66. Carlene drove with butterflies in her stomach. The only reason Tripp Barlow would come all the way from California to see her had to be the pictures. They would have to talk about those pictures.

She pulled up beside number 26, got out, and knocked. Tripp opened the door and looked at her with a big smile. He had to be the best-looking man she had ever seen in her life, and that included Jerry. She felt a little pang of disloyalty, but there it was. What was behind that smile, though, remained to be seen. Wolves had big shiny white teeth, too.

"Come in. Come in. Thank you for coming out here."

The room was the generic motel kind: beige walls, fake wood-grain particleboard furniture, plastic carpet that smelled like hundreds of cigarettes and late nights. Tripp's leather bag sat on the floor of the closet under a couple of hanging shirts, and the contents of a shaving kit were laid out on a clean towel beside the sink under the fluorescent light. There was a six-pack of beer, one of Coke, and a bucket of ice on the dresser.

"Can I get you a beer or a Coke? Sorry the choices are so limited. I had to drive ten miles to buy beer. I didn't realize Arkansas had this dry-county thing."

"Welcome to Arkansas, Tripp, the land of the deep-fat fry and the tee-totaling lawmakers—make that lawmakers with teetotaling voters. I'll have a Coke, if it's not too much trouble. I don't drink much—I work selling liquor and I see what it makes people act like." She knew she was babbling, but she couldn't seem to help herself.

"Good for you. I'm not too much of a drinker myself. A little beer once in a while." He put some ice in a glass and poured a Coke; handed it to her and poured himself a beer.

"So, Tripp Barlow. What made you come all the way to Arkansas from California to see me?"

"You get right to the point, don't you?"

"It's late, and I'm tired. It's the pictures, isn't it?"

The beer slid from his hand. It splashed over the rug and soaked his shoe and his left pant leg. He didn't bend to pick up the glass, which had rolled under the bed.

"Yeah. It's the pictures."

"How did you know I had them?"

Without answering, Tripp got up and went into the bathroom, then came back out with a towel. He wiped his leg and laid the towel over the dark wet spot. He poured himself another beer.

"Do you know how Jerry died?"

"Not really. They said it was a booby trap. I know he was real depressed over what happened at that village. It seemed like in his letters he sensed something was going to happen to him."

"Maybe he did. I don't know. A lot of us were pretty strung out about what happened at that village. How much did he tell you?"

"I'd guess all of it. If there was more, I don't want to know it. He told me how you saved those little girls, and then how y'all went around putting the nearly dead ones out of their misery. I know you didn't do any of the real bad stuff."

"Carlene, just being there was bad enough. It affected all of us in different ways, but nobody got out of it without being changed."

Tripp relaxed a little, as if he felt relieved that she knew and he could talk about it. He took a long drink and continued: "Of all the men there, he was one of the ones it hit the hardest. Jerry was probably the nicest guy I ever met—clean-living, a Christian. Didn't even cuss, which a lot of saints probably would have done in Vietnam. But he was just not cut out to be a soldier. I don't think he could live with what happened, and that's why he let himself get killed."

"Let himself?"

"We were out on patrol in an area we knew for a fact had a lot of booby traps. We'd been slogging along with no real goal, and our morale was bad. After My Lai, none of us even pretended to keep any order or have any pride in our outfit. The brass kept us out in the bush, and our mission was to try to surprise and kill the enemy, but we rarely saw any, even though we knew full well they were all around us. The way we crashed around would have alerted anybody within five miles we were out there. We didn't care.

322 · *Norris Church Mailer*

"We never got to go back to base for any downtime. The supplies weren't steady. Sometimes we didn't even have enough ammunition. We got in several firefights, and lost five men. Snipers shot at us all the time, and we never saw where they were coming from. They just wore us down to nothing. It seemed like the powers that be were hoping if they left us out there long enough, we'd all be killed and their problem of what to do with us would be solved. We all knew the cover-up of what happened at My Lai would be blown open one day. Too many people knew about it.

"Jerry kept reliving that day, over and over. He couldn't get it off his mind—especially one of the little kids. It was like that kid was haunting him. That one bothered me, too, and don't think I didn't have my own nightmares, but Jerry got to the point where he was half-insane, I think. The day he got killed, he spent most of the time mumbling to himself, looking up at the sky. Maybe he was talking to God. I don't know. He wouldn't eat anything all that day.

"We had been humping for several hours when the guy in front of me stepped on a mine and got his leg blown off. I dragged the guy off the trail, yelled for the medic. He came and did what he could for the guy and radioed for a dust-off. Jerry was right behind me, and I told him to give me a hand to carry him to the landing zone and put him on the chopper. He had a funny look on his face, and he said to me, 'There is something I have to take care of first. Stay here and don't follow me,' and then he took off running through the bush, without even looking for trip wires or anything, blundering past the trees as fast as he could go. I went after him, but he hadn't gotten a hundred yards when he hit a mine, and went up in the air like a rag doll. I think it was what he wanted. He went quick. I don't even know if he knew what hit him.

"His helmet landed almost at my feet. I picked it up and carried it back to camp with me, and later I found a picture of you and your baby tucked inside it, and the letter you wrote about getting the pictures. I should have put them with the rest of his things they sent to his family, but . . . I didn't."

Carlene took a sip of her Coke. She got up and walked around the little room, then went into the bathroom and closed the door. She gripped the edge of the sink, shook with silent sobs, then splashed cold water on her face. She looked in the mirror and said to herself, "Well—what did you expect?"

Tripp hadn't moved from his chair. Carlene sat down again, smoothed her skirt.

"Thank you for telling me," she said. "I was afraid it was something like that. It doesn't make it any easier, but I'm glad to know what happened. What I don't understand is why you are here now. Why did you wait all this time to come, if you knew I had the pictures?"

"A few months ago, they finally started a big investigation. A Colonel Wilson is going around tracking down all the guys he can find who were there that day. One of my buddies called and told me he had talked to Wilson and that he probably would be calling me. All of us could be court-martialed and could go to jail for life. Carlene, I don't know if you have it in your heart to help me or not, but I would appreciate it if you would give me the pictures back. Sooner or later I will have to talk to Colonel Wilson, and I would just as soon not have those mementos floating around."

"What if I thought this colonel needed to see them? Jerry wanted me to keep them until he got home, because he thought something ought to be done about what happened."

"Carlene, Jerry is dead. Would it do him or his family any good to have his name smeared with this? You know what went down that day. No matter what happens to all of us, those people aren't coming back, and neither is Jerry. It was war, and there was nothing Jerry or I could have done at the time to stop it. I will have to live with what I did the rest of my life. The real ones who ought to be court-martialed are Johnson and Westmoreland and McNamara, who started this war in the first place, and Nixon, who has kept it going, and you know that is not going to happen."

He was speaking in a calm tone of voice that somehow made you want to trust him. Everything he said made sense. Carlene listened as he went on:

"But as far as the pictures go, you do what you have to do. If you want to hand the pictures over to the army, I'll abide by that. It is between you and your memory of Jerry."

He got up and poured himself another beer.

"Do you want some more Coke?"

She chewed on her fingernail. She felt like her mind was in two pieces. Didn't she owe it to Jerry to try to do something about it? On the other hand, they were already doing something about it with this Colonel Wilson's investigation. Tripp wasn't one of the bad guys. He had saved those little girls. She didn't have the right to hand over the pictures and see him maybe get sent to the pen. Still, it might help convict the ones who were really guilty if she did give them to the army. Her head started to ache. She didn't want to have to think about it anymore. She had already spent too many sleepless nights thinking about those pictures, and she was sick of the whole mess. It had already killed Jerry. She couldn't let it kill her, too.

"They're out in the truck."

"What?"

"The pictures are out in the truck. You can have them. They're yours. I'd be happy never to have to look at them again. I'll go get them."

She went outside and brought in an envelope and handed it to Tripp.

His voice broke as he said, "Thank you."

"The negatives are in there, too. I didn't make any copies. What are you going to do with them? Burn them up?"

"I don't know."

"You might want to give them to this Colonel Wilson, yourself. At least some of them."

"Would you, if you were me?"

"I don't know. I probably would. It might call attention to the fact that this is not the greatest war that has ever been fought."

"Has there ever been a great war fought?"

"There have been ones, like World War Two, that were for more of a reason. I mean, the world couldn't just sit back and let Hitler drive his tanks in and take over ever single country, could it?"

"You're right. But World War Two was necessary, not great. That's the one trouble with necessary wars. They make you believe that all wars are worth fighting."

He took out a cigarette and handed the pack to Carlene. She tapped one out, and he lit it for her.

"Well, I guess you'll be heading back to California now that you got what you came after," she said, blowing out a stream of smoke.

"Not right away. I've decided to stay here awhile. There's some things in California I need to give a little space. I rented a house here in town today. Jerry used to talk about going to DuVall University, so I might go there and pick up a few more credits toward my degree. It seems like nice country around here."

"It's nice, all right. But let me warn you—if you move full-grown to a small southern town, you'll never belong."

"And if you leave full-grown, they never let you go?"

"We'll find out about that. I'm going to California myself, as soon as I can. Hollywood."

"You want to try acting?"

"Yeah. I'd like to give it a try. Who knows? Somebody's got to make it. Why not me?"

"You just might, Carlene. Wanting to bad enough is half of it." He raised his glass in a toast. "Okay then, it's a deal. We'll swap. You go to California and I'll stay in Sweet Valley."

They clinked their glasses. Carlene drained the last of the Coke, set her glass down, and picked up her purse.

"Well, I better get going."

Tripp walked her the few steps to the door. "Thank you, Carlene. For everything."

"That's all right. I'm glad it's out of my hands. You don't know how glad. Take it easy, Tripp. Maybe I'll see you around."

They stood looking at each other, neither quite knowing how to end it. It all had happened too quick, too easy. They each had a piece of Jerry, and they seemed to sense that when they went their separate ways, something of him would be split and lost forever.

"Carlene . . . do you think we could get together sometime? I don't know anybody in town, and if I'm going to stay awhile, it might be good if you could introduce me to some people."

"You met anybody at all?"

"Just my landlord. Nobody my own age."

"Sure. We could do that. When would you want to do it?"

"How about right now? You could give me a night tour of this booming metropolis—if you're not too tired."

"Well . . . why not? I'm getting my second wind. We'll take a ride in my pickup and hit the hot spots. You will be so dazzled, you'll thank God every night you moved here."

"You think so?"

"That was a joke, son. But let's get out of here. This motel room stinks like beer. I need some fresh air."

55. *Cherry*

 It was five-thirty by the time I got out to Baby's and woke her up. I thought she was going to faint just like I nearly did when she saw the pictures.

"Oh my Lord, Cherry. I can't believe it. Do you think Tripp killed all those people? If he did, that means he killed Carlene to keep her from telling on him!"

"I don't know what it means, but I can't believe Tripp could murder that many people. There's hundreds of them, it looks like. He is a decent, good guy. In spite of how it looks, I know in my heart he is, and I am not going to jump to any conclusions until I talk to him."

"Well, you're not going to talk to him by yourself, that's for sure. I think we should call Ricky Don and let him arrest Tripp."

"No! We're not calling Ricky Don. I am going to talk to Tripp before I do anything. He has a lot more than these pictures to explain, including one little thing you don't know: Tripp is married. To somebody named Faye. Ricky Don told me she called the sheriff's office, trying to track him down. That's what the Ouija board said, remember? 'Ask Faye.' Is that creepy or what?"

"Carlene tried to tell you. Oh, Cherry, please let's get somebody to help us!"

"Baby, cool your jets. We can't panic and do something stupid. Where do you think Tripp might be? I didn't hear from him yesterday, and he didn't come home last night. Do you think Bean might know?"

"We could call him and see. I think he's up on the Ridge."

We called Bean's house and his mother, sounding like we had woken her up, said he must have gone out early to tend to his garden. I don't think she had a clue what it was he grew.

"Let's go on up there and talk to Bean, Cherry. We'll get him to help us."

I had only been out to Bean's one time, and that was when I went with Baby to pick him up after his truck wouldn't start and he had to get to a gig. We were only there a minute, and I didn't get out of the car. I didn't really like going up that far back on the Ridge, and Bean wasn't in a big hurry to have his friends come out and visit, either. He had moved to an apartment in town when he got back from Nam, but he still went up to the homeplace to work his patch and take care of his business.

———

The house was a square wooden box propped up on crooked stacks of rocks at the corners, and looked like it had never come within a mile of a paintbrush. Chickens pecked in the yard, and a rusted-out wringer washer sat on the porch beside a dipper and bucket full of water on a washstand.

Three or four blue tick hounds went to baying at us when we pulled up in the yard. Bean's daddy was in his undershirt, lying on a cot in the shade, drinking something out of a flat brown bottle for his breakfast and reading a paperback western. His mother was sitting on the porch in an old armchair with the stuffing coming out the back; she was drinking a cup of coffee. Ramblin' Rose was parked out beside Bean's pickup.

I was scared to get out of the car, with the dogs barking and clawing at the door. Baby rolled down the window, and Mrs. Boggs yelled at the dogs.

"Get down from there, you dogs! Get on, old Bullet! Little Boy! Come on here! Let these girls out of the car!"

The dogs slunk back, but watched us out of the corner of their eyes to see if we were going to make a false move.

"Hi, Mrs. Boggs. Is Bean around?"

"Naw, I don't reckon, Baby. He was gone before y'all called this morning, or he may have even spent the night out there. I didn't hear him come in last night, but his truck's still here, his and that boy's that come up here last night. I don't know why he is so crazy about that old garden. He don't hardly ever bring us nothing to eat out of it. Maybe a few tomatoes once in a while. It seems like a waste of time to me."

"Do you think it would be all right if I left my car here and we went out there to say hi?"

"Suit yourself. I wouldn't want to go out through all that old brush and get covered in ticks and chiggers if it was me, but go right on ahead."

I wasn't too keen on going through all that brush and getting ticks and chiggers myself, but we set out across the road on a little trail that you couldn't see if you didn't know where to look.

"Have you been out here a lot, Baby?"

"Just one time. Bean took me out to show me how high his marijuana plants had grown. I'm not real sure I can find it, but we better holler loud before we get to it. He keeps a gun out there, and I'd hate for him to shoot first and ask questions later."

We whacked through trees and underbrush, ripping our panty hose and scratching up our legs and arms for what seemed like an hour, and Baby didn't recognize anything. I knew we had passed the same old knotty tree three times, but I was so turned around that I didn't know north from south. I never had a sense of direction, anyhow. Maybe if the sun was setting in a clear sky I could tell if it was west, but that was about it. It seemed like Baby didn't have much of a sense of direction, either. Why was I surprised?

"Let's just turn back and go home, Baby, and call Bean later. This is ridiculous, and I'm itching like crazy. I think that might have been a patch of poison oak we went through back there."

"I'd do that in a minute if I knew which way was back, Cherry. Do you know?"

"You mean we're lost?"

"Well, not lost, exactly . . ."

"Well then what, exactly?"

"We know we're on the Ridge. How lost can we be, finally? I mean, if we keep walking in one direction, we're bound to find somebody. It's not like the desert or anything. People do live up here."

"Great. We'll just wander until we hit a house. Baby, there are not all that many houses up here. Some of them are miles apart. And there are bears and cougars. Don't you remember when we heard a bear that one time?"

We came up not all that far from here to do some climbing on the rocks and camp out with the Girl Scouts when we were eleven, and while we were sitting around the fire telling ghost stories and roasting marshmallows, we heard a growl and that coughing sound bears make. It seemed like it was right in the trees outside our camp. We'd all heard stories of how bears went in people's kitchens and into campers' tents looking for food, and none of us wanted to get in the tents and go to sleep, even the leader, so we packed up, doused the fire like you're supposed to, and went home in the middle of the night. We didn't even get to climb any rocks, which we were looking forward to doing the next day.

"That might not have been a bear. I think the boys came up here to scare us. It was the boys, I'm pretty sure."

"Then why didn't they ever tell us and get the credit for it? It was a bear, I'm telling you."

"Well, stop telling me! It's bad enough that we're lost!"

"I'm going to yell. BEAN! WHERE ARE YOU? BEAN!"

"BEAN! BEAN!" we both yelled at once. At least maybe it would scare off any bears or cougars, even if he couldn't hear us.

"Cherry, I think I hear something. Keep yelling."

We kept screaming Bean's name, and sure enough there was a faint answer. It was hard to tell where it was coming from, but we took off in the most likely direction.

56. *Carlene*

 Tripp and Carlene drove toward town from the Ramada on Route 66, then turned off and went down the road that circled the lake, and passed by her trailer. The only light was a faint glow in her room, where Kevin was asleep on his little cot.

"That's where Mama and Kevin and I live. Not much, is it?"

"I've seen worse."

"I don't intend to live there forever—just a little while longer. I've almost saved enough to make the move." She turned down a road that branched off past her trailer. "Let's go on around the lake, and I'll show you the restaurant where I work. It's real nice, and not too far from here."

They went down the narrow dirt road to the Water Witch, deserted and dark, circled the parking lot, and Carlene noticed that the lights were on down in Frank's houseboat. He must have just gotten back in town. She hadn't heard from him in a couple of weeks. There was a little Honda motorcycle parked out by the dock. That was odd, but she couldn't think about stopping in to see Frank now, with Tripp in the truck. He would probably call her tomorrow.

They drove back to 66 again for a quick pass by the Freezer Fresh, closed at that hour, and made the loop back to the high school so Carlene could show Tripp where she got her education, such as it was, since she never did graduate.

They pulled into the parking lot, and she and Tripp walked around to the elementary school building and the playground, off behind the big brick high school. The seesaws, swings, and other equipment sat still in the July moonlight, waiting for September, when the noisy kids would come back and wrestle them to life.

"Come on, Tripp. I'll race you to the tommy-walkers! I bet you can't walk them." Carlene took off running.

"Hold on! That's not fair! You got a head start!"

Carlene beat him, but Tripp leaped up and walked the bars hand over hand, right behind her, and then without skipping a beat, they jumped down and ran to the tall wooden swings.

"This is how you do it, Tripp. You stand up, pump to go as fast as you can, then you sit down." She stood up and soon had her swing going in a high arc.

Tripp stood up on the swing and tried to pump, but couldn't get the hang of the sitting down part.

"I think you have to be eight to do this, Carlene!" His slick leather-soled shoes slipped just then, and he almost flew off. He barely saved himself by grabbing onto the chain, and dragged his feet to slow down.

"Ow, my hands! I can't believe you used to do this every day. Why weren't more kids here brain-damaged?"

"Who said they weren't? Come on. Don't be a baby. Let's do the merry-go-round!"

They took a couple of turns on the merry-go-round, pushing it to get going fast and then leaping on and off, like she swore the kids used to do.

"This is more fun than I had when I actually went to school here," Carlene said, trying to catch her breath as the merry-go-round slowed to a stop. "Whooee. I gotta give up these cigarettes. They're killing me."

"Yeah, me too. Wow." Tripp was a little winded himself. "So far, Sweet Valley is a groovy town. What else is there to see?"

"It's a surprise. Let's go. I saved the best for last. I'll even let you drive my pickup, and I don't let many people do that."

They got back in the truck and Carlene pointed him up the mountain road. Tripp ground down to second gear to pull the hairpin turns, until they leveled out on top of the Ridge.

"Turn here, Tripp, and I'll show you the best parking spot in Sweet Valley. Not that I want to seduce you or anything, so don't get any ideas. You just need to learn the ropes of our exciting social life if you're going to live around here, and for better or worse, parking is it."

They pulled up at the red airplane lights, got out, and sat down on the edge of the bluff.

"Now, that's some view. You were right. This is the top of the world."

"I come up here sometimes and pretend that I'm a Caddo Indian and it is hundreds of years ago, before the white man came and messed things all up, and there was no town, but just a few wigwams down in that sweet valley there in the moonlight. Wouldn't it be great to have lived then? No phones, no factories, no such of a thing as money. All we'd have to do was grow our food, hunt with a bow and arrow, play with our kids, and tend to living. Everybody working together to survive. I wish sometimes I could go someplace like that."

"It was a little like that in Nam. Or it was before the war, I would imagine. Pretty and primitive. The most valuable thing the people owned was their water buffalo."

Tripp lit up two cigarettes, like Paul Henreid did for Bette Davis, and handed one to Carlene. They leaned back on their elbows and smoked.

"What was Vietnam really like, Tripp? I don't mean the war. What was the place like before the war?"

"Before the war . . . I think it was warm and full of life and beautiful. The light was magic in the rainy season. Rain swept down every day at two o'clock and turned the rice paddies to silver. Little barefoot boys rode high up on the backs of water buffalo and never seemed to notice it was raining. People would be out on their bicycles going about their business, and when the rain started, they wouldn't miss a spin of the pedal as they pulled out bright-colored rain ponchos and covered themselves, turning the roads into rivers of moving color—purple, green, blue, pink, and yellow. Whole families rode on a single bicycle, kids sandwiched in between the parents. It was unbelievable, how much they could balance on those bikes—long loaves of bread, baskets piled high with mangoes or red dragon fruit and flowers, large trees, even things like windows for their houses.

"The women wore these long-sleeved, high-necked silk dresses, split up each side over narrow pants, and they looked like graceful flowers on their bicycles. The high school girls wore them in white silk, as uniforms. They never seemed to get dirty, even riding out in the rain and the mud. The people probably laughed a lot before the war. I think they used to be happy."

"I wish Jerry could have seen it like that. It seems like he only saw the bad side of it."

"He had beauty in his life. He had you."

"Did he talk to you about me?"

"He did. A lot. I can see why he liked you."

"I see why he liked you, too." They sat in companionable silence. Carlene started to say something, then stopped.

"What were you going to say?"

"Nothing. It's crazy."

"Tell me anyhow. I'm crazy, too, sometimes."

"All right, then. Would you think I was weird if I told you he came to me when he died?"

"No, I wouldn't think you were weird. Tell me about it."

"I might have imagined it, but I was out behind my trailer, sitting on this big rock where I go to be by myself sometimes. I was reading the last letter he sent me, for something like the fortieth time, and I heard him call my name as clear as day. As close to me as you are right now. He said, 'Carlene.' That's all—just my name. But it was his voice, as real as yours is. I looked around, thinking it was maybe somebody who sounded like him, but there wasn't anybody there. Of course, I thought I was going bananas or something, but then a couple of days later, his mother called and told me he had been killed. Nobody can ever tell me it wasn't him coming to say good-bye."

"I think it probably was. I've heard of strange things like that happening. People tend to believe in the supernatural more in California, for some reason. I don't laugh at it, Carlene."

"I like your accent. It sounds like California. The way you say 'Carlene' is nice. Do you like the name Carlene?"

"It's a good, strong name. Why? Don't you like it?"

"Not for a movie-star name. I was named after my daddy, Carl. Me and him didn't get along too well, and I thought I might change my name when I got to Hollywood."

"A lot of people do that. I think Tony Curtis is really Bernie Schwartz or something. Have you thought of one you like?"

"I don't know. Not really. Maybe you can help me figure one out. It needs to be something memorable and catchy but simple, like Marilyn Monroe, or Lana Turner."

"Hm. How about . . . Madeleine Morgan?"

"Nah. Too many *M*'s. Too much like Monroe. What do you think about Ramona Desmond?"

"Too old-fashioned. Sounds like that movie *Sunset Boulevard*. What about . . . Veronica Fairchild?"

"Too la-de-da. It's not the one, but I'm definitely changing it. I want to start all over, like a new person out in California. Leave the old me behind."

"It's a good place to do that." He took a last drag from his cigarette and ground it against the rock, snuffing out the ember; flipped it out into the air over the treetops. Carlene did the same.

The moon was waxing toward full and came out from behind a cloud, lighting up the night with blue-white light.

"You go on back to the truck, Tripp. I need to answer the call of nature. Cokes always do that to me. I'll just be down by the rocks. Go on, now."

"All right. I'll wait for you."

Carlene went down the little path and through Fat Man's Squeeze. She'd be out of sight there, in case Tripp was watching. She stumbled over something in the dark that clanked, and took out her lighter to see what it was. It was a can of red paint, left over from the kids who painted SE-NIORS OF '69 on Sweet Rock. The brush was in the can. Carlene swished it around a few times, poking through the dried-out skin on top, and found the paint was still wet.

"If I'm going to have a new name and a new life, I'm going to get rid of the old one. I'll lay you to rest, Ida Red, and leave you buried here at the bottom of Sweet Rock," she said out loud. "This will be your final resting place."

She wrote on the rock wall, IDA RED IS DEAD!! She didn't care if anybody ever saw it or not, or what they might think. Somehow finally killing the hateful name lifted her spirits. She hadn't told Tripp, but she had already decided on her new name. She was going to be Hedy, after Hedy Lamarr, the most beautiful actress in her mother's drawer of old pictures. She would be Hedy Golden, and if Jerry's parents didn't like it, too bad. It would have been her name if Jerry had lived; she was entitled to it, and she would take it. She couldn't tell Tripp, though. He might not approve, and that would spoil it a little. She would introduce herself as Hedy Golden, shiny and new, when she got to California, and nobody would ever know she had once been a poor girl from Sweet Valley, Arkansas, known as Ida Red.

———

"Ready, Tripp?" she called out as she climbed back up over the rocks. He was sitting on the tailgate, dangling his legs out of the back of the truck waiting for her, smoking a joint. He held it out and she took a toke.

"What's the deal around here about pot?" he asked.

"Well, you can go to jail for twenty years at a great place called Tucker Prison—famous for the Tucker Telephone, a little electric device they hook up to your balls and then dial your number—if they catch you with a single joint. If they find it in your car, they can confiscate the car and sell it at auction, usually to their brother-in-law, and there's nothing you can do about it. I'd watch myself if I were you. However, that said, I have a friend up here on the Ridge who raises just about the best homegrown you'll ever find anywhere, and it might be worth taking the chance."

"Would you introduce me?"

"Be happy to."

They finished the joint, and Tripp put the roach in a little tin box in his pocket. The stars had never been brighter. Funny, but Carlene wasn't really attracted to Tripp, in spite of how good-looking he was. It was almost a relief. There is nothing like having a great-looking guy for a pal when you don't have to worry about seducing him. A relief for the guy, too, since she didn't get any vibes from him that he was particularly attracted to her. Jerry was too strong a presence between them.

They lay down on the grass then, side by side, like eight-year-old chums, and looked up at the sky. Carlene was happier than she had been in more than a year. Part of it was, the responsibility of Jerry's pictures had sat on her like a heavy weight, and that had been lifted. She hadn't realized how much they were bothering her. Now it was out of her hands, and if nobody ever saw them, there was nothing she could do about it.

Another thing was that it was so nice to be out with somebody besides Frank, somebody who was her own age. It was so clear to her tonight that she didn't want to be with Frank. Playing on the swings, she had felt so light and free—like a kid again. She didn't enjoy the dirty games with Frank anymore. He had gotten too into them, and it wasn't fun like it had been at first. Her heart sank every time he dragged out that camera equipment. Maybe she could get the film and the pictures away from him and burn them. If she did become a star in Hollywood, it wouldn't be good to have pictures like that of her floating around, even if they were locked in a drawer—and certainly not a film. She made up her mind to tell Frank tomorrow. He might not like it, but she thought he would give them to her when she explained. Then nothing would stand between her and her future.

———

"It's hard to believe the astronauts are up there somewhere on their way to land on the moon," Tripp said. "I wonder if they are looking down here at us right now. That must be so bizarre."

"But the moon looks so close tonight, doesn't it? Like you could fly up to it in no time."

"Yeah. Or maybe it's just the pot making it seem that way. But whatever. This feels good, laying here under the stars like this. I haven't been this relaxed in a long time."

"Me neither. It's way better than sex."

"That's debatable, but I know what you mean."

"You have a girlfriend, Tripp?"

"Nope. I'm married."

"Oh really? Where's your wife?"

"Back in San Francisco. Two months before I was due to leave Nam, I stumbled into a punji trap, and they sent me to Chu Lai to the hospital. Faye was one of the Vietnamese nurses who took care of me. Her real name is Phuong, but I started calling her Faye, and it fits her. I thought she was an angel, and married her and brought her home with me. It was a crazy thing to do in a lot of ways, and even though it didn't work out, I'm glad I got her out of there.

"Part of the reason I'm staying here and going to DuVall is to give us a little time to think things over. She was not really in love with me, I soon discovered, but she sure is in love with America. That's cool. I'm probably not in love with her, either. We'll stay married, though, at least until she gets her citizenship. She knows where I am, but we agreed not to write or call or be in touch in any way for six months. Then we'll see what happens."

"Is she beautiful?"

"I think she is. She's tiny. Long hair, small hips; strong legs with big calves, like a lot of the Vietnamese women have. She'll do all right over here, since she speaks perfect English. Her father was a language professor before the war. She can always get a job as a nurse somewhere. Faye can take care of herself, I have no doubt."

"Well, I hope it works out for the best, whatever that is. What will you do until school starts?"

"I don't know. Maybe get some kind of a job. What do you think would be a good place to work for a few weeks?"

"Not much choice for a short-time job. The pickle plant, I guess, would be easiest to get on. It's hard work but the most interesting, if you're looking for interesting. You'd meet a lot of kids there. Everyone in Sweet Valley should definitely experience the pickle plant at least once. It's part of the local culture."

"Pickle plant, huh? Sure, why not? Sounds like a chapter for my memoirs."

57. *Cherry*

 "BEAN! KEEP YELLING! IT'S ME AND CHERRY!" Baby was screaming. Our voices echoed all over the place. There were a lot of high rock cliffs on this part of the Ridge, which made it really confusing to tell where the sound was coming from.

I didn't see how the law could ever find Bean's patch, because I didn't see how we would, and we knew it was there. My legs were all scratched up and stinging. When would I learn not to wear miniskirts on these excursions? I had on my favorite mint-green leather gillies, too, and they were getting beaten up. One of the laces had already caught on a stump and broke, and it was hard to walk with the shoe flopping with every step. I needed to have my head examined. I mean, who did I think would be up here in the woods to see me and say, "Oh, that Cherry Marshall is so chic in her green miniskirt, striped sweater, and matching shoes?" I'd never wear them again, so it was hard payment for a lesson learned.

After, it seemed like, another hour of crashing around, we heard our names being called, and this time there was no mistaking where it was coming from. It was close.

"Over there, Cherry! I see him!"

Sure enough, Bean was standing beside a rock cliff, waving his arms and yelling at us. We crawled over some dead logs and finally made it to the little clearing where Bean had his marijuana patch. I couldn't believe the size of them. They were higher than my head, and that's pretty high.

"Baby, what in the world are you doing coming out here at this time of the morning?" Bean didn't seem too happy to see us. "And why are you coming from that direction? That's the most roundabout way of getting here I ever saw. Didn't you know the way?"

"We wanted to take the scenic route, what do you think?" Baby seemed considerably less glad to see him than she was a minute earlier.

"Why did you bring her up here? You know not to bring people—no offense, Cherry."

"She knows all about it, Bean. She's been smoking your pot with your old pal Tripp Barlow, so she's hip."

"Look, Bean, you know you can trust me. We had to come up here to talk to you because we're looking for Tripp. It's kind of an emergency. We haven't seen him since night before last. We saw his car up at your house. Do you know where he is?"

"Yeah, I do. He's right down here in the cave."

"In a cave? There's a cave up here? What's he doing in there?"

"He's stuck and can't get out. I'm at the point where I need to get some help, but I can't hardly bring just anybody in to do it. You see the problem." Bean seemed a little nervous and upset.

"What do you mean stuck? You mean he's down in a hole? How long has he been in there?"

"Since late last night. Me and him came out to get a couple of bags from my stash, and while we were here, we dropped a few tabs of acid. After a while, I guess it hit him the wrong way, because he got scared and grabbed a flashlight and took off down into the cave. It ain't no big deal for me, but he's a lot bigger than me and not used to caves, and he fell into a tight place and got his leg stuck."

"Why didn't you try to get him out last night?" An alarm bell went off in my head, like something might be really wrong.

"I was pretty zonked-out myself, and didn't know he was in trouble until this morning when he didn't come back up. I wasn't at myself enough to go after him until a little while ago, when I heard him calling, and crawled down and found him. He seems to be okay, but his leg is hurt

338 · Norris Church Mailer

and he's pretty weak. I was getting ready to go down to town to get some tools and food and ropes and stuff when I heard you yelling."

I was thunderstruck. It was hard to grasp what Bean was telling us. He looked awful, all pale and sweaty, so he must have been through some-thing trying to rescue Tripp. I didn't know what to say.

"Did you know about this cave, Baby?"

"I did, but I've never been down in it. You know I don't like tight un-derground places. Bean is an expert caver, though. There's miles of them running all under the Ridge. Right, Bean?"

"Miles. I figure I've only explored maybe ten or twenty percent of it, and I've been doing it ever since I was a kid."

I didn't like tight underground places, either. I had only been in a cave one time myself, when our seventh-grade class went up in the Ozarks on a field trip to Diamond Cave, near Jasper. It had only been open to the public a little while and they didn't have it really fixed up yet—just a long wire, with a lightbulb every few feet, and no paved paths or steps or any-thing. There was one place where we had to all get down on our hands and knees in a line and crawl, which was already beginning to freak me out a little when the line stopped because one of the kids up ahead got scared and couldn't go on. Actually, come to think of it, it was Baby. There was no place to turn around and go back and no way to go forward. I got so claustrophobic that I went a little buggy and started screaming.

The teacher finally got through the tunnel and started grabbing kids right and left and pulling them through so she could get me out of there before all of them panicked, too. When I got out into the big room, I still was a little hysterical at the thought that I'd have to go back through that tunnel again, and Baby was not much better, so the teacher took me back by myself and then went and brought out Baby. We waited in the bus for the rest of them. I didn't even notice the stalagmites, and never had any desire to go back into a cave, especially a wild one like this here on the Ridge, which didn't even have a wire and lightbulbs.

"Cherry? Maybe it would be good if you could go in and talk to Tripp for a little bit while I get the tools and supplies. Cheer him up or some-thing."

The idea of going into a cave paralyzed me. But Tripp was down there. He was hurt. In spite of everything that had happened, I needed to go to him. Life is full of hard decisions, isn't it?

"How far down is he, Bean? Can I walk to where he is?"

"Part of the way, but you'd have to crawl in a few places to where he is. You don't have to go all the way in, just far enough for him to hear you. It'll be easy, skinny as you are. He's pretty scared, I think. I'll go with you. It ain't nothing. I do it all the time."

"Baby? Will you go with me too?"

"We don't all need to go," Bean said. "She better stay out here in case I need her when I get back."

"Bean will be with you, Cherry," Baby said. "He's right. Somebody needs to wait up here, don't you think?"

Her eyes were big. I could tell she was even more scared than I was.

I took a deep breath and squeezed through the crevice leading into the cave. Tripp needed me, and it looked like this was the only way I could get to him, but my knees were shaking. I said a little prayer to God to help me in spite of me being such a sinner. I hoped He heard me.

58. *Baby*

 Tatang wouldn't admit it to anybody, especially Auwling, but Pilar was his favorite child. She was, by a trick of nature, even more like his dead wife than her own child, Babilonia. Pilar was as like Maeling in beauty as if she were her reincarnation, and she had her beautiful voice and mischievous ways, too. Manang despaired that Pilar would ever get a husband, because she had no interest in things of the house, like learning to cook or sew, but Tatang just laughed when she was impudent and said that she had beauty and spirit and would always do well in life.

Where Baby was studious, Pilar barely passed her exams. She had a good memory and got by from listening in class, but she never read the assignment and seldom did her homework. She preferred to sit in her room and listen to records or talk to her friends on the phone.

Baby tried to talk sense into her, but Pilar was like the grasshopper, playing through the summer and never thinking of the winter to come, while Baby was like the ant. The two of them couldn't get along on anything.

"You're not my mother, Baby, so just butt out of my life and stop trying to boss me around. I'll do what I want to and there's nothing you can do about it. Your boyfriend is not such a goody-goody, either, you know. I know what all he does and what you do with him, so you just better not preach at me."

"Yes, Pilar, I know all about it, but I'm a lot older than you are. You'd do better to be a kid for a while. It passes too fast, as you'll find out, and one of these days you'll be sorry you wanted to grow up so quick."

Before Pilar approached her fourteenth birthday, she began to go out with boys. They were bad boys, older boys, who gave her beer and cigarettes and liked to watch her dance, her long hair swirling around her narrow hips, who didn't care that she was young, but loved the sparkle in her eye and her giggle and the red lips that were so tender to kiss. No matter what Manang said, Pilar couldn't be kept at home. She was afraid of no one, especially not her Tatang, who adored her no matter what she did, and in fact was blind to what was happening to his beloved daughter.

Manang knew well enough, but was helpless to stop her. Now, since the night last summer when that girl Carlene was thrown into the lake, the visits from the ghost of Maeling were becoming more and more frequent and Auwling began to sense that the message she was trying to give had something to do with her wild child, Pilar.

Manang was not the kind of mother who would search through her children's belongings—she respected everyone's need for privacy—but the feeling of disaster got stronger with every visit from Maeling, and one day it was so strong that while Pilar was at school Manang decided to search in her room for something, for anything that would show her what kind of danger her daughter was flirting with.

Pilar's room was always untidy. Piled on every surface were glasses with milk dried in the bottom, plates of stale cookie crumbs, and cheese covered with green fuzzy mold. Hamburger wrappers from the Freezer Fresh in grease-soaked bags lay in a mound in the corner, along with hard, dry french fries. Underwear draped a lamp, and most of her wardrobe was in disarray across the floor. In the corner, a salmon pink-and-white hi-fi record player sat on a table with dozens of albums strewn around: the Beatles, the Rolling Stones, Herman's Hermits, the Animals, the Who, and many others that Manang had heard at top volume over and over until even her gentle patience came to its end and she ached to throw them against the wall.

Auwling stood in the doorway in despair. She didn't know where in the chaos to start. She took a deep breath and went in. In the chest of drawers she found packages of cigarettes and matches, but that was no surprise. They weren't even hidden. Inside a box of Kotex napkins, there were small squares of foil wrapped around circle-shaped objects that Manang didn't recognize, but she sensed were not something a young girl should have. She would ask Dionisio about them. Maybe he would know what they were for. She didn't think Dionisio would approve of her snooping in Pilar's room, but there was nothing else she could do. He would see the necessity once she found something. And she was sure she would, though she didn't wish it.

Some of the records were lying on the floor out of their jackets. Manang didn't want to disturb the room too much, but Pilar would never notice if the records were put away. They were too expensive to ruin by scratching, even if Manang couldn't stand to listen to them. She picked up one called *Rubber Soul* and began looking for its cover, which she found under the bed, along with several pairs of shoes and a lot of dust. She tried to slide the record into the cardboard sleeve, but something was blocking the way. She reached her hand into the sleeve and pulled out a stack of photographs.

Manang sat down on the unmade bed and stared at the pictures. They were beautiful—of a girl with long black hair draped over her shoulder, face half in shadow, with small, perfect breasts and graceful, long legs tucked under a round naked bottom. There were other poses in the stack, six in all. The others were more explicit, showing fine pubic hair, and one even displayed the most private part of the beautiful girl as her shapely legs kicked high into the air. It took Manang a few moments before she realized she was looking at Pilar. Her hands began to shake.

—

Tatang was beside himself when she showed him the pictures. Auwling had never seen him so distraught, even on that night he had found Maeling dead in the jungle so many years ago. She thought he was going to have a stroke. His eyes bulged and the veins in his neck looked dangerously near to rupture.

"Please, Dionisio! Calm yourself! You will die if you do not stop this!"

But Dionisio would not be calmed. "Do not say anything to Pilar. Not yet. She would only lie. Wait and I will find out who is responsible for this, and he will pay."

It was hard to look at the girl that afternoon when she came home from school and not allow the sick feelings to show, but Manang was used to swallowing her feelings, and Pilar went into her room, which was exactly as Manang had found it—the *Rubber Soul* record cover under the bed with the pictures, the shoes, and the dust.

Tatang was not so good at hiding his feelings. He stayed late at the fish-and-bait store, pacing the floor and waiting for nightfall, for Pilar to go out. Then he would follow her. If she did not go tonight to the man who had done this to her, she would go soon enough. Tatang had plenty of patience. He had learned it in the jungles of the Philippines when he was a hunter of men.

59. Cherry

 I read somewhere that all caves are a constant fifty-four degrees, summer and winter. It was October, but it doesn't really get all that cold in Arkansas until late in the month, or even November, and then most times you only need a jacket, so it was colder in the cave than it was outside. The air held that kind of damp that oozes into your bones and chills you through and through. Tripp must have been freezing by now. I began to really worry about him. I wished to goodness he had never heard of LSD.

I could just barely snake my way through the crack that led into the cave. If anything, it was tighter than Fat Man's Squeeze. Bean slipped through easy enough. He seemed to be like a rat that could dislocate its bones and squeeze through something the size of a wedding ring. It hit me why his outfit in Vietnam called themselves tunnel rats.

The room we came into was something I would never in my wildest dreams have imagined being there. It was like a weird little apartment. There were kerosene lanterns and candles lit all around the room, and Bean had taken old quilts and pillows and draped them over rocks and made furniture. A big orange carpet remnant covered part of the ground. It smelled of mildew. There was a bed on a shelf of rock up off the floor and a fireplace in the middle, with a circle of stones around it. A rough wooden table sat against the wall loaded with marijuana plants laid out to dry. They gave off a really strong musty smell.

"How did you get all this stuff through that little crack, Bean?"

"That ain't the only way to get in here. There's a bigger one on down, but this one's the fastest from where we were."

In the flickering light, I noticed a skull set in a niche in the wall. It had a big candle burning on top of it, and the wax from countless other candles had dripped down around the eye sockets and made what looked like long hair flowing onto the floor. It had a grinning mouth of straight white teeth. Propped up next to it was a bundle of old decrepit straw that had been burned at one end and a pair of what might at one time have been moccasins.

"My Lord, Bean! Who is that!"

"It's an old Indian, I reckon. Them's his moccasins, and they look Indian. I don't know how long he had been down in there, but I found his skeleton back in a part of the cave that was real hard to get to. I can't hardly believe he got that far in there himself with just that rush torch, but I guess his light went out and he couldn't find his way back out and died. I left the rest of him down there, but it seemed like the thing to do to at least take his head back up and give him a little memorial."

It was creepy, to say the least, having that grinning, empty-eyed skull holding court over the room. Off to the side, behind the drying table, there was a dark passageway, and another one, in the back of the room, that went into the shadows.

"Where is Tripp, Bean? Is he down that passage?"

"Naw, it's the one back yonder. I feel real bad that I let him go off like that, but before I knew what was happening, he was gone. Come on, and I'll show you."

Bean picked up a little bag and a flashlight and gave me one, and we set out. It wasn't too bad for the first few yards, in spite of my flapping shoe. I could stand up, at least. Even though I had on a turtleneck sweater, I was cold. I wished I still had my long hair.

The walls were cold and wet, and I tried not to touch them, but I couldn't avoid it. I was beginning to get the first tiny feeling of panic, like I had in Diamond Cave, but there was enough fresh air, and it hadn't gotten too tight yet, so I took a couple of deep breaths and kept on going.

I followed Bean around a bend, and the passage opened up into a

344 · Norris Church Mailer

good-size room. I gasped, as my flashlight lit up what looked like a chandelier hanging from the ceiling.

"Oh, Bean! That's so beautiful! Is it a stalagmite?"

"It's a stalactite. It hangs from the ceiling. Stalagmites grow from the floor. Just think of stalactite—stick tight—to the ceiling, and you can remember the difference." Bean seemed a lot calmer now than he was outside. His voice had changed, and he seemed strangely unconcerned that Tripp might be in real trouble. If I didn't know what we were going down in the cave for, he would seem like a tour guide. Maybe Tripp was not in such bad shape, after all.

We went for what seemed like a half hour or more, through a few more small rooms and passages that were right on the verge of being too narrow and low. A couple, we had to crawl through, and I tried to concentrate on looking down and breathing. My mint-green panty hose had lost their knees a while ago, and my own knees were skinned up and killing me, but I had no choice except to go on.

This last passage opened up into a big room with a good-size pool of crystal-clear water. I shined my light over it and saw some white fish swimming around. Nearly albinos, like me, poor things. I wondered how they could see, living all the time in the dark, and Bean said they were blind. Hanging above the pond was a rock formation that looked like a bronzed waterfall. It took my breath away.

"That's flowstone. It was formed by a waterfall running over it millions of years ago. Before there was even any pyramids, that flowstone was here."

I was frankly amazed at what all was here under the ground. It was a whole lot better than Diamond Cave. If the public ever found out about it, they would take it over and make a theme park out of it, like Dogpatch. Bean could sell the land and be rich. We kept on going, and there were even more wondrous formations—stalactites and stalagmites that looked like lace curtains, like pipe organs, like straws. And everywhere there were big piles of fine-looking dirt.

"Don't step in that bat guano, if you can help it."

"Bat guano?"

"Yeah. Them's bats hanging up on the ceiling. They won't bother you if you don't bother them."

I shone my light up, and the ceiling was a mass of churning black bodies. Great. I was deep under the ground with a piddly little flashlight and hundreds of bats. That's some feeling, I don't have to tell you. It made my skin crawl. I started to ask how much longer we had to go until we got to Tripp, when Bean started calling out:

"Barlow! Barlow? Can you hear me? Cherry is here to see you."

"Tripp? Tripp sweetie? It's me. Can you hear me?"

"Cherry?" It sounded like he was at the bottom of a well, far away, but he was alive and we would get him out soon if I had anything to do with it.

60. *Carlene*

 It was nearly midnight when Carlene and Tripp got to Bean's house. Tripp insisted they go by before they left the Ridge and see if he was still up. Carlene thought Tripp and Bean would get along. They had a lot in common, both having been in Vietnam, and Bean grew pot—reason enough for Tripp to like him.

Tripp was having quite an education about Sweet Valley all in one night, and he seemed to love it. Even with all he said about needing to work out some things with his wife, Carlene still couldn't understand why he didn't just go back to California and work it out there, since he had the pictures. Sweet Valley was not exactly the ideal place you go to seek your fortune. Maybe he had other things to work out that she knew nothing about. You never could tell; maybe he would really like it here. He could always leave if he didn't. It was so easy for men with no kids just to pick up and go wherever they wanted to.

Bean's old man had passed out and his mother was watching TV and eating popcorn when Carlene and Tripp came in, so the three of them left her glued to the set and went out behind the house to the shed, sat on the broken-down tractor, and passed around a joint while Bean and Tripp got acquainted. Before long, they seemed like old buddies. Carlene took a few more tokes while she listened to them speak as if in a foreign language about Vietnam, then she started to crash.

"Y'all, I'm sorry, but I can't take any more of this. I got to get home. I'm exhausted. Mama has to go to work in the morning, and I have to get up and take care of Kevin."

"Don't go yet, Carlene. I'd like to give you a little present. You guys are the greatest friends I could have met here. You make me feel right at home, and I'd like to do something nice for you."

"What kind of a present?" Carlene asked. "You don't have to give me a present. You're a great guy, too, Tripp, and I'm happy to help you out any way I can."

Tripp pulled out a bottle of Visine eyedrops.

"Here in this little bottle is a piece of heaven—the ticket for the most wonderful trip you will ever take. I'd like to share it with my two new best friends."

"What is it, Barlow?"

"My friend, it is acid. Moondust and magic."

"Thanks but no thanks, Tripp. Pot is more than enough for me," Carlene said. "It's been fun, boys, and I hate to be a party pooper, but I need to get going. You coming, Tripp?"

"Why don't you stay, Barlow?" Bean said. "I can take you down. I got to go back to my apartment anyhow."

"Okay. Sure. Better than hanging out by myself at the Ramada smelling the beer somebody spilled. Right, Carlene?"

"Anything's better than that." She climbed down off the tractor, got her purse, and started across the yard to her truck. "Y'all be good. Don't do anything I wouldn't do. I'll see you, Tripp. If you need me to, call me tomorrow and I'll go with you out to the pickle plant to see about a job."

And she left them as Tripp put a drop of acid on Bean's tongue.

———

Carlene was still feeling rosy from the pot and all her Hollywood plans when she neared the turnoff to the Water Witch and a Honda motorcycle shot out in front of her and headed down the lake road. There was a young girl on it, black hair flying, and for a minute Carlene thought it was Baby, then realized it was her little sister, Pilar. With a jolt, it hit her that it must have been Pilar's motorcycle she saw down at Frank's houseboat. The girl couldn't be more than fifteen, if she was even that. It felt like all the blood drained out of her face, and Carlene turned the truck down the road and headed toward the Water Witch.

Carlene didn't know what she was going to do, but she had to confront Frank. She felt sick to her stomach, and wished she hadn't smoked so much—her brain seemed to be working in slow motion. Maybe she shouldn't confront him at all. Maybe she should just never mention it and never see him again. But she couldn't do that. It was Baby's little sister, and even if Pilar was a willing partner, she was still way too young. With sudden clarity, like on the day her daddy died, she saw the young girl she used to be lying in the dirt behind her trailer, the last of her childhood wrenched away from her. She couldn't let that happen to Baby's sister. Not by her own boyfriend. No, she couldn't let it go, even until morning.

Carlene drove nearly to the restaurant, then pulled the truck into a turnaround off the road, killed the motor, and walked the last several yards toward the houseboat. She didn't want to give Frank any warning.

The lights were on, and she saw Frank through the window. He was sitting at the table with rows of pictures spread out. He looked up as he heard footsteps cross the gangplank, but before he could do anything, she had opened the door and come inside.

"Carlene! Honey, what are you doing here this late?" He tried to slide the pictures into a stack, but there were too many. He left them and stood up, then noticed her distraught face.

"What's the matter?"

"You tell me if something is the matter, Frank. I just saw a fourteen-year-old girl leave here."

"Sweetheart, I don't know what you thought you saw, but there was no girl here. I've been alone all evening."

"Don't lie to me, Frank. I'm not as ignorant as you think I am. What are those pictures of?"

She crossed the room toward the table. Frank caught her by the arm and pulled her back.

"Those pictures have nothing to do with you. I think you're all upset over nothing, and maybe you should go home. We can talk in the morning when you feel better."

She jerked her arm free, moved quickly to the table, and picked up a stack of pictures. They were all like the ones they had taken, but they were not of her. She felt hot with shock. There were dozens of girls. Among them was Pilar. She held one of her up.

"So there was no girl here? This is the one I saw, and I know for a fact that she is not even fifteen." Her voice shook.

"Okay, Carlene. So I'm not a saint. You wanted to catch me and you did. But that girl is eighteen. Oriental girls just look young."

"I ought to know how old she is. That's Baby's little sister. You remember Baby. You met her at a banquet. Don't think I didn't see you talk to her that night and try to put the moves on her."

"I never had anything to do with Baby."

"That's because she wouldn't have anything to do with you. Oh God. I wish I had never met you."

She took off the diamond ring shaped like a leaf and threw it at him.

"Here's your ring. I'll give you back every cent you gave me, and you give me my pictures. I have it all. I didn't spend a penny."

"Carlene, be sensible. Let's talk about this, honey." He had the smarmy tone of a man trying to talk to an idiot child.

"And you leave Pilar alone or I will tell the police. I swear I will."

He stopped trying to placate her. His voice was like ice. "I don't think you better do that. The judge is a friend of mine. In fact, he was more than fond of your pictures."

"You showed Judge Greer my pictures?"

"I showed a lot of people your pictures. They are some of my bestsellers. You don't have to be ashamed. You have a beautiful body."

"You *sell* these pictures? Is that where you get all your money?"

"Carlene, don't be so naive. It's no worse than *Playboy* magazine. Maybe I didn't treat you right and let you in on what was happening, but I thought it would be better if you didn't know. I was going to tell you eventually, and I was sharing the money with you, wasn't I? Ask your girlfriends. They think it's a good way to make a lot of money. You didn't mind taking your share of the profits. And the films are worth a lot more. Stop and think about it, honey. It could be a gold mine for you as well as me."

She was horrified. He wasn't even sorry. He expected her to say, "You're right, let's take some more pictures."

She slapped his face, then burst into tears and ran out the door, into the night.

61. *Bean*

 Bean dropped Tripp off at the Ramada. It seemed like the acid wasn't going to hit, and it had been a long day. He had made a point of staying away from acid in Nam, because it was such an unpredictable drug. He knew every little nerve in his body that pot smoothed away, and it was a familiar old friend, but he had seen too many guys strung out on acid and unable to function, sometimes for days at a time. He needed his senses. Even so, he had always been curious about it. Now that he had taken some, it didn't seem like such a big deal. Maybe he was immune to it or something, but nothing was happening. Nothing at all.

Barlow, on the other hand, was off in some kind of la-la land. His eyes were glassy, and he had a hard time forming words. It was better to put him to bed and talk about it later.

"See you tomorrow, Barlow. I'll be by in the afternoon to pick you up and go with you over to the pickle plant. Okay? Hear me? We'll call Carlene and tell her she doesn't need to take you. You ought not to have any trouble getting on the night shift. Barlow? You listening, buddy?"

"Sure. Yes. Thanks, buddy. Buddy, buddy. Pickle plant. I know."

Bean took off down Route 66 and decided to drive around a little and clear his head. He had been sleepy before, but now all of a sudden he was wide awake. He rolled down the windows. He wasn't feeling so good. He had a headache, and his vision was doing strange things. Lights coming at him on the road from passing cars were so bright that he had to hold his hand in front of his eyes to keep them from splitting his head open. It seemed like there were animals looking at him from the side of the road. His heart was pumping hard, and he started to sweat. Big drops ran down his face and under his collar. His shirt felt soaked.

He turned down the road that went out by the lake, and a girl in purple pajamas, on a motorcycle, went around him, her long black hair flying. It was Nguyen. Wait a minute. Wasn't Nguyen dead? No, she couldn't be if she was here. She must have been pretending. Those Viet Cong are crafty, pretending to be dead when they really weren't, waiting for you to come up to them. Then they would raise up and blast you. You never took for granted that a VC was dead. Now here Nguyen was, alive and going to her tunnel, to wait for him in the dark. He must have taken a wrong turn back there on the road. He must have taken a wrong turn and wound up in Vietnam.

The trees along the road waved to him, beckoning as if they were alive. They reached out their long fingers as he passed and touched his elbow, propped up in the open window. Graceful, long fingers of the jungle trees caressed his arm. They were evil, those trees, hiding Viet Cong snipers in their branches. Bean looked for Nguyen, but she had disappeared. Gone down her tunnel to wait for him; gone to set a trap with a poison snake; a viper that would fall out of a bamboo tube and land on his head, curl around his neck and sink its fangs deep into his flesh. A quarter-step snake, they called it, since after it bit you, you only had time to take a quarter of a step before you fell down dead.

No, wait a minute. Nguyen wasn't down in her tunnel. Not yet. She was right here, walking down the side of the road. She had changed her clothes and tried to disguise herself, but it was her, all right. He pulled up beside her and opened the door.

"Get in. I've been looking for you."

62. Carlene

 Carlene was walking back to where she had parked in the turnaround when Bean's truck pulled up beside her. She didn't know why he was there or why he had been looking for her, but it occurred to her that he was just the person she needed to see. He could help her figure out how to tell Baby about Pilar, and then together they could decide what to do. She got in beside him, and he took off. She could come back and get her truck later.

"Oh, Bean, it's so good you came by. I just found out something horrible, and you need to hear about it so you can help me tell Baby. I don't know what to do or where to turn. It's about Pilar."

Bean was looking at her with a funny light in his eyes. "Are you on your way to the tunnel?" he asked.

"What tunnel? Bean, are you all right? Come on now, I need for you to focus. Listen to me. Something awful is happening, and I've accidentally been a part of it. There's a man out here, an older man, and he's been using Baby's little sister . . . Bean? What's wrong? Why are you staring at me like that?"

Nguyen was saying something in Vietnamese, but Bean couldn't tell what it was. Her voice sounded like chirping crickets. He had never noticed it before, but her voice was orange. She was probably lying to him, like she always did, telling him he was her GI number one when she was really plotting to kill him. Plotting to take his baby and kill it and kill him.

"Why didn't you tell me about the baby, Nguyen? Why didn't you have the guts to come out and tell me what you were instead of going off like that without a word? You and Charlie must have had a good laugh about what a fool I was, didn't you?"

"Bean? You're scaring me. Who is Noy-yen? What are you talking about? Bean?"

Bean slumped down, and the truck lurched from one side of the road to the other. Carlene grabbed the wheel to keep it from going in the ditch, and the glove compartment door fell open. In the dim light, Carlene saw a gun. She slammed the door shut and shook Bean's arm. He pushed her arm away, hard, then he shook his head, as if he had water in his ears, and took the wheel.

He must be losing it on the drugs, she thought. She had to get out of the truck. He was clearly out of his mind, and she didn't want him to grab that gun.

"I need to get out here, Bean. Just stop and let me out right here. We can talk in the morning. I mean it now, Bean. Stop the truck!"

Instead, in a panic, he floored the gas pedal. The jungle was closing in tighter now, the trees reaching out to grab him. There was a whole company of Viet Cong hiding in the trees, shooting at him. But he had Nguyen. She would be his hostage, his ticket out of there. He had to get to safety. He had to get to his tunnel. He'd be safe in his own tunnel.

He started up the mountain road.

Carlene was getting more and more scared, but there was no way she could jump out while the truck was going so fast. As soon as Bean slowed down enough, she would jump. She clung to the door handle and waited for her chance.

—

The truck never slowed down until Bean pulled up into his yard. Before the wheels stopped turning, Carlene opened the door and ran toward the house. Bean jumped out the other side and grabbed her. She twisted, pulled loose, and ran back to the truck; wrenched open the door and took the gun from the glove compartment. She turned to point it at him but fell before she got the chance. She never saw the blow. He hit her on the neck with the side of his hand, like they had taught him in the army; the chop silenced her.

She fell hard, like a sack of salt. He kneeled down beside her, picked up her hand. It was lifeless. He entwined his fingers with hers, but her hand didn't grasp them. Her fingers stuck out straight between his, like sausages. He kissed the fingers, rubbed them on his chin, then rocked back and forth, cradling her limp arm like a baby. Tears streamed down his cheeks.

"Why did you try to kill me, Nguyen? I never did anything but love you. Why did you cut me with that knife? Why did you take away my baby?"

After a moment, he shoved the gun into his pocket, picked her up, threw her over his shoulder, and set off through the woods to his tunnel. He would be safe there.

63. *Cherry*

 "Just hang on, buddy. We'll have you out of there soon." Bean called out, then he turned to me. "Talk to him, Cherry, and I'll be back in a while with the tools. You can get farther down the tunnel to where he is. Just lay on your stomach, pull with your elbows, and push with your toes."

"You're just going to leave me down here by myself with him? What if my light goes out? I'll never find my way out of here again!" I tried not to let on that I was about to panic, but I was.

"I won't be gone long, I promise."

I guess it hadn't hit me that Bean would leave so soon without me, but he did, and I was alone with Tripp. He was wedged in a narrow passageway, and I couldn't see myself pushing with my toes and pulling with my elbows to get down in it. I did scoot along far enough to beam the light down, though, and saw the top of his head and his arms and shoulders. He looked like he was probably in a cramp.

"Tripp, it's me, Cherry. Are you all right? Tripp? Can you hear me?"

"I can hear you, Cherry. I'm okay." His voice sounded weak and strained; papery and dry.

"You don't sound okay."

"I think my leg is broken. It's jammed between two rocks and I don't have any feeling in it. My foot is way swollen. Do you have any water?"

"No. But Bean has gone to get some tools and stuff. You'll be out soon."

"I need a drink bad. My throat feels like cotton. I think there is a pool somewhere down here. Can you get me some water?"

There was the pool we had passed, back a ways. Maybe I could get some water out of that, but it couldn't be very clean, with the blind fish swimming around in it and bats flying over it and pooping their guano. And I didn't have anything to put water in. But he needed it. I had to try.

"Tripp honey? I'll try to get you some water. Hang on."

I went slow, memorizing the rocks and the turns I took to get back to the pool. It wasn't all that far, but there was still the problem of what to put the water in. I squatted by the edge and dipped my hand in the pool. It was freezing. I scooped a little into my mouth, and it didn't taste too bad. It was good and clear. I hoped it wouldn't make us sick.

I looked around, but there was just nothing that would hold water. Nothing but my shoe. Thank goodness it was so big. Even so, it was a lace-up, and the water would probably leak out of the holes. But it was all I had, so I filled it up. By the time I carried the shoe of water back, trying to hold the flashlight steady, and scooted down to where he could reach it, there wasn't more than a swallow or two left in it.

"Oh my God. That is the best-tasting water I ever drank. Can I have more?"

I limped back with one bare foot and filled the shoe again. At this rate, it would take ten trips to get him a good drink, but at least I knew the way.

Finally, he said he'd had enough. I sat down by the opening to where he was and rested. The sock of my panty hose was torn all to pieces, and my foot was cold as ice. It wouldn't help to put it into the soggy shoe, though, so I rubbed it and tried to warm it up. My knees were still oozing, and they hurt every time I moved. I had to keep up my spirits for Tripp, but I felt like crying. I wanted to get out of there.

"Cherry? How did you know I was in here? What did Bean say?"

"Baby and I needed to talk to you, and we came up here looking for you. Bean said y'all took some acid and you ran off down here and got stuck. Is that right?"

"Not exactly. Bean brought me out here late last night to get a couple bags of weed. He wanted to drop some acid, so we sat in that rock room of his with the skull and tripped out for a while."

"Oh, Tripp. I wish you wouldn't take that LSD."

"I may have cured myself of it. But I do wish I had some pot right now. My leg is starting to really hurt."

"I can't go back up there and get any. I don't know the way. I'd never find you again. Just keep talking to me, and try not to think about it. So did you freak out and come all the way down here by yourself, or what?"

"No. Even stoned, I wouldn't be that crazy. Bean said he wanted to show me the cave, and fool that I was, I agreed. We were both still pretty far gone, but all the same, it was an incredible place, with all the formations and the bronze waterfall. I can't tell you what it was like on acid. It was fairyland."

He stopped and groaned. I could tell how hard it was for him to talk.

"Do you think I might be able to crawl down and help you get out?"

"I don't think so. We'll have to chip some of this rock away. I just have to think about something else, and hope he comes back soon."

He groaned again but continued talking.

"I was really enjoying the tour until we got to the room with the fish pond. Then all of a sudden, Bean started to flip out and began talking to somebody who wasn't there, like he was angry. He was cussing at them. Then I looked at the rocks where he was standing, and it looked like they were coated in something dark that might have been blood. I have to say, it freaked me out, and I took my flashlight and started to go back out by myself. I didn't know where I was going, though, and went the wrong way. Then I slipped and dropped my flashlight, which made me stumble and fall. I slammed into these rocks, hard, and my leg went right down between them. It's been more or less numb, but the feeling is starting to come back, and I'm pretty sure it's broken. I can't move it."

"Just rest a minute. You don't have to talk."

"No, I want to. You need to know this before Bean gets back."

"Well then, go on. Who was he talking to? Did he know you fell?"

"He heard me calling him and he came, but instead of trying to get me out, he started crying and telling me about this girl in Vietnam and her baby that he had killed down in some tunnel, and the more he rambled on, the crazier it got. He seemed to think the baby was his. And then I realized after a while, when he said it happened here in the cave over by the fish pond, that it wasn't a Vietnamese girl he was talking about. Cherry, I think it might have been Carlene."

"What are you saying, Tripp? Are you saying that Bean killed Carlene? That's crazy!"

"I know it is. But he took acid that night she and I were up here, and maybe he might have thought she was this Viet Cong girl, Nguyen, who had come back to get him. I think he must have brought Carlene here to the cave and killed her. It was all mixed up in his mind, but the details sounded so true I think it could have really happened."

"Wait a minute. Hold the phone. You were up here with Bean and Carlene the night she was murdered? I thought you never met her."

Waves of alarm were washing over me, but somehow I just kept concentrating on the rock wall in front of me and tried to make the ringing in my ears stop.

"No, I lied to you, and I'm sorry. I did meet her. Just once. She introduced me to Bean and then left us up here at his house and drove away, and I had no idea that he got back together with her later."

"It seems like you have been telling a lot of lies, Tripp. Please don't tell me any more."

"I had to lie about it. After I heard she had been killed, I couldn't tell anybody I was with her that night. I'm a stranger in town. I would be the first one anybody would suspect. But I swear on anything you want me to—she walked away from that house alive, and I never saw her again, and I didn't know anything about what happened later."

"That's the real reason why you came here to Sweet Valley, isn't it? To meet Carlene? You lied about that, so how do I know you aren't lying now? How do I know *you* didn't kill her for the pictures?"

"Because I didn't! She gave them to me!" He stopped. "How do you know about the pictures?"

"I know a lot of things, Tripp. I even know about Faye."

"Cherry, please. Tell me what's going on. If you ever in your life had any love for me, please believe that I didn't have anything to do with Carlene's death, and tell me what is going on."

I was so confused. I wanted to believe him, but then I didn't want to believe it was Bean who killed her, either. Bean was the only way I was going to get out of this cave.

"It seems like your wife didn't have a phone number for you, and she called the sheriff's office to try to get hold of you and tell you that somebody from the army is looking for you. Ricky Don told me."

"I bet he enjoyed that."

"Not as much as you'd think. Anyhow, I went over to your place early this morning to talk to you, and when you weren't there, I did some snooping around. I'm sorry, but I felt like I had to. I found the pictures in *Catch-22* and read Carlene's letter. You should think of better hiding places."

"I guess I better."

"Do you want to tell me the truth about it now?"

"I will. I'll tell you all of it if you can get to my pocket and pull out the box of roaches I have in there. I really need it. Please. I don't think I can stand this pain."

I was a little afraid to get that close to him, but he was hurting bad, and what could he really do to me, pinned down like that? I didn't know what was real—or who to trust, or who was a murderer—but I couldn't let him suffer like that, so I went for it. Somehow, I squirmed around and got the tin box and a pack of matches out of his pocket. I lit the marijuana butt for him and passed it down. He took a couple of deep tokes, then started to talk again.

He got wound up and told me everything—about how he met Carlene, then how Bean had picked him up the next afternoon and took him to the pickle plant, where they heard about the murder. It really shook Bean up, and the two of them went back to his apartment, had a few beers, and talked about what a great girl Carlene was. They speculated, but couldn't come up with anybody who might want to kill her. Then they had a few more beers and said they would never forgive themselves for not going home with her when she left, to make sure she was all right. They decided they should just keep between themselves the fact that they had been with her that night, so nobody would misunderstand.

Tripp took a few more tokes, and started telling me about My Lai and Jerry and the punji trap and Faye. I tried not to breathe the smoke in. I wanted to have a clear head to hear it all.

I really didn't need to know all the details that he went into, but he needed to tell them, I guess. I made myself sit there with my mouth shut, and tried to fight the feeling that I wanted to run out of that dark underground place into the sunlight. Tripp talked until he was hoarse, and I believed him. If he wasn't telling the truth, he should go to Hollywood and get an Oscar.

When he was through, neither of us said anything for a while.

There is no silence anyplace else like there is down in a cave. All I could hear was the drip of water echoing somewhere off in the dark. Finally, I stirred myself to speak.

"Well, I see. I guess the only thing you didn't tell me was where I fit into all this. And what you're going to do now."

"I'm in love with you, Cherry. What I said is true—I never met anybody like you. I don't want to lose you." He reached his hand up as far as he could. I scooted down a little more. His hand was ice-cold. I tried to warm it up by rubbing it.

"I never met anybody like you either, Tripp. I don't think there is anybody else like you."

Or at least anybody I had ever run across who could give me the feelings he did. Wasn't that love?

"I don't need to wait six months. I've made up my mind to get a divorce from Faye—just as soon as she gets her citizenship."

"How long will that take?"

"I don't know. I'll work to get it as fast as I can."

"Are you sure you want to break up a marriage that hasn't hardly started? You must have thought you loved her when you married her."

I couldn't believe I was trying to convince him to stay with his wife. What was the matter with me? I guess I just needed for him to be sure.

"I hadn't met you when I married her, or I wouldn't have done it. Sometimes that happens. You just marry the wrong one, and the sooner you find out and end it, the better it is for everyone."

"What if you meet somebody you like better than me? You'd leave me, too."

"No. This is different with you. I know it is. This is for keeps."

I didn't know what to say. If he divorced Faye, would he expect me to marry him? I hadn't even done my practice teaching yet. It was all well and good to think about getting married one day, in the future, but when it actually came down to it, I wasn't so sure.

Especially in light of what happened last night with Ricky Don. I started to tell him about that—because to tell the truth, being in the dark of that cave and not being able to look each other in the eye had sort of taken down whatever defenses we might have had with each other, and made us tell things that we normally wouldn't have—but something stopped me and I held back. It is always better to keep a little mystery in the relationship.

"Cherry? Am I in this all by myself? Did I read you wrong?"

"No. I love you too, Tripp. I really do. I just don't know if I'm ready to get married or not."

"We don't have to get married right away. But you do want to be with me, don't you?"

"Of course I do." But for the first time since I met him, the words sounded like a lie to my own ears. If I loved Tripp like I was supposed to, then why did I do what I did with Ricky Don? I sure didn't love or even want to be with Ricky Don at all. The last thing in the world I wanted was to stay in Sweet Valley my whole life and be married to the deputy sheriff. I'd have to join the Jaycettes and organize the craft fair. Right now, I didn't know what I wanted except to get out of this cave. All these plans might be for nothing if we couldn't get out.

I tried not to think of the Indian with the wax wig, but I couldn't help it. It had been a really long time since Bean had left and there was no sign of him. I didn't want to think that he had left us down there to die. And I was worried about Baby. If he had done something to Baby, that would be all she wrote, for all of us.

I tried to pray to God to get us out of there, but it felt like the prayer didn't rise above the ground. It was trapped, like us, down in this cave.

—

The flashlight started to get dim. I watched it flicker, then go out.

"Tripp? Oh my God. The light went out. What are we going to do?"

You have never in your life been in dark like there is in a cave. You don't know if your eyes are open or shut. It's the kind of dark that could suck the sanity out of you if you were in it long enough. In a flash, it gave me a whole new respect for blind people, and a taste of what it might have been like for Bean in the tunnels in Vietnam. It was a miracle that Tripp hadn't gone crazy this morning before we got to him.

There were only three matches left in the pack in the tin box, and we needed to save those for the roaches in case Tripp's pain got worse. The only thing we could do was hold tight to each other's hand, and wait in the dark for whatever was going to happen next.

64. Carlene

 When Bean came to himself, he was slumped on the cold stone floor of the cave next to a kerosene lamp—not in the tunnels in Vietnam, but his own cave on Nehi Mountain. He was sticky with blood. His head still hurt, and he couldn't figure out where all the blood had come from. He checked himself to see if he was cut, but there didn't seem to be any wound. He got to his feet and looked around. He was in the room with the pool and the blind fish. Lying not far from him was the body of a girl.

Now he remembered. Nguyen had come after him with a gun and he had killed her. But that didn't make any sense. Nguyen was dead in Vietnam. He walked over and looked down. It was Carlene, white and still. Bean's heart skipped a beat. It must have been Carlene he had killed. Nobody else could have done it and dragged her here. Adrenaline shot through his body and he started to shake. He got sick and gagged on his own vomit. He had to stay calm and think what to do. Her clothes were ripped half off, there was his gun lying beside her, and she was covered in blood. There was so much blood. He had to get it off himself. He couldn't stand the feeling of so much sticky blood. That was the part he never liked about killing people.

But first he had to do something with Nguyen. No, not Nguyen. Carlene. His head was still playing tricks. He squeezed his eyes tight shut and tried to focus his brain. He couldn't leave her down here in his cave. It was his place. His and the Indian's. They couldn't have someone else buried down here, someone who would stink up their cave like the Viet Cong used to stink up their tunnels, so that every breath was a torture of swallowing down violent nausea. He would have to take her home. If he took her home, maybe they could fix her.

He went up to his room, found an old tarp, and pulled a white sheet off the bed on the rock ledge. He wrapped Carlene, winding her like a mummy, first with the sheet, then with the tarp, to keep the blood off of him. He took off his own clothes, went down to the clear pool, and dove in, washing himself clean of the sticky blood. Then he got dressed in the extra clothes he kept in his room, and lifted the body. His knees nearly buckled. He was still woozy, and she was a sturdy girl, quite a bit bigger than him. It took all his strength, but he half carried, half dragged her through the passageways and then rested before hoisting her over his shoulder and carrying her through the woods to his truck.

—

She must have parked somewhere down the road that led to the Water Witch. That was where he had picked her up. He would put her in her truck, and whoever found her would have to deal with it. He hadn't meant to kill Carlene. He liked Carlene. He had meant to kill Nguyen, that lying, murderous VC, and somehow Carlene got in the way. It was just like Nguyen to throw him off the trail and make him kill someone else. If she could kill her own infant, she could kill anyone. Not her infant. His infant. His little girl. Killed by the Viet Cong. One chamber of his heart was ripped out that day. He was living with only three quarters of a heart. You could tell by the way it skipped every fourth beat. He wasn't stupid. He could do the math. His brain was still a little weird, though, and for a minute he wondered how Nguyen had managed to escape again and find him here in Arkansas. She was a slippery one. He would think about it later.

Bean couldn't find the truck. The road was dark, and a fog was rolling in over the lake. He had to put her someplace where she would be found by the Americans. It wasn't right to put her out by herself in the jungle. The Viet Cong might find her, and they would cut off her ears and mail them to her mother. Or cut off her arm and nail it to a tree. He had to find a safe place for her. He would take her to the restaurant where she worked. They would take care of her in the morning.

He parked and staggered up the road toward the restaurant, carrying the bundle in his arms. Then he looked out and saw the houseboat down by the dock. Didn't Carlene tell him her boyfriend lived on a houseboat out by the restaurant? Maybe he should take her there. Her boyfriend would take care of her. He wouldn't let the VC cut her.

Bean carried her down and laid her on the deck of the dark houseboat. His head felt better, but he was still confused. Was he in Vietnam or Arkansas? What river was this? He wished he could remember.

Driving down Route 66, he got a strong whiff of pickles and realized he was passing by the plant. He must be in Arkansas. Baby was in there working. He needed to see Baby and make sure she was all right; make sure Nguyen hadn't taken her and cut off her ears.

He pulled into the parking lot and walked out behind the plant. Better not to go in the front door and answer any questions. You never could tell who was working for the Viet Cong. Anything you said would be passed on to the enemy. He would just sneak in the back and take a quick look to make sure Baby was all right.

He stole up behind the big wooden vats out in the yard, hugging the shadows, and looked toward the clamor and the bustle and the yellow bug lights on the dock. There was a long conveyer belt set up under the shed, and there was Baby. She was sitting beside Cherry in a line of women who were picking out things and throwing them into cans. They were all laughing. He crouched in the shadow of the vat and watched her. She was so pretty. So smart. He loved her so much. She would never betray him like Nguyen had done. And he would never let anyone hurt her, as long as he lived.

Satisfied, he got into his truck, drove to his apartment and went to bed.

65. *Carlene*

 Frank couldn't sleep. He had been in bed for more than an hour, tossing and turning. He was disturbed by what Carlene had said about the Oriental girl. If she was really fourteen, it could be real trouble. Worse, it was a really stupid mistake to have said anything about Judge Greer seeing her pictures, or to have told her that he sold them. He had lost his head when she threatened to go to the police. Now there was no telling what she might do. Probably, he tried to convince himself, she would do nothing. Tomorrow, he would pack her pictures up and give them to her, and she would keep her mouth shut. She would be too embarrassed, and he knew she wouldn't want her mother to see them. She was a decent girl, and he liked her a lot, but she never should have been so jealous; she never should have spied on him. He wasn't going to settle down and marry some little waitress with an illegitimate kid. He thought she knew that.

She looked great in the pictures, though. He certainly went through enough to get her to do them. Most of the girls he had were eager to pose, but Carlene had been a tough one. That was part of her attraction. He liked a challenge. She was like a game. He knew she never would have done it if he had asked her head-on; he'd had to wine and dine her and pretend to be in love with her, but the results were worth it. And it wasn't all pretending. He always had a good time with her, and her pictures were some of his best-sellers. She had a real quality—earthy and sexy and wise and innocent all at the same time. It reminded him a little of what Marilyn Monroe had. The film was good, too. The boys in Memphis would take the raw footage and cut it in with several others and make a film worth several thousand dollars. There were always girls who had stars in their eyes and wanted to be in films, even this kind, and plenty of men who paid good money to see them.

Too bad about the kid, Pilar. She was a natural. A wild one. She had told him she was eighteen, and he had no reason not to believe her. Her sister looked young, too, and she was twenty-one when he met her a year ago. He needed an Oriental girl. Since the war had started, there was a high demand for them.

He hated to give Pilar up, but Judge Greer was only one judge and another one wouldn't wink an eye. If Carlene pursued this, she might be able to really do him some damage. He would have to find a way to keep her quiet. He would call her in the morning and offer the pictures. Maybe he would take her on another trip. He could handle Carlene.

He heard a noise, like something falling with a thud, on the deck. It might be a dog, but Frank didn't think so. Someone was out there. He pushed back the covers and crossed to the window. Although the moon was bright, it was beginning to get foggy, and the light was fading in and out. He crouched low and crept from one window to another, peering into the dark, but saw nothing. Cautiously, he opened the door, stepped outside, and stumbled over a bundle lying on the deck. It was soft but solid, like a person. He pulled back the tarp and gasped. Feeling weak, he leaned against the railing. Carlene's long red hair trailed out of the wrapping.

He looked up toward the restaurant, but there was no one around. A motor started somewhere in the distance, and soon it grew fainter. Whoever had left her was gone. This had to be some kind of message. Obviously, someone wanted to frame him for murder. Carlene had been with him only a few hours ago. He cringed at the thought that he had worried over what to do about her. Could someone have been listening outside the window during their fight?

He paced around the boat, but there were no lights anywhere, no fisherman within sight of the marina. If he called the police, they would never believe his story. Besides, he couldn't afford to have the cops poking around in his business. They would search his boat and find the pictures and the films. Not to mention his marijuana. There was no way to dispose of everything so quickly. His only choice was to get rid of the body, and soon.

The body. A living person becomes a body when she dies, a thing. He squatted beside the bundle and pulled back the tarp. This was a woman who had cared for him. She had been warm and funny and spunky, and he had hurt her horribly. He felt a pang, as if this were his doing. The sheet was soaked in blood. Carlene's face was so white in the moonlight. He brushed a lock of hair off her eye. Oh, Carlene, you should have been at home with your son. For the first time, maybe, in his life, he felt remorse. But that didn't solve his problem.

———

Frank wrestled the bundle into the bottom of the dinghy and pushed away from the pier. The fog had gotten thicker, and while that was good news in case anyone might be out fishing this late at night, as people tended to do around here in July, it didn't help him see where he was going. Frank had never been much of a fisherman. He just liked the gypsy quality of living on a houseboat; he could pull up and move on when a place got too familiar. But he didn't want to leave Sweet Valley if he didn't have to. This town had been good to him. He liked Jackie Lim, who let him do his business without asking too many questions, and he had made a lot of contacts here, like the judge. And with DuVall University, there were a lot of willing girls who always needed cash and helped him earn the bulk of his money. He should have never gotten so involved with Carlene. He would have to watch that in the future. If he got out of this in one piece.

Now, though, he had to concentrate on the task at hand. He kept rowing.

——

Frank had gone far enough, he figured. The water was deep here and the body would sink, even though he couldn't find anything to weigh it down except a few rocks. No one would find it for days, if ever. There was nothing to connect him to the murder. The tarp had protected his deck and his boat from the blood. He would have to keep his ears open, though. At least one person knew who he was if the body had been left at his place. He would have to be careful.

He wrestled the body up, and as it hung over the edge of the boat, it moved. Carlene wasn't dead. He cursed as she let out a moan. Too late to do anything about it now. He pushed her on over the side, and she floated for a moment, then started to sink. He just hoped nobody was out there to hear. She probably wouldn't have lived long anyhow, with all the blood she had lost, so it wasn't like he was killing her. Even if he had taken her the minute he found her, she would more than likely have died before he could get her to the hospital.

Better to let her go this way. Cleaner. Get it over and stop her suffering. If he had tried to save her, there would be all kinds of questions he couldn't answer.

He stared into the inky water. He could just about make out a dark form, drifting downward. It was out of his hands now. He paddled away as fast as he could.

Maybe he wouldn't have to give up Pilar after all.

Funny thing about fog—it makes your eyes play tricks. He looked up and saw what seemed like a silver figure floating above his head. It almost looked like Pilar. He shivered. Probably a reflection of the moon. Probably nerves. He threw his back into it and rowed toward the marina.

——

Carlene came to as she hit the cold water. She didn't know where she was or how she had gotten there, but the shock of hitting the water jolted her, and she opened her eyes. There was a white sheet wrapped around her face, and she clawed it aside in a panic, coughing against the water that surged into her lungs. For a moment, she struggled to understand where she was. It was so dark. She couldn't remember anything.

Then she felt a warmth on her face and looked up to see a bright light shining through the green water. A figure swam toward her, silhouetted. At first Carlene thought it might be the Aswang, but for some reason she was not afraid. In fact, she had never felt calmer. Waves of happiness washed over her with every motion of the water, as if she had been waiting all her life for this moment. It was pure joy. As the figure came nearer, she could see its face, shining and golden.

"Jerry! What are you doing here? I thought you were dead." He laughed, the biggest, most glorious happy laugh. It made her want to laugh, too.

"Come on, Carlene! You won't believe the place we're going. It will blow your mind, baby. It will totally blow your mind."

"Can we live there together always? Can Kevin come too?"

"We can live there together always. And Kevin can come too, just as soon as he is ready."

The sheet fell away and drifted down into the cold green depths as he took her by the hand. They began to swim together toward the surface of the lake, toward the bright shining light.

66. Baby

Baby sat on a rock beside the cave entrance. She had checked out the plants, explored around the crevice, and paced back and forth for what seemed like hours. She had even tried to climb the rocks, like they were going to do with the Girl Scouts, and got several feet off the ground before she got scared she would fall and jumped down.

She looked up at the sky. They had gotten here before seven, and the sun was high overhead now, burning hot on her shoulders. She wished she wore a watch, but they always bothered her on her wrists. She would have to get one on a chain she could wear around her neck.

Bean should have come back a long time ago. He said he was going to take Cherry down to where Tripp was, then come right back up and go get some tools. Something must be wrong. He knew the caves too well to get lost. Cherry had been so afraid of going down in the cave. Baby felt guilty for staying behind. But it wasn't her fault. Bean had said she should. Still, that was just an excuse. She was too scared to go down, but she had thrown her best friend in the world to the wolves. Baby didn't know what she would do if something happened to Cherry.

Baby grew more and more frightened. She couldn't sit there one more minute. Now she was sure something had gone wrong. She would go back to Bean's house. Maybe he had come out some other way. Maybe they were all at his house now, waiting for Baby to come back. If they were, she would be so mad at them for scaring her like that! But she knew that wasn't what had happened. They were all still in the cave. And she was the only one who knew they were down there, the only one who could save them.

She set off in what she thought was the right direction. At least it was a different direction from the one where she and Cherry had come from. She would go to Bean's house and call Ricky Don. She didn't care if he saw the marijuana plants or not. Ricky Don would know what to do to get them all out.

Baby almost changed her mind about guardian angels, because she hadn't gone far before she stumbled onto a trail and, in a short time, emerged from the woods. She was scratched up and bitten by bugs, but she hardly noticed as she ran across the road and leaped up the rickety old wooden steps two at a time. Bean's mother was in the kitchen rinsing dishes in the wash pan when Baby burst in.

"Lordy mercy, Baby, you scared me half to death. What's got after you?"

"Have you seen Bean or Tripp or Cherry, Mrs. Boggs?"

"No, I sure haven't. Ain't they with you? Is anything the matter?"

"I don't know. I think they're down in the cave, and they should have been back out by now. I'm going to call and get somebody to come help."

"They're probably all right. Bean has crawled around in them old caves for years. I wouldn't worry if I was you."

"I hope you're right, but I can't help it. I need to use your phone."

Ricky Don was not at the office, but the girl promised she would get him on the radio and tell him to come up to Bean's as soon as he could. All Baby could do was fidget and wait.

67. Baby

 Dioniso sat in his store until long after the lights were out and the house was quiet. Perhaps Pilar was going to stay in her room tonight, he thought, looking at her dark window. His mind went back to July, three months ago, and the night Auwling had come home, breathless, to tell him she had seen a girl being thrown into the lake. The image wouldn't leave him, except in his mind it wasn't the murdered girl he saw; it was his daughter. There was danger in that lake, and Pilar was so young and heedless; she flirted with danger, as the moth flirts with the flame. But short of chaining her to the bed, there was no way to control her. He should have been harder on her long ago. Now it was he who would have to somehow right his wrongs.

Still no movement from her room. He would wait another half hour, then go to bed. He would be out early, before Pilar got up for school, so he could avoid talking to her in the morning. But he couldn't avoid her forever.

Twenty-five minutes passed, and just as Dionisio prepared to leave the store, the back door opened and his beautiful daughter emerged and got on one of the little motorcycles that Denny and J.C. had parked out back. She pushed it, making no sound, until she was a distance from the house, and then stood up on the starter and roared toward the bend in the road that led around the lake.

Dionisio got into his car, leaving off the lights, and followed as Pilar turned down the road that led to the Water Witch. Dionisio knew it well. Park bought all his fish from the store, and the two men had become friends, as two foreigners will.

Dionisio left his car and followed on foot. He kept to the trees lining the road, melting into the shadows, as he had done on so many nights long ago in the Philippines.

Down by the marina, he saw the little Honda parked beside a house-boat. The lights were on, and music floated over the water. Dionisio crept down to the dock and boarded the boat, making no sound. He looked in the window, through the crack below the shade.

What he saw forced him to exert all of his self-control, because there in the bedroom was his precious daughter Pilar, stripping off her clothes and dancing for a man with gray hair, who was standing behind a movie camera filming her.

His soul screamed, but he did not utter a sound. His body was cold. He withdrew, making no noise, and crouched in the shadow of the dock, never taking his eyes off the door. Time passed slowly, but Dionisio was used to waiting.

—

The door opened finally, and Pilar got on the Honda, passing no more than three feet from the place where her father waited, hidden. On one of her hands, the sparkle of a diamond ring, shaped like a leaf, caught his eye.

As she rode up the ramp and out of sight, the man with the gray hair opened his door and stood on the deck, looking out over the lake. He took out a cigarette, put it into his mouth, and flicked a lighter.

Before he had even inhaled the first puff, he felt rather than heard a presence. He turned in surprise to see an upraised machete glint in the moonlight. Before a scream had time to form in his throat, his head hit the deck.

68. *Cherry*

 Tripp smoked all the roaches down to nothing and ate the last ash. Then, to distract him from the pain, he and I told each other every story we could think of, going back to grade school and all the kids we knew who had shoved beans up their noses and peed on themselves and thrown up vegetable soup in class. We admitted that we had both, at one time or another, peed on our ownselves, and then we confessed to every single naughty thing we had ever done, from stealing a comic book to inching somebody's chair out from under them while they stood in class to read so they sat on the floor. He had done a lot more naughty things than I had, but then he was a Catholic. Then we told all the jokes we could think of, clean and dirty, and finally we tried to sleep. I thought about trying to feel my way back out to the entrance of the cave, but I knew that was insane. I kept thinking about what had happened to the old Indian, and he, I'm pretty sure, was better at directions than I was.

Surely to goodness Bean wouldn't just leave us down here. But if he had killed Carlene, he was capable of anything. He hadn't seemed mad at Tripp or anything, though. He had called him buddy. But that could have just been to lull us into thinking he was really coming back so we wouldn't try to follow him. I was heartsick thinking that Bean had killed Carlene. A lot of bad things probably happened to him over in Vietnam, and he must have started to lose his mind. That must be why he had gotten so bad with Baby. The drugs probably finished the job. That's all it could have been.

But surely, even crazy, he wouldn't do anything like that to us or to Baby. He was madly in love with Baby. As soon I thought it, that fact made me worry about her all the more.

Baby was outside. What if Bean had kidnapped her and taken off across the country? She wouldn't be able to get to a phone and let anybody know where we were. Nobody would ever think to look for us down here—hardly anybody even knew these caves existed.

I prayed then like I had never prayed in my life. I promised God that if He would get us out of this fix, I would stop every sinful thing I was doing and go to church every Sunday, Sunday night, and Wednesday night, and volunteer to teach at Vacation Bible School. I hoped He bought it, but I was afraid that God was wise to people who only prayed to Him when they were in bad trouble and wouldn't believe I would follow through on my promises. But I meant it. I really did. I prayed hard enough for it to get up to the surface and all the way to heaven.

—

"Tripp? Are you okay?" He hadn't said anything in a long time. Maybe he was asleep. I may have dozed off myself, and I was in a cramp, but I was afraid if I let go of Tripp's hand I would never find it again, so I shifted as best I could and kept hanging on. "Tripp?" I shook his hand. He stirred. Thank goodness he was still alive.

"Okay, Cherry . . . I'm okay. My leg hurts . . . I'm . . . just tired."

His voice had gotten so weak. I tried to squeeze his hand to let him know it would be all right, but it was hard for me to flex my fingers. I had to move, though, or my arm was going to fall asleep. It was starting to hurt. If I could back out of this passage into the big room, I would be able to stand up and stretch. I wouldn't go far. I would stay close enough to reach out and feel the entrance.

It was harder to back out than it had been to get in. I could just about get up on my knees, but they were so skinned that it killed me to put much pressure on them. I tried to push myself up on the tips of my toes and my elbows and scoot out backward, which took forever, because I kept collapsing. I never could do one single push-up in gym, and I wished now I'd worked harder at it.

It's weird, but somehow the dark made it seem less claustrophobic, and while I can't say I was getting used to it, I wasn't as panicky as before. If I could get into the bigger room, I could yell. Maybe there were people looking for us right now.

I managed to get out and stand up. The air was a lot better outside the passage. I tried to remember what the room looked like. I know there were two big stalagmites right beside the entrance. But I was afraid to move more than a step or two.

I heard what sounded like a whirring sound. Oh Lord. It was the bats. They seemed like they were gearing up to take off. How did they get out of here, anyhow? There must be a hole nearby. Maybe somebody would be passing by the place where they flew out and would hear me if I yelled.

"HELP! CAN ANYBODY HEAR ME? HELP! WE'RE DOWN HERE!"

I yelled until my throat was raw, then I sat down inside the beginning of the passage. It must be nearly night if the bats were leaving. I felt the air move as they flapped their wings, making a sound like dead leaves rustling. I was afraid they would bump into me and get tangled in my hair, so I tucked myself into as small a ball as I could and huddled in the entrance to the passage where Tripp was. And for the first time all day, I cried.

69. Baby

 "Forgive me, Park, for awakening you at this hour, but I must tell you something of great import."

"Dionisio, come in." Park rubbed his eyes, then held the screen door open. "What has happened? You look awful."

"I am afraid there is a dead man down by your restaurant."

—

Dionisio sat in the kitchen of Park's little house on the banks of the lake, and while Park made coffee, told him the story of Pilar and Frank and the film. It was difficult for Dionisio to talk, because he had always kept his own counsel, but this was one secret he couldn't carry alone.

Park clenched his teeth, and his hands shook with rage. "If you hadn't done it, Dionisio, I would have. I knew that O'Reilly was trouble, from the way he used the waitresses, but I never thought he would prey on children. Where is this film?"

"In my car. I will burn it tonight. Should I call the sheriff? What should I do? Help me, Park."

"No. We cannot call the sheriff. He is not to be trusted, and would never understand. Come. I will go with you to the Water Witch. We will take care of this ourselves."

—

The body lay where it had fallen. The head had rolled against the wall, leaving a slick trail of blood. The weathered boards of the deck were stained with a thick splash of red, already coagulated to jelly.

"Dionisio, my friend, go home. You have done your part, and now I will do mine. Go. Burn the film, and we will never speak of this evening again. You will have enough to do dealing with your daughter. You are blessed, Dionisio, with four beautiful daughters. I would have done the same if they were mine. Now, go."

Dionisio did as his friend suggested, and Park stood for a moment in thought, then went inside the houseboat. He looked across to the cliffs of

Nehi Mountain, then peered at the other boats in the marina, deserted and shuttered against the chill October nights. There was no movement, and no sound, anywhere.

It would be impossible to drag the body into the houseboat without smearing a lot of blood, but it wouldn't matter. Park picked up the feet, shod in the soft leather loafers with little tassels, and struggled until he got the body inside, on the floor of the small kitchen. Then he went back, picked the head up by its hair, and carefully arranged it in its proper position on the neck.

Stepping around the body, he opened the cabinet doors until he found what he was looking for.

"Wesson oil or bacon fat? I think bacon fat, don't you, Frank? You did like bacon, didn't you?" Underneath a counter were several large coffee cans full of the bacon drippings, soupy and pale brown, pungent and rich. Park took the first one and poured it over the head and body of Frank O'Reilly, until it oozed onto the floor. Then he dribbled a trail into the living room and out onto the deck of the boat. He poured the remainder on boxes of pictures and spools of film he found in closets and drawers, then brought the cans back and laid one on the floor beside the body. He stacked the others neatly under the cabinet.

Reaching into the container of matches that hung beside the stove, he took one and struck it, then watched the fat become transparent as it melted. Soon, flames began to spread across the body.

—

Park stood for a moment in the driveway of the Water Witch looking at the familiar green-and-white awning. It was like a beautiful woman who hid a cancer inside. He loved the restaurant, as he loved his brother, but neither Jackie nor the Water Witch would ever change. They would always be rotten under the skin.

He walked back to his little house on the banks of the lake, washed the coffeepot and cups, and went to bed.

70. *Cherry*

 I don't know how much time went by after the bats all left, but I went back into the big room and passed it by yelling awhile and then sitting awhile, doing toe touches and jumping jacks to keep the blood flowing, and then yelling some more.

I had crawled back into the passage entrance, trying to talk to Tripp, who was drifting in and out of consciousness, when I heard somebody calling my name. I forgot where I was and jumped right straight up, whacking my head on a rock. I know now what they mean when they talk about seeing stars. It was the first light I had seen in hours. Or maybe there was a real light flickering off in the distance. I started yelling.

"Here! We're down here!" I kept it up until I saw for sure that it was a light, and then I was hugging Baby and hugging Ricky Don and hugging another girl I had never seen before. She was Oriental, and for a minute I thought she must be some relation to Baby.

"Who are you?" I said after I had practically broken her ribs hugging her so hard.

"Faye Barlow. Tripp's wife. Where is Tripp?"

I have never been so speechless in my whole life.

"Down there." I pointed.

She took her flashlight and didn't even hesitate; she crawled right down to him. Ricky Don took off a pack and set up a lantern. It was almost as bright as sunlight to my eyes.

"How did you find us? Where's Bean?"

"I thought Bean was down here with you," Baby said. "He never came out after y'all left me up there. I finally went and called Ricky Don, and he came driving up here with Faye in the front seat beside him."

"How'd she wind up with you, Ricky Don?"

"She flew into Little Rock this morning, rented a car, and come into the office looking for Barlow. I took her over to his house, but he wasn't there, so I called up at Bean's, and his mama said Barlow was up here and so were you and Baby. We had done started up the mountain when the call from Baby came in on the radio."

Faye and Tripp were talking, but as hard as I strained, I couldn't hear what they were saying. His voice was faint, but at least he was conscious.

"It was a good thing she was with Ricky Don, Cherry. She used to play in the tunnels in Vietnam they dug during the war with the French when she was a kid, and wasn't at all scared of this cave. Ricky Don couldn't get through the crack, but Faye did, easy, and she found a bigger opening. We've been looking for you for the last hour. Finally, we heard you screaming."

"I'm grateful to her, then. But we need to get Tripp out of there. His leg is hurt bad."

—

It took a long time to get Tripp out. Ricky Don could just about get down to where he was trapped, and went to work chiseling a piece of rock off to get his leg out. He couldn't do it for long, though, in that cramped space, so we all took turns crawling down and hammering on the rock, even Baby. Funny how you get used to things. The second or third time she went in, it didn't bother her at all. Finally, the rock broke, and we got the leg free. When we tried to move him, Tripp passed out, and that was for the better. His leg was bloody, and it stuck out at an odd angle. Faye rigged up a splint and we wrapped him in one of Bean's old quilts and carried him out as gently as we could. In some places, we had to lay him on the ground and drag him. He kept waking up and moaning and taking on something awful until he finally passed out for good. I don't know who was more upset, Faye or me. It was weird. We didn't say anything to each other, but she didn't act like a woman who wasn't in love with him. There would be time enough later for us to talk, but we definitely needed to.

We put Tripp in the backseat of Ricky Don's cruiser, and Faye plopped herself down next to him and put his head on her lap. I had to get in the front with Ricky Don, and Baby followed us in my VW. Bean had still not come back when we got to the house. I hadn't said anything to them about Bean killing Carlene. There didn't seem to be a good moment. But then there probably wouldn't ever be a good moment to tell Baby. I couldn't imagine what she would say or do. I sure dreaded it. If he really had killed Carlene, he might be halfway to California by now, but I couldn't do anything about it. The important thing was to get Tripp to the hospital.

Ricky Don pulled out onto the road and got on the radio to let the hospital know we were coming. Then he flipped the red lights on, and we raced on down the mountain with the siren blasting. As we passed the red airplane lights, I glanced out across the valley and it looked like there was a big fire down there. I guessed we'd find out what it was later. For now, all I could worry about was Tripp.

71. *Cherry*

 We got Tripp into the emergency room, and all of us went out to the waiting room while they cleaned and X-rayed his leg. It turned out to be a compound fracture, which we knew already, and they prepped him for surgery.

Faye took right over, talking to the doctor in nurse language and filling out the papers, telling everyone she was the wife. I went and called Mama and Daddy and told them I was all right. They wanted to come out, but I said I would be home to tell them the whole story later. I can tell you, I wasn't looking forward to it any more than I was to telling Baby about Bean.

They finally let me in to see Tripp just before they took him to the operating room. He had already been given a shot, and was pretty groggy.

"Hey, Tripp. It's me, Cherry. You're going to be all right. You'll have to wear a cast for a little while, but you'll be good as new in no time. How do you feel?"

"Fine. Good stuff in that shot. Primo. This is peanuts compared to a punji trap." He smiled a goofy smile at me and reached for my hand. "You look so cute. I never even noticed you had a haircut. You look like a cute little fuzzy little wuzzy little lamb." He was beginning to slur.

"Little lamb? You're really out of it, aren't you?" The nurse stuck her head in and said I only had a couple more minutes before I'd have to leave.

"I'll go on now and let you get your operation, Tripp, but I'll be right outside. I won't leave you. We'll all be outside."

"Faye too?"

"Faye too."

"That's nice."

I got a little pain in my heart when he said that. He drifted off to sleep, and the nurse came in to take him to surgery.

—

Baby said they'd be down in the coffee shop, so I went to look for her and Ricky Don. They weren't there, but Faye was. She stood up, and I realized she came up to my armpit. It was the first time I had really taken a good look at her. She was about the same size as Baby, but more delicate—like a cat. Her eyes were wide set and slanted up at the corners like a cat's, too. She was wearing a midriff-baring top and the lowest pair of hip-hugger pants I ever saw. I don't know how she kept them up without her crack showing. I guess it was warmer in California than it was here. She had black shoulder-length hair and long fingernails, painted silver.

"Well. How are you doing, Faye?" I had no idea what to say to her. I wondered where Ricky Don and Baby were. They must have set this up, the rats.

"I'm fine. Would you like some coffee?" She spoke really good English, with a cute accent.

"Sure." I went to the machine, put my dime in, and pressed LIGHT. I suspected that the milk they put in wasn't real, but it was the only thing you could get here.

"You are beautiful," she said.

"So are you." She was. It was hard not to be jealous, even though Tripp said he was divorcing her. She had a thick gold band on her wedding-ring finger.

"Well, it has been some day. I want to thank you for what you did for Tripp and me. I am grateful you were there to help us."

"Of course I would help Tripp, and also you. He is my husband. Did you know that?"

"I know that. He's a friend of mine."

"You don't have to pretend, Cherry. I know he has been seeing you. He told me when I was with him a little while ago."

"Oh. What did he say?"

"He told me he was in love with you."

"Oh." So, even out of it on painkillers, he had told her he loved me. Maybe he really did. I kind of felt sorry for her.

"Are you in love with him?"

"Well, Faye . . . this is sort of awkward. I mean, I just met you and all. In fact, I only found out about you yesterday. If I had known all this time that Tripp was married, I would never . . ."

"I am going to fight for him. He thought he married Vietnam and I married America. That is why he ran away—he was running from Vietnam. But he was wrong. I am more than Vietnam. I am a woman. I understand him, and I love him."

"You're going to fight . . . what do you mean?"

"I am not going to pull your hair, if that is what you are afraid of. But I will not go away and leave him here for you, either."

"I think Tripp will have some say in that decision, don't you? But I guess he's worth fighting for, all right. You do what you think you have to do, and I will too. I have to go now."

This was awful. I thought she didn't love him, and there would be no problem with us being together. I thought she had just married him to get to the States. It was so much easier when I didn't have to look a flesh-and-blood wife but could just think of her as a problem to get past. After us going through what we had in the cave, I thought he had been completely truthful with me. Now I didn't know again.

———

I went back to the waiting room and found Baby and Ricky Don. They turned, as one, and looked at me.

"Thanks, guys, for warning me about Faye. I really appreciate it."

"We thought it would be better if you talked to her alone. Are you mad at us?"

"No. I don't know who to be mad at, you or her or Bean or Tripp or myself." I started to cry, just a little. The day had been kind of a strain, to say the least. Baby scooted over to make room for me on the couch, and I sat down next to her. She put her arm around me, pulled my head down on her shoulder and let me cry. Ricky Don went outside. I don't know what he thought, and I really didn't care.

"Cherry, what do you think happened to Bean? I'm not worried about him being lost, but it is really weird that he never came back. Do you think he's all right?"

I had to stop feeling sorry for myself when she was going through just as much as I was.

"Oh, Baby. I've been so worried about Tripp and all that I just couldn't say anything."

"Say about what? Do you know something about Bean?"

"Baby . . . don't go crazy on me here, but Tripp thinks Bean might have killed Carlene." I just blurted it out. There was no soft way to say it.

Her eyes bugged out, and her mouth tried to make a sound, but nothing came out.

"You know he hasn't exactly been his old self since he came home. You said it enough times. Right?"

"Right. But that doesn't mean . . . what did Tripp say?"

"The night it happened, Tripp gave Bean some LSD, and he thinks it kicked something loose in Bean's brain."

Baby wouldn't look me in the face. She started to shred a Kleenex, making a little pile on the arm of the chair.

"That still doesn't mean he would kill Carlene. He liked her."

"He didn't know it was Carlene. He thought she was some girl back in Vietnam, somebody he had already killed."

"Did he say her name?"

"He did, but I don't really remember it. Noy Ann, or something like that."

Baby listened, but she kept looking down at her lap. She started in on a second Kleenex. I got really uncomfortable.

"I didn't say I thought it was so, Baby, just that Tripp did."

"Well. I don't know. I do know he knew somebody named Nguyen." She kept looking at her lap, like she didn't want to meet my eyes.

"Baby—do you think it is possible?"

She carefully picked up all the pieces of the Kleenex and wadded them into a ball, then threw it toward the wastebasket. It missed.

"He's not the same guy he was, Cherry. Ever since Carlene was murdered, I have been more scared of him than I let on. Now that you told me what you did, I think it might possibly be true, but I didn't want to see it before. Little things he did and said are starting to add up, though."

"Do you think we ought to tell Ricky Don?"

"I think we have to."

We grabbed each other and held on. Now both of us were crying.

———

Ricky Don came in with some sandwiches for us and, finally, I had to tell him what Tripp had said.

He shook his head. "Let's don't jump to conclusions. The first thing we need to do is go back down in there and see if we can find some evidence. I'll have to get some of the state forensics guys. Then what we have to do is find Bean. No telling where he might be. Y'all be careful. If he gets in touch, don't let on that you know anything. See if you can get him to come here to the hospital."

"If he did do it, Ricky Don, it wasn't really Bean," Baby said. "It was something that the war made out of him. We think that the war is happening halfway around the world, but it's not. It's digging its claws into the boys and they are bringing it home with them."

"You're right about that, Baby. You sure are right about that. I got to go now. Y'all hang in. I'll let you know what happens."

72. *Cherry*

 Tripp had been in the operating room over an hour when Baby and I heard noise outside and looked out the window. In the street in front of the hospital, there must have been a thousand or more people walking by holding candles. They were all wearing black armbands. It was the moratorium. I had forgotten all about it. We had been planning it at the university for weeks, but it hadn't entered my head once all day. All over the country, people were marching tonight to protest the Vietnam War. Our art fraternity, Kappa Pi, had planned to march all together, with most of the other ones. It seemed like such a long time ago that I had sat next to Tripp in drawing class, planning on going to the march, and didn't have anything on my mind more serious than what I was going to wear. It almost seemed like that was some other girl.

Baby had been sitting there like a zombie, and nothing I said seemed to get her out of it. She needed to get some air. I took her by the hand and made her get up, and we went outside and stood on the sidewalk watching the marchers. I must have looked awful, with my ragged, dirty clothes and skinned-up knees, but I didn't even care. I would guess most of the kids from DuVall were out there, and a whole lot of teachers and just plain people, including a lot of older ones. Rainy Day and John Cool went by and waved, and so did Rocky and Denny and J.C. I saw my drawing teacher go by with Father Leo from St. Juniper's. He was wearing his long black priest robe and a black band around his forehead, carrying a blazing candelabra and smoking a cigar.

Queen Esther McVay saw us and waved, then came over with some armbands. We all put them on.

"Where you been, girl? I thought you two were going to march with Kappa Pi."

"We were going to, Queen, but something came up. My boyfriend got in an accident and they are operating on his leg right now."

"Oh, that's awful. I hope he's all right. I'll say a prayer for him. Here, let me get you a candle." She yelled to her boyfriend, "Marcus, bring over some of those candles."

Marcus was the handsomest black guy I ever saw in my life. He brought over a box of candles, and Baby and I each lit one and held them up as the crowd filed by. Queen Esther and Marcus stayed with us and she started to sing "We Shall Overcome" in her strong alto voice, and we sang with her. The crowd heard us and gradually joined in, and all ever-how-many hundreds of us sang the whole song, right there in front of the hospital. It made chills go up my spine. It was the most moving thing I ever was part of, us singing and all those candle flames flickering, like a thousand fireflies passing in the night.

I heard a sweet, small voice behind me. It was Faye, singing right along with us. She knew all the words. I handed her my candle, and the two of us stood side by side and sang until the last notes of the song died away. Then the marchers moved on and we all went back upstairs, Baby, me, and Faye, to wait for Tripp to get out of surgery. I wanted to be mad at Faye, but I couldn't. She had probably saved my life. That had to have been one of those "God's plan" moments, because there was no other way she would have turned up in Sweet Valley on the exact same morning that we had gotten trapped in a cave if God hadn't had a hand in it. I guess He heard me after all.

I remembered then that I hadn't even thanked God for saving me, after all that heavy praying and promises I had made Him. I guess I was no better than anybody else who makes promises when they are in trouble, but

He probably knew that before He answered my prayers. I thanked Him then and said a prayer for Tripp, and another one for Bean, wherever he was. He would need it.

73. *Bean*

 When Bean left Cherry with Tripp, he took a different route out of the cave. He couldn't believe that Cherry and Baby had picked this morning of all mornings to come up here. He had just come out of the cave and was on his way to get his truck and take off when he heard them calling. They would have to know that Barlow was with him if they had been to the house and seen his car. Barlow would probably never be able to get out of that hole, and while the idea of him starving down there wasn't pretty, there was always the chance he would free himself and find a way out. It would take him a good long time, though. Enough time for Bean to get some stuff together and make it to Mexico.

He didn't really remember what all he had told Barlow last night, but it was enough to scare him and send him running for the exit. He must have told him about killing the girl. Nguyen. Or maybe he told him it was Carlene. The two of them ran together in his head. Whoever it was, he was sure of one thing—he had killed somebody down by the pool in the flowstone room.

He couldn't see why Barlow had been so freaked about him killing the girl gook, though. Barlow had been in some heavy killing, himself, to hear him tell it. It shouldn't shock him. It was war. You had to kill people in war. That's what we are over here for. We have to make a high body count so we can win the war. Anyone would tell you that.

One minute they were having a good time looking at the wonders of his cave, then the next minute he turned around and there was Barlow, running off to tell on him for doing his job. That's not how a buddy acts. A buddy helps you, watches your back. Barlow wasn't his friend, so he must be working for the VC. They were the only ones who would be mad if he killed one of them. His commanding officers gave him medals for killing VC. He had a drawer full of them.

He would have had to stop Barlow from telling, but Barlow had done the job himself by falling into the hole. And it was just Cherry's bad luck that she happened into the tunnel when she did. They would be down there a good long time before they realized he wasn't coming back.

The worst of it was, he had to leave Baby. He would like to take her with him, but she would never go and leave Cherry. Sometimes he thought she liked Cherry more than she liked him. Baby would be all right without him. Even if she tried to get some help, it wouldn't be for hours. And who was there to help her, anyhow, who knew the caves? Baby would never go down in them. She was even afraid to go into his Indian room at the entrance. Once Cherry was out of the picture, he would send for Baby to come and join him in Mexico. She would love him more when Cherry was no longer around. He would just have to wait until then. But now, he had to figure out how to get out of this tunnel. Sometimes it was so hard to think.

He couldn't leave by an entrance near his patch, because Baby would see him. Instead, he would have to go in deeper and join up with a trail that led to a different entrance.

Bean stopped beside a fork in the rocks and tried to figure out which way to go. His flashlight was getting weak. It wasn't more than a mile or two underground to the waterfall, if he remembered right. He had plenty of batteries in his pack, and extra bulbs. He could change a bulb in pitch-dark with one hand in less than five seconds if he needed to.

There was an underground stream that came out in a little waterfall on the far side of Nehi Mountain. He would just climb down the mountain and go to the highway and hitch a ride with a trucker. Truckers didn't mind giving rides to kids. He would rather drive himself, but the Viet Cong might recognize him and come after him if he was in his truck. Or was it the cops? It didn't matter. The cops were probably working for the Viet Cong, too. You couldn't trust any of them. If he got lucky, he could be across the border in a couple of days, in a whole new country that didn't have anything to do with war. He would be safe. Soon, Baby would come and join him. It would be a good life in Mexico. Maybe they would get a little house on the beach somewhere and he would play the guitar and sing in a cantina at night. Baby looked kind of Mexican, and he could grow a mustache and look more like one. Before long, they could have a baby. It would be the same baby that Nguyen had killed, he knew. His baby girl, who had gone back to heaven to wait to be born to him again. It would be perfect.

All he had to do now was find his way out of the cave and get a ride with a trucker. Then he would be in business.

74. Cherry

 Tripp got out of the hospital a couple of weeks later. He had to stay in and get some heavy-duty antibiotics because of all the dirt and guano that had gotten into the wound. I had gone to see him every day, and Faye probably had too, although we never ran into each other. I made sure of that by checking in at the nurses' station before I went over. He hadn't said anything about Faye in all that time, and neither had I, but when I asked him if he wanted me to pick him up from the hospital and take him home he told me, a little apologetically, that Faye was coming to get him in Ramblin' Rose. So she had moved into his house and was driving his car. Okay. I guess she had to have someplace to stay. But we had to get this straightened out soon. So far, I had managed to not tell Mama and Daddy about Tripp being married, but sooner or later, somebody was going to spill the beans. Lucille knew about it, of course, and if the girls at the beauty school found out, it would be all over. I hoped to goodness Lucille would keep her mouth shut. I had no control over Faye, though, and she would probably go around saying she was Mrs. Tripp Barlow to anybody who would listen. I couldn't do anything about it, but I was a wreck. It was hard to concentrate in class.

Baby was as nervous as a cat, too. They still hadn't found Bean. If he had come out of the cave, he probably was long gone. If he hadn't, then . . . I didn't know. Baby said he was capable of living down there forever if he had to. The state sheriff's department had brought in some forensics guys and a team of cavers. They had found plenty of evidence— a lot of dried blood and an army revolver that had been thrown into the pool. The whole town, of course, was talking about it. It was on the news on TV, and Ricky Don was being treated like a hero, even though there was no suspect in custody. They had brought in cameras while Ricky Don and Melvyn Arbus burned up the marijuana plants, and that made the news, too. Sweet Valley was on the map in a big way. Thank goodness Ricky Don didn't tell them about Tripp and me being in the cave. I think the main reason was that he wanted all the glory for himself, but also he did us a favor, because I would not have liked to have my picture splashed across the TV in close connection to a murder and a drug bust, and he knew that. I guess he really does care about me, in his way.

Baby and I were really upset, too, about the fire I had seen from the top of the mountain. It turned out to be the Water Witch and the whole marina. Every single boat was burned to a crisp, and there was nothing left of that beautiful restaurant but a black hole in the ground and a naked brick chimney.

Nobody was in the restaurant at the time, thank goodness, but Frank O'Reilly had been killed on his boat. In fact, they think he was the one who started it all with a grease fire in his kitchen, and they thought the fire ran up the wooden walkway from the pier and set the restaurant on fire.

There was an investigation, and Judge Greer ruled it was an accident, so the insurance company will have to pay Jackie Lim. I don't know whether he is going to try to rebuild or not. Park has gone back to Hong Kong, and I don't know if he will come back or stay over there. A new Chinese restaurant without Park's cooking wouldn't be as good. And frankly, after what Baby had told me about the banquets and all, I would just as soon the place stay closed. I think Baby had mixed emotions, though. In spite of everything, I think she still has a secret soft spot for Jackie. She called him and told him how sorry she was, and she said he seemed glad to hear from her. I just hope to goodness she doesn't get started with him again. But that is the last thing on her mind right now, since they still haven't located Bean.

I felt a little bad about Frank, but not too much, considering how he had tried to get Lucille involved in porn and Lord knows what all else he had done. Now we would never know who the pictures were of that Lucille thought looked like Baby. They were probably burned up along with everything else. It was just as well. I never did figure out a way to get a look at them without him knowing.

I felt a little funny about it, since I knew Faye was probably there, but I dropped by Tripp's house to see him the day after he came home from the hospital. Sure enough, there she was in the kitchen, cooking something in a frying pan, wearing her little hip-huggers. It felt like the house had already been taken over by a woman. Her stuff was all over the place, and it was considerably less neat than it used to be. I wondered how Tripp felt about that. I bet she wouldn't wipe down the wall behind the stove with Lysol every time she cooked, like he did. There was a whole different vibe there now. I noticed the painting of me that Tripp had been working on was leaning with its face against the wall. I was really uncomfortable.

"Hi, Tripp. Hi, Faye. I just stopped by to see how you were doing and if there was anything I could get for you."

"Thanks, Cherry, but I'm fine. Faye is taking good care of me. She's a nurse."

"Yeah. I know. That's handy."

Boy, this was awkward. I could tell he would have liked to say more, the way he looked at me, but she was standing right there. Okay. I would just pretend that this was a friendly visit.

"That was lucky, her coming right when she did, wasn't it?" I continued. "We might still be down there."

My heart broke at the way she went over and sat down beside him on the bed we had spent so many nights together in, like it was her bed now. They hadn't asked me to sit, but I put my purse down and perched on the edge of the chair beside the bed. I wasn't going to just stand there like an idiot and then leave, like she probably thought I would. I had a right to be there, too, in a way.

"So have you been doing any painting, Tripp?" I looked over at the back side of my picture. I knew it would never be finished now. Faye smiled.

"Not really. Too much on my mind, I guess. Colonel Wilson is coming tomorrow, and I've decided to give him the pictures and tell the whole story. I'm ready to take my punishment, if it comes to it, and then try to get past it and get on with my life."

"That's good, Tripp. I think you will feel a lot better after you talk to him. You shouldn't have anything to worry about. Just tell the truth."

I wasn't so sure about that, but I was trying to look on the bright side. My private feeling was that probably the whole platoon was going to get court-martialed and go to jail, although in a situation like that, it would be hard to pin down who did what.

"Then what are you going to do after you talk to him and get back on your feet? Have you figured it out?"

I was really asking what he was going to do about Faye. She leaned against him and tucked her legs up into one of her little cat poses.

"I don't know. Finish out the semester if I can. Maybe go back to California. I don't know."

It was plain that Faye was going to stay and finish out the semester, too. While she was sitting right there between us, I couldn't say anything like I wanted to say to him. I reached down to get my purse. I might as well wrap this up. There was no point in staying any longer now.

"Tripp, we are out of orange juice," Faye said suddenly, standing up. "I need to go to the store and get some. Do you mind?"

"No, Faye. I'll be all right. You go on." She put on her jacket and started for the door.

"Faye?" I called after her. She turned around. "Hey, thanks."

"I won't be gone long, Cherry." She raised one eyebrow.

———

We were alone, him in the bed with his leg propped up, me sitting in a chair beside him. He reached out and touched my knee. I had skinned it up pretty bad, crawling through the cave. Both my knees were still scabbed over.

"You better take care of those scrapes."

"I wash them in soap and water."

"You better put some alcohol on them. Here, I have some."

"No, it's all right. I never use it. Doc McGuire told me when he pierced my ears not to ever use alcohol on them, or on any cut for that matter. He said, 'Just wash your ears every morning with plain old soap and water, Cherry, and you'll never get an infection. That goes for every cut and scrape, too. Soap will kill the germs better than that stinging old alcohol, and it doesn't hurt half as bad.' I did it and I have never had an infection yet. See, the knees are scabbed over real nice."

I was nattering to cover over how nervous I felt. He took my hand, and all of a sudden tears started to run down my cheeks.

"It's over, isn't it, Tripp? I can tell. You're going to stay with Faye, aren't you?"

"Cherry—I just don't know. I still love you, but I don't know what to do about Faye. She seems set on staying here and taking care of me."

"She's a nurse. That's her job. And she is in love with you, whether you know it or not."

"Are you in love with me?"

"I thought I was."

"But now you're not sure?"

I remembered what Mama had said about marrying the first boy that showed you what a thrill was. Tripp had been the first one, and it sure was a thrill, to use an understatement. A little part of me would always love him, but I knew in my heart I wouldn't marry him, even if he divorced Faye tomorrow. I don't think I could fight her for him. He should have told me the truth about being married and everything. I think part of me just couldn't get over the idea that he would lie to me, like marriage was nothing. I don't think I could ever really trust him again. And I knew I would never be comfortable with somebody who liked drugs as much as he did. But it still hurt.

"Now I'm not sure." I wiped my eyes. He pulled me down and kissed me then, a sweet sad kiss, like maybe it would be the last one. Even his sad kisses were perfect. I had to get out of there. I was going to lose more respect for him and me both if I didn't.

"I'll run on now, Tripp, but we'll talk in a day or two." He took my hand and kissed the palm. It gave me that little electric shock.

"I don't think it's all over between us, do you?"

"I don't know, Tripp. Like Mama says, never say never."

I left before Faye got back from the store. Just out of curiosity, I looked on my way to the door, and there was a full carton of orange juice in the fridge.

75. *Cherry*

 The phone rang. I jumped like I had been shot, and groped on the bedside table for the receiver, knocking it off onto the floor. It took me a few minutes to untangle it and turn on the light. I looked at the clock. It was three-fifteen. It could only be bad news if somebody calls at that hour. The dead hour, Daddy called it. In this little town, as soon as anybody passed on, people ran to their phones and called everybody they knew to tell them, no matter what time it was.

"Hello?"

388 · Norris Church Mailer

"It's me, Cherry." Baby.

"What's the matter, Baby? Are you all right?"

"They've found Bean." She started to cry.

"Where? What happened? Baby? Talk to me. You're scaring me."

"He was down in Austin, trying to get to Mexico. A trucker from Arkansas gave him a ride and got suspicious because he had seen his picture on the news up here. He called the cops from a truck stop and they picked him up tonight. Ricky Don called me. They're bringing him back to Little Rock for trial. Oh, Cherry, I don't think I can go through a trial with the papers and TV and all."

"I'll be there with you, Baby. You won't be by yourself. Just be thankful they found him. I haven't spent one night without worrying he was going to try to do something to you. He would have left Tripp and me to die in the cave—you know that. He needed to be caught. Don't think he didn't, Baby."

"I don't think he meant to kill you. If he wanted to kill you, he would have. He just wanted time to get away. He's sick, Cherry. They can't lock him away forever in jail. He just lost his mind after what all happened in Vietnam. You can't just go from being a killer one day back to being a normal boy the next."

"Baby, listen to me. Guys come back from Vietnam every day and they aren't killers. Look at Ricky Don and Tripp. They were soldiers. There must have been something bad wrong with Bean for a long time—probably before he even went over there. I agree that he needs help, but they aren't just going to put him back out on the street. He needs to be locked up where he can't hurt himself or anybody else."

She was sobbing now.

"Do you want me to come over? Baby? Do you hear me?"

"Would you? The boys are out, and I'm all by myself."

"I'll be right over." I got up and started hunting in the closet for some clothes. Mama was awake, standing outside my door in her marabou slippers and baby-blue negligee.

"Cherry? What's the matter?"

"They found Bean, Mama. I'm going over to Baby's."

She came in and sat on my bed while I dressed.

"Well, it's come to a head now. Poor Baby. I feel like all of this mess with Bean started when that Tripp Barlow came to town. I wish he had never come here. And I wish to goodness I had never said what I did to you that day out in the yard, about sleeping with him and all. Maybe you wouldn't have got in so deep with him. I've worried and worried about that. I feel like somehow all this is my fault."

"Mama! That's crazy! You didn't do anything. I was going to do what I did with Tripp no matter what you said, and you better believe that. And what Bean did might have happened anyhow, even if he hadn't got hold of that LSD. You sure didn't have anything to do with that! What's the matter with you?"

"I don't know. I know it's silly, but I guess when you're a mother, you just feel like you can fix any problem your child has. When you were little, I could sew your torn dress or glue your broken doll or make you laugh when somebody said something mean to you. Then one day I realized you all had bigger problems than I ever dreamed of, and I wasn't able to fix anything at all."

"Yes, you can. I don't know what I would do without you, Mama. I know that you are always there for me, and you would back me up in any fight. Like the first time you took me to the movies, remember? When we saw Elvis? You would have beat Brother Wilkins black and blue if he had tried to make me go to the altar and repent, like he did Bernadine Taylor."

"You better believe I would! I still would. Somebody should have kicked that old goat in the rear end a long time ago."

I kneeled down, and she took me in her arms, like she used to do when I was little. We hugged for a long minute, then I had to go.

"I'll call you, Mama, when we find out anything. Pray for Bean. Pray for all of us."

"Don't worry. I will. Tell Baby to come and stay over here with us. She doesn't need to be out there by herself."

———

Manang and Tatang had taken Pilar and the little girls to the Philippines for a long visit with Manang's mother, Lula. I didn't know why they did it in the middle of the school year or what exactly was going on, but Baby said they clamped down hard on Pilar, who had gotten more and more cheeky and disobedient, and wanted to get her away for a while. Good luck to them. I'm sure there were things for her to get into in the Philippines, too, although probably not as much as here. The boys were going to have to run the store while they were gone, so we will see how that goes. If it is still standing when Tatang and them get back, I'll be surprised.

—

Baby and I sat up the rest of the night drinking coffee and talking about Bean and Tripp and everything that had happened and wondering if we would ever find anybody normal to fall in love with. Ricky Don stopped by at six to say that Bean was in custody and on his way to Little Rock. He said it took five of them to hold him down when they found him at the truck stop. He was ranting about the Viet Cong, clearly out of his mind.

"I hate it that it all had to happen, Baby," he said. "I know you loved Bean."

She looked hard at the bottom of her empty coffee cup, not meeting his eyes. "I guess I did used to love him. At least I loved the idea of him. It's hard to tell the difference, isn't it?" She smiled, and it came out a little lopsided. "But wasn't he just the sexiest thing in the world when he was up on the stage, singing, strutting back and forth, slinging that hair around? He had the power, didn't he? He was really good and decent then. I know he was. If it hadn't been for that old war . . ." Her face crinkled up, and she started to sob. "I don't know why men always have to go to war!"

I put my arm around her. Men had always gone to war, from day one, and probably always would, even after this one was over and done.

"Do you remember what you talked about last summer when we were out on the relish belt with the rat and all?" I said, to get her to stop crying.

She wiped her eyes. "That seems like a long time ago. What did I say?"

"You said how you thought the windchill was nature lying to us, making us think it was cooler than it really was, and then we all said men were like that, too, saying one thing when they really meant something else. Remember?"

"Yeah?"

"Well, I think that goes for this war as well. The government is blowing a chill wind over the country to try to make us believe we are fighting a good and honorable war to save Vietnam from Communism when it's really causing more evil than anything. It seems like men just have a born need to dominate and kill each other, and in spite of all the protesting and marching, we can't do anything to change human nature any more than we can stop the wind from blowing."

She nodded, blew her nose. "I know it. That's true. Some things you just have to try to accept and go on. I guess I always knew, too, down deep inside, that Bean was teetering on the edge, but I didn't want to see it." She patted my hand, got up, and poured another cup of coffee. "Don't worry about me. I'll be all right." She poured a second cup and handed it to Ricky Don, who was still standing, hat in hand, looking uncomfortable. "Come on and sit down and have a cup of coffee, Ricky Don. Don't pay any attention to us. Tell us a funny joke or two, and then Cherry and I have to take off for painting class. We still have to try to graduate."

Baby was going to be all right. I would see to it that she was, if it was the last thing I did.

76. *Cherry*

 It was November 24, and the whole family was over at our house ganged around the TV, watching Walter Cronkite. He talked to the audience for a little while, clearly upset, trying to prepare us for what we were about to see, and then up there, in living color, they splashed the My Lai pictures across the nation. Mama and the aunts got pale.

"Oh my Lord and stars. What has happened over there?" Mama put her hand over her heart, and I watched her out of the corner of my eye in case she fainted. Daddy and Uncle Jake got grim around the mouth.

Aunt Juanita looked thunderstruck. "Thank God in heaven that G. Dub is safe and out of that awful mess," she said. Uncle Ray, for the first time maybe, agreed with her. He had been pretty cold after G. Dub ran off, and hadn't written or called him. I hoped he would now.

Lucille stared in fascination. I'm sure she was trying to figure out how much duct tape and dowel rods it would have taken to get all those poor dead Vietnamese ready for viewing.

It was hard for me to sit there and keep my mouth shut, knowing what I did and all, but I didn't want anybody to know that Tripp—and Jerry, God rest his soul—had been a part of it. Maybe it would never come out.

It had been bad enough when they found out that Tripp was married. I don't want to go into the awfulness of *that* when I had to tell them.

Of course the pictures bothered me, but I had already seen photographs just like them. Maybe these were even some of the ones Tripp gave to Colonel Wilson. It was hard to tell.

Tripp had talked for the better part of an afternoon with the colonel, and said he was a good, decent guy. At one point, the two of them even broke down and cried. I didn't know what was going to happen to everyone in Charlie Company, but I felt like they should at least send Calley away for life, and probably some of the others. I hoped Tripp wouldn't have to do any jail time. Faye would be right there with him if he did, though; you could bet on that. She hadn't left his side for more than five minutes, except to get that orange juice, ever since she came to Sweet Valley.

And here's another little piece of news: She was pregnant. She called and told me herself, and it was funny, but my heart didn't even skip a beat. I had given up on Tripp already, and frankly, it was a relief to not have to be on that emotional roller coaster and have to lie all the time to Mama and Daddy. In fact, as strange as it seems, I was at the point where I kind of liked Faye, and we talked on the phone every once in a while. She had gotten a job at the hospital, and it seemed like she and Tripp would be staying here, at least for the time being. Maybe Baby and I would ask her to go out with us shopping or something. There was a neat place to buy maternity clothes that Lucille knew about. If it was a girl, maybe Lucille would give her some of Tiffany LaDawn's old dresses. She had enough to open the Tiffany LaDawn Hawkins Pink Ruffled Dress Museum.

A team of psychiatrists worked on Bean, giving him all kinds of tests, and the judge down in Little Rock found him not guilty by reason of insanity, which strikes me as stupid. Why couldn't he be *guilty* by reason of insanity? He did it, sane or not. Anyhow, he is going to be in the criminal part of the mental hospital down at Little Rock for a good long time. I felt so sorry for his poor mother and daddy. He was their only son, and even though they never really understood him, they were so proud that he was making something out of himself as a singer. They sure didn't have a lot else to be proud of.

I went with Baby up to visit him the first time she went, and it was hard on her. She promised him she would come back and see him again, but I don't think it is good for either one of them. We'll see how that goes. She hasn't been in a hurry to go back. I think she needs to try to move on, but it's not for me to say.

Rocky was just about undone by Bean's arrest. He does go to see him at the mental hospital pretty often, and I think Bean is allowed to play the guitar some. Rocky is trying to get the band together again, but it is not much good without Bean. John Cool was so flipped-out about the whole thing that he said he was retiring from music. They are so busy at the Family Hand that he doesn't really have time for the band anyhow. I'll keep working there through Christmas, and then I'll have to quit to practice-teach.

Here's good news—Baby is going to do her practice teaching up at Buchanan High School, the same town where St. Juniper's is located. It is too far away for us to drive every day, especially over those steep Ozark Mountain roads, so we are going to get an apartment together, maybe up at the monastery. Until January, she will be living out in the house with her brothers, and then they will be on their own while she's away. I seriously doubt that Denny and J.C. can keep the fish business going, since they're not really all that into it. They, at least, make some money fixing old cars and motorcycles, and they're going to start their own garage. They're calling it Moreno's Speed and Stuff, and it should do pretty well. Baby and I painted them a really cool sign, with psychedelic letters, like she did at the Family Hand. Rocky may have to run the fish store. If anything brings Manang and Tatang back home, that will. I know Baby misses all of them like crazy, and I do, too.

—

Frannie Moore and Brother Dane got married a couple of days ago. It was at our church, and was a real pretty wedding. Mama made them a big white cake, and Frannie looked beautiful in a periwinkle-blue silk organza dress with a veil-on-a-hat thing and a long train that looked like something out of King Arthur's Court. I still don't know where she gets those clothes. She must make them herself. Brother Dane was real handsome in a tuxedo, and little Kevin wore a berry-red velvet suit with a white satin collar. He strutted down the aisle, carrying the ring on a green silk pillow, and stood beside Brother Dane as the best man. He was so cute, with his little kneesocks and his shiny red hair. I wish Carlene could have been there to see him. She would have been so proud. Happiness just filled the whole church, and I didn't even get annoyed when Brother Wilkins said "Ah" too many times, like he always does. Not too much.

Being the wife of an evangelist is not easy with all the traveling Brother Dane has to do, but they bought a house here in town, and Frannie is taking piano lessons, since the preacher's wife needs to know how to play the piano in case there is nobody else to do it. I bet it won't be long before he settles down and takes a church as the pastor. I pray Brother Wilkins will retire and it would be ours.

Lucille is taking off to visit Jim Floyd in Dallas for Thanksgiving. I pity the poor thing. I should send him a big bottle of Geritol to take before she gets there. Aunt Rubynell is keeping Tiffany LaDawn, but she said I could take her out and buy her some clothes. She doesn't like pink any better than I do. As long as Lucille is gone, Tiffany LaDawn will wear T-shirts and jeans and at least get to be comfortable for a little while.

—

G. Dub has settled up in Vancouver and found a job at a service station. He loves it up there; says the country is the most beautiful he has ever seen—even prettier than the Ozarks—and he has a girlfriend already. Aunt Juanita and Uncle Ray are going up for Christmas to be with him. It will be the first Christmas we haven't all been together, but in the light of what all was happening in Vietnam right now, it's a small price to pay.

—

It seemed like Christmas was right around the corner, and then the semester would be over. I couldn't wait. We actually had a couple of inches of snow yesterday, which is a good sign for a white Christmas, maybe. It feels so clean and fresh, the first snow of the year. It gives you hope—like a whole new year is beginning. This year it will be a whole new decade—1970. Maybe it will be better than the old one. It would have a ways to go to be worse.

I still can't think about what I want to do after graduation. I hate to say it out loud, but I would like to go to New York City and try to be a fashion model, like in *Vogue*. That awful Frank, bless his heart, said I could, and even if he was a sleaze-o, he seemed like he knew a lot about the modeling world. I know it seems shallow and all to want to have your picture in magazines, but I don't care. I never pretended to be deep. If I don't try, I will always wonder if I could have made it. I don't want to be nearly forty, like Mama, and not ever have done anything but get married, have a kid, and go to church. I can always do that later. It might be hard at first, but girls do it every day. Somebody has to succeed—why not me? They say New York is dangerous, but on TV you see women pushing baby carriages right out on the streets, so how bad could it be? I haven't really discussed it with Baby yet, but I know she would come, too, and I bet we could get some kind of jobs and still paint while I am trying to model. Maybe we could teach or get jobs in an art gallery, and maybe even show our work in one. There's a lot of art galleries in New York.

But we'll cross that bridge when we get to it. It's pretty scary to think about. For now, I just want to think about Christmas and practice teaching at St. Juniper's and not worry about what happens in the future. Or about men, for that matter.

Speaking of which, Ricky Don has called a few times to ask me out, but I told him I wasn't ready to see him or anybody else right now, that I needed to cool out and wind down. He is thinking about running for sheriff when Melvyn Arbus retires, although he shouldn't hold his breath, if you ask me. But I hope one day he does. He would be a good one. Ricky Don is the kind of solid guy who will get married and have a bunch of kids and coach Little League and live forever right here in Sweet Valley, where he grew up, and I think that's great. Somebody has to do it.

I asked him what he thought about me going to New York someday, and he said, "Cherry, I don't know what you are looking for, but it doesn't seem like it's anything in Sweet Valley. I would hate to see you leave, but you might be nutty enough to make it. And this town is not going anywhere. You can always come back, if you need to."

I'm not sure what I'm looking for, either. I love my family and all, but there is a big world out there, and I have never been any farther than Vian, Oklahoma, to visit Aunt Juanita's folks.

Anyhow, like he said, if I go and don't like New York, I don't have to stay. There will always be Sweet Valley, and Mama and Daddy to come home to. For a lot of years to come.

ACKNOWLEDGMENTS

Thanks is a poor word for what I owe to Aurora Huston for her inspiration and help on the Philippine parts of the book, and for her unflagging friendship these last thirty years. James Shinn gave me a generous lesson in the funeral business, and Susan Gibson Shinn, the first person who read the manuscript, has encouraged my writing since we were six. Robert Jay Lifton's work on the My Lai veterans was invaluable, as were the materials Randy Fertel sent me from the My Lai hearings and Michael Bilton and Kevin Sim's fine book *Four Hours in My Lai*. I am grateful to my superb agent, John Taylor Williams, for his expertise and encouragement, and to Jason Epstein for bringing this book to Random House. To the friends and family who read and reread the various drafts with enthusiasm, I thank you from the bottom of my heart. Last but not least, I would like to send kudos to Courtney Hodell, my editor and friend, for shepherding this first effort with no pain and a lot of joy.

Windchill
Summer

NORRIS CHURCH MAILER

A Reader's Guide

A Conversation with Norris Church Mailer

Kim Harington is a former high school English teacher, a member of two book groups, and a book reviewer for the Arkansas Democrat Gazette. Like Norris Church Mailer, she is a native of Arkansas, and married to a novelist. She and the author have discovered a number of commonalities, among them a shared birthday. Harington is at work on a novel herself.

KH: While *Windchill Summer* is glorious in imaginative detail, it is set in Sweet Valley, a town not unlike your own hometown of Atkins, Arkansas. Did you feel the need to disguise Atkins as Sweet Valley? You call My Lai by its actual name.

NCM: Sweet Valley is probably closest to Atkins, population 1,391 when I was there, but has characteristics of several other Arkansas towns, plus quite a lot of made-up details. I didn't want to be bound by reality, or to imply that the fictitious events in the book actually happened by putting them in a real place.

On the other hand, the events described in the novel did indeed take place in My Lai, or did as closely as I could ascertain from my research. At one point, I considered giving the village a fictitious name, calling the officers by other names, and making it a My Lai-like event, but I didn't because My Lai was a turning point in America's consciousness of the war, and a big part of history.

Q: You have stated that a writer of fiction draws from real life experiences, research, and imagination. How much of you is in Cherry?

NCM: Warren Beatty once said that if an actor has even five percent of a character in him, he can successfully portray that person, and I think the same holds true for a writer.

Just as Sweet Valley was a composite of several places, Cherry is assembled with bits and pieces and quirks of people I know (like a friend who is obsessed with her big feet), and her sensibilities are filtered through mine. But then, so is everyone else in the book, even the bad guys!

Obviously, I have more than five percent of Cherry in me, but Cherry's life and ideas, while not too far removed from mine, are certainly her own. She is probably a lot nicer than I am, maybe a little more naïve, and she certainly held on to her virginity longer.

Q: (laughter) But Cherry has a tendency to underestimate her own strength and her intelligence. Her self-reflective statement comes to mind: "I never pretended to be deep." Is this not contradicted by the wisdom with which she views the people and events of her narrative?

NCM: I wrote that with secret irony, because, although Cherry totally believes it—that self-effacement is part of her charm—she is, in fact, a deep person. She deals with death, war, religion, and love—subjects, I believe, anyone would say are deep. In her own way, Cherry is a philosopher, having the courage to ask questions of her religion, country, and friends that don't have hard and fast answers, and to make decisions herself.

Q: When you were Cherry's age, how conscious were you of the events taking place in Vietnam? How concerned were you?

NCM: I started this book in a creative writing class at Arkansas Tech, while my first husband was in Vietnam and I was finishing my degree, pregnant with our son, Matthew. The war was an obsession with me, as it naturally would be in that situation, and I was glued to the TV and the mailbox. Although those first pages I wrote were vastly different than this finished book, they were the genesis of it, and it was helpful to me at the time to channel some of my fear and frustration into the work. Like Cherry, I went to anti-war rallies and believed it was a horrible war—as if any wars are not—but as Tripp says, some wars are more honorable than others, and it was hard to find any honor in the Vietnamese war. We didn't take land or give it back—we just killed people.

Q: Have you, by the way, heard from any Vietnam vets who have read *Windchill Summer*? If so, what stands out among the comments?

NCM: Most of the veterans I have spoken to aren't happy that My Lai was the defining incident in the book, but I felt like I was pro-soldier, although anti-war, in the tone. I wanted to understand and portray the circumstances that might build up and lead young boys of eighteen or nineteen to eventually commit the events that happened at My Lai, and I think I succeeded to some degree, at least to myself. Besides this, most of the vets I spoke to thought the portrayal of the war, the language, and the feelings were pretty true to life.

Q: Did you enjoy the necessary research you undertook in order to write authentically of the Vietnam experience? You made a trip to Saigon (Ho Chi Minh City) to research the novel. How helpful was that visit?

NCM: There is so much good research material out there that it would have been possible to write this book without going to Vietnam, but the book is a lot richer because of the trip. Just to get my hands in the dirt, smell the air, and go into the Cu Chi tunnels was worth it. One of the tunnels has been turned into a tourist attraction, with a bored former VC tunnel fighter as a guide. It has been made larger, for the fat American tourists, with lights along the way, but even so, the feeling of claustrophobia and fear of what lies ahead is pretty easy to visualize from in there.

Q: I'm wondering, is there a character closest to your heart?

NCM: That is a little like asking which is your favorite child, but, aside from Cherry, if I had to pick one I loved, it would be Lucille, because she lives out loud and does exactly what she wants to do without any self-consciousness or shame or guilt, which neither Cherry nor I am able to do. I called my friend Aurora in Arkansas after I had written Carlene's funeral scene, and said, "Can you believe it? Lucille wore a pink dress to the funeral!" The characters were that real to me.

Q: Carlene's story—her romance, early motherhood, her father's death, her secrets—is especially dramatic and quite poignant, far more than the lives of Baby or Cherry. Did you have a special fondness for Carlene?

NCM: Yes, I did, more and more as she developed. She was the operative definition of "Nobody Ever Said It Had To Be Fair," the personification of our own dreams and our worst nightmares—that bad things can happen to good people through no fault of their own. I had to let Carlene go to Heaven with Jerry, though, in all fairness. That was a particularly favorite passage of mine. I cried the whole time I was writing it.

Carlene's death was also a metaphor, for me, of the senseless killing in war—at the same time she was killed, thousands of innocent people were dying over in Vietnam.

Q: **What happens underwater and underground in tunnels and caves is significantly symbolic of the secrets your characters hold. Did you consciously decide at some point to make effective dramatic use of underworlds—water and ground—to represent secrets, the unknown? Or did this connection spring up as a function of the mysterious and illusive creative process?**

NCM: Much to our annoyance, there are times when someone will say to a writer, usually with the great excitement of discovery, "You don't know what you've written!" and although my first comment would be, "Yes, I do! I wrote it, didn't I?" sometimes we, as writers, aren't always aware of all the connections and elements of our work until it is viewed through the fresh perspective of another's eyes. I never consciously said, "Oh, the cave and the lake are such great metaphors!" but obviously they are.

Lakes and caves have always been fascinating to me, dangerous and mysterious and somehow other-worldly. I have gone several times to Blanchard Springs Caverns, up in the Ozarks, and ever since I read Tom and Huck, I loved the idea of an adventure taking place in a cave. An Indian skeleton was actually found in the Blanchard Springs Caverns, too, so I appropriated that for Bean's cave, and we could possibly find many layers of symbolism in that!

The Philippine stories of the Aswang mermaid and her underwater world fed nicely into Carlene's death and journey from the lake to Heaven, and it made the lake a bit more sinister as a backdrop for The Water Witch, Baby's family, and Frank's houseboat.

**Q: You are also a painter, and with this novel have joined a small but se-
lect group of creative people who split their talents between the verbal
and visual arts. *Windchill Summer* is inarguably visually powerful. Do
you feel your visual sense stems from your hands-on art?**

NCM: I had a double major in college, Art and English, and since I believed I had small chance of earning my living in Arkansas as either a
painter or writer, I got a teaching degree in both subjects. It must be said
that teaching Art was a lot more fun. I always kept an easel in the class-
room, doing my own work at odd moments, and after I moved to New
York, I had nine one-woman shows of my paintings and numerous group
shows.

Painting does teach one to observe details, and visualizing a scene is
richer for the elements that might also go into a painting. I believe the
two disciplines are the same, and that only the tool is different—a picture
is created with a brush or with words. Thinking in these terms, one scene
of the novel in particular comes to mind—where Carlene is molested by
her father. As she lay on the ground afterward, it was so clear to me,
through her eyes, that I could see the curl of the rusted beige siding on the
trailer (burnt sienna); the cloudless blue sky (cerulean mixed with a little
cobalt and white); the dirt smeared on her hands and elbows (burnt
umber and yellow ochre); the blood laced across her legs (alizarin crim-
son and Chinese red); the sap green of the pine trees . . . I could paint
it now.

**Q: While writing *Windchill Summer,* were you obsessed with your
work? How would you characterize your writing habits?**

NCM: It did take me over completely, especially toward the end when the
story became involved and I was on a roll. I hated to stop for the day and
go downstairs to cook dinner. My poor husband ate cereal a lot, or cooked
himself. Since he is a writer too, fortunately he understood.

My habit is to take care of the minutiae of life in the morning, have
lunch, and then start work around two in the afternoon and work until six
or seven. I try to treat it like a job, and even if I am not in the mood, just

the act of sitting at the computer and reading what I wrote the previous day usually primes the pump for new work.

Q: And did you find that during the writing process you experienced a number of emotions?

NCM: Of course! Writing a scene such as the rape of Carlene by her father, or her death, or My Lai, or Cherry's first sexual experience with Tripp, are powerful, emotional scenes and in creating them, a writer, like an actor, has to experience the emotion—at least the first time it goes down on paper. The next time the writer goes over the scene should be done with the cold clear eye of the writer-as-editor, which polishes the writing, but leaves the power and emotion of the scene intact.

Q: To me, one of the novel's major strengths is the interconnectedness of its characters and their entwined secrets. Subplots bump up against each other deliciously. Equally complicated is the handling of time in the novel's development. The reader gets information in a piecemeal fashion, as you juggle the past and present, and reveal events as though they were part of a jigsaw puzzle. What informed your sense of the effective unfolding of events?

NCM: As unbelievable as it might seem, the chapters unfolded pretty much as they are in the book. There was no real diagram, just a gut instinct and the characters leading me on. I did work hard to keep the events clear as to time and place, which is why I used the name and little drawing in the chapter headings—so readers would know at a glance who was going to be the focus of the chapter before they began reading it.

Q: The characters led you on, yet none of them know all. They know only bits and pieces of what has happened in Sweet Valley. The reader, though, is privy to all details, a powerful technique and one that grants the reader a certain power. In this way, the reader feels a sense of participation. Was that your objective?

NCM: Very much so.

Q: Cherry struggles with the concepts of sin and wrong-doing coupled with her own recent pleasurable experiences. How did your own religious background prepare you to write this novel?

NCM: I was raised in the Free Will Baptist church, which is somewhat like the Holiness church Cherry attends, but rather more reserved. As a child, I did frequent a Holiness church with my cousin, and it was so much more exciting than ours because they spoke in tongues, and played guitars, and had healing services where everyone fell down on the floor, and people shouted and danced in the aisles. I chose to make Cherry Holiness, I admit, because it was more interesting to write about, although the questions she struggles with could be found in any religion. I wanted to treat the religious aspects with the utmost seriousness, and to not make fun of any of it, because it was serious to Cherry and it is serious to me.

Q: You have been married to Norman Mailer for more than twenty-six years. What is it like for a first-time novelist to be married to such a famous and distinguished writer?

NCM: I had aspirations to be a writer when I met Norman, and in fact had written over three hundred pages of a novel that was the genesis for *Windchill Summer*, but I suppose at that time I wasn't secure enough in my own writing abilities to pursue it. However, I continued to write on various levels and gain experience—plays produced at the Actors Studio, screenplays, film treatments, and a short piece for a magazine. Living with Norman over the years has been an ongoing education in writing, too, because I have read each draft of all his books, been part of the editing process, and have seen what it takes to go to work every day and be a professional. I think I became a better writer almost by osmosis.

The obvious question is: Did Norman help get my book published? The short answer is No, since we decided he wouldn't read it until it was in hardcover, but it would be folly not to acknowledge that because of him I knew a lot of people in publishing, and they were curious to read my manuscript. Still, no matter *who* writes a book, publishing houses have their reputation to consider, and if they don't believe a book is good and will make money, they won't publish it. I went with Random House, my husband's publisher, but in fact there were several other offers, which was gratifying.

Q: So tell me this: Is publishing an act of courage?

NCM: Of course I would say yes, but really, the first time you show your work to *anyone*, preferably someone who loves you, is scary. If they like it, as you suspect they will, then you have to gather the courage to show it to an agent or publisher who could turn you down and crush several years of your work, life, and self esteem.

Then when, wonder of wonders, they decide to take it, you have to hand the manuscript—which has known no other hand but your own—over to an editor, and *then*, once it is published, critics who, you believe, hardly read it much less understood it, take it apart in print for everyone to see. It all requires courage. Still, the thrill of holding the first book in your hands, like a newborn baby, makes it all worth while.

Reading Group Questions and Topics for Discussion

1. If you were to tell a friend about *Windchill Summer*, how would you describe it without giving away a single detail of the plot?

2. Why do you think the author chose to write Cherry's chapters in the first person while writing all the other character's chapters in the third person?

3. From your point of view, is Cherry indeed the central character? Explain why or why not. Does another character "steal the show"?

4. If you were to pinpoint the novel's essential theme in only a few words, what would it be?

5. Nguyen, Bean's Vietnamese lover, could be said to represent Bean's wartime experience, symbolic of his fears. The violent act he commits in Sweet Valley is meshed with his confused memories of her. Was Nguyen created strictly for this purpose, to serve as horrific memory, or is she a character in her own right? How believable is Bean's distortion of reality?

6. Two women in the novel, the mothers of Cherry and Carlene, feel constricted in their marriages. Cherry's mother, married to a very religious man, takes pleasure in jewelry, cosmetics, and movies her husband would not approve of, while Carlene's mother is a free-spirited woman who communes with nature in order to escape. What, if anything, do you think the author is saying about the state of marriage, the essential nature of women, or the need for individualism? How do these two characters differ in these respects from Baby's Manang?

7. In what way did the reading of *Windchill Summer* change your view of the Vietnam War?

8. Do you find the title of the novel an apt one?

9. While Cherry's voice is one of wit and affability, there are other passages far more somber, such as Jerry's letters from Vietnam or the worrisome troubled edge that Baby brings to the story. How did such variation in tone affect your reading experience?

10. How does the author use humor in this novel?

11. Which character do you find most sympathetic and why?

12. Consider the main characters as they each undergo a change or experience a revelation during the course of the novel. In what way do each of them change? Whose transformation is most dramatic? Whose is most startling or unexpected?

13. Mysticism plays a role in the understanding of Baby's heritage. How does knowledge of her family's past affect her?

14. Friendship is at the core of this novel, setting the stage for the exploration of trust, secrecy, loyalty, betrayal, and reunion. Is there any message about friendship that you take away from your reading of *Windchill Summer*?

15. Carlene's circumstances are particularly difficult. What, given the confines of her situation, might she have done differently? Does she have other viable choices? How does her relationship with her mother shape her direction? Her relationship with Jerry?

16. What passages in the novel are especially riveting for you? In what ways does the author engage our senses?